THE WORLD'S BEST
FAIRY TALES

A READER'S DIGEST ANTHOLOGY

THE WORLD'S BEST FAIRY TALES

Edited by
BELLE BECKER SIDEMAN

Illustrations by
FRITZ KREDEL

The Reader's Digest Association, Inc.
Pleasantville, New York   Montreal

The acknowledgments that appear on page 832 are
hereby made a part of this copyright page.

Library of Congress Catalog Card Number: 67-27762
ISBN: 0-89577-001-6

Printed in the United States of America

Tenth Printing, October 1978

INTRODUCTION

FAIRY TALES and other folk-tales are among the oldest works of man. The most ancient stories in this book probably originated in Asia, then passed through Europe and Africa. And every people adapted the tales to their own life, shifting the details to fit local customs. Worn smooth by ages of telling, the stories acquired that distinctive conciseness of form and rapidity of movement which are among their principal charms.

Folktales were not especially intended for children. Their audience was the young and old alike. The tales were of all kinds: myths, legends, sagas, fables, comic stories, allegories. The sort that most children like best today is the one we call "fairy tales."

The fairy story takes place in a strange world inhabited by ordinary people as well as by all manner of extraordinary creatures—giants and dwarfs, witches and fabulous beasts. In the midst of everyday affairs wonderful things happen. Animals talk, and even trees. People are transformed into birds and fish, into objects, and then back again. In this world, virtue is always rewarded, evil is punished, the weak are helped and the youngest can be the winner. The fairy tale offers re-assurance, at the same time that it appeals to the taste for the marvelous.

A fairy tale may exist in many different versions, recorded in many places. In this book the earliest stories to be written down were those in the *Arabian Nights*. The first of these came from India, and were translated into Persian in the ninth century. The entire work had assumed its present form by the thirteenth century.

Next in time came the stories by Charles Perrault, who wrote them in his lively and witty style to entertain the seventeenth-century court of Louis XIV of France. Of course something is lost in translation, but at times there is an unexpected delight. Cinderella's glass slipper is one of the happy mistakes—in the original it was made of fur.

The first systematic recording of ancient tales was done early in the nineteenth century by the Grimm brothers, who set down the stories word for word as the German peasants told them. Their versions are notable for simplicity and vividness.

The greatest storyteller of all was Hans Christian Andersen of Denmark, who arrived somewhat later. His stories enchant the reader with that personal voice which mingles the plaintive and the humorous, whether they are based on traditional material, such as "The Tinderbox," or are wholly original, for example, "The Steadfast Tin Soldier."

This book has a generous sampling of stories from many lands, and each has the special flavor of the country from which it comes. "The Three Bears" deserves particular note. Written by the English poet Robert Southey in the early nineteenth century, it traveled throughout the world and was soon generally thought to be an ancient folktale.

The World's Best Fairy Tales is a rich storehouse containing all the well-known and best-loved stories. There are some for every taste and a good version of each story—good to read and good to read aloud. Listening to them or reading them, children will experience some of the enduring wisdom of other times, when the sense of wonder was very much alive.

Maria Cimino, Formerly Librarian-in-Charge,
Central Children's Room, The New York Public Library

CONTENTS

THE PIED PIPER OF HAMELIN

A VERY LONG time ago, the town of Hamelin in Germany was invaded by bands of rats, the likes of which had never been seen before nor ever will be again. They were great black creatures which ran boldly in broad daylight through the streets and swarmed all over the houses, so that people at last could not put hand or foot down anywhere without touching one.

When dressing in the morning they found rats in their breeches and petticoats, in their pockets and in their boots; and when they wanted a morsel to eat, the voracious horde had swept away everything from cellar to garret. The nighttime was even worse. As soon as the lights were out, these untiring nibblers set to work. And everywhere—in the ceilings, in the floors, in the cupboards, at the doors—there was a chase and a rummage, and so furious a noise of gimlets, pincers and saws that a deaf man could not rest for even one hour. Neither cats nor dogs, nor poison nor traps, nor prayers, nor candles burned to all the saints—nothing did any good. The more rats they killed the more came.

But one Friday there arrived in the town a man with a queer face, who played the bagpipes and sang this refrain:

> Who lives shall see:
> This is he,
> The ratcatcher.

He was a tall, gawky fellow, dry and bronzed, with a crooked nose, a long rattail mustache, two great yellow piercing and mocking eyes under a large felt hat set off by a scarlet cock's feather. He was dressed in a green jacket with a leather belt and orange breeches, and on his feet were sandals fastened by thongs passed around his legs in the gypsy fashion. That is how he may be seen to this day, painted on a window of the cathedral of Hamelin.

He stopped in the great marketplace before the town hall, turned his back to the church and went on with his music, singing:

> Who lives shall see:
> This is he,
> The ratcatcher.

The town council had just assembled to consider once more this plague of Egypt, from which no one could save the town. The stranger sent word to the councilors that if they would make it worth his while, he would rid them of all their rats before night fell.

"Then he is a sorcerer!" cried the citizens with one voice. "We must beware of him."

The chief town councilor, who was considered clever, reassured them. He said, "Sorcerer or no, if this bagpiper speaks the truth, it was he who sent us this horrible vermin he wants to rid us of today for money. Well, we must learn to catch the devil in his own snares. You leave it to me."

"Leave it to the town councilor," said the citizens one to another.

And the stranger was brought before them. "Before night," said he, "I shall have dispatched all the rats in Hamelin if you will but pay me a schilling a head."

"A schilling a head!" cried the citizens. "But that will come to millions of taler!"

The town councilor simply shrugged his shoulders and said to the stranger, "A bargain! The rats will be paid for at one schilling a head as you ask."

The bagpiper announced he would begin that very evening when the moon rose. He added that the inhabitants should at that hour leave the streets free and content themselves with looking out of their windows at the pleasant spectacle that was passing.

When the people of Hamelin heard of the bargain, they too exclaimed, "A schilling a head! But this will cost us a deal of money!"

"Leave it to the town councilor," said the town council with a malicious air. And the good people of

Hamelin repeated, "Leave it to the town councilor."

Toward evening the bagpiper reappeared in the marketplace. As at first, he turned his back to the church, and the moment the moon rose on the horizon, the bagpipes resounded: *Trarira, trari!*

It was first a slow, caressing sound, then more and more lively and urgent, and so sonorous and piercing that it penetrated the farthest alleys and retreats of the town. Soon—from the bottom of cellars, the top of garrets, from under all the furniture, from all the nooks and corners of the houses—out came the rats, searching for the door, flinging themselves into the street, and—trip, trip, trip—they began to run in file toward the front of the town hall, so squeezed together that they covered the pavement like the waves of a flooded torrent.

When the square was quite full, the bagpiper faced about and, still playing briskly, turned toward the river that runs at the foot of the walls of Hamelin.

Arriving there, he turned around; the rats were following. "Hop! Hop!" he cried, pointing with his finger to the middle of the stream where the water whirled and was drawn down as if through a funnel. And, hop, hop, without hesitating, the rats took the leap, swam straight to the funnel, plunged in head foremost and disappeared.

The plunging continued thus without ceasing till midnight. At last, dragging himself with difficulty, came a big rat, white with age, who stopped on the bank. It was the king of the band.

"Are they all there, Friend Blanchet?" asked the bagpiper.

"They are all there," replied the white rat.

"And how many were they?"

"Nine hundred and ninety thousand, nine hundred and ninety-nine."

"Well reckoned?"

"Well reckoned."

"Then go and join them, old sire, and *au revoir*."

And the old white rat sprang in his turn into the river, swam to the whirlpool and disappeared.

When the bagpiper had thus concluded his business, he went to bed at his inn. And for the first time in three months the people of Hamelin slept quietly through the night.

The next morning at nine o'clock, the bagpiper appeared at the town hall, where the town council awaited him. "All your rats took a jump into the river yesterday," said he to the councilors, "and I guarantee that not one of them comes back. They were nine hundred and ninety thousand, nine hundred and ninety-nine, at a schilling a head. Reckon!"

"Let us reckon the heads first. One schilling a head is one head the schilling. Where are the heads?"

The piper did not expect this treacherous stroke. He paled with anger, and his eyes flashed fire. "The heads!" cried he. "If you care about them, go and find them in the river."

"So," replied the chief councilor, "you refuse to honor the terms of your agreement? We ourselves could refuse you all payment. But you have been of use to us, and we will not let you go without a recompense." With this, he offered him fifty taler.

"Keep your recompense for yourself," replied the piper proudly. "If you do not pay me, I will be paid by your heirs." Thereupon he pulled his hat down over his eyes, went hastily out of the hall and left the town without speaking to a soul.

When the people of Hamelin heard how the affair had ended, they rubbed their hands and, with no more scruple than their town councilors, laughed about the bagpiper who, they said, had been caught in his own trap. But what made them laugh above all was his threat of getting himself paid by their heirs. Ha! They wished they could only have such creditors for the rest of their lives.

Next day, which was a Sunday, they went gaily to church, thinking that afterward they would at last be able to eat some good thing that the rats had not tasted before them. They never suspected the terrible surprise that awaited them on their return home: no children anywhere! They had all disappeared!

"Our children! Where are our poor children?" was the cry that was soon heard in all the streets.

Then through the east gate of the town came three little boys who cried and wept, and this is the story they told:

While the parents were at church, a wonderful music had sounded in the streets. Soon all the little boys and all the little girls who had been left at home, attracted by the magic sounds, had gone out to the great marketplace. There they found the piper playing his bagpipes. Then the stranger started to walk quickly, and they had followed—running, singing and dancing to the sound of the music, as far as the foot of the mountain which one sees on entering Hamelin. At their approach the mountain had opened a little, and the bagpiper had gone in with them, after which it had closed again.

Only the three little ones who told of the adventure had remained outside, as if by a miracle. One was lame and could not run fast enough; the second, who had left the house in haste, one foot shod, the other bare, had hurt himself against a big stone and could scarcely walk; the third had arrived on time, but while hurrying to go in had struck so violently against the wall of the mountain that he fell backward at the moment it closed upon his comrades.

Hearing this story, the parents redoubled their lamentations. They ran with pikes and mattocks to the mountain and searched till evening to find the opening through which their children had disappeared, without success. At last, the night falling, they returned desolate to Hamelin.

But the most unhappy was the town councilor who had bargained with the piper, for he had lost three boys and two girls, and to crown all, the people of Hamelin overwhelmed him with reproaches, forgetting that the day before they had agreed with him.

What had become of these unfortunate children?

The parents always hoped they were not dead and that the piper, who certainly must have come out of the mountain, would have taken them with him to his own country. That is why for several years they sent in search of them to different countries, but no one ever found a trace of the poor little ones.

It was not till much later that anything was to be heard.

About a hundred and fifty years after the event, when there were no longer any of the fathers, mothers, brothers or sisters of that day left, there arrived one evening in Hamelin some merchants of Bremen returning from the East, who asked to speak with the citizens. They told how, in crossing Hungary, they had sojourned in a mountainous country called Transylvania where the inhabitants spoke only German, while all around them nothing was spoken but Hungarian. These people also declared that they came from Germany, but they did not know how they chanced to be in this strange country.

"Now," said the merchants of Bremen, "these Germans cannot be other than the descendants of the lost children of Hamelin."

The people of Hamelin did not doubt it; and since that day they have regarded it as certain that the Transylvanians of Hungary are their countryfolk, whose ancestors, as children, were taken from Hamelin by the bagpiper. There are more difficult things to believe than that.   CHARLES MARELLES, ANDREW LANG COLLECTION

SNOW WHITE AND ROSE RED

A POOR WIDOW once lived in a little cottage, in front of which grew two rose trees, one bearing white roses and the other red. She had two little girls who were just like the two trees. One was called Snow White and the other Rose Red, and they were the sweetest and best children in the world.

Rose Red loved to run about the fields and meadows and to pick flowers and catch butterflies, but Snow White sat at home with her mother and helped her in the household or read aloud to her when there was no work to do. The two children loved each other so dearly they always walked about hand in hand whenever they went out together, and when Snow White said, "We will never desert each other," Rose Red answered, "No, not so long as we live." And the mother added, "Whatever one gets she shall share with her sister."

They often roamed about in the woods gathering berries, and no beast ever hurt them; on the contrary, they came up to them in the most confiding manner. The little hare would eat a cabbage leaf from their hands, the deer grazed beside them, the stag would bound past them merrily, and the birds remained on the nearby branches and sang to them. No evil ever befell them. If they forgot about the time and night overtook them, they lay down on the moss and slept till morning, and their mother knew they were quite safe and never felt anxious about them.

Once, when they had slept the night in the wood and had been wakened by the morning sun, they perceived a beautiful child in a shining white robe sitting close to their resting place. The figure looked at them kindly, but said nothing and vanished into the wood. And, when they looked around, they saw they had slept quite close to a precipice, over which they would certainly have fallen had they gone on a few steps farther in the darkness.

When they told their mother of their adventure, she said what they had seen must have been the angel that guards good children.

Snow White and Rose Red kept their mother's cottage so clean and neat it was a pleasure to step into it. In summer Rose Red looked after the house and, every morning before her mother awoke, she placed two flowers beside the bed, a rose from each tree. In winter Snow White lit the fire and put a shining brass kettle on to boil.

In the long winter evenings when snowflakes fell, their mother would say, "Snow White, go close the shutters." They gathered around the fire, while their mother put on her spectacles and read aloud from a big book. The two girls listened and spun quietly. Beside them on the ground lay a little lamb, and behind them perched a little white dove with its head tucked under its wing.

One evening, as they sat thus cozily together, someone knocked at the door. The mother said, "Rose Red, open the door quickly. It must be some poor traveler seeking shelter from the snow and cold."

Rose Red hastened to unbar the door and thought she saw a poor man standing in the darkness outside. But it was a Bear who poked his thick black head through the door. Rose Red screamed aloud and sprang back in terror, the lamb began to bleat, the dove flapped its wings, and Snow White ran and hid behind her mother's bed. But the Bear said, "Don't be afraid. I won't hurt you. I am half frozen and only wish to warm myself a little."

"You poor Bear," said the mother, "lie down by the fire, but take care not to burn your fur."

Then she called, "Snow White and Rose Red, come out. The Bear will do you no harm; he is a good, honest creature."

So they both came out of their hiding places, and gradually the lamb and dove drew near too, and they all forgot their fear. The Bear asked the children to beat the snow out of his fur, and they fetched a brush and scrubbed him till he was dry. Then the beast stretched himself in front of the fire and growled happily and comfortably. The girls soon grew quite playful with him and treated their guest like a big dog. They rolled him about here and there and teased him gaily, and if he growled they only laughed.

The Bear submitted to everything with the greatest good nature, only when they went too far, he cried:

> Oh, spare my life!
> Snow White and Rose Red,
> Don't beat your lover dead.

When it was time to retire for the night, and the others went to bed, the mother said to the Bear, "You can lie there on the hearth; it will be a shelter for you from the cold and wet outside."

As soon as day dawned the children let him out, and he trotted off through the snow into the wood. From this time on the Bear came every evening at the same hour and lay down by the hearth and let Snow White and Rose Red play what pranks they liked with him. They grew so accustomed to his visits that the door was never locked at night till their friend had made his appearance.

When spring came, and all the world outside was green, the Bear said one morning to Snow White, "Now I must leave you and I will not return again the whole summer."

"Where are you going, dear Bear?" asked Snow White.

"I must go to the forest and protect my treasure from the wicked dwarfs. In winter, when the earth is frozen hard, they remain underground, for they cannot work their way through. But now, when the snow has thawed and the sun has warmed the ground, they come out to spy the land and steal what they can. Anything that falls into their hands and disappears into their caves with them is not easily brought to light again."

Snow White was quite sad over their friend's departure. When she unbarred the door for him, the Bear caught a piece of his fur in the door knocker as he stepped out, and Snow White thought she caught sight of glittering gold beneath it, but she could not be certain. The Bear ran hastily away and soon disappeared behind the trees.

A short time later, their mother sent the children into the wood to collect brushwood. They came upon a big tree fallen on the ground, and on the trunk among the long grass they noticed something jumping up and down, but what it was they could not distinguish.

When they came closer they perceived a dwarf with a wizened face and a beard a yard long. The end of the beard was caught in a cleft of the tree, and the little man sprang about like a dog on a chain and did not seem to know what to do. He glared at the girls with his fiery red eyes and screamed out, "What are you standing there for? Come and help me!"

"What were you doing, little man?" Rose Red asked him.

"You stupid, inquisitive goose!" replied the dwarf. "I wanted to split the tree in order to get chips of wood for our kitchen fire. I drove in the wedge, and all was going well, but the wood was so slippery it suddenly sprang out. There was no time to remove my beautiful white beard, so here I am caught fast. I can't get away, and you silly, smooth-faced, milk-and-water girls just stand and laugh at me! Ugh, what wretches you are!"

The girls did everything in their power, but they could not get the little man's beard out; it was wedged in far too firmly.

"I will run and fetch somebody," said Rose Red.

"Blockheads!" snapped the dwarf. "What is the good of calling anyone else? You two are already too many for me. Does nothing better occur to you than that idea?"

"Do not be so impatient," said Snow White. "I will help you." And taking her scissors out of her pocket she snipped the end off his beard. As soon as the dwarf was free, he seized a bag full of gold which was hidden among the roots of the tree, and muttered aloud, "Curse these rude wretches, cutting off a piece of my splendid beard!" With these words he swung the bag over his back and disappeared without another look at the children.

A few days later Snow White and Rose Red went out to catch some fish for supper. As they approached the stream they saw something which looked like an enormous grasshopper springing toward the water as if it were going to jump in. They ran forward and recognized their old friend the dwarf.

"Where are you going?" asked Rose Red. "You are surely not going to jump into the water?"

"I am not such a fool!" screamed the dwarf. "That wretched fish is trying to drag me in!"

The little man had been sitting on the bank fishing, when the wind had unfortunately entangled his beard in the line. Immediately afterward, a big fish bit, but the feeble little creature had no strength to pull it out and the fish was dragging the dwarf toward him. He clung with all his might to every rush and blade of grass, but it did not help him much. He had to follow every movement of the fish and was in great danger of being dragged into the water.

The girls had come just at the right moment. They held him firm and did all they could to disentangle his beard from the line; but in vain, for beard and line were in a hopeless muddle. Nothing remained but to produce the scissors and cut the beard, and a small part of it was sacrificed.

When the dwarf saw what they were doing, the ungrateful little man yelled, "Do you call that manners, to disfigure a fellow's face? It wasn't enough that you shortened my beard before, but now you cut off the best bit of it. I won't dare show myself like this before my own people. I wish you'd never come at all." Then he picked up a sack of pearls that lay among the rushes, and, without saying another word, he dragged it away and disappeared behind a stone.

Soon after this the mother sent the two girls to the town to buy needles, thread, laces and ribbons. The road led over a field where huge boulders of rock lay scattered. As they walked along they saw a big bird hovering in the air, circling slowly above them, but always descending lower, till at last it settled on a rock not far from them. Immediately afterward they heard a sharp, piercing cry.

They ran forward and saw with horror that the eagle had pounced on their old friend the dwarf and was about to carry him off. The tenderhearted girls seized hold of the little man and struggled so long with the bird that at last he let go his prey. When the dwarf had recovered from the first shock he screamed in his screeching voice, "Couldn't you have treated me more carefully? You have torn my fine little coat all to shreds, awkward hussies that you are!" Then he took up a bag of precious stones and vanished under the rocks into his cave.

The girls were accustomed to his ingratitude, and continued on to the town. On their way home, they passed the field again and were surprised to see the dwarf pouring out his precious jewels on an open space, for he had thought no one would pass by at so late an hour. The evening sun shone on the glittering stones, and they sparkled so beautifully that the girls stood still and gazed at them.

"What are you two standing there gaping for?" shrieked the dwarf, and his ashen-gray face became scarlet with rage.

He was about to run off with these angry words when a sudden growl was heard, and a black Bear trotted out of the wood. The dwarf jumped up in great fright, but he had no time to reach his hiding place, for the Bear was already upon him. Then he cried in terror, "Dear Mister Bear, spare me! I'll give you all my treasure. Look at those beautiful precious stones lying there. Spare my life! What pleasure would you get from a poor, feeble little fellow like me? You wouldn't feel me between your teeth. There, lay hold of these two wicked girls; they will be a tender morsel for you, as fat as young quails. Eat them instead."

The Bear, paying no attention to his words, gave the evil little creature one blow with his paw, and he never moved again. The girls had run away, but the Bear called after them, "Snow White and Rose Red, do not be afraid. Wait, and I will come with you." Then they recognized his voice and stood still. When he was quite close to them his bear skin suddenly fell off, and a handsome young man stood beside them, all dressed in gleaming gold.

"I am a king's son," he said, "and was bewitched by that wicked dwarf. Not only had he stolen my treasure, but I was doomed to roam about the woods as a wild bear till his death should set me free. Now he has the punishment he deserves."

Snow White married the Prince, and Rose Red married his brother, and they divided the great treasure the dwarf had collected between them. The old mother lived peacefully with her children for many years. She carried the two rose trees with her. They stood in front of her window, and every year they bore the loveliest red and white roses.

JAKOB AND WILHELM GRIMM, TRANSLATED BY MAY SELLAR

IT'S PERFECTLY TRUE!

"**I**T'S A DREADFUL business," said a hen, and she said it in a part of the town where the incident had not taken place.

"It's a dreadful business to happen in a hen house. I wouldn't dare to sleep alone tonight. Thank goodness there are so many of us up here on the perch!"

And then she told the story she had heard in such a way that the feathers of the other hens stood on end as she spoke, and even the Rooster's comb drooped. It's perfectly true!

But let's begin at the beginning.

It happened in a hen house at the other end of the town. The sun went down, and the hens flew up. One of them was a white-feathered, short-legged little thing who laid her eggs regularly—a most respectable hen in every way. She settled on the perch, preening herself with her beak. As she did this, one tiny feather fluttered down.

"There's that feather gone!" said the Hen. "Well, well, the more I preen myself, the prettier I shall become, no doubt!"

She said it only in fun, you know. She was the life and soul of that crowd, but otherwise, as we've said, most respectable. Then she fell asleep.

All was dark. There sat the hens, packed closely together.

But the white Hen's neighbor wasn't asleep; she had heard and not heard, as one must do in this world for the sake of peace and quiet.

But she couldn't resist telling her neighbor on the other side: "Did you hear? Well, my dear, I won't mention names, but there's one hen I know who is going to pluck out all her feathers just because she thinks it makes her look smart. Humph! If I were a rooster I should simply treat her with the greatest contempt."

Up above the hens lived Mother Owl, Father Owl and all the little Owls. They were a sharp-eared family, and they heard every word; they rolled their eyes, and old Mother Owl flapped her wings. "Don't take any notice—you heard what she said, of course, and I heard it with my own ears. Upon my word, I don't know what the world is coming to! One of the hens, so utterly lost to all sense of henly decency, is sitting there plucking out her feathers with the Rooster looking on the whole time!"

"Little pitchers have big ears," said Father Owl, motioning toward their children. "Be careful what you are saying!"

"Oh, but I shall have to tell the owl across the road," said Mother Owl. "She is somebody well worth associating with, you know." And off she flew to spread the news.

"Tu-whit, tu-whoo, tu-whit, tu-whoo," they hooted together outside the pigeon house over the way. "Have you heard the news? Have you heard the news? There is a hen who has pulled out all her feathers just to please the Rooster. She is freezing to death, if she isn't dead already—tu-whit, tu-whoo, tu-whit, tu-whoo. . . ."

"Where? Where?" asked the pigeons.

"In the yard opposite; I saw it, so to speak, with my own eyes! It's not at all a nice story to tell, but it's perfectly true!"

"Trrrue, too trrrue—trrrue, too trrrue," cooed the pigeons, and they immediately flew down to tell the story in the chicken run below. "There's a hen—in fact, some say there are two hens—who have plucked out all their feathers to be different from the rest and to attract the attention of the Rooster. It was certainly a dreadful thing to do, what with the risk of chills and fever; and they caught cold and died, both of them!"

"Cock-a-doodle-doo! Wake up! Wake up!" crowed the Rooster, flying up onto the fence. He was still half asleep, but he crowed all the same. "Three hens have died of a broken heart, all for the sake of the Rooster;

they've plucked out all their feathers, and now they are dead! It's a dreadful business, it really is, but it's no good trying to keep it quiet. Tell anyone you please!"

"We'll tell, we'll tell!" squeaked the bats; and the Rooster crowed and the hens clucked, "Tell, tell, tell, tell," and so the story flew from one hen house to another, until at last it came back to the place where it had really started: "Five hens . . ." (that's how it was told) "five hens have plucked out all their feathers to show which one has lost the most weight for love of the Rooster; then they pecked at one another till they bled and all five dropped down dead—a shame and a disgrace to their relations, and a serious loss to their owner!"

The Hen who had dropped the little loose feather naturally didn't recognize her own story and, as she was a respectable hen, she exclaimed, "I despise such hens! But there are others just as bad! Things like that ought not to be hushed up; I must do what I can to make certain that the story gets into the papers, then it will soon be known throughout the country and it will surely serve the wretches right and their relations too!"

It was put into the papers, all clearly written in plain print. And it's perfectly true—one little feather can easily become five hens.

HANS CHRISTIAN ANDERSEN, TRANSLATED BY PAUL LEYSSAC

Ɪɴ ᴛʜᴇ ᴅᴀʏs of the great King Arthur there lived a mighty magician called Merlin, the most learned and skillful enchanter the world has ever seen.

This famous magician, who could take any form he pleased, was once traveling about as a poor beggar and, being very tired, he stopped at the cottage of a peasant to rest himself, and asked for food.

The farmer bade him welcome, and his wife, who was a goodhearted woman, soon brought him some milk in a wooden bowl and some coarse brown bread on a platter.

Merlin was much pleased with the kindness of the peasant and his wife, but he could not help noticing that though everything was neat and comfortable in the cottage, they both seemed to be very unhappy. He therefore asked them why they were so melancholy, and learned that they were miserable because they had no children.

The poor woman said, with tears in her eyes, "I should be the happiest creature in the world if I had a son; even if he was no bigger than my husband's thumb, I would be satisfied.''

Merlin was so amused with the idea of a boy no bigger than a man's thumb that he determined to grant the poor woman's wish.

Accordingly, in a little while the peasant's wife had a son who, wonderful to relate, was not a bit bigger than his father's thumb.

The Queen of the Fairies, wishing to see the little fellow, came in the window while his mother was sitting up in bed admiring him. The Queen kissed the child and, giving him the name of Tom Thumb, sent for some of the fairies, who dressed her little godson according to her orders:

> An oak-leaf hat he had for his crown;
> His shirt of web by spiders spun;
> With jacket wove of thistle's down;
> His trousers were of feathers done.
> His stockings, of apple-rind, they tie
> With eyelash from his mother's eye:
> His shoes were made of mouse's skin,
> Tanned with the downy hair within.

Tom never grew any larger than his father's thumb, which was only of ordinary size; but as he got older he became very cunning and full of tricks. When he was old enough to play with the boys and had lost all his own marbles, he would creep into the bags of his playfellows and fill his pockets with theirs. Then, getting out without their noticing him, Tom would again join in the game.

One day, however, as he was coming out of a bag of marbles, where he had been stealing as usual, the boy to whom it belonged chanced to see him. "Ah, ah, my little Tommy," said the boy, "so I have caught you stealing my marbles at last, and you shall be rewarded for your thievish tricks." On saying this, he drew the string tight around Tom's neck and gave the bag such a hearty shake that poor little Tom's legs, thighs and body were sadly bruised. He roared out with pain and begged the fellow to let him out, promising never to steal again.

A short time afterward Tom's mother was making a batter-pudding, and, being very anxious to see how it was made, he climbed up to the edge of the bowl. But his foot slipped, and he plumped head over heels into the bowl without his mother noticing him. She stirred him into the pudding and set him into the pot to boil.

The batter filled Tom's mouth and prevented him from crying out. But the hot water began to scald him, and he kicked and struggled so much in the pot that his mother thought the pudding was bewitched and, pulling it out of the pot, she threw it outside the door. A poor tinker who was passing by picked up the pudding and, putting it into his knapsack, walked off.

As Tom had now got his mouth cleared of the batter, he began to cry aloud, which so frightened the tinker that he flung down the pudding and ran away. The pudding broke to pieces in the fall, and Tom crept out, covered all over with the batter, and walked home. His mother, who was very sorry to see her darling in such a woeful state, put him into a teacup and soon washed off the batter, after which she kissed him and put him into bed.

Soon after the adventure of the pudding, Tom's mother went to milk her cow in the meadow, and she took Tom along with her. The wind was very high, and, fearing he would be blown away, she tied him to a thistle with a piece of fine thread. The cow soon observed Tom's little oak-leaf hat and, liking the appearance of it, took poor Tom, his hat and the thistle at one mouthful.

While the cow was chewing the thistle, Tom was afraid of her great teeth which threatened to crush him in pieces, and he roared out as loud as he could, "Mother, Mother!"

"Where are you, Tommy, my dear Tommy?" said his mother.

"Here, Mother, in the red cow's mouth."

His mother began to cry and wring her hands. But the cow, surprised at the odd noise in her throat, opened her mouth and let Tom drop out.

Fortunately his mother caught him in her apron as

he was falling, or he might have been dreadfully hurt. She then put Tom inside her blouse and quickly ran home with him.

Tom's father made him a whip of a barley straw to drive the cattle with, and having one day gone into the fields, Tom slipped and rolled into a furrow. A raven which was flying past picked him up, flew with him over the sea and there dropped him.

A large fish swallowed Tom the moment he fell into the sea. Soon after, this fish was caught and bought for the table of King Arthur. When they opened the fish in order to cook it, everyone was very astonished at finding such a little boy. Tom was quite delighted at being free again. They carried him to the King, who made Tom his dwarf, and he soon became a great favorite at court. By his tricks and gambols he not only amused the King and Queen, but the Knights of the Round Table as well. It is said that when the King rode out on horseback he often took Tom along, and if a shower came, Tom would creep into His Majesty's vest pocket and sleep till the rain was over.

King Arthur one day asked Tom about his parents, wishing to know if they were as small as he was and whether they were well off. Tom told the King that his father and mother were as tall as anybody in the court, but that they were in poor circumstances. On hearing this, the King carried Tom to his treasury, where he kept his money, and told him to take as much money

as he could carry home to his parents, which made the poor fellow caper with joy. Tom went to procure a purse, which was made out of a water bubble, and King Arthur gave him a large silver piece to put into it.

Our little hero had some difficulty in lifting the burden upon his back, but at last he succeeded in getting it placed to his liking, and set forward on his journey. Without meeting with any accident, and after resting himself more than a hundred times by the wayside, in two days and two nights he reached his father's house in safety. Tom had traveled forty-eight hours with a huge silver piece on his back and was almost tired to death when his mother ran out to meet him and carried him into the house. But he soon returned to King Arthur's court.

As Tom's clothes had suffered much in the batter-pudding and the inside of the fish, His Majesty ordered him a new suit of clothes, and announced he would be mounted as a knight on a mouse.

Of butterfly's wings his shirt was made,
His boots of chicken's hide;
And by a nimble fairy blade,
Well learnèd in the tailoring trade,
His clothing was supplied.
A needle dangled by his side;
A dapper mouse he used to ride;
Thus strutted Tom in stately pride!

It was certainly very diverting to see Tom in this dress and mounted on the mouse as he rode out hunting with the King and nobility, who were ready to expire with laughter at the sight of Tom and his fine prancing charger.

The King was so charmed with his manner that he ordered a little chair to be made, in order that Tom might sit upon the Round Table, and a palace of gold, a foot high, with a door an inch wide, to live in. He also gave Tom a coach drawn by six small mice.

The Queen was so enraged at the honors that were being conferred on Sir Thomas that she resolved to ruin him, and told the King that the little knight had been saucy to her.

The King sent for Tom in great haste, but being fully aware of the danger of royal anger, Tom crept into an empty snail shell where he lay for a long time until he was almost starved with hunger. At last he ventured to peep out and, seeing a fine large butterfly on the ground near his hiding place, he got close to it and, jumping astride it, was carried up into the air. The butterfly flew with him from flower to flower and from tree to tree and from field to field and at last returned to the court, where the King and nobility all strove to catch hold of him, but poor Tom finally fell from his seat into a watering pot, in which he was almost drowned.

When the Queen saw him, she was angry and said

he should be beheaded, and so Tom was put into a mousetrap to wait for his execution.

However, a cat, observing something alive in the trap, patted it about till the wires broke, and set Thomas at liberty.

The King received Tom into favor once again. But Tom did not live to enjoy it, for a large spider one day attacked him, and although he drew his sword and fought well, the spider's poison at last overcame him.

> He fell dead on the ground where he stood,
> And the spider sucked every drop of his blood.

King Arthur and his whole court were so sorry at the loss of their little favorite that they went into mourning and raised a fine white marble monument over his grave with the following epitaph:

> Here lies Tom Thumb, King Arthur's knight,
> Who died by a spider's cruel bite.
> He was well known in Arthur's court,
> Where he afforded gallant sport;
> He rode a tilt and tournament,
> And on a mouse a-hunting went.
> Alive he filled the court with mirth;
> His death to sorrow soon gave birth.
> Wipe, wipe your eyes, and shake your head
> And cry, Alas! Tom Thumb is dead!

OLD ENGLISH TALE, RETOLD BY JOSEPH JACOBS

THE NIGHTINGALE

IN CHINA, the Emperor is Chinese, as you can well understand, and all his courtiers are also Chinese. It happened many years ago, but the story is worth telling again, before it is forgotten.

The Emperor's palace was the most splendid in the world, all made of priceless porcelain, but so brittle and delicate one had to take great care in touching it. In the garden were the most beautiful flowers, and the loveliest of them were hung with silver bells which tinkled as you passed—you could not help admiring them. Everything was admirably arranged for a pleasing effect, and the garden was quite large; even the gardener himself did not know where it ended. Beyond it was a stately forest with great trees and deep lakes. The forest sloped down to the sea, which was a clear blue. Large ships could sail in under the branches of the trees, where lived a Nightingale.

This Nightingale sang so beautifully that even the poor fisherman, who had much to do, stopped to listen when he came at night to haul in his nets. "How beautiful it is!" he said. But he had to attend to his work and forgot about the bird.

Travelers came to the Emperor's capital from many countries and were astonished at the palace and the garden. But as they heard the Nightingale, they all said, "This is the finest of all!"

The travelers told about it when they returned home, and learned scholars wrote many books about the town, the palace and the garden. But they did not forget the Nightingale. She was praised above everything else in the empire, and the poets composed splendid verses about the Nightingale in the forest by the deep blue sea.

These books were sent everywhere in the world, and some of them reached the Emperor. He sat in his golden chair and read and read. He nodded his head now and then, for he liked the brilliant accounts of the town, the palace and the garden. "But the Nightingale is the most wonderful," the books said.

"What!" said the Emperor. "I don't know anything about the Nightingale. Is there such a bird in my empire, and in my own garden? I have never heard of her. Fancy reading about her for the first time in a book written by someone who never lived here!"

He called his first lord, who was so grand that if anyone of lower rank ventured to speak to him, he would say only "Pfft!"—and that means nothing at all.

"There is said to be a most remarkable bird called

a Nightingale," said the Emperor. "They say she is the most glorious wonder of my kingdom. Why has no one ever said anything to me about her?"

"I have never before heard the Nightingale mentioned," said the first lord. "I know that she has never been presented at court! But I will seek her out!"

But where was she to be found? The first lord ran upstairs and downstairs, through the halls and corridors; but no one he met had ever heard of the Nightingale. So the first lord ran again to the Emperor and told him that it must all be imagination on the part of those who had written the books.

"Your Imperial Majesty cannot really believe whatever is written. There are some inventions called the black art."

"But one book in which I read this," said the Emperor, "was sent me by the powerful Emperor of Japan, so it cannot be untrue. The Nightingale must be here this evening! She has my gracious permission to appear before me, and if she does not, the whole court shall be trampled underfoot after supper!"

"Tsing pe!" said the first lord; and he ran upstairs and downstairs, through the halls and corridors, and half the court ran with him, for they did not want to be trampled underfoot.

Everyone was asking about the wonderful Nightingale, of which all the world knew except those at the court of the Chinese Emperor.

At last they met a poor little maid in the kitchen who said, "Oh, I know the Nightingale well. How she sings! Every evening I carry the leftover scraps from the court table to my poor sick mother. When I am going home at night, tired and weary, and I stop to rest for a while in the woods, then I hear the Nightingale singing. It brings tears to my eyes, and I feel as if my mother were kissing me."

"Little kitchen maid," said the first lord, "I will give you a place as the court cook, and you shall have leave to see the Emperor at dinner every night, if you will lead us to the Nightingale. She is invited to appear at court this evening."

So they all went into the forest where the Nightingale usually sang, and half the court went too. On the way they heard a cow mooing.

"Oh," said one of the courtiers, "we have found her! What wonderful power for such a small creature! I am sure I have heard her before."

"No, that is a cow mooing," said the little kitchen maid. "We are still a long way off."

Then the frogs began to croak in the marsh.

"Splendid," said the court chaplain. "That must be the Nightingale. It sounds like distant church bells."

"No, no, those are frogs," said the little kitchen maid. "But I think we shall soon hear her now!"

Then the Nightingale began to sing.

"There she is!" cried the girl. "Listen! She is sitting

there." And she pointed to a small gray bird up in the branches.

"Is it possible?" said the first lord. "I should never have thought it. How ordinary she looks! She must have lost her color, seeing so many distinguished men around her."

"Dear little Nightingale," called the kitchen maid, "our gracious Emperor would like to have you sing for him."

"With the greatest of pleasure," said the Nightingale, and she sang so gloriously that it was a joy to hear her.

"It sounds like crystal bells," said the first lord. "Look how her tiny throat throbs! It is strange we have never heard her before. She will be a great success at court."

"Shall I sing once more for the Emperor?" asked the Nightingale, thinking that he was one of the men standing below.

"My esteemed little Nightingale," said the first lord, "I have the honor to invite you to court this evening, where his gracious Imperial Highness will be enchanted with your charming song!"

"My song sounds best among the trees," said the Nightingale; but she went with them gladly when she heard that the Emperor wished it.

At the palace everything was prepared for the glorious occasion. The porcelain walls and floors glittered in the light of many thousands of golden lamps; gorgeous flowers with tinkling bells were placed in the corridors. There was such hurrying and doors opening and closing that all the bells jingled so one could scarcely hear oneself speak.

In the center of the great hall, where the Emperor sat on his throne, a golden perch had been placed for the Nightingale. The whole court was there, and the little kitchen maid was allowed to stand behind the door, now that she was court cook. Everyone was dressed in his best, and everyone was looking toward the little gray bird to whom the Emperor nodded most kindly.

The Nightingale sang so gloriously that tears came into the Emperor's eyes and rolled down his cheeks. Then the Nightingale sang even more beautifully, and her music melted every heart.

The Emperor was filled with such delight that he said she should wear his gold slipper around her neck. But the Nightingale thanked him and said she had reward enough already: "I have seen tears in the Emperor's eyes; that is the richest reward. An Emperor's tears have great power." Then she sang again with her entrancingly sweet voice.

"That is the most charming coquetry I have ever heard," said the ladies, and all of them held water in their mouths that they might make a jug-jugging sound whenever anyone spoke to them. Then they thought themselves nightingales. The lackeys and chambermaids announced they also were pleased, which means a great deal, for they are most difficult of all to satisfy. In short, the Nightingale was a real success.

She had to stay at court now. She had her own cage, with permission to walk out twice in the day and once at night. She was given twelve servants, each of whom held a silken ribbon which was fastened around one of her tiny legs, so there was not much fun in an outing like this.

The whole town was talking about the wonderful bird, and, when two people met, one would say "Nightin—" and the other "—gale," and then they would sigh and understand each other. Yes, and eleven grocers' children were named after the Nightingale, but not one of them could sing a note.

One day the Emperor received a large parcel, on which was written, "The Nightingale."

"Here is another new book about our famous bird, I am sure," said the Emperor.

It was not a book, however, but a little mechanical toy, which lay in a box—an artificial nightingale, very like the real one, but studded with diamonds, rubies and sapphires. When it was wound up, it could sing one of the songs the real bird sang, and its tail moved up and down, glittering with silver and gold. Around its neck was a little collar on which was written, "The

Nightingale of the Emperor of Japan is nothing compared to that of the Emperor of China."

"Wonderful!" everyone said, and the man who had brought the artificial bird received the title of "Bringer of the Imperial First Nightingale."

"Now they must sing together. What a duet we shall have!"

And so they sang together, but their voices did not blend, for the real Nightingale sang in her way, and the other bird sang waltzes.

"It is not its fault!" said the music master. "It always keeps very good time and is quite correct in every way."

Then the artificial bird had to sing alone. It gave just as much pleasure as the real one, and some said it was much prettier to look at, for it sparkled like bracelets and necklaces. Three-and-thirty times it sang the same piece without being tired.

The courtiers wanted to hear it once again, but the Emperor thought that the living Nightingale should sing for them now—but where was she? No one had noticed that she had flown out of the open window, back to her green woods.

"What shall we do?" said the Emperor.

And all the court scolded and said that the Nightingale was very ungrateful.

"But we still have the better bird!" they said joyfully. Then the artificial one had to sing again, and that was the thirty-fourth time they had heard the same piece, but they did not yet know it by heart; it was much too difficult.

The music master praised the bird and assured them it was better than a real nightingale, not only because of its beautiful diamond-studded plumage, but because of its mechanical interior as well.

"For see, my lords and ladies and Your Imperial Majesty, with the real Nightingale one can never tell which song will come out, but with the artificial bird everything is set beforehand. You can explain its mechanism and show people how man's skill arranged the waltzes and how one note follows the other in perfect order!"

"That is just what I think!" said everyone, and the music master requested permission to show the bird to the people the next Sunday. "They shall hear it sing," commanded the Emperor. And they heard it and were as pleased as if they had had too much tea, after the Chinese fashion. They all said, "Oh!" and held up their forefingers and nodded time. But the poor fisherman who had heard the real Nightingale suddenly remembered its voice and said, "This one sings well enough, but there is something wanting. I don't know what."

The real Nightingale was banished from the kingdom, while the artificial bird was put on a silken cushion by the Emperor's bed. All the presents which it received of gold and precious stones lay around it. It was given the title of "Imperial Night Singer, First from the Left." The Emperor considered that side the more distinguished, for even an Emperor's heart is on the left.

And the music master wrote twenty-five volumes about the artificial bird, all learned, lengthy and full of the hardest Chinese words—yet the people in the court said they had read and understood them, for they remembered that once they had been very stupid about a book and had been trampled underfoot in consequence.

So a whole year passed. The Emperor, the court and the other Chinese knew every note of the artificial bird's song by heart, and they liked it the better for that. They could even sing with it, and they did so. The young street boys sang "Tra-la-la-la-la," and the Emperor sang with the bird too, sometimes. It was indeed delightful.

But one evening, when the artificial bird was singing its best, and the Emperor lay in bed listening to it, something inside the bird snapped! Whir-r-r! All the wheels ran down and then the music ceased. The Emperor sprang up and had his physician summoned, but what could he do?

Then the watchmaker came, and, after a great deal of talking and examining, he repaired the bird as well as he could. But he said the bird must be used as little as possible, as the works were nearly worn out and could not be replaced.

Here was a calamity! Only once a year was the artificial bird allowed to sing, and even that was almost too much for it; but then the music master made a little speech full of difficult words, saying that it was just as good as before, and so, of course, it was just as good as before.

Five years passed, and then a great sorrow befell the nation. The Chinese were fond of their Emperor, and now he lay ill and, it was said, was not likely to live. Already a new Emperor had been chosen, and the people stood in the street and asked the first lord how the old Emperor was.

"Pfft!" said he, and shook his head.

Cold and pale lay the Emperor in his regal bed; all the courtiers believed him dead, and one after the other left him to pay their respects to the new Emperor. Everywhere in the halls and corridors cloth was laid down so no footstep could be heard, and everything was still—very, very still—and nothing came to break the silence.

The Emperor longed for something to relieve the monotony of this deathlike stillness. If only someone would speak to him. If only someone would sing to him. Music would carry his thoughts away and break the spell lying on him. The moon shone in at the open window, but that, too, was silent, quite silent.

"Music! Music!" cried the Emperor. "Precious little golden bird, sing! Sing! I gave you gold and jewels; I hung my gold slipper around your neck with my own hand. Sing! Sing!"

But the bird was silent, for there was no one to wind it up. And everything was silent, terribly still!

All at once there came in through the window the most glorious burst of song. It was the little living Nightingale, who had been sitting on a bough outside. She had heard of the need of her Emperor and had come to sing to him of comfort and hope. As she sang, the blood flowed quicker and quicker in the Emperor's weak body, and life began to return.

"Thank you, thank you," said the Emperor, "you divine little bird. I know you. I banished you from my kingdom, and yet you have given me life again. How can I reward you?"

"You have done that already," said the Nightingale. "I brought tears to your eyes the first time I sang; I shall never forget that. They are jewels that rejoice a singer's heart. But now sleep and grow strong again. I will sing you a lullaby."

And the Emperor fell into a deep, calm sleep as the Nightingale sang.

The sun was shining through the window when he awoke, strong and well. None of his servants had come back yet, for they thought he was dead. But the Nightingale still sang to him.

"You must stay with me always," said the Emperor. "You shall sing only when you like, and I will break the artificial bird into a thousand pieces."

"Don't do that," said the Nightingale. "It did what it could. Keep it as you have done. I cannot build my nest in the palace and live here, but let me come whenever I like. In the evening I will sit on the branch outside the window and sing something to make you feel happy. I will sing of joy and of sorrow; I will sing of the evil and the good which lie hidden from you. The little singing bird flies everywhere—to the poor fisherman's hut or the farmer's cottage, to all those who are far away from you and your court. I love your heart more than your crown, though that has about it a brightness as of something holy.

"Now I will sing to you again, but you must promise me one thing."

"Anything that you ask," said the Emperor, standing up in his beautiful imperial robes, which he had put on himself, and fastening on his sword richly embossed with gold.

"One thing only I beg of you! Do not tell anyone you have a little bird who tells you everything; it will be much better not to have it known."

Then the Nightingale flew away.

When the servants came in to attend their dead Emperor, the Emperor said, "Good morning!"

HANS CHRISTIAN ANDERSEN, ANDREW LANG COLLECTION

CHICKEN LITTLE

ONCE UPON a time there was a tiny little chicken whom everyone called Chicken Little. One day, while she was out in the garden (where she had no right to be), a rose leaf fell on her tail. Away she ran in great fright, for she thought the sky was falling.

As she ran along she met Henny Penny.

"Oh, Henny Penny," cried Chicken Little, "the sky is falling!"

"How do you know that?" asked Henny Penny.

"Oh, I saw it with my eyes; I heard it with my ears; and part of it fell on my tail," said Chicken Little.

"Let us run and tell the King," said Henny Penny.

So they ran along together until they met Ducky Lucky.

"Oh, Ducky Lucky," cried Chicken Little, "the sky is falling!"

"How do you know that?" asked Ducky Lucky.

"Oh, I saw it with my eyes; I heard it with my ears; and part of it fell on my tail," said Chicken Little, "and we are going to tell the King."

"May I go, too?" asked Ducky Lucky.

"Oh, yes," said Chicken Little, and they all ran along together. Presently they met Goosey Loosey.

"Oh, Goosey Loosey," cried Chicken Little, "the sky is falling!"

"How do you know that?" asked Goosey Loosey.

"Oh, I saw it with my eyes; I heard it with my ears; and part of it fell on my tail," said Chicken Little, "and we are going to tell the King."

"May I go, too?" asked Goosey Loosey.

"Oh, yes," said Chicken Little, and they all ran along together. Presently they met Turkey Lurkey.

"Oh, Turkey Lurkey," cried Chicken Little, "the sky is falling!"

"How do you know that?" asked Turkey Lurkey.

"Oh, I saw it with my eyes; I heard it with my ears; and part of it fell on my tail," said Chicken Little, "and we are going to tell the King."

"May I go, too?" asked Turkey Lurkey.

"Oh, yes," said Chicken Little, and they all ran along together. Presently they met Foxy Loxy.

"Oh, Foxy Loxy," cried Chicken Little, "the sky is falling."

"How do you know that?" asked Foxy Loxy.

"Oh, I saw it with my eyes; I heard it with my ears; and part of it fell on my tail," said Chicken Little, "and we are going to tell the King."

"Come with me," said Foxy Loxy, "and I will show

you where the King lives." So Chicken Little, Henny Penny, Ducky Lucky, Goosey Loosey and Turkey Lurkey all followed Foxy Loxy; but, oh! he led them into his den, and they never, never came out again!

ENGLISH FOLK TALE, RETOLD BY CLARA M. LEWIS

THE FROG PRINCE

IN THE OLDEN days, when wishing was still of some use, there lived a King. He had several beautiful daughters, but the youngest was so fair that even the sun, who sees so many wonders, could not help marveling every time he looked into her face.

Near the King's palace lay a large, dark forest, and there, under an old linden tree, was a well. When the day was very warm, the little Princess would go off into this forest and sit at the rim of the cool well. There she would play with her golden ball, tossing it up and catching it deftly in her little hands. This was her favorite game and she never tired of it.

Now it happened one day that, as the Princess

tossed her golden ball into the air, it did not fall into her uplifted hands as usual. Instead, it fell to the ground, rolled to the rim of the well and then into the water. Plunk, splash! The golden ball was gone.

The well was deep and the Princess knew it. She felt sure she would never see her beautiful ball again, so she cried and cried and could not stop. "What is the matter, little Princess?" said a voice behind her. "You are crying so that even a hard stone would have pity on you."

The little girl looked around and there she saw a Frog. He was in the well and stretching his fat, ugly head out of the water. "Oh, it's you—you old water-splasher!" said the girl. "I'm crying over my golden ball. It has fallen into the well."

"Oh, as to that," said the Frog, "I can bring your ball back to you. But what will you give me if I do?"

"Whatever you wish, dear old Frog," said the Princess. "I'll give you my dresses, my beads and all my jewelry—even the golden crown on my head."

The Frog answered, "Your dresses, your beads and all your jewelry, even the golden crown on your head —I don't want them. But if you can find it in your heart to like me and take me for your playfellow, if you will let me sit beside you at the table, eat from your little golden plate and drink from your little golden cup, and if you are willing to let me sleep in your own little bed besides: if you promise me all this, little Princess, then I will gladly go down to the bottom of the well and bring back your golden ball."

"Oh, yes," said the Princess, "I'll promise anything you say if you'll only bring back my golden ball to me." But to herself she thought: What is the silly Frog chattering about? He can only live in the water and croak with the other frogs; he could never be a playmate to a human being.

As soon as the Frog had heard her promise, he disappeared into the well. Down, down, down, he sank; but he soon came up again, holding the golden ball in his mouth. He dropped it on the grass at the feet of the Princess, who was wild with joy when she saw her favorite plaything once more. She picked up the ball and skipped away, thinking no more about the little creature who had returned it to her. "Wait!" cried the Frog. "Take me with you, I can't run that fast."

But what good did it do him to cry out his "Quark! Quark!" after her as loud as he could? She didn't listen to him but hurried home, where she soon forgot the poor Frog, who now had to go back into his well again.

The next evening, the Princess was eating her dinner at the royal table when—plitch, plotch, plitch, plotch—something came climbing up the stairs. When it reached the door, it knocked and cried:

Youngest daughter of the King,
Open the door for me!

The Princess rose from the table and ran to see who was calling her. When she opened the door, there sat the Frog, wet and green and cold! Quickly she slammed the door and sat down at the table again, her heart beating loud and fast. The King could see well enough that she was frightened and worried, and he said, "My child, what are you afraid of? Is there a giant out there who wants to carry you away?"

"Oh, no," said the Princess. "It's not a giant, but a horrid old Frog!"

"And what does he want of you?" asked the King.

"Oh, dear Father, as I was playing under the linden tree by the well, my golden ball fell into the water. And because I cried so hard, the Frog brought it back to me; and because he insisted so much, I promised him that he could be my playmate. But I never, never thought that he would ever leave his well. Now he is out there and wants to come in and eat from my plate and drink from my cup and sleep in my little bed. But I couldn't bear that, Papa, he's so wet and ugly and his eyes bulge out!"

While she was talking, the Frog knocked at the door once more and said:

> Youngest daughter of the King,
>   Open the door for me.
> Mind your words at the old well spring;
>   Open the door for me!

At that the King said, "If we make promises, Daughter, we must keep them. So you had better go and open the door."

The Princess still did not want to do it but she had to obey. When she opened the door, the Frog hopped in and followed her until she reached her chair. Then he sat on the floor and said, "Lift me up beside you."

She hesitated—the Frog was so cold and clammy— but her father looked at her sternly and said, "You must keep your promise."

After the Frog was on her chair, he wanted to be put on the table. When he was there, he said, "Now shove your plate a little closer so we can eat together like real playmates."

The Princess shuddered, but she had to do it. The Frog enjoyed the meal and ate heartily, but the poor girl could not swallow a single bite. At last the Frog said, "Now I've eaten enough and I feel tired. Carry me to your room so I can go to sleep."

The Princess began to cry. It had been hard enough to touch the cold, fat Frog, and worse still to have him eat out of her plate, but to have him beside her in her little bed was more than she could bear.

"I want to go to bed," repeated the Frog. "Take me there and tuck me in."

The Princess shuddered again and looked at her father, but he only said, "He helped you in your trouble. Is it fair to scorn him now?"

There was nothing for her to do but pick up the creature—she did it with both hands—and carry him up into her room, where she dropped him in a corner on the floor, hoping he would be satisfied. But after she had gone to bed, she heard something she didn't like. Ploppety, plop! Ploppety, plop! It was the Frog, hopping across the floor, and when he reached her bed he said, "I'm tired and the floor is too hard. I have as much right as you to sleep in a good soft bed. Lift me up or I will tell your father."

At this the Princess was bitterly angry, but she picked the Frog up and put him at the foot of her bed. There he stayed all night; but when the dark was graying into daylight, the Frog jumped down from the bed, out of the door and away, she knew not where.

The next night it was the same. The Frog came back, knocked at the door and said:

> Youngest daughter of the King,
>   Open the door for me.
> Mind your words at the old well spring;
>   Open the door for me!

The only thing the Princess could do was let him in. Again he ate out of her golden plate, sipped out of her golden cup, and again he slept at the foot of her bed. In the morning he went away as before.

The third night he came again. But this time he was not content to sleep at her feet. "I want to sleep under your pillow," he said. "I'd like it better there."

The girl thought she would never be able to sleep with a horrid, damp, goggle-eyed Frog under her pillow. She began to weep softly to herself and couldn't stop until at last she cried herself to sleep.

When the night was over and the morning sunlight burst in at the window, the Frog crept out from under her pillow and hopped off the bed. But as soon as his feet touched the floor something happened to him. In that moment he was no longer a cold, fat, goggle-eyed Frog—he had turned into a young Prince with handsome, friendly eyes!

"You see," he said, "I wasn't what I seemed to be! A wicked old woman bewitched me. No one but you could break the spell, little Princess, and I waited and waited at the well for you to help me."

The Princess was speechless with surprise, but her eyes sparkled.

"And will you let me be your playmate now?" said the Prince, laughing. "Mind your words at the old well spring!"

At this the Princess laughed too, and they both ran out to play with the golden ball.

For years they were the best of friends and the happiest of playmates, and it is not hard to guess, I'm sure, that when they were grown up they were married and lived happily ever after.

JAKOB AND WILHELM GRIMM, TRANSLATED BY WANDA GÁG

CINDERELLA

O<small>NCE THERE</small> was a gen-
tleman who married, for his second wife, the proudest
and most haughty woman that was ever seen. She had,
by a former husband, two daughters who possessed
their mother's temper and who were, indeed, exactly
like her in all things. The man had a young daughter of
his own, who had an unusually sweet disposition
which she took from her mother, who had been the
nicest person in the world.

No sooner were the ceremonies of their wedding
over than the stepmother began to show her true colors. She could not bear the good qualities of her pretty
stepdaughter, and all the less because they made her
own daughters appear the more odious. She employed
her in the meanest work of the house: scouring the
dishes and tables and scrubbing madam's room and
those of her daughters. The girl slept in a miserable
garret upon a wretched straw bed, while her sisters occupied fine rooms with beds of the very newest fashion, and where they had looking glasses so large they
could view themselves from head to foot.

The poor girl bore all of this patiently and dared not tell her father, who would have scolded her, for his wife ruled him entirely. When she had done her work, she used to go into the chimney corner and sit down among the cinders and ashes, which is the reason why they called her Cinderwench. But the younger of the sisters, who was not so rude and mean as the elder, called her Cinderella. However, Cinderella, notwithstanding her shabby attire, was a hundred times more beautiful than her sisters, though they were always dressed very richly.

It happened that the King's son gave a ball and invited all persons of fashion to it. The two sisters were among those invited, for they cut a very grand figure. They were delighted with this invitation and became wonderfully busy choosing such gowns, petticoats and headdresses as might become them. This meant new trouble for Cinderella, for it was she who ironed her sisters' linen and pleated their ruffles, while they talked of nothing but how they should be dressed for the ball.

"For my part," said the elder, "I will wear my red velvet suit with French trimming."

"And I," said the younger, "shall have my usual silk skirt. But then, to make amends for that, I will put on my gold-flowered cloak and my diamond necklace, which is far from being the most ordinary one in the world."

They sent for the best milliner to make up their

headdresses and adjust their double-frilled caps, and they ordered their rouge and beauty patches from Mademoiselle de la Poche.

Cinderella was also consulted in all these matters, for she had excellent ideas, and she offered her services to dress their hair, which they were very willing she should do. As she was doing this, they said to her, "Cinderella, would you not like to go to the ball?"

"Alas," she said, "it is not for such as I."

"You are right," they replied. "It would make people laugh to see a cinderwench at a palace ball."

The two sisters went almost two days without eating, so much were they transported with joy. They broke more than a dozen laces in trying to be laced up tightly so that they might have fine slender shapes, and were continually at their looking glasses. At last the happy day came. They went to court, and Cinderella followed them with her eyes as long as she could and, when she had lost sight of them, she began to cry.

Her godmother found her all in tears, and asked her what was the matter. "I wish I could——I wish I could——" But Cinderella was not able to speak the rest, being interrupted by her tears and sobbing.

This godmother of hers, who was a fairy, said, "You wish to go to the ball—is that not so?"

"Yes," cried Cinderella, with a great sigh.

"Well," said her godmother, "be a good girl, and I will arrange that you shall go!" Then she said to Cinderella, "Run into the garden and bring me a pumpkin."

Cinderella went immediately to gather the finest one and brought it to her godmother, not being able to imagine how this pumpkin could help her go to the ball. Her godmother scooped out all of the inside, leaving nothing but the rind. Then she struck it with her wand, and the pumpkin was instantly turned into a fine coach. She then found six live mice in the mousetrap. She told Cinderella to lift up the little door, and—after she gave each mouse, as it went out, a little tap with her wand—every mouse was turned into a fine horse. Altogether they made a very handsome set of six beautiful horses with blond manes.

Being at a loss for a coachman, Cinderella said, "I will go and see if there is a rat in the rattrap—we may make a coachman of him."

"Yes," replied her godmother. "Go and look."

Cinderella brought the trap to her, and in it there were three huge rats. The fairy chose the one which had the largest beard, and, touching him with her wand, she turned him into a fat, jolly coachman with the smartest mustachios that eyes ever beheld. Then she said to Cinderella, "Go again into the garden, and you will find six lizards; bring them to me."

Cinderella had no sooner done so than her godmother turned them into six footmen, who skipped up immediately behind the coach, their green liveries trimmed with silver.

The fairy then said to Cinderella: "Well, you see here an equipage fit to take you to the ball."

"Oh, yes," cried Cinderella, "but must I go as I am, in these old rags?"

Her godmother barely touched her with her wand, and at that same instant her rags were turned into clothes of silver, all trimmed with gold and jewels. This done, she gave her a pair of glass slippers, the prettiest in the whole world. Thus decked out, Cinderella climbed into her coach. Then her godmother commanded her above all things not to stay after midnight, telling her that—if she stayed one moment later —the coach would be a pumpkin again, her horses mice, her coachman a rat, her footmen lizards and her clothes would become just as they were before.

Cinderella promised her godmother she would not fail to leave the ball before midnight. And then away she drove, scarcely able to contain herself for joy. The King's son, who was told that a great Princess, whom nobody knew, had come, ran out to receive her. He gave her his hand as she alighted from the coach and led her into the hall, among all the company. There was immediately a profound silence; the other guests stopped dancing, and the violins ceased to play, so attentive was everyone to the singular beauties of the unknown newcomer. Nothing was then heard but: "Ha! How lovely she is! Ha! How lovely she is!"

The King himself, old as he was, could not help

watching her, and he told the Queen softly that it was a long time since he had seen so beautiful a creature. All the ladies were busy observing her clothes and headdress, so they might have some made next day after the same pattern, provided they could find such fine materials and able hands to make them.

The King's son conducted her to the seat of honor, and afterward took her out to dance with him, and she danced so gracefully that all admired her more and more. A fine supper was served, but the young Prince ate nothing, so intently was he gazing on Cinderella.

She sat down by her sisters, showing them a thousand civilities, giving them part of the oranges and lemons with which the Prince had presented her, and this surprised them very much, for they did not recognize her. While Cinderella was thus amusing her two sisters, she heard the clock strike eleven and three quarters; she immediately made a curtsy to the company and hastened away as fast as she could.

Reaching home, she ran to seek out her godmother and, after having thanked her, said she could not but heartily wish she might go to the ball the next day, because the King's son had asked her. As she was eagerly telling her godmother all that had happened that evening, her two sisters knocked at the door, which Cinderella ran and opened.

"How long you have stayed!" she cried, rubbing her eyes and stretching herself as if she had just been waked out of her sleep. (She had not, of course, had any inclination to sleep since they had left home.)

"If you had been at the ball," said one of her sisters, "you would not have been tired with it. There came unexpectedly the finest Princess, the most beautiful ever seen with mortal eyes; she showed us a thousand civilities and gave us oranges and lemons."

Cinderella seemed very indifferent, but she asked them the name of that Princess. They told her they did not know it and that the King's son would give all the world to know who she was. At this Cinderella smiled and replied, "She must, then, be very beautiful indeed. How happy you have been! Could I not see her? Ah, dear Miss Charlotte, do lend me your yellow dress which you wear every day."

"Ah, to be sure," cried Miss Charlotte, "lend my clothes to a dirty cinderwench! I should be a fool."

Cinderella, indeed, had expected such an answer and was very glad of the refusal, for she would have been sadly put to it if her sister had done what she asked for jestingly.

The next day the two sisters were at the ball, and so was Cinderella, but dressed more magnificently than before. The King's son was always by her side and never ceased his compliments and kind speeches to her. All this was so far from being tiresome that she quite forgot what her godmother had commanded her. At last, she counted the clock striking twelve when she had thought it to be no more than eleven. She then rose up and fled, as nimble as a deer.

The Prince followed but could not overtake her. But she lost one of her glass slippers, which the Prince picked up most carefully. Cinderella reached home quite out of breath and in her old clothes, having nothing left of her finery but one of the little slippers, mate to the one she had dropped.

The guards at the palace gate were asked if they had seen a Princess go out. But no, they had seen nobody except a young girl, very poorly dressed, who had more the air of a country wench than a gentlewoman.

When the two sisters returned from the ball, Cinderella asked them if they had been well entertained, and if the fine lady had been there. They told her yes, but that she had hurried away immediately when it struck twelve and with such haste that she dropped one of her little glass slippers, which the Prince had picked up. He had done nothing but look at her during the ball, and he was very much in love with the beautiful girl who owned the glass slipper.

What they said was true, for a few days afterward the King's son caused it to be proclaimed, by sound of trumpet, that he would marry her whose foot this slipper would just fit. His gentlemen-in-waiting began to try it upon the princesses, then the duchesses and all the court, but in vain. It was brought to the two sisters, who each did what she possibly could to thrust her foot into the slipper. But they could not manage it. Cinderella, who knew her slipper, said to them, smiling, "Let me see if it will not fit me."

Her sisters burst out laughing and began to tease her. The gentleman who was sent to try the slipper looked earnestly at Cinderella and, finding her very lovely, said it was only fair that she should try and that he had orders to let everyone do so.

He bade Cinderella sit down and, putting the slipper to her foot, he found it went on easily and fitted her as if it had been made of wax. The astonishment of her two sisters was great, but it was greater still when Cinderella pulled out of her pocket the other slipper. At this, there appeared her godmother, who touched Cinderella's clothes with her wand, making them more magnificent than any she had ever worn before.

Her two sisters threw themselves at her feet to beg pardon for all the ill-treatment they had made her undergo. Cinderella embraced them and cried that she forgave them with her whole heart and desired them always to love her.

She was conducted to the young Prince. He thought her more charming than ever and, a few days afterward, married her. Cinderella, who was no less good than she was beautiful, gave her two sisters lodging in the palace and, that very same day, matched them with two great lords of the court.

CHARLES PERRAULT, ANDREW LANG COLLECTION

THE PRINCESS AND THE PEA

HERE WAS once upon a time a Prince who wanted to marry a princess, but she had to be a true princess. So he traveled through the whole world to find one, but there was always something against each one he met. There were plenty of princesses, but he could not find out if they were true princesses. In every case there was some little defect which showed the right person had not yet been found. So he came home again in very low spirits, for he had wanted very much to have a true princess for his bride.

One night there was a dreadful storm; it thundered, the lightning flashed and the rain streamed down in torrents. It was fearful! In the midst of the storm there was a knocking heard at the palace gate, and the old King went to open it.

There stood a Princess outside the gate; but, oh, in what a sad plight she was from the rain and the storm! The water was running down from her hair and her dress into the tips of her shoes and out at the heels again. And yet this girl said that she was really a true princess!

Well, we shall soon find out! thought the old Queen, when the King had brought her in. But she said nothing and went into one of the bedchambers, took off the bedclothes and laid a pea on the bottom of the bed.

Then she put twenty mattresses on top of the pea and twenty eiderdown quilts on top of the mattresses. And this was the bed in which the Princess was to spend the night.

The next morning the Queen asked the girl how she had slept.

"Oh, very badly!" said the Princess. "I scarcely closed my eyes all night! I am sure I don't know what was in the bed. I lay on something so hard that my whole body is black and blue. It is dreadful!"

Now they perceived that she was indeed a true princess, as she had claimed, because she had felt the pea through the twenty mattresses and the twenty eiderdown quilts.

No one, surely, but a true princess could be as sensitive as that.

So the Prince married her, for he knew that at last he had found a true princess. And the pea was put into the Royal Museum, where it is still to be seen if no one has stolen it.

Now, this is a true story.

HANS CHRISTIAN ANDERSEN, COLLECTION OF
KATE DOUGLAS WIGGIN AND NORA ARCHIBALD SMITH

ALI BABA AND
THE FORTY THIEVES

IN A TOWN in Persia there dwelled two brothers, one named Cassim, the other Ali Baba. Cassim was married to a rich wife and lived in wealth and plenty, while Ali Baba had to maintain his wife and children by cutting wood in a neighboring forest and selling it in the town.

One day, when Ali Baba was in the forest, he saw a troop of men on horseback coming toward him in a cloud of dust. He was afraid they were robbers and climbed up among some rocks for safety.

When they came up to him and dismounted, he counted forty of them. They unbridled their horses and tied them to trees.

The finest man among them, whom Ali Baba took to be their captain, went a little way into the bushes and said, "Open, Sesame!" so plainly that Ali Baba heard him. A door opened in the rocks and, having made the troops go in, the captain followed them, and the door shut again of itself.

They stayed some time inside, and Ali Baba, fearing

they might come out and catch him, was forced to sit patiently hidden in the rocks. At last the door opened again, and the forty thieves came out. As the captain had gone in last he came out first and made them all pass by him. He then closed the door, saying, "Shut, Sesame!" Every man bridled his horse and mounted, the captain put himself at their head, and they departed as they had come.

Then Ali Baba climbed down and went to the door concealed in the bushes and said, "Open, Sesame!" and it flew open. Ali Baba, who expected a dull, dismal place, was greatly surprised to find it large and well lighted and hollowed by the hand of man in the form of a vault, which received the light from an opening in the ceiling. He saw rich bales of merchandise—silk stuffs and brocades all piled together, gold and silver in heaps, and money in leather purses. He went in, and the door shut behind him. He did not look at the silver but brought out as many bags of gold as he thought his donkeys, which were browsing outside, could carry, loaded them with the bags and covered the bags with firewood.

Using the words "Shut, Sesame!" he closed the door after him and went home.

Then he drove his donkeys into his own yard, shut the gates, carried the bags to his wife and emptied them out before her. He bade her keep his adventure a secret and told her that he would bury the gold.

"Let me first measure it," said his wife. "I will borrow a measure from someone while you dig the hole."

So she ran to the wife of Cassim and borrowed a measure. Knowing Ali Baba's poverty, the sister-in-law was curious to find out what sort of grain his wife wished to weigh and artfully put some suet at the bottom of the measure. Ali Baba's wife went home and set the measure on the heap of gold and filled it and emptied it often, to her great content. She then took the measure back to her sister-in-law, without noticing that a piece of gold was sticking to it.

Cassim's wife saw it as soon as her back was turned. She grew very curious and said to her husband when he came home that evening, "Cassim, your brother is richer than you. He does not count his money; he measures it."

He begged her to explain this riddle, which she did by showing him the piece of money and telling him where she had found it. Then Cassim grew so envious that he could not sleep and went to his brother in the morning before sunrise.

"Ali Baba," he said, showing him the gold piece, "how is it that you pretend to be poor and yet you measure gold?"

By this Ali Baba realized that, through his wife's folly, Cassim and his wife knew his secret, so he confessed all and offered Cassim a share.

"That I expect," said Cassim, "but I must know

where to find the treasure, otherwise I will try to discover it for myself and you will lose it all."

Ali Baba, more out of kindness than fear, told him of the cave and the very words to use. Cassim left Ali Baba immediately, meaning to reach the cave before his brother and get the treasure for himself. He rose early next morning and set out with three mules loaded with great chests. He soon found the place and the door in the rock.

He said, "Open, Sesame!" and the door opened and shut behind him.

He could have feasted his eyes all day on the treasure, but he now hastened to gather together as much of it as possible; but when he was ready to go he could not remember what to say, for he was thinking only of his great riches. Instead of "Open, Sesame!" he said, "Open, Barley!" and the door remained fast. He named several other sorts of grain—for sesame is a kind of grain—all but the right one, and the door still stuck fast. He was so frightened at the danger he was in that he had as much forgotten the word as if he had never heard it.

About noon the robbers returned to their cave and saw Cassim's mules roving about with great chests on their backs. This gave them the alarm. They drew their sabers and went to the door, which opened on the captain's saying, "Open, Sesame!"

Cassim, who had heard the trampling of their

horses' feet, resolved to sell his life dearly, so when the door opened he leaped out and threw the captain down. In vain, however, for the robbers soon killed him with their sabers. On entering the cave they saw all the bags laid ready and could not imagine how he had entered in without knowing their secret. They cut Cassim's body into four quarters and nailed them up inside the cave in order to frighten anyone who should venture in. Then they went away in search of more treasure.

As night drew on, Cassim's wife grew very uneasy, and she ran to her brother-in-law to tell him where her husband had gone. Ali Baba did his best to comfort her and set out for the forest in search of Cassim. The first thing he saw on entering the cave was his dead brother. Full of horror, he put the body on one of the mules and bags of gold on the other two and, covering all with firewood, returned home. He drove the two mules laden with gold into his own yard and led the other to Cassim's house. The door was opened by the slave Morgiana, whom Ali Baba knew to be both brave and cunning.

Unloading the mule, he said to her, "This is the body of your master, who has been murdered, but whom we must bury as though he had died in his bed. I will speak with you again, but now tell your mistress that I have come."

The wife of Cassim, on learning the fate of her husband, broke out into cries and tears, but Ali Baba offered to take care of her for life if she would promise to keep his counsel and leave everything to Morgiana. She agreed to this and dried her eyes.

Morgiana, meanwhile, sought out an apothecary and asked him for some lozenges. "My poor master," she said, "can neither eat nor speak and no one knows what his illness is." She carried home the lozenges and returned next day, weeping, and asked for an essence only given to those almost dead. Thus, in the evening, no one was surprised to hear the shrieks and cries of Cassim's wife and Morgiana, telling everyone that Cassim had just died.

The next day Morgiana went to an old cobbler named Baba Mustapha, who opened his stall early near the gates of the town. She put a piece of gold in his hand and, having bound his eyes with a handkerchief, bade him follow her with his needle and thread. She took him to the room where the body lay, pulled off the bandage and bade him sew the quarters together, after which she covered his eyes again and led him back to his stall.

Then they buried Cassim, and Morgiana, his slave, followed him to the grave, weeping and tearing her hair, while Cassim's wife stayed at home uttering lamentable cries. Next day Ali Baba and his family went to live in Cassim's house, and Cassim's shop was given to Ali Baba's eldest son.

The forty thieves, meanwhile, on their return to the cave were much astonished to find Cassim's body gone as well as some of their money bags.

"We are certainly discovered," said the captain, "and shall be undone if we cannot find out who it is that knows our secret. Two men must have known it; we have killed one—we must now find the other. To this end one of you who is bold and artful must go into the city, dressed as a traveler, and discover whom we have killed and whether men talk of the strange manner of his death. If the messenger fails, he must lose his life, lest we be betrayed."

One of the thieves started up and offered to do this; and, after the rest had highly commended him for his bravery, he disguised himself and happened to enter the town at daybreak, just by Baba Mustapha's stall. The thief bade Baba Mustapha good day, saying to him, "Honest man, how can you possibly see to stitch at your age?"

"Old as I am," replied the cobbler, "I have very good eyes, and you will believe me when I tell you that I have sewn a dead body together in a place where I had less light than I have now."

The robber was overjoyed at his good fortune and, giving the cobbler a piece of gold, desired to be shown the house where he had stitched up the dead body. At first Mustapha refused, saying that he had been blindfolded. But when the robber gave him another piece of gold he began to think he might remember the turnings if blindfolded as before. This means succeeded. The robber partly led him and was partly guided by him right to the front of Cassim's house, the door of which the robber marked with a piece of chalk.

Then, well pleased, he bade farewell to Baba Mustapha and returned to the forest. By and by Morgiana, going out, saw the mark the robber had made, quickly guessed that some mischief was brewing and, fetching a piece of white chalk, marked two or three doors on each side, without saying anything to her master or mistresses.

The thief, meanwhile, told his comrades of his discovery. The captain thanked him and bade him show them the house he had marked. But when they came to it they saw that five or six of the houses were chalked in the same manner. The guide was so confounded that he knew not what answer to make, and when they returned to the cave he was at once beheaded for having failed in his mission.

Another robber was dispatched and, having won over Baba Mustapha, marked the house in red chalk. But Morgiana was again too clever for them, and the second messenger was put to death also.

The captain now resolved to go himself but, wiser than the others, he did not mark the house but looked at it so closely he could not fail to remember it. He returned and ordered his men to go into the neighboring villages and buy nineteen mules and thirty-eight leather jars, all empty, except one which was full of oil. The captain put one of his men, fully armed, into each, rubbing the outside of the jars with oil from the full vessel. Then the nineteen mules were loaded with the jar of oil and thirty-seven robbers in jars, and they reached the town at dusk.

The captain stopped his mules in front of the house and said to Ali Baba, who was sitting outside in the cool evening air, "I have brought some oil from a distance to sell at tomorrow's market, but it is now so late that I know not where to pass the night, unless you will do me the favor to take me in."

Though Ali Baba had seen the captain of the robbers in the forest, he did not recognize him in the disguise of an oil merchant. He bade him welcome, opened his gates for the mules to enter and went to Morgiana to bid her prepare a bed and supper for his guest. He brought the stranger into his hall and, after they had supped, went again to speak to Morgiana in the kitchen, while the captain went into the yard under the pretense of seeing after his mules but really to tell his men what to do.

Beginning at the first jar and ending at the last, he said to each man, "As soon as I throw some stones from the window of the chamber where I lie, cut the jars open with your knives and come out, and I will be with you in a trice."

He returned to the house and Morgiana led him to his chamber. She then told her fellow slave, Abdallah, to make some broth for her master, who had gone to bed. Meanwhile, her lamp had gone out and there was no more oil in the house.

"Do not be uneasy," said Abdallah. "Go into the yard and take some out of one of those jars."

Morgiana thanked him for his advice, took the oil pot and went into the yard. When she came to the first jar the robber inside said softly, "Is it time?"

Any other slave but Morgiana, on finding a man in the jar instead of the oil she wanted, would have screamed and called for help. But she, knowing the danger her master was in, bethought herself of a plan and answered quietly, "Not yet, but presently."

She went to all the jars, giving the same answer, till she came to the jar of oil. Morgiana now saw that her master, thinking he was entertaining an oil merchant, had let thirty-eight robbers into his house. She filled her oil pot, went back to the kitchen and, having lit her lamp, went again to the oil jar and filled a large kettle full of oil. As soon as it boiled, she went and poured enough oil into every jar to stifle and kill the robber inside. When this brave deed was done she went back to the kitchen, put out the fire and the lamp and waited to see what would happen.

In a quarter of an hour the captain of the robbers awoke, got up and opened the window. As all seemed quiet, he threw down some little pebbles which hit the jars. He listened and, when none of his men stirred, he grew uneasy and went down into the yard. On going to the first jar and saying, "Are you asleep?" he smelled the hot boiled oil and knew at once that his plot to murder Ali Baba and his household had been discovered. He found all the thieves were dead and, missing the oil out of the last jar, became aware of the manner of their death. He then forced the lock of a door leading into a garden and, climbing over several walls, made his escape.

Morgiana saw all this and, rejoicing at her success, went to bed and fell asleep.

At daybreak Ali Baba arose and, seeing the oil jars there still, asked why the merchant had not left with his mules. Morgiana bade him look in the first jar and see if there was any oil. Seeing a man, he started back in terror. "Have no fear," said Morgiana, "the man cannot harm you; he is dead."

Ali Baba, when he had recovered from his astonishment, asked what had become of the merchant.

"Merchant!" said she. "He is no more a merchant than I am!" And she told him the whole story, assuring him that it was a plot of the forty robbers of the forest, of whom she thought three were still alive, and that the white and red chalk marks had something to do with it. Ali Baba at once gave Morgiana her freedom, saying that he owed her his life. They then buried the bodies in Ali Baba's garden, while the mules were sold in the market by his slaves.

The captain returned to his lonely cave, which seemed frightful to him without his lost companions, and firmly resolved to avenge them by killing Ali Baba. He dressed himself carefully and went back into the town, where he lodged at an inn. In the course of a great number of journeys to the forest, he carried away many rich stuffs and much fine linen and set up a shop opposite that of Ali Baba's son. He called himself Cogia Hassan and, as he was both civil and well dressed, he soon made friends with Ali Baba's son and through him with Ali Baba, whom he was continually asking to sup with him.

Ali Baba, wishing to return his kindness, invited him into his house and received him smiling, thanking him for his kindness to his son. When the merchant was about to take his leave, Ali Baba stopped him, saying, "Where are you going, sir, in such haste? Will you not stay and sup with me?"

The merchant refused, saying that he had a reason and, on Ali Baba's asking him what that was, he replied, "It is, sir, that I can eat no foods that have any salt in them."

"If that is all," said Ali Baba, "let me tell you there shall be no salt in either the meat or the bread that we eat tonight."

He went to give this order to Morgiana, who was

much surprised, as custom made sacred the friendship of those who partook of salt together.

"Who is this man you speak of," she said, "who eats no salt with his meat?"

"He is an honest man, Morgiana," returned Ali Baba, "therefore do as I bid you."

But she could not withstand a desire to see this strange man, so she helped Abdallah carry up the dishes and saw in a moment that Cogia Hassan was the robber captain and carried a dagger under his garment. "I am not surprised," she said to herself, "that this wicked man who intends to kill my master will eat no salt with him, but I will hinder his plans."

She sent up the supper with Abdallah, while she made ready for one of the boldest acts that could be thought of. When the dessert had been served, Cogia Hassan was left alone with Ali Baba and his son, whom he thought to make drunk and then murder.

Morgiana, meanwhile, put on a headdress like a dancing girl's and clasped a jeweled belt around her waist, from which hung a dagger with a silver hilt. She said to Abdallah, "Take your tambourine, and let us go and divert our masters and their guest."

Abdallah took his instrument and played before Morgiana until they came to the door, where Abdallah stopped playing and Morgiana made a low curtsy.

"Come in, Morgiana," said Ali Baba. "Let Cogia Hassan see how you can dance."

Cogia Hassan was by no means pleased, for he feared that his chance of killing Ali Baba was gone for the present, but he pretended great eagerness to see Morgiana, and Abdallah began to play and Morgiana to dance. After she had performed several dances she drew her dagger and made passes with it, sometimes pointing it at her own breast, sometimes at her masters', as if it were part of the dance. Suddenly, out of breath, she snatched the tambourine from Abdallah with her left hand and held it out to her master, clutching the dagger in her right. Ali Baba and his son put a piece of gold into it, and Cogia Hassan, seeing that she was coming to him, pulled out his purse to make her a present, but while he was putting his hand into it Morgiana plunged the dagger into his heart.

"Unhappy girl!" cried Ali Baba and his son. "What have you done to ruin us?"

"It was to preserve you, master, not to ruin you," answered Morgiana. "See here"—opening the false merchant's garment and showing the dagger—"see what an enemy you have entertained! Remember, he would eat no salt with you; what more would you have? Look at him! He is both the false oil merchant and the captain of the forty thieves."

Ali Baba was so grateful to Morgiana for thus saving his life that he offered her in marriage to his son, who readily consented; and the wedding was celebrated with great splendor a few days after.

At the end of a year, Ali Baba, having heard nothing of the two remaining robbers, judged they were dead and set out to the cave. The door opened on his saying, "Open, Sesame!" Going in, he saw that nobody had been there since the captain had left it. He brought away as much gold as he could carry and returned to town. He told his son the secret of the cave, which his son handed down in turn, so the children and grandchildren of Ali Baba were rich to the end of their lives.

ARABIAN NIGHTS, TRANSLATED BY ANTOINE GALLAND

THE GOLDEN GOOSE

THERE WAS once a man who had three sons. The youngest of them was called Simpleton, and he was sneered and jeered at and snubbed on every possible opportunity. One day it happened that the eldest son wished to go into the forest to cut wood, and before he started out his mother gave him a fine rich cake and a bottle of wine so that he might be sure not to suffer from hunger or thirst.

When he reached the forest he met a little gray old man who wished him "Good morning" and said, "Do give me a piece of that cake you are carrying and a drink from your bottle of wine—I am so hungry and thirsty."

But this clever son replied, "If I give you my cake and wine I shall have none for myself; you just go your own way." And he left the little gray man standing there and went farther on into the forest. There he began to cut down a tree, but before long he made a false stroke with his axe, and cut his own arm so badly that he was obliged to go home and have it bound up by his mother.

Then the second son went to the forest, and his mother gave him a good cake and a bottle of wine as she had to his elder brother. He too met the little gray old man, who begged him for a morsel of cake and a drink of wine.

But the second son spoke most sensibly also, and said, "Whatever I give to you I deprive myself of. Just go your own way, will you?"

Not long afterward his punishment overtook him, for no sooner had he struck a couple of blows with his axe than he cut his leg so badly that he had to be carried back home.

Then the youngest son said, "Father, let me go out and cut wood."

But his father answered, "Both your brothers have

injured themselves. You had better not; you know nothing about it."

The boy begged him so hard to be allowed to go that at last his father said, "Very well, then—go! Perhaps when you have hurt yourself, you may learn to know better." His mother gave him only a very plain cake, made with water and baked in the cinders, and a bottle of sour beer.

When he came to the forest, he too met the little gray old man, who greeted him and said, "Give me a piece of your cake and a drink from your bottle. I am so hungry and thirsty."

The boy replied, "I have just a cinder cake and some sour beer, but if you care to have that, let us sit down and eat."

So they sat down, and when the boy brought out his cake he found it had turned into a fine rich loaf, and the sour beer into excellent wine. Then they ate and drank all they wanted.

When they had finished eating, the little gray man said, "Now I will bring you luck, because you have a kind heart and are willing to share what you have with others. There stands an old tree. Cut it down, and among its roots you'll find something."

With that the little man took his leave.

Then the boy began at once to hew down the tree, and when it fell he found among its roots a goose whose feathers were all of pure gold. He lifted it out, carried it off and took it with him to an inn where he meant to spend the night.

Now the landlord of the inn had three daughters, and when they saw the goose they were filled with curiosity about this wonderful bird, and each longed to have one of its golden feathers.

The eldest said to herself, "No doubt I shall soon find a good opportunity to pluck out one of its feathers," and the first time Simpleton happened to leave the room she caught hold of the goose by its wing. But, lo and behold! her fingers seemed to stick fast to the goose, and she could not take her hand away. Soon afterward the second daughter came in and thought to pluck a golden feather for herself too; but hardly had she touched her sister than she stuck fast as well. At last the third sister came with the same intention, but the other two cried out, "Keep off! For Heaven's sake, keep off!"

The youngest sister could not imagine why she was to keep off, and thought: If they are both there, why should not I be there too? So she sprang toward them; but no sooner had she touched one of them than she stuck fast to her. And they all three had to spend the night with the goose.

Next morning the boy tucked the goose under his arm and went off, without in the least troubling himself about the three girls who were hanging on to it. They just had to run after him right or left as best they could. In the middle of a field they met the parson, and when he saw this procession he cried, "For shame, you bold girls! What do you mean by running after a young fellow through the fields like that?"

And with that he caught the youngest girl by the arm to draw her away. But directly he touched her he stuck on and had to run along with the rest.

Not long afterward the town clerk came that way and was much surprised to see the parson following the footsteps of the three girls. "Why, where is Your Reverence going so fast?" cried he. And he ran after him, grabbed his coat and hung on to it himself.

As the five of them trotted along in this fashion one after the other, two peasants were coming from their work with their hoes. On seeing them, the parson called out and begged them to come and rescue him and the clerk. But no sooner did the first one touch the clerk than they were stuck too, and so there were seven of them running after Simpleton and his goose.

After a time they came to a town where a King reigned whose daughter was so serious and solemn that no one could ever manage to make her laugh. So the King had decreed that whoever should succeed in making her laugh could marry her.

When Simpleton heard this he marched before the Princess with his goose and its appendages, and as soon as she saw these seven people continually running after each other, she burst out laughing and could not stop

herself. Then he claimed her as his bride, but the King, who did not much fancy him as a son-in-law, made all sorts of objections and told him he must first find a man who could drink up a whole cellarful of wine.

Simpleton bethought him of the little gray old man, who could, he felt sure, help him. So he went off to the forest, and on the very spot where he had cut down the tree he saw a man with a most dismal expression on his face.

He asked the man what he was taking so much to heart, and the man answered, "I don't know how I am ever to quench this terrible thirst I am suffering from. Cold water doesn't suit me at all. To be sure, I've emptied a whole barrel of wine, but what is one drop on a hot stone?"

"I think I can help you," said the boy. "Come with me, and you shall drink to your heart's content."

So he took him to the King's cellar, and the man sat down before the huge casks and drank and drank till he had drunk up the whole contents of the cellar before the day closed.

Then Simpleton asked once more for his bride, but the King felt vexed at the idea of a stupid fellow whom people called Simpleton carrying off his daughter, and he began to make fresh conditions. He required Simpleton to find a man who could eat a mountain of bread. The boy did not wait to consider long but went straight off to the forest, and there on the same spot sat a man who was drawing in a strap as tightly as he could around his body, and making a most woeful face the while.

Said he, "I've eaten up a whole ovenful of loaves, but what's the good of that to anyone who is as hungry as I am? I declare my stomach feels quite empty, and I must draw my belt tight if I'm not to die of starvation."

Simpleton was delighted, and said, "Get up and come with me, and you shall have plenty to eat," and he brought him to the King's court.

Now the King had given orders to have all the flour in his kingdom brought together and to have a huge mountain baked of it. But the man from the wood just took up his stand before the mountain and began to eat, and in one day it had all vanished.

For the third time Simpleton asked for his bride, but again the King tried to make some evasion, and demanded a ship which could sail on land or water. "When you come sailing in such a ship," said he, "you shall have my daughter without further delay."

Again the boy started off to the forest, and there he found the little gray old man with whom he had shared his cake and who said, "I have eaten and I have drunk for you, and now I will give you the ship. I have done all these things for you because you were kind and merciful to me."

Then he gave him a ship which could sail on land or

water, and when the King saw it he felt he could no longer refuse him his daughter. So they celebrated the wedding with great rejoicings, and after the King's death Simpleton succeeded to the kingdom, and lived happily with his wife for many years.

JAKOB AND WILHELM GRIMM, TRANSLATED BY MAY SELLAR

WHY THE SEA IS SALT

Once upon a time long, long ago, there were two brothers, the one rich and the other poor. When Christmas Eve came, the poor one had not a bite in the house, either of meat or bread. So he went to his brother and begged him, in Heaven's name, to give him something for Christmas Day. It was by no means the first time his brother had been forced to give some food to him, and he was no more pleased at being asked now than he generally was.

"If you will do what I ask you, you shall have a whole ham," said he. The poor one immediately thanked him and promised.

"Well, here is the ham, and now you must go

straight to Dead Man's Hall," said the rich brother, throwing the ham to him.

"Well, I will do what I have promised," said the poor man, and he took the ham and set off. He went on and on for the livelong day, and at nightfall he came to a place where there was a bright light. I have no doubt this is the place, thought the man with the ham.

An old man with a long white beard was chopping yule logs.

"Good evening," said the man with the ham.

"Good evening to you. Where are you going at this late hour?" asked the old man.

"I am going to Dead Man's Hall, if only I am on the right track," answered the poor man.

"Oh, yes, you are right enough, for it is here," the old man said. "When you go inside they will all want to buy your ham, for they don't get much meat to eat there. But you must not sell it unless you can get for it the hand mill which stands behind the door. When you come out again I will teach you how to stop the hand mill, which is useful for almost everything."

So the man with the ham thanked the other for his good advice and rapped at the door. When he went in, everything happened just as the old man had said. All the people, great and small, came around him like ants on an anthill, and each tried to outbid the other for the ham.

"By rights, my old woman and I should have it for

our Christmas dinner, but since you have set your hearts upon it, I must just give it up to you," said the man. "But, if I sell it, I will have the hand mill standing there behind the door."

At first they would not hear of this, and haggled and bargained with the man, but he stuck to what he had said, and the people were forced to give the hand mill to him. When the man returned to the yard, he asked the old woodcutter how to stop the hand mill. And when he had learned that, he thanked him and set off with all the speed he could, but did not arrive home until after the clock had struck twelve on Christmas Eve.

"But where in the world have you been?" asked the old woman, his wife. "Here I have sat waiting for you hour after hour, and have not even two sticks to lay across each other underneath the Christmas porridge pot."

"Oh, I could not come before. I had something of importance to see about, and a long way to go, too. But now you shall just see!" said the man. Then he set the mill on the table and bade it first grind light, then a tablecloth, then meat and beer and everything else that was good for a Christmas Eve supper.

And the mill ground all that he ordered.

"Bless me!" said the old woman, as one thing after another appeared. She wanted to know where her husband had gotten the mill, but he would not tell her.

"Never mind where I got it. You can see it is a good one, and the water that turns it will never freeze," said the man. So he ground meat and drink and all kinds of good things, to last through Christmastide, and on the third day he invited friends to come to a feast.

Now when the rich brother saw what there was at the banquet and in the house, he was both vexed and angry, for he grudged everything his brother had. On Christmas Eve he was so poor he came to me and begged for a trifle, and here he gives a feast as if he were both a count and a king! thought he. "But, for Heaven's sake, tell me where you got your riches," said he to his brother.

"From behind the door," said he who owned the mill, for he did not choose to satisfy his brother on that point. But later in the evening, when he had taken a drop too much, he could not refrain from telling how he had come by the hand mill. "There you see what has brought me all my wealth!" And he brought out the mill from the cupboard and made it grind first one thing and then another.

When the brother saw that, he insisted on having the mill and after a great deal of persuasion got it. But he had to give three hundred dollars for it, and the poor brother was to keep it till haymaking time, for he thought: If I keep it that long, I can make it grind meat and drink that will last many a long year.

During that time the mill did not grow rusty, and, when hay harvest came, the rich brother took it, but the other had taken good care not to teach him how to stop it. It was evening when the rich man reached home, and in the morning he bade the old woman who tended his rooms and kitchen go out and spread the hay after the mowers, for he would attend to the house himself that day.

So, when dinner time drew near, he set the mill on the kitchen table and said, "Grind herrings and milk pudding, and do it both quickly and well."

So the mill began to grind herrings and milk pudding, and first all the dishes and tubs were filled, and then it covered the kitchen floor. The man twisted and turned the mill and did all he could to make it stop, but howsoever he turned it and screwed it, the mill went on grinding, and in a short time the pudding rose so high that the man was almost drowned. So he threw open the parlor door, but it was not long before the mill had ground the parlor full too, and it was with difficulty and danger that the man got through the mess of pudding and grabbed hold of the door latch. When the door was open, he did not stay long in the room, but ran out, and the herrings and pudding came after him and streamed out over both farm and field.

Now the old woman, who was out spreading the hay, began to think dinner was long in coming, and

said to the women and the mowers, "Though the master does not call us home, we may as well go. It may be he finds he is not good at making dinner, and I should go to help him." So they began to straggle homeward, but a little way up the hill they met the herrings and pudding, all pouring forth and winding about one over the other, and the man himself in front of the flood.

"Would to Heaven that each of you had a hundred stomachs! Take care that you are not drowned in the pudding!" he cried as he ran by them as if Mischief were at his heels, down to where his brother dwelled. Then he begged him to take the mill back again, and to do so in that instant, for, said he, "If it grind one hour more the whole district will be destroyed by herrings and pudding!" But the brother would not take it until the other paid him another three hundred dollars, and that he was obliged to do.

Now the poor brother had both the money and the mill again. So it was not long before he had a farmhouse much finer than his brother's, but the mill ground him so much money that he covered his house with blocks of gold, and, as it lay close by the seashore, it shone and glittered far out to sea. Everyone who sailed by put in to visit the rich man in the gold farmhouse, and everyone wanted to see the wonderful mill, for the report of it spread far and wide, and there was no one who had not heard tell of it.

After a long, long time there came a skipper who wished to see the mill. He asked if it could make salt. "Yes, it can make salt," said he who owned it, and when the skipper heard that, he wished with all his might and main to have the mill, no matter what it cost. He thought that if he had it he would not have to sail far away over the perilous sea for his cargo of salt. At first the owner would not hear of parting with the mill, but the skipper begged and prayed, and at last the man sold it to him, for many, many thousands of dollars. When the skipper had the mill he did not stay long, for he was afraid the man would change his mind, and he had no time to ask how he was to stop it grinding, but went on board his ship as fast as he could.

When he had gone a little way out to sea he took the mill on deck. "Grind salt, and grind both quickly and well," said the skipper.

So the mill began to grind salt, till it spouted out like water, and when the skipper had the ship filled he wanted to stop the mill, but whichsoever way he turned it, and howsoever he tried, it went on grinding, and the heap of salt grew higher and higher, until at last the ship sank.

There lies the mill at the bottom of the sea, and still, day by day, it grinds on: and that is why the sea is salt.

PETER C. ASBJÖRNSEN AND JÖRGEN E. MOE,
ANDREW LANG COLLECTION

THE UGLY DUCKLING

It was so lovely in the country—it was summer! The wheat was yellow, the oats were green, the hay was stacked in the meadows and the stork went tiptoeing about on his red legs, jabbering Egyptian, a language his mother had taught him. Around the fields and meadows were great forests, and in the midst of those forests lay deep lakes. Yes, it was indeed lovely in the country! An old manor house stood there, bathed in sunshine, surrounded by a deep moat, and from the walls down to the water's edge the bank was covered with great wild rhubarb leaves which were growing so high that little children would have been able to stand upright under the biggest of them. The place was as much of a wilderness as the densest forest.

There sat a Duck on her nest, busy hatching her ducklings, but she was almost tired of it, because sitting is such a tedious business, and she had very few callers. The other ducks thought it more fun to swim about in the moat than to come and have a gossip with her under a wild rhubarb leaf.

At last one eggshell after another began to crack open. "Cheep, cheep!" All the yolks had come to life and were sticking out their heads.

"Quack, quack," said the Duck, and her little ducklings came scurrying as fast as they could, looking about under the green leaves, and their mother let them look as much as they liked, because green is good for the eyes.

"How big the world is!" said the ducklings, for they felt far more comfortable now than when they were lying in their eggs.

"Do you imagine this is the whole of the world?" asked their mother. "It goes far beyond the other side of the garden, right into the rector's field, but I've never been there yet. I hope you're all here," she went on, and hoisted herself up. "No, I haven't got every one of you even now; the biggest egg is still there. I wonder how much longer it will take! I'm getting rather bored with the whole thing." And she squatted down again on the nest.

"Well, how are you getting on?" asked an Old Duck who came to call on her.

"That last egg is taking an awfully long time," said the Mother Duck. "It won't break; but let me show you the others, they're the sweetest ducklings I've ever seen. They are all exactly like their father; the scamp— he never comes to see me!"

"Let me look at the egg that won't break," said the

Old Duck. "You may be sure it's a turkey's egg. I was fooled like that once, and the trouble and bother I had with those youngsters, because they were actually afraid of the water! I simply couldn't get them to go in! I quacked at them and I snapped at them, but it was no use. Let me see the egg—of course, it's a turkey's egg. Leave it alone, and teach the other children to swim."

"Oh, well, if I've taken so much trouble I may just as well sit a little longer," said Mother Duck.

"Please yourself," said the Old Duck, and she waddled off.

At last the big egg cracked. "Cheep, cheep!" said the youngster, scrambling out. He was so big and ugly! Mother Duck looked at him.

"What a frightfully big Duckling that one is," she said. "None of the others looked like that! I wonder if he could possibly be a turkey chick. Well, we'll soon find out; he'll have to go into the water, even if I have to kick him in myself!"

The next day the weather was simply glorious, and Mother Duck appeared with her family down by the moat. Splash! There she was in the water! "Quack, quack," she said, and one duckling after another plunged in. The water closed over their heads, but they were up again in a second and floated beautifully. All of them were out in the water now, and even the ugly gray creature was swimming along with them.

"That's no turkey!" she said. "Look how nicely he uses his legs, and how straight he holds himself! He isn't really so bad when you take a good look at him. Quack, quack—come along with me, I'll bring you out into the world and introduce you to the duck yard, but keep close to me or you may get stepped on, and look out for the cat!"

So they made their entrance into the duck yard. What a pandemonium there was! Two families were quarreling over an eel's head; but in the end the cat got it after all.

"There you are, that's the way of the world!" said Mother Duck, licking her lips, for she did so want the eel's head herself. "Now use your legs," she said. "Move about briskly and bow to the Old Duck over there; she is the most aristocratic person here and of Spanish blood; that's why she is so stout. And be sure to observe that red rag around her leg. It's a great distinction and the highest honor that can be bestowed upon a duck. It means that her owner wishes to keep her and that she is to be specially noticed by man and beast. Now hurry! Don't turn your toes in; a well-brought-up duckling turns his toes out just as his father and mother do—like that."

And they did as they were told; but the other ducks looked at them and said out loud, "There now, have we got to have that crowd, too? As if there weren't enough of us already. Ugh, what a dreadful-looking

creature that Duckling is! We won't put up with him."
And immediately a duck rushed at him and bit him in
the neck.

"Leave him alone," said the mother. "He's not
bothering any of you."

"I know," said the duck who had bitten him, "but
he's too big and funny looking. What he wants is a
good smacking."

"Those are pretty children you've got, Mother,"
said the Old Duck with the rag around her leg. "They
are all nice looking except that one—he didn't turn out
so well."

"Your Grace," said Mother Duck, "he's not handsome, but he's as good as gold, and he swims as well
as any of the others, I daresay even a little better. He
was in the egg too long, that's why he isn't properly
shaped." And she pecked his neck and brushed up the
little creature. "As it happens, he's a drake," she
added, "so it doesn't matter quite so much."

But the poor Duckling who was the last to be
hatched, and who looked so ugly, was bitten and buf-
feted about and made fun of by all the ducks as well as
the hens.

"He's too big!" they all said. And the turkey-cock,
who was born with spurs and consequently thought he
was an emperor, blew himself up like a ship in full sail
and made for him, gobbling and gabbling till his wat-
tles were quite purple. The poor Duckling did not

know where to turn: he was so miserable because of his ugliness and because he was the butt of the whole barnyard.

And so it went on all the first day, and after that matters grew worse and worse. His own brothers and sisters were downright nasty to him and always said, "I hope the cat gets you, you skinny bag of bones!" And even his mother said, "I wish you were miles away!" And the ducks bit him and the hens pecked him, and the girl who fed them tried to kick him with her foot.

So one day, half running and half flying, he scrambled over the fence.

The little birds in the bushes rose up in alarm. That's because I'm so ugly, thought the Duckling, and closed his eyes, but he kept on running and finally came out into the great marsh where the wild ducks lived. There he lay the whole night long, very tired and very sad.

In the morning the wild ducks flew up and looked at their new companion. "What sort of a fellow are you?" they asked, and the Duckling turned in all directions, bowing to everybody around him as nicely as he could.

"You're appallingly ugly!" said the wild ducks, "but why should we care so long as you don't marry into our family?"

Poor thing! As if he had any thought of marrying!

All he wanted to do was to lie among the reeds and to drink a little marsh water.

So he lay there for two whole days, and then came two wild geese, or rather ganders, for they were young males. They had not been out of the egg very long, and that was why they were so cocky.

"Listen, young fellow," they said. "You're so ugly that we actually like you. Will you join us and be a bird of passage? There are some lovely wild geese, all nice young girls, in a marsh nearby. You're so ugly that you might appeal to them."

Two shots rang out—bang! bang! Both ganders fell dead among the reeds, and the water was reddened with their blood. Bang! bang! was heard again, and large flocks of wild geese flew up from the reeds. Then —bang! bang! bang! again and again. A great hunt was going on. The men were lying under cover around the marsh, and some of them were even up in the trees. Blue smoke drifted in among the dark trees and was carried far out over the water. Through the mud came the gundogs—splash! splash!—sniffing through the reeds and rushes. The poor Duckling was scared out of his wits and tried to hide his head under his wing, when suddenly a ferocious-looking dog came close to him, his tongue hanging far out of his mouth and his wild eyes gleaming horribly. He opened his jaws wide, showed his sharp teeth and—splash! splash!—off he went without touching the Duckling.

"Thank Heaven!" he sighed. "I'm so ugly that even the dog won't bother to bite me!" And so he lay perfectly still, while the shots rattled through the reeds as gun after gun was fired.

It was toward evening when it was quiet again; even then the poor Duckling dared not stir. He waited several hours before he looked about him, and then hurried away from the marsh as fast as he could. He ran over field and meadow, hardly able to fight against the strong wind.

Late that night he reached a wretched little hut, so wretched, in fact, that it did not know which way to fall, and that is why it remained standing upright. The wind whistled so fiercely around the Duckling that the poor thing simply had to sit down on his tail to keep from being knocked over.

The storm grew worse and worse. Then he noticed that the door had come off one of its hinges and hung so crookedly that he could slip inside through the opening, and that is what he did.

An old woman lived here with her Tomcat and her Hen. The Cat, whom she called "Sonny," knew how to arch his back and purr; in fact, he could even give out sparks, but for that she had to rub his fur the wrong way. The Hen had little short legs and was called "Stumpy." She produced many, many eggs, and the old woman loved her as her own child.

Next morning they at once noticed the strange

Duckling; the Cat began to purr and the Hen to cluck. "What's the matter?" asked the old woman, looking all about her; but her eyes were not very good and so she mistook the Duckling for a fat duck that had lost her way.

"What a windfall!" she said. "Now I shall have duck's eggs—if it doesn't happen to be a drake. We must make sure of that." So the Duckling was taken into the house on trial for three weeks, but not a single egg came along.

Now the Cat was master of the house, and the Hen was mistress, and they always said, "We, and the world," for they imagined themselves to be not only half the world, but by far the better half.

The Duckling thought that other people might be allowed to have an opinion too, but the Hen could not see that at all.

"Can you lay eggs?" she asked.

"No."

"Well, then, you'd better keep your mouth shut!"

And the Cat said, "Can you arch your back, purr and give out sparks?"

"No."

"Well, then, you can't have any opinion worth offering when sensible people are speaking."

The Duckling sat in a corner, feeling very gloomy and depressed; then he suddenly thought of the fresh air and the bright sunshine, and such a longing came over him to swim in the water that he could not help telling the Hen about it.

"What's the matter with you?" asked the Hen. "You haven't got anything to do, that's why you get these silly ideas. Either lay eggs or purr and you'll soon be all right."

"You don't understand me," said the Duckling.

"Well, if we don't understand you, then who would? You surely don't imagine you're wiser than the Cat or the old woman—not to mention myself, of course. Don't give yourself such airs, child. Believe me, I only wish you well. I tell you unpleasant things, but that's the way to know one's real friends. Come on, hurry up, see that you lay eggs, and do learn how to purr or to give out sparks!"

"I think I had better go out into the wide world," said the Duckling.

"Please yourself," said the Hen.

So the Duckling went away. He walked on the land and swam in the water and dived down into it, but he was still snubbed by every creature because of his ugliness.

Autumn set in. The leaves turned yellow and brown; the wind caught them and whirled them about; and up in the air it looked very cold. The clouds hung low, heavy with snowflakes, and on the fence perched the raven, trembling with the cold, and croaking, "Caw! Caw!" The mere thought of it was enough to make anybody shiver. The poor Duckling was certainly to be pitied!

One evening, when the sun was setting in all its splendor, a large flock of big handsome birds came out of the bushes. The Duckling had never before seen anything quite so beautiful as they were—dazzlingly white, with long supple necks—they were swans! They uttered a most uncanny cry, and spread their splendid great wings to fly away to warmer countries and open lakes. They rose so high, so very high in the air that a strange feeling came over the ugly little Duckling as he watched them. He turned around and around in the water like a wheel, craned his neck to follow their flight and uttered a cry so loud and strange that it frightened him.

He could not forget those noble birds, those happy birds, and when they were lost to sight he dived down to the bottom of the water; then when he came up again he was quite beside himself. He did not know what the birds were called, nor where they were flying to, and yet he loved them more than he had ever loved anything. He did not envy them in the least; it would never have occurred to him to want such beauty for himself. He would have been quite content if only the ducks would have put up with him—the poor ugly creature!

And the winter grew so cold, so bitterly cold. The Duckling was forced to swim about to keep the water

See page 124

from freezing altogether, but every night the opening became smaller and smaller; at last it froze so hard that the ice made cracking noises, and the Duckling had to keep on paddling to prevent the opening from closing up. In the end he was exhausted and lay quite still, caught in the ice.

Early next morning a farmer came by, and when he saw him he went onto the ice, broke it with his wooden shoe and carried him home to his wife. There the Duckling revived.

The children wanted to play with him, but he thought they meant to do him harm, so he fluttered, terrified, into the milk pail, splashing the milk all over the room. The farmer's wife screamed and threw up her hands in fright. Then he flew into the butter tub, and from that into the flour barrel and out again. What a sight he was! The woman shrieked and struck at him with her tongs. Laughing and shouting, the children fell on each other trying to catch him. Fortunately, the door was open, so the Duckling dashed out of the house and into the bushes and lay there in a daze in the newly fallen snow.

It would be too sad, however, to tell of the trouble and misery he had to suffer during that cruel winter. But when the sun began to shine warmly he found himself once more in the marsh among the reeds. The larks were singing—it was spring, beautiful spring!

Then suddenly he spread his wings; the sound of

their whirring made him realize how much stronger they had grown, and they carried him powerfully along. Before he knew it, he found himself in a great garden where the apple trees stood in bloom and the lilac filled the air with its fragrance.

It was so lovely here, so full of the freshness of spring. And floating down the stream in front of him came three beautiful white swans, ruffling their feathers proudly. The Duckling recognized the glorious creatures, and felt a strange sadness come over him.

"I will fly near those royal birds, and they will peck me to death for daring to bring my ugly self near them. But that doesn't matter in the least! Better to be killed by them than to be bitten by the ducks, pecked by the hens, kicked by the girl in charge of the hen run and suffer untold agony in winter."

Then he flew into the water and swam toward the beautiful swans. They saw him and dashed at him with outspread, rustling feathers. "Kill me," said the poor creature, and he bowed his head down upon the surface of the stream, expecting the worst. But what was this he saw mirrored in the clear water? He saw beneath him his own image, but it was no longer the image of an awkward, dirty, gray bird, ugly and repulsive—he himself was a swan!

It does not matter if one was born in a duck yard, if only one has lain in a swan's egg.

The great swans swam around him and stroked him

with their beaks. He felt quite glad to have been through so much trouble and adversity, for now he could fully appreciate not only his own good fortune, but also the beauty that greeted him.

Some little children came into the garden to throw bread and corn into the water, and the youngest exclaimed, "There's a new one!" And the other children chimed in, "Yes, there's a new one!" They clapped their hands, danced about and ran to fetch their father and mother.

Bread and cake were thrown into the water, and everyone said, "The new one is the most beautiful! He's so young and handsome!" And the old swans bowed to him.

That made him feel quite embarrassed, and he put his head under his wing, not knowing what it was all about. An overwhelming happiness filled him, and yet he was not a bit proud, for a good heart never becomes proud. He remembered how once he had been despised and persecuted; and now he heard everyone saying that he was the most beautiful of beautiful birds.

And the lilac bushes dipped their branches into the water before him, and the sun shone warm and mild. He rustled his feathers and held his graceful neck high, and from the depths of his heart he joyfully exclaimed, "I never dreamt that so much happiness was possible when I was the Ugly Duckling."

HANS CHRISTIAN ANDERSEN, TRANSLATED BY PAUL LEYSSAC

JACK AND THE BEANSTALK

ONCE UPON a time there was a poor widow who lived in a little cottage with her only son Jack, who was a simple but kindhearted boy. There had been a terribly hard winter, and the poor woman saw there would be no means of keeping Jack and herself from starvation but by selling her cow. So one morning she said to her son, "I am too weak to go myself, Jack. You must take the cow to market for me and sell her."

"Cheer up, Mother, I'll go and get work somewhere," said Jack.

"We've tried that before and nobody would take you," said his mother.

So Jack took the cow and left for the market. On the way, he met a butcher who had some beautiful beans in his hand.

Jack stopped to look at the beans, and the butcher told the boy that they were very valuable, and persuaded the silly lad to sell him the cow in exchange for these beans.

When he brought them home to his mother instead

of the money she had expected, she was vexed and shed many tears, scolding Jack for his folly. He was very sorry, and when mother and son went to bed sadly that night their last hope seemed gone.

At daybreak Jack rose and went out into the garden. At least, he thought, I can sow the wonderful beans. Mother says that they are just common scarlet runners and nothing else, but I may as well try and see. So he took a piece of stick, made some holes in the ground and put in the beans.

That day they had very little dinner and again went sadly to bed, knowing that the next day there would be none. Jack, unable to sleep from grief and vexation, got up at dawn and went out into the garden.

What was his amazement to find that the beans had grown in the night, and had climbed up and up till they covered the high cliff that sheltered the cottage and disappeared above it! The stalks had twined themselves together till they formed a sturdy ladder.

It would be easy to climb it, thought Jack. And, having thought of it, he at once resolved to do so. So climb he did, and went up and up on the ladderlike beanstalk till everything he had left behind him—the cottage, the village and even the tall church tower—looked quite small, and still he could not see the top of the beanstalk.

Jack felt tired and thought for a moment that he would go down again; but he was a very persevering boy and he knew that the way to succeed in anything is not to give up. So after resting for a few minutes he went on.

After climbing higher and higher, till he grew afraid to look down for fear he would become dizzy, Jack at last reached the top of the beanstalk and found himself in a beautiful country with fine meadows dotted with grazing sheep. A crystal stream ran through the pastures, and not far from the place where he had gotten off the beanstalk stood a fine, strong castle.

While Jack was standing looking at the castle, a very strange-looking woman came out of the wood and advanced toward him. She wore a pointed cap of quilted red satin turned up with ermine, her hair streamed loose over her shoulders and she walked with a staff. Jack took off his cap and made her a bow.

"If you please, ma'am," said he politely, "is this your house?"

"No," said the old woman. "Listen, and I will tell you the story of that castle.

"Once upon a time there was a noble knight who lived in this castle, which is on the borders of Fairyland. He had a fair and beloved wife and several lovely children. And as his neighbors, the little people, were very friendly toward him, they bestowed on him many excellent and precious gifts.

"Rumor whispered of these treasures, and a monstrous giant, who lived at no great distance and who

was a very wicked being, resolved that he would take possession of them.

"So he bribed a false servant to let him inside the castle, when the knight was asleep, and he killed him as he lay. Then he went to the part of the castle which was the nursery and also killed all the poor little ones he found there.

"Happily for her, the knight's lady was not there. She had gone with her infant son, who was only two or three months old, to visit her old nurse who lived in the valley, and she had been detained there all night by a storm.

"The next morning, as soon as it was light, one of the servants who had managed to escape from the castle came to tell the poor lady of the sad fate of her husband and her pretty babes. She could scarcely believe him at first, and, in her sorrow, was eager at once to go back and share the fate of her dear ones. But the old nurse, with many tears, besought her to remember that she still had a child and that it was her duty to live for his sake.

"The lady yielded to this reasoning and consented to remain in concealment at her nurse's house, for the servant told her that the giant had vowed, if he could find her, he would kill both her and her baby. Years went by. The old nurse died, leaving her cottage and its few articles of furniture to her poor mistress, who lived in it, working as a peasant for her daily bread.

Her spinning wheel and the milk of a cow which she had purchased with the little money she had with her sufficed for the scanty subsistence of herself and her growing son. There was a nice little garden attached to the cottage, in which they cultivated peas, beans and cabbages, and the old lady was not ashamed to go out and work in the fields to supply her son's wants.

"Jack, that poor lady is your mother. This castle was once your father's and must again be yours."

Jack uttered a cry of surprise. "My mother! Oh, ma'am, what ought I to do?"

"Your duty requires you to win it back for your mother," the woman said. "But the task is a very difficult one and full of peril, Jack. Have you courage to undertake it?"

"I fear nothing when I am doing right," said Jack, bravely.

"Then," said the lady in the red cap, "you are one of those who slay giants. You must get into the castle, and if possible gain possession of the hen that lays golden eggs and the harp that talks. Remember, all the giant possesses is really yours."

As she ceased speaking, the lady of the red hat suddenly disappeared, and of course Jack then knew she was a fairy.

Jack determined at once to attempt the adventure. He advanced and blew the horn which hung at the castle portal. The door was opened in a moment by a frightful giantess with one great eye in the middle of her forehead.

As soon as Jack saw her he turned to run away, but the giantess caught him and began to push and pull him toward the castle.

"Ho, ho!" she laughed terribly. "You didn't expect to see me here, that is clear! No, I shan't let you go. I am overworked, and I don't see why I should not have a page the same as other ladies. And you shall clean the knives and black the boots and make the fires, and help me generally when the giant is out. When he is at home I must hide you, for he has eaten up my other pages, and you would be a dainty morsel, my little lad."

While she spoke she dragged Jack right into the castle. The poor boy was very frightened, but he struggled to be brave and make the best of things. "I am quite ready to help you and do what I can to serve you, madam," he said, "only I beg you be good enough to hide me from your husband, for I should not like to be eaten at all."

"That's a good boy," said the giantess, nodding her head. "Come here, child. Go into my wardrobe; he never ventures to open that. You will be safe there."

She opened a huge wardrobe which stood in the great hall and shut him into it. The keyhole was so large that it admitted plenty of air, and through it Jack could see everything that took place in the room. By and by he heard a heavy tramp on the stairs, like the

lumbering along of a great cannon, and then a voice
booming:

> Fee-fi-fo-fum,
> I smell the blood of an Englishman.
> Be he alive or be he dead,
> I'll grind his bones to make my bread.

"Wife," cried the giant, "there is an Englishman in
the castle. Let me have him for breakfast."

"You have grown old and stupid," cried the giantess
in her loud tones. "It is only a nice fresh elephant steak
which you smell. Sit down and have breakfast."

And she placed a huge dish before him of savory
steaming meat, which greatly pleased him and made
him forget his idea of an Englishman being in the castle. When he had breakfasted he went for a walk, and
then the giantess made Jack come out to help her,
which he busily did all day. She fed him well and, when
evening came, put him back in the wardrobe.

The giant came in to supper. Jack watched him
through the keyhole and was amazed to see him pick
a wolf's bone and put half a fowl at a time into his
enormous mouth. When the supper was ended he bade
his wife bring him his hen that laid the golden eggs.

"It lays as well as it did when it belonged to that
paltry knight," he said. "Indeed I think the eggs are
heavier than ever."

The giantess went away, and soon returned with a

little brown hen, which she placed on the table before her husband.

"And now, my dear," she said, "I am going for a walk, if you don't want me any longer."

"Go," said the giant, "I shall be glad to have a nap in a little while."

Then he took up the brown hen and said to her: "Lay!" And she instantly laid a golden egg.

"Lay!" said the giant again. And she laid another.

"Lay!" he repeated the third time. And again a golden egg lay on the table.

Now Jack was sure this hen was the one of which the fairy had spoken. By and by the giant put the hen down on the floor, and soon went fast asleep, snoring so loudly that it sounded like thunder.

When Jack perceived that the giant was fast asleep, he pushed open the door of the wardrobe and crept out. Very softly he stole across the room and, picking up the hen, hurried away. He knew the way to the kitchen, the door of which he found ajar. He opened it, then shut and locked it after him, and flew back to the beanstalk, which he descended just as fast as his feet would move.

When his mother saw him she wept for joy, for she had feared the fairies had carried him off or that the giant, whom she had always secretly feared, had found him. But Jack put the brown hen down before her, and told her he had been in the giant's castle, and all his adventures. She was very glad to see the hen, which would surely make them rich.

Jack made another journey up the beanstalk to the giant's castle one day while his mother had gone to the market; but first he dyed his hair and disguised himself. The old giantess did not recognize him and dragged him in as she had done before to help do the work; but she heard her husband coming and hid him in the wardrobe, not thinking that he was the same boy who had stolen the hen. She bade him stay quite still there, afraid the giant would eat him.

Then the giant came in, saying:

> Fee-fi-fo-fum,
> I smell the blood of an Englishman.
> Be he alive or be he dead,
> I'll grind his bones to make my bread.

"Nonsense!" said the wife. "It is only a roasted ox that I thought would be a tidbit for your supper. Sit down and I will bring it at once."

The giant sat down, and soon his wife brought up a roasted ox on a large dish, and they began their supper. Jack was amazed to see them pick its bones as if it had been a small bird. As soon as they had finished their meal, the giantess rose and said, "Now, my dear, with your leave I am going up to my room to finish the story I am reading. If you want me, call for me."

"First," answered the giant, "bring me my money

bags, that I may count my gold pieces before I sleep."

The giantess obeyed. She soon brought two large bags over her shoulders, which she put down by her husband. "There," she said, "that is all that is left of the knight's money. When you have spent it you must go and take another baron's castle."

"That he shan't do, if I can help it," Jack vowed to himself.

The giant, when his wife was gone, took out heaps and heaps of gold pieces, counted them and put them in stacks, till he was bored. Then he swept them back into their bags and, leaning back in his chair, fell fast asleep, snoring so loudly that no other sound was audible.

Jack stole softly from the wardrobe and, taking up the bags of money, which were really his own because the giant had stolen them from his father, he ran off. After descending the beanstalk with great difficulty, he laid the bags of gold on his mother's table. She had just returned from town and was crying because Jack was not at home.

"There, Mother, I have brought you the gold that my father lost."

"Oh, Jack, you are a very good boy, but I wish you would not risk your precious life in the giant's castle! Tell me how you came to go there again."

And Jack told her all about it. His mother was very glad to have the money, but she did not like him to run any risk for her. But after a time Jack made up his mind to go again to the giant's castle.

So he climbed the beanstalk once more and blew the horn at the giant's gate. The giantess soon opened the door. She was very stupid and did not recognize him. She stopped a moment before she took him in, because she feared another robbery. But Jack's fresh face looked so innocent she bade him come in, and again she hid him away in the wardrobe.

By and by the giant came home, and as soon as he had crossed the threshold, he roared out:

> Fee-fi-fo-fum,
> I smell the blood of an Englishman.
> Be he alive or be he dead,
> I'll grind his bones to make my bread.

"You stupid old giant," said his wife, "you only smell the nice sheep I grilled for your dinner."

The giant sat down, and his wife brought up a whole sheep for his dinner. When he had eaten it all, he said, "Now bring me my harp, and I will have a little music while you take your walk."

The giantess obeyed and returned with a beautiful harp. The framework was all sparkling with diamonds and rubies, and the strings were all of gold.

"This is one of the nicest things I took from the knight," said the giant. "I am very fond of music, and my harp is a faithful servant."

So he drew the harp toward him, and said, "Play!"
And the harp played a very soft, sad air.

"Play something merrier!" said the giant.
And the harp played a gay tune.

"Now play me a lullaby," roared the giant. And the harp played a sweet lullaby, and at the sound its master fell asleep.

Then Jack stole softly out of the wardrobe and went into the huge kitchen to see if the giantess had gone out. He found no one there, so he went to the door and opened it softly. Then he entered the giant's room, seized the harp and ran away with it. But as he jumped over the threshold the harp called out loudly, "Master! Master!"

The giant woke up. With a tremendous roar he sprang from his seat and in two strides reached the door. Jack was very nimble and he fled like lightning with the harp, talking to it as he went, for he saw it was a fairy, and told it he was the son of its old master, the knight. Still the giant came on so fast that he was quite close to poor Jack and he stretched out his great hand to catch him. But, luckily, just at that moment he stepped upon a loose stone, stumbled and fell flat on the ground, where he lay at his full length.

Jack had just time to get on the beanstalk and hasten down it; but as he reached their own garden he beheld the giant descending after him. "Mother! Mother!" cried Jack. "Make haste and give me the axe."

His mother ran to him with the axe in her hand, and Jack with one tremendous blow cut through all the beanstalks except one. "Now, Mother, stand out of the way!" said he.

Jack's mother shrank back, and it was well she did, for just as the giant took hold of the last branch of the beanstalk, Jack cut the stem through and darted away. Down came the giant with a terrible crash, and that was the end of him. Before Jack and his mother had recovered from their alarm, a beautiful lady stood before them.

"Jack," said she, "you have acted like a brave knight's son and deserve to have your inheritance restored to you. Dig a grave and bury the giant, and then go and kill the giantess."

"But," said Jack, "I could not kill anyone unless I were fighting with him, and I could not draw my sword upon a woman. Moreover, the giantess was always very kind to me."

The fairy smiled on Jack. "I am much pleased with your generous feeling," she said. "Nevertheless, return to the castle, and act as you will find needful."

Jack asked the fairy to show him the way to the castle, as the beanstalk was now down. She told him she would drive him there in her chariot, which was drawn by two peacocks. Jack thanked her and sat down in the chariot with her.

The fairy drove him a long distance till they reached

a village which lay at the bottom of the hill. Here they found a number of wretched-looking men assembled. The fairy stopped her carriage and addressed them. "My friends," said she, "the cruel giant who oppressed you and ate up all your flocks and herds is dead, thanks to this young gentleman. He is the son of your kind old master, the knight."

The men gave a loud cheer at these words and pressed forward to say that they would serve Jack as faithfully as they had served his father. The fairy bade them follow her to the castle, and they marched there in a body. When they arrived, Jack blew the horn and demanded admittance.

The old giantess saw them coming from the turret loophole. She was very frightened, for she guessed that something had happened to her husband. As she came downstairs very quickly she caught her foot in her dress and fell from the top to the bottom.

When the people outside found that the door was not open, they took crowbars and forced the portal. Nobody was to be seen, but on going into the castle they found the body of the dead giantess at the foot of the stairs.

Thus Jack took possession of the castle. The fairy brought his mother to him, with the hen and the harp. He had the giantess buried and endeavored to help those whom the giant had robbed. Before her departure for Fairyland, the fairy explained to Jack that she had sent the butcher to meet him with the beans, to test what sort of lad he was.

"If you had looked at the gigantic beanstalk and just wondered stupidly about it," she said, "I should have left you where misfortune had placed you, only restoring her cow to your mother. But you showed an inquiring mind and great courage and enterprise, therefore you deserve to rise; and when you mounted the beanstalk you climbed the ladder of fortune."

She then took her leave of Jack and his mother.

OLD ENGLISH TALE, ANDREW LANG COLLECTION

TWO FROGS

ONCE UPON a time, in the country of Japan, there lived two Frogs, one of whom made his home in a ditch near the town of Osaka, on the seacoast, while the other dwelled in a clear little stream which ran through the city of Kyoto. At such a great distance apart, they had never even heard of each other; but, oddly enough, the idea came into both their heads at the same time that they should like to see a little of the world, and the Frog who lived in Kyoto wanted to visit Osaka, and the Frog who lived near Osaka wished to go to Kyoto, where the great Mikado had his palace.

So one fine morning in the spring they both set out along the road that led from Kyoto to Osaka, one Frog coming from Osaka and the other from Kyoto. The journey was more tiring than they expected, for they did not know much about traveling nor that halfway between the two towns there rose a mountain which had to be climbed. It took them a long while and a great many hops to reach the top, but there they were at last, and what was the surprise of each to see another frog before him!

They looked at each other for a moment without speaking and then fell into conversation, explaining the cause of their meeting so far from their homes. It was delightful to find that they both felt the same wish —to learn a little more of their native country—and, as there was no sort of hurry, they stretched themselves out in a cool, damp place and agreed that they would have a good rest before they parted to go their separate ways.

"What a pity we are not bigger," said the Osaka Frog, "for then we could see both towns from here and tell if it is worth our while going on."

"Oh, that is easily managed," returned the Kyoto Frog. "We have only to stand up on our hind legs and

hold on to each other, and then we can each look at the town we are traveling to."

This idea pleased the Osaka Frog so much that he at once jumped up and put his front feet on the shoulders of his friend, who had risen also. There they both stood, stretching themselves as high as they could, and holding to each other tightly so that they might not fall down.

The Kyoto Frog turned his nose toward Osaka, and the Osaka Frog turned his nose toward Kyoto. But the foolish things forgot that when they stood up their great eyes lay in the back of their heads, and that, though their noses might point to the places to which they wanted to go, their eyes beheld the places from which they had come.

"Dear me," cried the Osaka Frog, "Kyoto is exactly like Osaka! It is certainly not worth such a long journey. I shall go home!"

"If I'd had any idea that Osaka was only a copy of Kyoto I should never have traveled all this way!" exclaimed the Frog from Kyoto. And as he spoke he took his hands from his friend's shoulders and they both fell down on the grass.

Then the two Frogs took a polite farewell of each other and set off for home again, and to the end of their lives they believed that Osaka and Kyoto, which are as different to look at as two towns can be, were alike as two peas. FROM TALES OF JAPAN, ANDREW LANG COLLECTION

THE SNOW QUEEN

THERE WAS once a dread-fully wicked hobgoblin. One day he was in high good spirits because he had made a mirror which reflected everything that was good and beautiful in such a way that it dwindled almost to nothing, but anything that was bad and ugly stood out very clearly and appeared much worse. The most beautiful landscapes looked like boiled spinach. The nicest people looked repulsive or seemed to stand on their heads or had no middles, and their faces were so distorted that they could not be recognized. And if anyone had a single freckle you might be sure it would look as if it had spread over his whole nose and mouth. That's the funniest thing about it, thought the hobgoblin.

One day the hobgoblin was flying high among the clouds, maliciously flashing his mirror on all the countries below. Suddenly it slipped from his hands and crashed to the earth, shattered into millions and billions of pieces. And now came the greatest mischief of all, for most of the pieces were hardly as large as a grain of sand, and they flew about all over the world.

If anyone got a speck of the mirror in his eye there it stayed. From then on he would see everything crooked, or else could see only the ugly side of things. For every tiny splinter of the glass possessed the same power as the whole mirror.

Some people got a splinter in their hearts, and that was dreadful, for then the heart would turn into a lump of ice. A few of the fragments were large enough to be used as windowpanes, but how terrible it would be to look at one's friends and neighbors through such a window!

The hobgoblin was so pleased he laughed till his sides ached, as the tiny bits of glass continued to whirl about in the air.

And now we will hear what happened.

A Little Boy and a Little Girl

In a large town, where there were so many people and houses that there was not enough room for everybody to have a garden, lived two poor children. They were not brother and sister, but they loved each other just as much as if they were. Their parents lived opposite one another in two attics, and each family had planted a rose tree and sweet peas in a window box. In summer the two children were allowed to sit out underneath the rose trees and play lovely games together all afternoon.

In the winter they could not do this, so they heated pennies on the stove and put them against the frozen windowpanes. These made perfect peepholes through which they could gaze at each other across the frozen gutters.

His name was Kay, and hers was Gerda.

One day it was snowing very hard.

"Those are the white bees swarming," said the old grandmother.

"Have they got a queen bee too?" asked the little boy, for he knew that the real bees have one.

"To be sure," said the grandmother. "She flies wherever they swarm the thickest. She is the Snow Queen and is the biggest of them all. She never remains still upon the earth, but always returns to the black clouds. Often at midnight she flies through the streets of the town and peeps in at all the windows, and then the snowflakes freeze in pretty patterns and look like flowers."

"Yes, we have seen that," said both children; they knew that it was true.

"Can the Snow Queen come in here?" asked the little girl.

"Just let her!" cried the boy. "I would put her on the stove and melt her!"

But the grandmother stroked his hair, and told some more stories.

That evening, when little Kay was going to bed, he

jumped on the chair by the window and peeped through the little hole. A few snowflakes were falling, and one of them, the largest, lay on the edge of one of the window boxes. The snowflake grew larger and larger till it took the form of a maiden, dressed in finest white gauze.

She was so beautiful and delicate, but all ice—hard, glittering ice.

She nodded at the window, and beckoned to Kay with her hand. The little boy was frightened at the sight of her and sprang down from the chair. Suddenly it seemed as if a great white bird had flown past the window.

The next day the weather cleared. Not long after, a thaw set in—and spring appeared. With the warm spring sunshine, the countryside turned a soft green, the swallows worked busily on their nests and Kay and Gerda played together once more in their little garden high on the rooftop. They knew that summer had come at last when their little rose trees burst into glorious bloom.

One day the children were looking at a picture book. The clock in the great church tower had just struck five, when Kay suddenly exclaimed, "Oh! Something has stung my heart, and now I've got something in my eye!" Gerda threw her arms around his neck. He blinked his eyes again and again; but no, she could see nothing in them.

"I think it is gone now," said he. But it had not gone. It was one of the tiny splinters from the magic mirror we have heard about, the mirror that turned whatever was fine and good reflected in it into something small and ugly. And a splinter had found its way to poor Kay's heart, which began to change into a lump of ice. His heart did not hurt him at all, but the splinter was still there.

"Why are you crying?" he asked Gerda. "It makes you look so ugly! There's nothing the matter with me. Just look! That rose is all worm-eaten, and this one is stunted! What ugly roses they are!"

And he began to pull them to pieces.

"Kay, what *are* you doing?" cried the little girl, and she threw up her hands.

When he saw how frightened she was he pulled off another rose and ran inside to his window, away from dear little Gerda.

When she came later on with a picture book, he said that it was only fit for babies, and when his grandmother told them stories, he always interrupted with, "But——" and then he would get behind her and put on her spectacles and mimic everything she did. Very soon he could imitate whatever was odd or ugly about the people who lived on their street.

When winter came, he began to love the cold. Each day he would take a magnifying glass and hold it over his blue coat while the snowflakes fell on it. "Look in

154

the glass, Gerda! They are much more perfect than real flowers. If only they did not melt!"

One morning Kay went out with his warm gloves on and his little sled hung over his shoulder. He shouted to Gerda, "I don't want to play with you. I am going to the marketplace to be with the other boys," and away he went.

In the marketplace the boldest boys often used to fasten their sleds to the rears of the carts of the farmers, and then they got a good ride. That day, when Kay and the other boys were in the middle of their games, there drove into the square a large white sleigh, and in it sat a figure dressed in a white fur cloak and a white fur cap.

The sleigh drove around the square twice. Suddenly it came to a short stop, and Kay fastened his little sled behind it and was pulled away. The sleigh began to go more and more quickly. The driver turned around from time to time and nodded to Kay in a friendly way, as if they had known each other before. Every time Kay tried to unfasten his sled the driver nodded again, and Kay sat still, and so they drove swiftly out of the town.

The snow began to fall so thickly that the little boy could not see his hand before him as they sped along. He tried to unfasten the cord to get free of the big sleigh, but it was no use; his little sled could not be loosened and on they went like the wind. He cried out, but nobody heard him. He was dreadfully frightened.

The snowflakes grew larger and larger till they looked like great white birds. All at once the large sleigh stopped, and the figure who was driving stood up. It was a lady, tall and slim and glittering. Her fur cloak and cap were made entirely of snow. It was the Snow Queen.

"We have made good time," she said. "But you are almost frozen. Creep in under my cloak."

And she held him close to her in the sleigh and drew the cloak over him. He felt as though he were sinking into a snowdrift.

"Are you still cold?" she asked, and kissed him on the forehead. The kiss was as cold as ice and reached down to his heart, which was already frozen into half a lump of ice.

"My sled! Don't forget my sled!" He thought of that first, and they fastened it to one of the white birds, who flew behind with the sled on its back.

The Snow Queen kissed Kay again, and he forgot all about little Gerda, his grandmother and everybody else at home.

"Now I must not kiss you anymore," she said, "or I will kiss you to death."

Then away they flew over forests and lakes, over sea and land. Around them whistled the cold wind, the wolves howled and the snow hissed; over them flew the black shrieking crows. But high up the moon shone

large and bright, and thus Kay passed the long, long winter night. During the day he slept at the Snow Queen's feet.

The Old Woman and Her Magic Garden

But what happened to little Gerda when Kay did not come back? What had become of him? Nobody knew. The other boys told how they had seen him fasten his sled to a large one which had driven out of the town gate. Gerda cried a great deal. The winter was long and dark to her.

Then the spring came and with it the warm sunshine. "I will go and look for Kay," said Gerda.

So she went down to the river and climbed into a little boat that lay on the bank. Presently the stream began to carry it away. The boat glided along, passing trees and fields; then Gerda saw a large cherry orchard, in which stood a house with strange red, blue and yellow windows and a straw roof. Before the door stood two wooden soldiers at attention.

Gerda thought they were alive and called to them, but naturally they did not answer. The current swept the boat straight toward the bank. Gerda called still louder, and a very old woman came out of the house. She leaned upon a crutch and wore a large sun hat painted with the most beautiful flowers.

"You poor child!" said the old woman.

And then she stepped into the water, brought the boat in close with her crutch and lifted little Gerda out.

"And now come and tell me who you are and how you came here," she said, and taking Gerda's hand she led her into the house and shut the door.

The windows were very high and painted red, blue and yellow, so that the light came through in strange colors. On the table was a bowl of the most delicious cherries, and the old woman let Gerda eat as many as she liked, while she combed her hair with a gold comb. The beautiful sunny hair rippled and shone around the friendly face. "I have always longed to have a dear little girl like you," said the old woman. "You shall see how happy we will be together."

And as she combed Gerda's hair, Gerda thought less and less about Kay, for the old woman was a witch, but not a wicked witch. She only enchanted now and then to amuse herself. She did want to keep little Gerda very much, and so she went into the garden and waved her crooked stick over all the rosebushes, and they disappeared into the black earth, leaving no trace of where they had been. The witch was afraid that if Gerda saw the roses they would remind her of her own roses and of Kay, and she would run away.

Then she led Gerda out into the garden. How glorious it was, and what lovely scents filled the air!

Gerda jumped for joy and played in the garden till the sun set behind the tall cherry trees. Then she went to sleep in a beautiful bed with red silk pillows filled with violets, and she slept soundly and dreamed as a queen does on her wedding day.

The next day she played again among the flowers in the warm sunshine, and so many days passed by. Gerda knew every flower, but although there were so many, it seemed to her as if one was missing, but she could not remember which.

One day she happened to look at the old woman's sun hat, the one with painted flowers on it, and there she saw a rose. The good witch had forgotten about that one when she made the other roses disappear into the black earth. It is so difficult to think of everything! "Why, there are no roses here!" cried Gerda, and then she sat down and cried, but her tears fell on the spot where a rosebush had sunk, and when her warm tears watered the earth, the bush came up in full bloom just as it had been before. Gerda kissed the roses and thought of the lovely ones at home, and with them came the thought of Kay. "Oh, what have I been doing!" said the little girl. "I wanted to look for Kay."

She ran to the end of the garden. The gate was shut, but she pushed against the rusty lock so that it swung open, then ran barefoot out of the garden. No one came after her. At last she could not run any longer, and she sat down on a large stone. When she looked around she saw that the summer was over; it was late autumn. The seasons had never changed in the old woman's beautiful garden, where there were sunshine and flow-ers all the year round.

"My goodness, how much time I've wasted," said Gerda. "It's almost winter! I cannot rest any longer!" And she sprang up to run on.

Oh, how tired and sore her little feet were, and all around her it became colder and colder.

The Prince and the Princess

After a while, Gerda had to rest again. While she was sitting, she looked up and there on the snow in front of her was a large Crow.

It had been looking at her for some time, and it nodded its head and said, "Caw! Caw! Good day." Then it asked the little girl where she was going all alone like that in the world. Gerda told the Crow her story, and asked if he had seen Kay.

The Crow nodded very thoughtfully and said, "It might be! It *might* be!"

"What! Do you think you have?" cried the little girl, and she smothered him with her kisses.

"Gently, gently," said the Crow. "It might be little Kay, but now he has forgotten you for the Princess!"

"Does he live with a Princess?" asked Gerda.

Then the Crow told her everything he knew.

"In the kingdom in which we are now sitting lives a Princess who is dreadfully clever. She has read all the newspapers in the world and then forgotten them again. She is as clever as that. The other day she was sitting on the throne, and that is not such fun as people think. Then she began to say, 'Why should I not marry?' But she wanted a husband who knew how to answer when spoken to, not one who would stand up stiffly looking superior—that would be too boring.

"When she told all the ladies of the court, they were delighted. You can believe every word I say," continued the Crow. "I have a tame sweetheart in the palace, and she tells me everything." (Of course his sweetheart was a crow.)

"Every newspaper came out next morning with a border of hearts and the Princess' initials, and inside you could read that every handsome young man might come into the palace and speak to the Princess, and whoever spoke best should become her husband.

"Indeed," said the Crow, "you can certainly believe me. It is as true as that I am sitting here.

"Young men arrived in streams, but nothing came of it on the first or the second day. The suitors were talkative enough in the streets, but once they went inside the palace gates and saw the guards in silver-braided uniforms and the footmen in gold-braided uniforms lining the stairs and the great hall all lit up, then their wits left them entirely. When they stood in front of the throne where the Princess sat, they could think of nothing to say except to repeat the last word she had spoken, and she did not care to hear that again. It seemed as if they were walking in their sleep until they went out into the street again and were able to speak once more.

"There was a line of young men stretching from the town gate up to the castle. They were hungry and thirsty, but in the palace they did not even get a glass of water. Some of the cleverest had thought to bring slices of bread and butter with them, but they did not share with their neighbor, for they thought: If he looks hungry, the Princess will not have him!"

"But what about Kay?" asked Gerda. "When did he come? Was he in the crowd?"

"Wait a bit; we are coming to him! On the third day, a little figure without horse or carriage walked jauntily up to the palace. His eyes shone as yours do; he had lovely curly hair, but very shabby clothes."

"That was Kay!" cried Gerda with delight. "Oh, I have found him!" And she clapped her hands.

"He had a little bundle on his back," said the Crow.

"It must have been his sled."

"Possibly," said the Crow, "I did not see for certain. But I know, from my sweetheart, that when he came to the palace gate and saw the royal guards in silver and the footmen in gold on the stairs, he was not the least bit put out. He nodded to them, saying, 'It must be rather dull standing on the stairs. I would rather go inside.'

"The halls were ablaze with lights; counselors and ambassadors were walking about carrying gold trays. It was enough to make one nervous! The boy's boots creaked noisily, but he was not frightened."

"That must be Kay!" said Gerda. "I know he had new boots on; I've heard them creaking in his grandmother's room!"

"They did creak, certainly!" said the Crow. "And, not one bit afraid, up he went to the Princess, who was sitting on a large pearl as round as a spinning wheel. All the ladies-in-waiting were standing around with their attendants, and the lords-in-waiting with their attendants."

"It must have been dreadful," said little Gerda. "And Kay did win the Princess?"

"I heard from my tame sweetheart that he was cheerful and quick-witted. He had not come to woo, he said, but to listen to the Princess' wisdom. And the end of it was that they fell in love with each other."

"That must have been Kay! He was always so clever; he could do sums with fractions. Oh, won't you lead me to the palace?" begged Gerda.

"That's easily asked!" said the Crow, "but how are we to manage that? I must talk it over with my tame sweetheart. She may be able to advise us, but I may as well tell you that a little girl like you could never get permission to enter the palace."

"Oh, I will get in!" said Gerda. "When Kay hears

that I am there he will come out at once and fetch me!''

"Wait for me by the fence," said the Crow, and he nodded his head and flew away.

It was late in the evening when he came back.

"Caw, caw!" he cried, "I am to give you her love, and here is a little roll for you. She took it out of the kitchen; there's plenty there, and you must be hungry. The guards in silver braid and the footmen in gold will not allow you to come into the palace. But don't cry! You shall get in all right. My sweetheart knows a little back staircase which leads to the bedchamber, and she knows where to find the key."

Later that evening they went into the palace garden, and when the lights were put out one by one, the Crow led Gerda to a back door.

Oh, how Gerda's heart beat with anxiety and longing! It seemed as if she were going to do something wrong, but she only wanted to know if it was little Kay. Yes, it must be he! She remembered so well his clever eyes, his curly hair. She could see him smiling as he did when they were at home under the rose trees! He would be so pleased to see her and to hear how they all were at home.

Now they were on the stairs; a little lamp was burning, and on the landing stood the tame Crow. She put her head on one side and looked at Gerda, who bowed as her grandmother had taught her.

"My fiancé has told me many nice things about you,

my dear young lady," the Crow said. "Will you take the lamp while I go in front? We go this way so as to meet no one."

They walked through many beautiful rooms until they came to the bedchamber. In the middle of it were two beds shaped like lilies, one all white, in which the Princess lay, and the other red, in which Gerda hoped to find Kay. She pushed aside the curtain, and saw a slim brown neck. Oh, it *was* Kay! She called his name out loud, holding the lamp toward him.

He woke up and turned his head, and she saw that it was *not* Kay!

It was only his neck that was like Kay's, but he was young and handsome. The Princess sat up in her lily-bed and asked who was there. Then Gerda cried, and told her story and all that the Crows had done.

"You poor child!" said the Prince and Princess, and they praised the Crows and said that they were not angry with them, but that they must not do it again. Now they should have a reward.

"Would you like to fly away free?" the Princess asked the birds, "or will you take a permanent place as Court Crows with what you can get in the kitchen?"

They both bowed and asked for a permanent appointment, for they thought of their old age.

They put Gerda to bed, and she folded her hands, thinking, as she fell asleep, "How good people and animals are to me!"

The next day she was dressed from head to foot in silk and satin. The Prince and Princess wanted her to stay on in the palace, but she begged for a little carriage, a horse and a pair of shoes so that she might go out again into the world to look for Kay.

They gave her a muff as well as some shoes. She was warmly dressed, and when she was ready, there in front of the door stood a coach of pure gold, with a coachman, footmen and outriders, all wearing fine gold crowns.

The Prince and Princess helped her into the carriage and wished her good luck.

"Good-bye, good-bye!" called the Prince and Princess; and little Gerda cried, and the Crow cried.

The wild Crow, who was now married, drove with her for the first three miles; his wife could not come because she had a bad headache.

When the wild Crow had said good-bye, he flew up to a tree and flapped his big black wings for as long as the carriage was in sight.

The Little Robber Girl

They drove on and came to a dark forest, which the coach lit up like a torch as it passed through. When a band of robbers saw the carriage, they rushed out, exclaiming, "Gold! It's gold!"

And they seized the horses, killed the coachman,

footmen and outriders, and dragged Gerda out of the carriage.

"What a plump and tender morsel! I will eat her for my supper," said the old robber queen, and she drew her long knife, which glittered horribly.

"You shall not kill her!" cried the queen's little daughter. "She shall play with me. She shall give me her muff and her beautiful dress, and she shall sleep with me in my bed."

The little robber girl was as big as Gerda, but she was stronger and broader, with dark hair and black eyes that looked a little sad. She threw her arms around Gerda and said, "I will not let them kill you, so long as you do not make me angry. Are you a princess?"

"No," answered Gerda, "I'm not," and she began to tell all that had happened to her, and how dearly she loved little Kay.

The robber girl listened attentively and, when the tale was finished, she took Gerda to a corner of the robbers' camp where she slept.

Perched on rafters all around were more than a hundred Pigeons, who seemed to be asleep, but who fluttered a little when the two girls appeared. A Reindeer came up and nuzzled the robber girl while she teased it by tickling it with her long sharp knife.

Gerda lay awake for some time, for she did not know whether she was going to live or die in the robbers' camp.

"Coo, coo!" said the Pigeons. "We have seen little Kay. A white bird carried his sled while he was sitting in the Snow Queen's sleigh. They drove over the forest as we were sitting in our nests. She breathed on our young, and all died except two. Coo, coo!"

"What are you saying up there?" cried Gerda. "Where was the Snow Queen going? Do you know anything at all?"

"She was probably traveling to Lapland, where there is always ice and snow. Ask the Reindeer."

"There is marvelous ice and snow there!" said the Reindeer. "One can run about in the great sparkling valleys. There the Snow Queen has her summer palace, but her best palace is up by the North Pole, on one of the islands called Spitsbergen."

In the morning Gerda told the little robber girl all that the Pigeons had said. She nodded. "Do you know where Lapland is?" she asked the Reindeer.

"Who should know better than I?" said the beast, and his eyes sparkled. "I was born and bred there on the snowfields."

"Listen!" said the robber girl to Gerda, "you see that all the robbers have gone. Only my mother is left, and she takes a nap in the afternoon—then I shall do something for you!"

When her mother had fallen asleep, the robber girl went up to the Reindeer and said, "I am going to set you free so that you can run to Lapland. But you must go quickly and carry this little girl to the Snow Queen's palace, where her playmate is. You must have heard all that she told me, for she spoke loud enough!"

The Reindeer leaped high for joy. The robber girl lifted up little Gerda and tied her firmly onto the Reindeer. She even gave her a little pillow for a saddle.

"You must wear your fur boots," she said, "for it will be cold; but I shall keep your muff, it's such a pretty one! And I'm going to give you my mother's big fur gloves so that you won't freeze. They will come right up to your elbows."

And Gerda wept for joy.

"Don't make such faces!" said the robber girl. "You should look very happy now. And here are two loaves of bread and a sausage, so you won't be hungry!"

When these were tied to the Reindeer's back, the robber girl opened the door, called in all the big dogs, cut through the Reindeer's halter with her sharp knife and said to him, "Off with you now! But take good care of the little girl."

And Gerda stretched out her hands with the large fur gloves toward the little robber girl and said, "Good-bye!"

Then the Reindeer flew over the ground, through the great forest, as fast as he could. The wolves howled, the ravens screamed, the sky seemed on fire. "Those are my dear old Northern Lights," said the Reindeer. "Look how they glow."

And he ran faster and faster still, day and night. The loaves and the sausage were eaten, and then they came to Lapland.

The Lapp Woman and the Finn Woman

They stopped at a wretched little house. The roof almost touched the ground, and the door was so low that you had to creep in and out. There was no one in the house except an old Lapp woman who was cooking fish over an oil lamp. The Reindeer told Gerda's whole history, but first he told his own, for that seemed to him much more important, and Gerda was so cold that she could not speak.

"Ah, you poor creatures!" said the Lapp woman. "You have still farther to go! You must go over a hundred miles into Finland, for there the Snow Queen lives, and every single night she burns blue flares. I will scribble a few words on a dried codfish, for I have no paper, and you must give it to the Finn woman, for she can give you better advice than I can."

And when Gerda was warmed up and had had something to eat and drink, the Lapp woman wrote a few lines on a dried cod and told Gerda to take care of it. Then she tied her securely onto the Reindeer's back, and away they went again.

The whole night was ablaze with Northern Lights, and then they came to Finland and knocked at the Finn woman's chimney, for it was so cold she had no door at all.

Inside it was so hot that the Finn woman wore almost nothing. She drew off Gerda's fur gloves and boots and loosened her clothes. Finally she read what was written on the codfish. She read it over three times, till she knew it by heart, and then put the fish in her saucepan to cook, for she never wasted anything.

Soon the Reindeer told his story and, after his, little Gerda's, and the Finn woman blinked her eyes but said nothing.

"You are very clever, I know," said the Reindeer. "Won't you give the little girl a drink so that she may have the strength of twelve men and overpower the Snow Queen?"

"The strength of twelve men!" said the Finn woman. "That would not help much. It's true that little Kay is with the Snow Queen, and he likes everything there very much and thinks it the best place in all the world. That is because he has a splinter of glass in his heart and a tiny chip of it in his eye. If these do not come out, he will never be free, and the Snow Queen will keep him in her power."

"But can't you give little Gerda something so that she can have power over the Snow Queen?"

"I can give her no greater power than she already has. Don't you see how great it is? Don't you see how men and beasts help her when she wanders into the wide world with her bare feet? She is powerful already, because she is a dear little innocent child. If she herself cannot conquer the Snow Queen and remove the glass splinters that are in little Kay, *we* cannot help her! The Snow Queen's garden begins two miles from here. You can carry the girl so far; put her down by the large bush with red berries that stands in the snow. And you must come back here as fast as you can." Then the Finn woman lifted Gerda onto the Reindeer, and away he sped.

"Oh, I have left my gloves and boots behind!" cried Gerda. She missed them in the piercing cold, but the Reindeer did not dare to stop. On he ran till he came to the bush with red berries. There he sat Gerda down and kissed her, and big tears ran down his cheeks. Then he ran back, leaving the poor girl without shoes or gloves in the middle of the bitter cold of Finland.

She went on as fast as she could. A regiment of gigantic snowflakes came against her, but they melted even before they touched her, and she continued with fresh courage.

The Snow Queen's Palace

And now we must see what Kay was doing. He was not thinking of Gerda and never dreamed that she was standing right outside the Snow Queen's palace.

The walls of the palace were built of driven snow,

and the doors and windows of piercing winds. There were more than a hundred halls in it—the largest several miles long—all made of frozen snow. The bright Northern Lights lit them up, and very large and empty and cold and glittering they were! In the middle of the great hall was a frozen lake which had cracked in a thousand pieces. Here the Snow Queen used to sit when she was at home.

Little Kay was almost black and blue with cold, but he never felt it, for the Snow Queen had kissed away his feelings and his heart was a lump of ice. He was sitting in the hall, pulling about some sharp, flat pieces of ice and trying to put them together into a pattern. He thought they were beautiful, but that was because of the splinter of glass in his eye. He was able to fit them into a great many shapes, but he really wanted to make them spell the word "Love." The Snow Queen had said, "If you can spell out that word you will be your own master. I shall give you the whole world and a new sled." But Kay could not do it.

"Today I must fly to warmer countries," said the Snow Queen. "I must go and stir up my black kettles!" (This was what she called Mount Etna and Mount Vesuvius.) And off she flew, leaving Kay alone in the great hall trying to do his puzzle. He sat so still that you would have thought he was frozen.

Then little Gerda stepped into the palace hall. The raging winds quieted down as if they had fallen asleep when she appeared. She caught sight of Kay and ran to put her arms around his neck, crying, "Kay! Dear little Kay! I have found you at last!"

But Kay sat quite still and cold. Gerda wept hot tears, which fell on his breast and thawed his heart so that the glass splinter was dissolved. He looked at her and burst into tears. He cried so much that the splinter swam out of his eye. Then he recognized her and cried out, "Gerda! Dear little Gerda! Where have you been so long? And where have I been?"

And he looked around him. "How cold it is here! How huge and empty!" He threw his arms around Gerda, and she laughed and wept for joy. It was such a happy time that the pieces of ice even danced around them for joy. When they grew tired, Kay and Gerda lay down, and as they slept they melted the ice, forming the word that the Snow Queen had said Kay must spell in order to become his own master.

Gerda kissed his cheeks and they grew rosy. She kissed his eyes and they sparkled like hers. She kissed his hands and feet and he became warm and glowing. The Snow Queen might come home now, but they had his release—the word "Love" stood written in the sparkling ice.

They took each other's hands and wandered out of the great palace. They talked about the grandmother and the roses in the window boxes, and wherever they went the winds calmed down and the sun came out.

When they reached the bush with red berries there stood the Reindeer waiting for them.

He carried Kay and Gerda first to the Finn woman, who warmed them in her hot room and gave them advice for their journey home.

Then they went to the Lapp woman, who gave them new clothes and let them borrow her sleigh until they reached the border of their own country. The Reindeer ran alongside the sleigh till they came to fields fresh with the first spring green. There he said good-bye.

When they reached the forest, which was bursting into bud, there came riding out of it a young girl on a splendid horse. She was wearing a red cap and carrying pistols in her belt. It was the little robber girl, who was tired of staying at home and wanted to go out into the world. She and Gerda recognized each other at once.

"You are a fine one!" she said to Kay. "I wonder if you deserve to be run after all over the world!"

But Gerda patted her cheeks and asked after the Prince and Princess.

"They are traveling about," said the robber girl.

"And the Crow?" asked Gerda.

"Oh, the Crow is dead," answered the robber girl. "His tame sweetheart is a widow now and hops about with a bit of black crepe on her leg. She makes a great fuss, but it's all nonsense. Now tell me what happened to you, and how you found him."

And Kay and Gerda told her all.

"What a story!" said the robber girl. She shook hands with them and promised that if she ever passed through their town she would come and see them. Then she rode on.

Gerda and Kay went home hand in hand. There they found the grandmother and everything just as it had been, but when they went through the doorway they found they were grown up.

There were the roses in the window boxes. It was summer—warm, glorious summer.

HANS CHRISTIAN ANDERSEN, ANDREW LANG COLLECTION

SIX SILLIES

ONCE UPON a time there was a girl who had reached the age of thirty-seven without ever having had a suitor, for she was so foolish that no one wanted to marry her.

One day, however, a young man arrived to pay court to her, and her mother, beaming with joy, sent the girl down to the cellar to draw a jug of beer.

As her daughter did not come back, the mother

went down to see what had become of her and found her sitting on the stairs, her head in her hands, while by her side the beer was running all over the floor, for she had forgotten to close the tap.

"What are you doing?" asked the mother.

"I was thinking what I shall call my first child, after I am married to that young man. All the names in the calendar are taken already."

The mother sat down on the staircase beside her daughter and said, "I will think about it with you, my dear."

The father, who had stayed upstairs with the young man, was surprised that neither his daughter nor his wife came back, and he in turn decided to go down to look for them.

He found them both sitting on the stairs, while beside them the beer was running all over the ground from the tap, which was wide open.

"What are you doing there? The beer is running all over the cellar."

"We were thinking what we should call the children that our daughter will have when she marries that young man. All the names in the calendar are taken already."

"Well," said the father, "I will think about it with the two of you."

As neither daughter nor mother nor father came upstairs again, the suitor grew impatient waiting for them and went down into the cellar to see what they could all be doing.

He found the three sitting on the stairs, while beside them beer was running all over the ground from the tap, which was still wide open.

"What in the world are you all doing that you don't come upstairs and that you allow the beer to run all over the cellar?"

"Yes, I know the beer is flowing, my boy," said the father, "but if you marry our daughter, what shall you call your children? All the names in the calendar are already taken."

When the young man heard this answer he replied, "Well, good-bye, I am going away. When I have found three people sillier than you, I will come back and marry your daughter."

So he started his journey and, after walking a long way, he reached an orchard. There he saw a man knocking down walnuts from a tree and trying to throw them into a cart with a fork.

"What are you doing there?" the young man asked.

"I want to load the cart with walnuts, but cannot manage to do it."

The young man advised him to get a basket and put all the walnuts in it, and then turn the basket over into the cart.

"Well," he said to himself, "I have already found someone more foolish than those three."

So he went on his way, and by and by he came to a wood. There he saw a man who wanted to give his pig some acorns to eat and was trying with all his might to make the pig climb up the oak tree.

"What are you doing, my good man?" asked he.

"I want to make my pig eat some acorns, but I can't get him to go up the tree."

"If you were to climb up and shake down the acorns, the pig would pick them up."

"Oh, I never thought of that."

"Here is the second foolish one," said the young man to himself.

Some way farther along the road, he came upon a man who had never worn any trousers and who was trying to put on a pair. He had fastened them between two trees and was jumping with all his might high up in the air and trying to hit the two legs of the trousers as he came down.

"It would be much better if you held them in your hands," said the young man, "and then put your legs in, one after the other."

"Dear me, to be sure! You are sharper than I am, for that never occurred to me."

And, having found three people more foolish than the girl or her father or her mother, the young man went back to marry the young lady. And, in the course of time, they had a great many children.

HENRI CARNOY, ANDREW LANG COLLECTION

THE HEDGEHOG AND
THE RABBIT

THIS IS A lying story, my children, but it's true just the same, for my grandfather, who told it to me, used to say: "It must be true, my child, or else how could one tell it, after all?"

But this is the way the story goes:

It happened on the Buxtehuder Heath on a Sunday morning at harvesttime, just as the buckwheat was coming into flower. The sun was climbing up into the heavens, a breeze blew gently over the stubble, larks trilled in the sky, bees buzzed in the buckwheat and everybody was going to church in their Sunday best— in short, all creatures, great and small, were contented; and the Hedgehog was, too.

This Hedgehog, he was standing in his doorway with his arms crossed on his chest, pointing his nose to the wind and singing a little tune—that is, as good or bad a tune as a hedgehog might be expected to sing on a lovely Sunday morning.

While he was humming contentedly to himself in this charming fashion, a thought came into his head.

While my wife is busy washing and brushing the little ones, he thought, I might as well go for a Sunday stroll and take a look at my turnip patch. The turnip patch was in the field next to his house and belonged to a farmer, but, because the Hedgehog and his family had fallen into the habit of eating there, they had come to think of it as their own.

Well, no sooner said than done. The Hedgehog closed the door after him and sauntered down the road. But just as he reached the blackthorn bush which grew beside the turnip patch, he met a Rabbit who was out on the same business—that is to say, he had come to see how his garden, the cabbage patch, was getting along on this fine day.

Bowing and smiling, the Hedgehog wished the Rabbit a pleasant good morning, but the Rabbit—who was a grand gentleman in his own community, and most haughty about it, too—this Rabbit did not return the Hedgehog's neighborly greeting. Instead, he said with a mocking air, "Hm! And how do you happen to be running around in this field so early on a Sunday morning?"

"It's such a fine Sunday," said the Hedgehog. "I'm just out for a little stroll."

"A stroll!" jeered the Rabbit. "I should think you could put your legs to better use than that!"

This remark wounded the Hedgehog beyond words, for he was very sensitive about his legs, which were short and somewhat crooked. So now he bristled up and cried in fury, "Oh, yes? You must think that your legs are better than mine!"

"That's exactly what I think," replied the Rabbit calmly.

"Yes, that's what you think," cried the Hedgehog, "but I'll wager that if we ran a race, I'd win it."

"That's a joke!" cried the Rabbit. "You with your stumpy little legs! However, if you are so bent on making a fool of yourself, I'll take you on. What shall be the prize for the winner?"

"A golden coin and a bottle of brandy," said the Hedgehog.

"Agreed!" cried the Rabbit. "Get in line and let's start."

"Oh, no hurry about it," said the Hedgehog, carelessly. "I haven't even had breakfast yet. You get the prizes; I'll be right back here on the same spot in half an hour."

With that they parted, for the Rabbit was satisfied with this plan.

On the way home, the Hedgehog was busy with his thoughts. That Rabbit will depend upon his long, fleet legs, he thought. My legs are—well, they're neither long nor fleet, but I'll beat him to it all the same. He may be a grand gentleman, yes—but he's an old muddle-noodle; and as for me, I'm not as stupid as I may look.

Upon reaching home, the Hedgehog said to his wife, "Come, hurry and get yourself ready. I need you out in the field."

"What's going on, then?" asked his wife.

"Oh, nothing much. I told the Rabbit I would run a race with him, and I'd like to have you around while it's going on."

"My heavens, man!" cried his wife. "Are you out of your head? How could you ever hope to win a race against a rabbit?"

"No words, wife!" cried the Hedgehog sternly. "That's my business. Don't poke your nose into men's affairs. March along now! Are you ready?"

What could the wife do? She had to obey whether she wanted to or not, and as they waddled along side by side, the Hedgehog said to her, "Now listen well to what I'm telling you. In this big field is where we'll run our race, the Rabbit and I. See these long deep furrows?"

"Yes," said his wife, "but———"

"Silence!" cried her husband, and then continued: "The Rabbit of course will run in one furrow and I in the next, and we'll start over there at the upper end of the field. Now, all you have to do is to sit at the lower end of my furrow. Understand? Don't move from that place; just sit there quietly, and when you hear the Rabbit coming along, just pop up your head and say, 'Here I am already!'"

So that's the way it was done. The Hedgehog left his wife hiding in the lower end of his furrow, had a final meeting with the Rabbit, and—one, two, three!—off they went like a whirlwind down the field.

That is, the Rabbit did. The Hedgehog only ran a few steps, then ducked down in his furrow and crouched there, out of sight and quiet as a mouse.

The Rabbit ran for his life, his ears flapping in the wind. He thought he was doing remarkably well, but as he neared the lower end of the field someone cried, "Here I am already!"

The Rabbit couldn't believe his ears and, when he looked over into the next furrow, he could hardly believe his eyes, either. What he saw, of course, was the Hedgehog's wife but, since she looked exactly like her husband, the Rabbit couldn't tell the difference between them.

Well, it's the Hedgehog all right, he thought. Just the same, I don't like the looks of the whole thing. Then, still panting for breath, he cried, "Another race! The other way around!" and off he went, so fast that it was a wonder his ears stayed on his head.

The Hedgehog's wife didn't move; she still stayed quietly in the lower end of the furrow.

In a twinkling-and-a-half the Rabbit had returned to the upper end of the furrow, yet there sat the Hedgehog, calling, "Here I am already!"

The Rabbit, now almost out of his head with fury, cried out wildly, "Another race—the other way around again!"

"As often as you wish, for all I care," said the Hedgehog.

Back and forth went the Rabbit, forth and back, then back and forth again—but always when he reached the end of the furrow it was the same old story: there sat the Hedgehog, calling, "Yoo hoo! Here I am already."

Seventy-three times he tried, this racing Rabbit, but at the seventy-fourth try he had to give up. His legs folded up under him, his ears flopped sideways over his head, and then, with his breath coming in weary gasps, he sank down in his furrow and lay there with closed eyes.

The Hedgehog picked up the prizes and called his wife out of the furrow, saying, "The race is over and, as you see, I won it."

Then they both went home together in great delight, and, if they're not dead, for all I know they're living there still.

Yes, that is the way the story goes, my children, and it must be true—or how could it be that, ever since that time, no rabbit in the Buxtehuder Heath has dared to pass a remark about a hedgehog's legs? Yes? No? Well, what do you think about it?

JAKOB AND WILHELM GRIMM, TRANSLATED BY WANDA GÁG

THUMBELINA

THERE WAS once a woman who wanted to have a tiny little child, but she did not know where to get one. So one day she went to an old witch and said to her, "I should so much like to have a tiny little child. Can you tell me where I might get one?"

"Oh, we have one ready now!" said the witch. "Here, take this barleycorn. It's not the kind the farmer sows in his field or feeds the cocks and hens with, I can tell you. Put it in a flowerpot and then you will see what happens."

"Oh, thank you," said the woman and gave the witch twelve pennies, for that was what the barleycorn cost. Then she went home and planted it. Immediately there grew from it a large and beautiful flower which looked like a tulip, but the petals were tightly closed as if it were still only a bud.

"What a beautiful flower!" exclaimed the woman and she kissed the red and yellow petals. As she kissed them the flower burst open. It was a real tulip, the kind we usually see, but in the middle of the blossom on the soft velvety petals, sat a tiny girl, delicate and pretty. She was scarcely as big as a thumb, so the woman and her husband called her Thumbelina.

An elegant polished walnut shell served Thumbelina as a cradle, the blue petals of a violet were her mattress and a rose petal was her quilt. There she lay at night, but in the daytime she used to play about on the table. Here the woman had put a bowl, which was surrounded by a ring of flowers, their stems dipping into the water, where a great tulip petal floated. In this, Thumbelina sat and sailed from one side of the bowl to the other, rowing herself with two white horsehairs for oars. It was such a pretty sight! She would sing, too, with a voice more soft and sweet than had ever been heard before.

One night, when she was lying in her pretty bed, an old Toad crept in through a broken pane in the window. She was very ugly and clumsy, and she hopped onto the table where Thumbelina lay asleep under the red rose petal.

"This would make a beautiful wife for my son," said the Toad. Taking up the walnut shell with Thumbelina inside, she hopped with it through the window into the garden.

Here there flowed a great wide stream, with slippery and marshy banks, where the Toad lived with her son. Ugh, how ugly and clammy he was, just like his mother!

"Croak, croak, croak!" was all he could say when he saw the pretty little girl asleep in the walnut shell.

"Don't talk so loud, or you'll wake her," said the old Toad. "She might escape us even now. She is as light as a feather. We will put her out on a broad water-lily leaf in the stream. She is so small and light it will be just like an island for her. She can't run away from us there, while we are preparing the guest room under the marsh where she will live."

Growing in the stream were many water lilies with broad green leaves which looked as if they were float-ing on the water. The farthest leaf was the largest, and to this the old Toad swam with Thumbelina in her walnut shell.

The tiny Thumbelina woke up very early in the morning, and when she saw where she was she began to cry bitterly. On every side of the great green leaf was water and she could not get back to the land.

The old Toad was down under the marsh, decorat-ing her room with rushes and yellow marigold petals to make it grand for her new daughter-in-law. After she had finished she swam out with her ugly son to the leaf where Thumbelina lay. She wanted to take the pretty cradle to the room before Thumbelina herself went there. The old Toad bowed low in the water be-fore her, and said, "Here is my son. You shall marry him and the two of you will live in great magnificence down under the marsh."

"Croak, croak, croak!" was all the son could say. Then they took the neat little cradle and swam away with it. Thumbelina sat alone on the great green leaf and wept, for she did not want to live with the Toad or marry her ugly son.

The little fishes swimming about under the water had seen the old Toad quite plainly and heard what she said. They raised their heads to see Thumbelina and thought her so pretty they were very sorry she was going down to live with the ugly Toad. No, that must not happen, they decided. They assembled in the water around the green stalk which supported the leaf on which the tiny girl was sitting and nibbled the stem in two. Away floated the leaf down the stream, bearing Thumbelina far beyond the reach of the Toad.

On she sailed past several towns, and the birds sitting in the bushes saw her and sang, "What a pretty little girl!" The leaf floated farther and farther away. Thus Thumbelina left her native land.

A beautiful little white Butterfly fluttered above her and at last settled on the leaf. Thumbelina pleased him and she, too, was delighted. Now the Toads could not reach her, and everything was so beautiful where she was sailing. The sun shone on the water and made it sparkle like the brightest silver. She took off her sash and tied one end around the Butterfly; the other end she fastened to the leaf, so that he glided along with her faster than ever.

Soon after, a great Beetle came flying past. He caught sight of Thumbelina and in a moment had put his legs around her slender waist and had flown off with her to a tree. The green leaf floated away down the stream and the Butterfly with it, for he was fastened to the leaf and could not get loose. How terrified poor little Thumbelina was when the Beetle flew off with her to the tree! And she was especially distressed for the beautiful white Butterfly because she had tied him to the leaf. If he did not get away he might starve to death.

But the Beetle did not trouble himself about that. He sat down with her on a large green leaf, gave her honey out of the flowers to eat and told her she was very pretty, although she wasn't in the least like a beetle. Later on, all the other beetles who lived in the same tree came to pay calls. They examined Thumbelina closely, and remarked, "Why, she has only two legs! How disgusting!"

"She has no feelers!" cried another.

"How ugly she is!" said all the lady beetles—and yet Thumbelina was really very pretty.

The Beetle who had stolen her knew this very well. But when he heard all the ladies saying she was ugly, he began to think so too and decided not to keep her. She could go wherever she liked. So he flew down from the tree with her and put her on a daisy. There she sat and wept, thinking she must be very ugly, because the

Beetle would have nothing to do with her. Yet she was the most beautiful creature imaginable, so soft and delicate, like the loveliest rose petal.

The whole summer poor little Thumbelina lived alone in the great wood. She wove a bed for herself of blades of grass and hung it up under a clover leaf so she was protected from the rain. She gathered honey from the flowers for food and drank the dew on the leaves every morning. Thus the summer and autumn passed. But then came winter—the long, cold winter. All the birds who had sung so sweetly about her had flown away. The trees had shed their leaves, the flowers were dead. The great clover leaf under which she lived had curled up and nothing remained but the withered stalk. She was terribly cold, for her clothes were ragged and she herself was so small and thin. Poor little Thumbelina would surely be frozen to death very soon. It began to snow, and every snowflake that fell on her was like a whole shovelful, for she was only an inch high. She wrapped herself up in a dead leaf, but since it was torn in the middle, it gave her no warmth. She was trembling with cold.

Now, just outside the wood where she was living lay a great grainfield. The grain had been harvested a long time before. Only dry, bare stubble was left standing in the frozen ground. This made a forest for her to wander about in. All at once she came across the door of a Field Mouse, who had a little hole under a knoll. There the Mouse lived warm and snug, with a storeroom full of grain, a splendid kitchen and dining room. Poor little Thumbelina went up to the door and begged for a little piece of barley, for she had not had anything to eat for two days.

"Poor little creature!" said the Field Mouse, for she was a kindhearted old thing. "Come into my warm room and have some dinner with me." Because Thumbelina pleased her, she said, "As far as I am concerned you may spend the winter with me. You must keep my room clean and tidy and tell me stories, for I like them very much." And Thumbelina did all that the kind Field Mouse asked and did it remarkably well, too.

"I am expecting a visitor tonight," said the Field Mouse. "My neighbor comes to call on me once a week. He is in better circumstances than I am, has great big rooms and wears a fine black velvet coat. If you could only marry him, you would be well provided for, though he is blind. You must tell him all the prettiest stories you know."

But Thumbelina did not trouble her head about him, for he was only a mole. He came and paid them a visit in his black velvet coat.

"He is so rich and accomplished," the Field Mouse told her. "His house is twenty times larger than mine. He possesses great knowledge, but he cannot bear the sun and the beautiful flowers and speaks slightingly of them, for he has never seen them."

Thumbelina had to sing to him, so she sang "Lady-bird, ladybird, fly away home!" and other songs so prettily that the Mole fell in love with her. He did not say anything. He was a very cautious man. A short time before, he had dug a long passage through the ground from his own house to that of his neighbor. He gave the Field Mouse and Thumbelina permission to walk in this as often as they liked, but he begged them not to be afraid of the dead Bird that lay in the passage. It was a real bird with beak and feathers and must have died a long time ago. It now lay buried just where the Mole had made his tunnel.

One day the Mole led Thumbelina and the Field Mouse into the tunnel. He took a piece of tinder wood in his mouth, for that glows in the dark, and went ahead of them, lighting their way through the long dark passage. When they came to the place where the dead Bird lay, the Mole put his broad nose against the ceiling and pushed a hole through so the daylight could shine down. In the middle of the path lay a dead Swallow, his pretty wings pressed close to his sides, his claws and head drawn under his feathers; the poor Bird had evidently died of cold.

Thumbelina was very sorry, for she was fond of all little birds. They had sung and twittered so beautifully to her all through the summer. But the Mole kicked the Bird with his bandy legs and said, "Now he can't sing anymore! It must be miserable to be a little bird! I'm thankful that none of my children are. Birds always starve in winter."

"Yes, you speak like a sensible man," said the Field Mouse. "What has a bird, in spite of all his singing, in the wintertime? He can only starve and freeze, and that must be very unpleasant for him, I must say!"

Thumbelina did not say anything. When the other two had passed on, she bent down to the Bird, brushed aside the feathers from his head and kissed his closed eyes gently. "Perhaps he sang to me in the summer," she said. "How much pleasure he did give me, dear little Bird!"

The Mole closed up the hole which let in the light and then escorted the ladies home. But Thumbelina could not sleep that night. She got out of bed and wove a big blanket of straw and carried it off and spread it over the dead Bird. She piled upon it thistledown as soft as cotton wool, which she had found in the Field Mouse's room, so that the poor little thing should lie warmly buried.

"Farewell, pretty little Bird!" she said. "Farewell, and thank you for your beautiful songs in the summer, when the trees were green and the sun shone down warmly on us!" Then she laid her head against the Bird's heart. But the Bird was not dead. He had been frozen, but now that she had warmed him, he was coming to life again.

In autumn the swallows fly away to foreign lands.

But there are some who are late in starting and then they get so cold that they drop down as if dead, and the snow comes and covers them over.

Thumbelina trembled, she was so frightened. The Bird was very large to her, for she was only an inch high. But she took courage, piled up the down more closely around the poor Swallow, fetched her own little quilt and laid it over his head.

Next night she crept out again to him. There he was, alive but very weak. He could only open his eyes for a moment and look at Thumbelina, who was standing in front of him with a piece of tinder wood in her hand, for she had no other lantern.

"Thank you, pretty little child!" said the Swallow to her. "I am so beautifully warm! Soon I shall regain my strength and I shall be able to fly out once more into the warm sunshine."

"Oh," she said, "it is very cold outside. It is snowing and freezing! Stay in your warm bed. I will take care of you!"

Then she brought him water in a petal, which he drank. He told her how he had torn one of his wings on a bramble so he could not keep up with the other swallows, who had flown far away to warmer lands. At last he had dropped down exhausted, and then he could remember no more. The whole winter he remained down there, and Thumbelina looked after him and nursed him tenderly. She told neither the Mole nor the Field Mouse anything of this, for they could not bear the poor Swallow.

When the spring came, and the sun warmed the earth again, the Swallow said farewell to Thumbelina, who opened for him the hole in the roof the Mole had made. The sun shone brightly down upon her, and the Swallow asked her if she would go with him. She could sit upon his back. Thumbelina wanted very much to fly far away into the greenwood, but she knew that the old Field Mouse would be sad if she ran away. "No, I mustn't come!" she said.

"Farewell, dear good little girl!" said the Swallow, and flew off into the sunshine. Thumbelina gazed after him with tears in her eyes, for she was very fond of the Swallow.

"Tweet, tweet!" sang the Bird, and flew into the greenwood. Thumbelina was very unhappy. She was not allowed to go out into the warm sunshine. The grain which had been sowed in the field over the Field Mouse's home grew up high into the air and made a thick forest for the poor little girl, who was only an inch high.

"Soon you are to be a bride, Thumbelina," said the Field Mouse one day, "for our neighbor has said he wishes to marry you. What a piece of fortune for a poor child like you! Now you must set to work on your trousseau, for nothing must be lacking if you are to become the wife of our neighbor, the Mole!"

Thumbelina had to sew all day long, and every evening the Mole visited her and told her that when the summer was over the sun would not shine so hot. Now it was burning the earth as hard as a stone. Yes, when the summer had passed, they would have the wedding.

But she was not at all pleased about it, for she did not like the stupid Mole. Every morning when the sun was rising, and every evening when it was setting, she would steal out of the house door, and when the breeze parted the stalks of grain so that she could see the clear sky through them, she thought how bright and beautiful it must be outside and longed to see her dear Swallow again. But he never came. No doubt he had flown far away into the great greenwood.

By the autumn Thumbelina had finished her whole trousseau.

"In four weeks you will be married," said the Field Mouse, but Thumbelina wept and declared she would not marry the ugly old Mole.

"Don't be obstinate, or I shall bite you with my sharp white teeth! You are getting a fine husband. The King himself does not possess such a velvet coat. His storeroom and cellar are full, and you should be thankful for that."

The wedding day arrived. The Mole had come to fetch Thumbelina to live with him deep down under the ground, never to come out into the warm sun again, for that was what he didn't like. The poor little girl was very sad, for now she must say good-bye to the beautiful sun.

"Farewell, bright sun!" she cried, stretching out her arms toward it and taking another step outside the house. Now the grain had been harvested and only the stubble was left standing. "Farewell, farewell!" she said, and put her arms around a little red flower that grew there. "Give my love to the dear Swallow when you see him!"

"Tweet, tweet!" sounded in her ear all at once. She looked up. There was the Swallow flying past! He was delighted when he saw Thumbelina. She told him how unwilling she was to marry the ugly Mole, because then she would have to live underground where the sun never shone, and while she said this she could not help bursting into tears.

"The cold winter is coming now," said the Swallow. "I must fly away to warmer lands. Will you come with me? You can sit on my back, and we will fly far away from the ugly Mole and his dark house, over the mountains to the warm countries. There the sun shines more brightly than here. There it is always summer and beautiful flowers always bloom. Do come with me, dear little Thumbelina, who saved my life when I lay frozen in the dark tunnel!"

"Yes, I will go with you," said Thumbelina, and climbed on the Swallow's back, with her feet on one of his outstretched wings. Up into the air he flew, over woods and seas, over the great mountains always covered with snow. When she felt cold she crept under his warm feathers, only keeping her little head out to admire all the beautiful things in the world beneath. At last they came to warm lands. There the sun was brighter, the sky seemed twice as high, and in the hedges hung the finest green and purple grapes. In the orchards grew oranges and lemons. The air was scented with myrtle and mint and on the roads were pretty little children running about and playing with great gorgeous butterflies. But the Swallow flew on farther, and the country became more and more beautiful. Under the most splendid green trees beside a blue lake stood a glittering white marble castle. Vines trailed from the high pillars and at the top there were many swallows' nests. In one of these lived the Swallow who was carrying Thumbelina.

"Here is my house!" said he. "But it won't do for you to live with me. I am not tidy enough to please you. Find a home for yourself in one of the pretty flowers that grow down there. Now I will set you down and you can do whatever you like."

"That will be lovely!" said she, clapping her hands.

There lay a great white marble column which had fallen to the ground and broken into three pieces, but between these grew the most beautiful white flowers. The Swallow flew down with Thumbelina and set her upon one of the broad leaves. There, to her astonish-

ment, she found a tiny little man sitting in the middle of the flower, as white and transparent as if he were made of glass. He had the prettiest golden crown on his head and the most beautiful wings on his shoulders. He himself was no bigger than Thumbelina. He was the spirit of the flower. In each blossom there lived a tiny man or woman. But this one was King of them all.

"How handsome he is!" whispered Thumbelina to the Swallow.

The little King was very much frightened by the Swallow, for in comparison with one as tiny as himself the Bird seemed a giant. But when he saw Thumbelina, he was delighted, for she was the loveliest girl that he had ever seen. He took his golden crown off his head and put it on hers, asking her her name and if she would be his wife, and then she would be Queen of all the flowers. Yes, he was a different kind of husband from the son of the Toad and the Mole with the black velvet coat. So she said "Yes" to the King. And out of each flower came a lady or a gentleman, so tiny and pretty that it was a pleasure to see them. Everyone brought Thumbelina a present, but the best of all was a pair of lovely wings which they fastened to her back, and now she too could fly from flower to flower. They wished her joy, and the Swallow sat above in his nest and sang the wedding march as well as he could. But he was sad, as he was very fond of Thumbelina and did not want to be separated from her.

"You shall not be called Thumbelina!" said the spirit of the flower. "That is an ugly name, and you are much too pretty. We will call you May Blossom."

"Farewell, farewell!" said the little Swallow with a heavy heart, and he flew away to farther lands, far, far away, to the country of Denmark. There he had a little nest above the window of a man who tells such nice fairy stories. "Tweet, tweet!" he sang to the man. And that is the way we learned the whole story.

HANS CHRISTIAN ANDERSEN, ANDREW LANG COLLECTION

THE SORCERER'S APPRENTICE

A MAN FOUND himself in need of a helper for his workshop, and one day as he was walking along on the outskirts of a little hamlet he met a boy who was carrying a bundle slung over his shoulder.

Stopping him, the man said, "Good morning, my lad. I am looking for an apprentice for my shop. Have you a master?"

"No," said the boy, "I have just this morning said

good-bye to my mother and am now off to find myself a trade."

"Good," said the man. "You look as though you might be just the lad I need. But wait, do you know anything about reading and writing?"

"Oh, yes!" said the boy.

"Too bad!" said the man. "You won't do after all. I have no use for an apprentice who is able to read and write."

"Pardon me?" said the boy. "If it was reading and writing you were talking about, I misunderstood you. I thought you asked if I knew anything about eating and fighting—those two things I am able to do well, but as to reading and writing, those are things I know nothing about."

"Well!" cried the man. "Then you are just the fellow I want. Come with me to my workshop, and I will show you what to do."

The boy, however, had had his wits about him. He could read and write well enough and had only pretended to be a fool. Wondering why a man should prefer to have an unschooled helper, he thought to himself, I smell a rat. There is something strange about all of this business, and I had better keep my eyes and ears open.

While he was pondering over this, his new master was leading him into the heart of a deep forest. Here in a small clearing stood a house, and as soon as they entered it the boy could see that this was no ordinary workshop.

At one end of a big room was a huge hearth with a copper caldron hanging in it; at the other end was a small alcove lined with many big books, and from the ceiling there hung a huge, many-toothed fish. A mortar and pestle stood on the floor; bottles and sieves, measuring scales and oddly shaped glassware were strewn about on the table.

Well! It did not take the clever young apprentice very long to realize that he was working for a magician or sorcerer of some kind and so, although he pretended to be quite stupid, he kept his eyes and ears open and tried to learn all he could.

"Sorcery—that is a trade I would dearly love to master!" said the boy to himself. "A mouthful of good chants and charms would never come amiss to a poor fellow like me, and with them I might even be able to do some good in the world."

There were many things the boy had to do. Sometimes he was ordered to stir the evil-smelling broths which bubbled in the big copper caldron; at other times he had to grind up herbs and berries—and many things too gruesome to mention—in the big mortar and pestle. It was also his task to sweep up the workshop, to keep the fire burning on the big hearth and to gather the strange materials needed by the man for the broths and brews he was always mixing.

This went on day after day, week after week and month after month, until the boy was almost beside himself with curiosity. He was most curious about the thick heavy books in the alcove. How often he had wondered about them and how many times had he been tempted to take a peep between their covers! But, remembering that he was not supposed to know how to read or write, he had been wise enough never to show the least interest in them. At last there came a day when he made up his mind to see what was in them, no matter what the risk.

I'll try it before another day dawns, he thought.

That night he waited until the sorcerer was sound asleep and snoring loudly in his bedchamber. Then, creeping out of his straw couch, the boy took a light into the corner of the alcove and began paging through one of the heavy volumes. What was written in them has never been told, but they were conjuring books, each and every one of them; and from that time on, the boy read them silently, secretly, for an hour or two, night after night. In this way he learned many magic tricks: chants and charms and countercharms; recipes for philters and potions, for broths and brews and witches' stews; signs mystic and cabalistic; and other helpful spells of many kinds.

The boy memorized all these tricks of the magician carefully, and it was not long before he sometimes was able to figure out what kind of charms his master was working, what brand of potion he was mixing, what sort of stews he was brewing.

And what kind of charms and potions and stews were they? Alas, they were all wicked ones! Now the boy knew that he was not working for an ordinary magician, but for a cruel, dangerous sorcerer. And because of this, the boy made a plan, a bold one.

He went on with his nightly studies until his head was swarming with magic recipes and incantations. He even had time to work at them during the day, for the sorcerer sometimes left the shop for hours—working harm and havoc on mortals, no doubt. At such times the boy would try out a few bits of his newly learned wisdom. He began with simple things, such as changing the cat into a bee and back to the cat again, making a viper out of the poker, an imp out of the broom and so on. Sometimes he was successful, but often he was not; so the boy said to himself, "The time is not yet ripe."

Not long after, the sorcerer again went forth on one of his mysterious trips. The boy hurried through his work and had just settled down with a large conjuring book on his knees, when the master returned unexpectedly. The boy, thinking fast, pointed smilingly at a few of the pictures, after which he quietly closed the book and went on with his work as though nothing were amiss.

But the sorcerer was not deceived. If the wretch

can read, he thought, he may learn how to outwit me. And I can't send him off with a beating and a "Bad speed to you," either. Doubtless he knows too much already and will reveal all my fine mean tricks, and then I can't have any more sport working mischief on man and beast.

He acted quickly. With one leap he rushed at the boy, who in turn made a spring for the door.

"Stop!" cried the sorcerer. "You shall not escape from me!"

He was about to grab the boy by the collar when the quick-witted lad mumbled a powerful incantation by which he changed himself into a bird, and—wootsch!—he had flown into the woods.

The sorcerer, not to be outdone, shouted a charm, thus changing himself into a larger bird, and—whoosh!—he was after the little one.

With another incantation the boy changed himself into a fish, and—whish!—he was swimming across a big pond.

But the master was equal to this, for with a few words he made himself into a fish too, a big one, and swam after the little one.

At this the boy changed himself into a still bigger fish, but the magician, by a master stroke, turned himself into a tiny kernel of grain and rolled into a small crack in a stone where the fish couldn't touch him.

Quickly the boy changed himself into a rooster, and

See page 208

—peck! peck! peck!—with his sharp beak he snapped at the kernel of grain and ate it up.

That was the end of the wicked sorcerer, and the boy became the owner of the magic workshop. And wasn't it fine that all the powers and ingredients which had been used for evil by the sorcerer were now in the hands of a boy who would use them only for the good of man and beast?

JAKOB AND WILHELM GRIMM, TRANSLATED BY WANDA GÁG

RED RIDING HOOD

ONCE UPON a time there was a sweet little maiden who was loved by all who knew her, but she was especially dear to her grandmother, who did everything she could for the child. Once she gave her a little red velvet cloak. It was so becoming and the little girl liked it so much that she would never wear anything else, and so she got the name of Red Riding Hood.

One day her mother said to her, "Come here, Red Riding Hood! Take this cake and bottle of wine to

Grandmother. She is weak and ill, and they will do her good. Go quickly, before it gets hot. Don't loiter by the way, nor run, or you will fall and break the bottle, and then there will be no wine for Grandmother. And when you get to her house, don't forget to say 'Good morning' prettily to Grandmother, without staring about you."

"I will do just as you tell me," Red Riding Hood promised her mother.

Her grandmother lived far into the wood, a good half-hour from the village. When she got to the wood, Red Riding Hood met a Wolf, but she did not know what a wicked animal he was, so she was not a bit afraid of him.

"Good morning, Red Riding Hood," he said.

"Good morning, Wolf," she answered.

"Whither away so early, Red Riding Hood?"

"To Grandmother's."

"What have you in your basket?"

"Cake and wine. We baked yesterday, so I'm taking a cake to Grandmother. She needs something to make her well."

"Where does she live, Red Riding Hood?"

"A good quarter of an hour farther into the wood. Her house stands under three big oak trees, near a hedge of nut trees which you must know," said Red Riding Hood.

The Wolf thought: This tender little creature will

be a plump morsel! She will be much nicer to eat than the old woman. I must be very cunning and snap them both up.

He walked along with Red Riding Hood for a while, then he said, "Look at the pretty flowers, Red Riding Hood. Why don't you look about you? I don't believe you even hear the birds sing. You are as solemn as if you were going to school, and everything else is so gay out here in the wood."

Red Riding Hood raised her eyes, and when she saw the sunlight dancing through the trees, and all the bright flowers, she thought: I'm sure Grandmother would be pleased if I took her a bunch of fresh flowers. It is still quite early. I shall have plenty of time to pick them.

So she left the path and wandered off among the trees to pick flowers. Each time she picked one, she always saw another even prettier one farther on. So she went deeper and deeper into the forest.

In the meantime the Wolf went straight off to the grandmother's cottage and knocked at the door.

"Who is there?"

"Red Riding Hood, bringing you a cake and some wine. Open the door!"

"Lift the latch," called out the old woman. "I am too weak to get up."

The Wolf lifted the latch and the door sprang open. He went straight in and up to the bed without saying a word, and ate up the poor old woman. Then he put on her nightdress and cap, got into bed and drew the curtains.

Red Riding Hood picked flowers till she could carry no more, and then she remembered that she had promised not to loiter on the way to her grandmother's. She was astonished when she got to the house to find the door open, and when she entered the room everything seemed so strange. She felt quite frightened but she did not know why.

"Good morning, Grandmother," she cried. But she received no answer.

Then she went up to the bed and drew the curtain back. There lay her grandmother, but she had drawn her cap down over her face and she looked very odd.

"Oh, Grandmother, what big ears you have," she said.

"The better to hear you with, my dear."

"Grandmother, what big eyes you have."

"The better to see you with, my dear."

"What big hands you have, Grandmother."

"The better to catch hold of you with, my dear."

"But, Grandmother, what big teeth you have."

"The better to eat you with, my dear."

Hardly had the Wolf said this when he made a spring out of bed and swallowed up poor little Red Riding Hood. When the Wolf was quite full, he went back to bed, and soon he was snoring loudly.

A huntsman went past the house and thought: How loudly the old lady is snoring! I must see if there is anything the matter with her. He went into the house and up to the bed, where he found the Wolf fast asleep. "So—do I find you here, you old sinner?" he said. "Long enough have I looked for you!"

He had just raised his gun to shoot, when it occurred to him that perhaps the Wolf had eaten up the old lady and that she might still be saved. So he took a knife and began cutting open the sleeping Wolf. At the first cut he saw a little red cloak, and after a few more slashes, the little girl jumped out and cried, "Oh, how frightened I was! It was so dark inside the Wolf!" Next the old grandmother came out, alive but hardly able to breathe.

Red Riding Hood brought some big stones with which they filled the Wolf. He woke up and tried to dash away, but the stones dragged him back and he fell down dead.

They were all happy now. The huntsman skinned the Wolf and took its fur home. The grandmother ate the cake and drank the wine which Red Riding Hood had brought, and she soon felt quite strong.

And Red Riding Hood said to herself, "I will never again wander off into the forest as long as I live, when my mother forbids it."

JAKOB AND WILHELM GRIMM, COLLECTION OF
MRS. E. V. LUCAS, LUCY CRANE AND MARIAN EDWARDES

THE LITTLE MERMAID

FAR OUT AT sea, the water is as blue as the bluest cornflower and as clear as the clearest crystal, but it is very deep—deeper than any anchor cable can fathom. Many church steeples would have to be piled one on top of the other to reach from the very bottom to the surface of the water. And down in the depths live the sea folk.

Now, don't imagine for a moment that there is nothing but bare white sand on the bed of the ocean—no, the most fantastic trees and flowers grow there, and all kinds of fishes, big and small, flit in and out among the branches, just as birds do in the air up here. At the very lowest depth stands the palace of the Sea King; the walls are made of coral and the high, pointed windows of the clearest amber, but the roof is made of mussel shells which open and close with the gentle motion of the water. It is a wonderful sight, for every mussel shell contains gleaming pearls—any single one of which would be a perfect ornament for a queen's crown.

The Sea King had been a widower for many years,

but his old mother kept house for him. She was very intelligent, although proud of her noble birth, and that is why she went about with twelve oysters on her tail, while the other highborn ladies were allowed just six. Apart from this, she deserved a great deal of praise because she was so fond of her grandchildren, the Princesses. They were six beautiful little girls, but the youngest was the prettiest of them all: her skin was as clear and delicate as a rose petal, her eyes were as blue as the deepest sea, but, like the other mermaids, she had no feet, only a fish's tail.

All day long they used to play down in the palace, in the great galleries where living flowers grew out of the walls. When the tall amber windows were opened, fishes swam in just as swallows fly into our rooms when we open the windows, but the fishes swam right up to the little Princesses, ate from their hands and allowed themselves to be patted.

Outside the palace there was a large garden with trees of fiery red and deep blue, their fruits glimmering like gold, and flowers like a blazing fire, ceaselessly moving their stems and leaves. The ground itself was of the finest sand, but blue as a sulfur flame. Down there a strange blue mist enveloped everything; you would have thought you were standing high in the air, with only the sky above and beneath you, and not down in the depths of the ocean. When the surface was dead calm you could just faintly perceive the sun, looking like a crimson flower from which streamed a flood of light.

Each of the small Princesses had her own little plot in the garden where she could dig and plant as she liked. One of them gave her flower bed the shape of a whale, another thought it nicer to have hers formed like a mermaid, but the youngest made hers as round as the sun and used only flowers as red as the sun itself. She was a strange child, quiet and pensive, and, while the other sisters decorated their gardens with all kinds of extraordinary things that they had taken from sunken ships, she would have nothing in hers but a beautiful statue and her red flowers. It was the statue of a handsome boy, in the purest white marble, that had sunk to the bottom of the sea after a shipwreck. Next to the statue she planted a rose-red weeping willow which grew splendidly and shaded the statue with its delicate branches.

Nothing gave the youngest Princess greater pleasure than to hear about the world of human beings up above. She made her grandmother tell all she knew about ships and towns, people and animals; but what fascinated her beyond words was that the flowers on earth were scented, while those at the bottom of the sea were not, that the woods were green and that the fishes one saw among the branches could sing so loudly and sweetly that it was a delight to hear them. Grandmother called the little birds of the air fishes, because otherwise the mermaids would not have understood her, for they had never seen a bird.

"As soon as you are fifteen," said their grandmother, "you will all be allowed to rise up above the water and sit on the rocks in the moonlight to watch the big ships sail by."

The following year the eldest sister was to have her fifteenth birthday, but as there was one year between each of them, the youngest still had five whole years to wait before her turn came to see what things are like on the earth. And the very one who had the longest time to wait was the most curious of them all. Many a night she stood by the open window and looked up through the dark blue sea where the fishes were lashing the water with fins and tails. She could just perceive the moon and the stars, though their light was very faint, but through the water they looked much bigger than they do to us; and if something like a black cloud passed under them, she knew that it was either a whale swimming above her or a ship with many people on board. They probably never dreamed that a lovely little mermaid was standing below, raising her white hands toward the keel of their ship.

The eldest Princess had now reached her fifteenth birthday, and was allowed to rise above the surface.

When she came back, she had hundreds of things to tell the others. But the most wonderful of all, she said, was to lie in the moonlight on a sandbank in the calm sea, gazing at the huge town close to the shore, where the lights twinkled like hundreds of stars; to listen to the music and the church bells, and to the noise and stir of carriages and people. But just because she could not get there, that was the very thing the mermaid longed to do most of all.

Oh, how eagerly the youngest sister listened; and whenever after this she stood at the open window in the evening looking up through the deep blue sea, she thought of the great town with its noise and bustle, and seemed to hear the sound of the church bells coming right down to her.

The following year, the second sister was allowed to rise up through the waves. She reached the surface just at sunset, and that sight was the most magnificent she had ever seen. The heavens looked like liquid gold, she told them, and the clouds, well, she never tired of describing their beauty—all rosy-red and violet as they sailed over her. Faster than the clouds, like a long white veil flung out toward the sky, a flock of wild swans flew away over the water beyond which the sun was setting. She swam toward the sun, but it sank, and the rosy tint faded away from sea and cloud.

The year after that, the third sister went up; she was the most daring of them, so she swam up a broad river which flowed into the ocean. She saw beautiful green hills and vineyards; palaces and farms were faintly visible among splendid forests. In a tiny cove she found a crowd of little human children, splashing about quite naked; she wanted to play with them, but she gave them a fright, and they ran away. Then came a little black animal—it was a dog, but she had never seen one before. It barked at her so furiously that she was frightened and took refuge in the open sea, but she could never forget the beautiful woods, the green hills and the lovely children who could swim in the water although they had no fishes' tails.

The fourth sister was not so daring: she remained far out in the stormy ocean and told her sisters that staying there was the best part of her adventures. You could see for miles and miles around, and the sky above was like a great glass dome. She had seen ships, but only far, far away; they looked like sea gulls. The amusing dolphins had turned somersaults, and the gigantic whales had spouted water through their nostrils, giving the effect of hundreds of fountains playing.

Now it was the turn of the fifth sister. Her birthday happened to be in the winter, so she saw things which none of the others had seen when they first went up to the surface. The sea was quite green, and large icebergs were floating about; they looked like pearls, she said. They appeared in the most wonderful shapes and sparkled like diamonds. She sat down on one of the largest, and every ship gave it a wide berth when the sailors saw her sitting there with her long hair floating in the wind. Late in the evening, the sky became overcast, thunder crashed and lightning stabbed the sky, while the black waves lifted the huge icebergs high up on their crests. Sails were furled on all the ships, the sailors stood in fear and trembling, but she sat quietly on her floating iceberg, watching the blue lightning flash in zigzags down into the shining sea.

The first time the sisters rose above the water, they were all delighted with the new and beautiful things they had seen, but as they were now grown up and were allowed to go up to the surface whenever they liked, they lost interest in it. They longed for their home, and after a month had gone by, each said that no place was more delightful than the bottom of the sea— besides, one felt so comfortably at home there.

Many an evening the five sisters would appear on the surface arm in arm. They had beautiful voices, more beautiful than those of any human beings, and when storms threatened to wreck the ships, the mermaids would swim in front of them. They sang their most seductive songs of the wonders in the depths of the sea and tried to persuade the people not to be afraid of coming down to them. But the seafarers could not understand them; they thought it was the storm they heard. Nor did they ever see the promised splendors, for when the ships sank, they drowned, and never reached the palace of the Sea King alive.

At night, when the sisters rose up through the water, the youngest remained behind quite alone, gazing after them. She would have wept, but a mermaid has no tears, and so she suffers all the more.

"Oh, if I were only fifteen!" she said. "I know I shall love that Upper World!"

At last she, too, reached the age of fifteen.

"Well, now we are getting you off our hands," said her grandmother, the old Dowager Queen. "Come here, let me dress you up like your sisters!" And she put a wreath of white lilies on her head, but each petal was formed of half a pearl; then the old Queen made eight large oysters fasten themselves to the Princess' tail to show her high rank.

"Oh, how it hurts!" said the little mermaid.

"Well, one must suffer to be beautiful," declared her grandmother.

The youngest mermaid would gladly have shaken off all this finery and laid aside the heavy wreath. The red flowers in her garden suited her much better, but she did not dare to change. "Good-bye, good-bye," she said and she rose up through the waters.

The sun had just set when her head appeared above the surface, but the clouds were still tinted with rose and gold, and in the pink-flushed sky the evening star twinkled bright and clear. The air was mild and fresh and the sea dead calm. She saw a big three-masted ship with only a single sail set, for not a breath of wind stirred, and sailors were sitting on the rigging.

She heard music and singing on board the ship,

and as the darkness was gathering, hundreds of colored lanterns were lighted; they looked like the flags of every nation waving in the air. The little mermaid swam right up to the porthole of the cabin, and every time the swell lifted her, she could see crowds of people in evening dress, but the handsomest of them all was a young Prince with great coal-black eyes. He could hardly have been more than sixteen years old; it was his birthday, and that was the reason for the party. The sailors danced on deck, and when the Prince appeared among them, hundreds of rockets shot up into the air, turning night to day and frightening the little mermaid so much that she had to dive under the water; but she soon ventured to put her head up again, and it looked as if all the stars were falling down to her from the sky. Never had she seen such a display. It was so light on board ship that one could see every rope, to say nothing of the people. Oh, how handsome the young Prince was, laughing and smiling while the music rang out in the beauty of the night.

It got quite late, but the little mermaid could not turn her eyes away from the ship and the beautiful Prince. The colored lanterns were put out, no more rockets shot up through the air, no more guns were fired, but deep down in the sea there was a dull humming and rumbling. The water was lifting her up and down so that she could look into the cabin, but the ship started to move, sail after sail opened to the wind, the waves grew mightier, great clouds gathered, and lightning flashed along the horizon. Oh, there was terrible weather ahead, so the sailors furled the sails. The great ship plowed on, pitching and tossing in the angry sea; waves, like enormous black mountains, were threatening to crash down upon the mast, but the ship disappeared like a swan in the trough of the waves and was lifted again the next moment to the top of their towering crests. The ship creaked and groaned, the thick planks cracked under the blows of the waves, the mast broke in two like a reed, and the ship rolled over so far to one side that water rushed into the hold.

Then the little mermaid saw that the people were in peril, while she herself had to beware of the beams and pieces of wreckage which were floating about in the sea. At one moment it was pitch-dark and she could see nothing at all; then there came a flash of lightning which lit up everything on board. She looked particularly for the young Prince, and when the ship split apart, she saw him sink into the sea. Her first impulse was one of joy because he was coming down to her, but then she remembered that human beings could not live under the water and that he could not come alive down to her father's palace. No, die he must not! So she swam in among the drifting beams and planks, quite forgetting that they might crush her. She dived deep into the sea, rose high up again among the waves and at last reached the young Prince, who could hardly keep on swimming in the stormy ocean. His arms and legs were beginning to fail him, his beautiful eyes were closing, he would have died had not the mermaid been there. She held his head above the water and let the waves carry her with him wherever they pleased.

At dawn the storm was over; not a trace of the ship was to be seen. The sun rose red and shining out of the water and seemed to bring life and color back into the Prince's cheeks, but his eyes remained closed. The mermaid kissed his high, noble brow and stroked back his wet hair. She thought he looked like the marble statue down in her little garden; she kissed him again and wished from the bottom of her heart that he might live.

In front of her she saw land, with snow-capped mountains in the distance. Near the shoreline were glorious green forests, and close by was a church or a convent—she could not be certain just what it was. Lemon and orange trees grew in the garden, and outside the gate were tall palm trees. There the sea had formed a cove where the fine white sand had been washed up. She swam toward it with the handsome Prince, and laid him on the sand with his head turned to the warm rays of the sun.

Then the bells rang out from the white building, and a group of young girls came through the garden. The little mermaid swam farther out and hid behind some large rocks, covering her hair and her breast with sea foam so that no one could catch sight of her face, and then kept watch to see who would come to the rescue of the poor shipwrecked Prince.

It was not long before one of the young girls arrived. For a moment, she seemed quite frightened, but she ran for help, and the mermaid saw the Prince come to and smile at those who stood around him. But he did not smile at her far out in the sea, for he did not know that she had saved him. She felt very sad, and when he was carried into the great building, she dived sorrowfully down into the depths of the water and returned to her father's palace. There her sisters asked what she had seen on her first visit to the surface, but she would tell them nothing.

Many an evening and many a morning she rose up to the place where she had left the Prince. She saw how the fruit in the garden ripened and was gathered, how the snow melted on the distant mountains, but she never saw the Prince, so she would return home sadder than before. Her only consolation was to sit in her little garden and throw her arms around the beautiful marble statue which was so like him. She neglected her flowers, and they grew into a wilderness all over the paths and wove their long stems and leaves in and out of the branches of the trees until the whole place was shrouded in darkness.

When she could endure it no longer, she confided in one of her sisters. At once the others knew about it, but nobody else—except for a few more mermaids who told just their most intimate friends. One of them knew who the Prince was; she too had seen the party held in his honor and heard where his kingdom lay.

"Come, little sister," said the other Princesses, and with their arms about each other's shoulders, they rose in a long line up through the water opposite the place where they knew the Prince's palace stood.

It was built of a kind of pale yellow stone, with a great flight of marble steps leading down to the sea. Splendid gilded cupolas were seen above the roof, and in between the pillars surrounding the whole building stood marble statues which looked as if they were alive. Through the clear glass windows one looked into magnificent halls where costly silk curtains and tapestries were hung and where all the walls were covered with large paintings. In the middle of the biggest hall a great fountain was playing, its jets soaring high up toward the glass dome through which the sun shone down upon the water and upon the beautiful plants growing in the great basin.

Now she knew where he lived, and many an evening and many a night she haunted the palace. She swam much closer to land than any of her sisters had dared to do, and she even went up the narrow creek running under the splendid balcony which cast its long shadow upon the water. Here she would sit and gaze at the young Prince, who thought he was quite alone in the bright moonlight.

Often in the evening she saw him sailing to the sound of music in a splendid new ship with waving flags. She peeped through the reeds, and if the wind caught her long silver-white veil, those who saw it thought it was a swan spreading its wings.

Many a night she heard the fishermen praising the young Prince and she rejoiced that she had saved his life. She thought how closely his head had rested on her bosom and how lovingly she had kissed him, though he knew nothing about it and could not even dream of her.

She became more and more fond of human beings, and more and more did she long to be among them. Their world seemed much larger than her own: they were able to fly over the sea in ships and climb the lofty mountains; the lands they possessed stretched farther than her eyes could reach. There was so much she wanted to know, but her sisters could not answer all her questions, so she asked her old grandmother who knew so well that Upper World, as she rightly called the countries above the sea.

"If human beings aren't drowned," asked the little mermaid, "can they live forever? Don't they die as we do down here in the depths of the sea?"

"Yes," answered the old lady, "they must die too, and their lifetime is even shorter than ours. We can live to be three hundred years old, but when we cease to exist, we turn to foam on the water, and so we don't even have a grave down here among our dear ones. We have no immortal soul, we never have another life; we are like the green reed—once it is cut, it never grows again. Human beings, on the contrary, have a soul which lives forever, which lives after the body has turned to dust. It rises up through the limpid air, up to the shining stars! Just as we rise out of the water and see the countries of the earth, so do they rise up to unknown beautiful regions which we shall never be able to see."

"Why were we not granted an immortal soul?" asked the little mermaid in a melancholy voice. "I know that I would gladly give the three hundred years I have to live if I could be a human being for only one single day, and then have some part in that heavenly world!"

"You must not brood over that," said her grandmother. "We have a much happier life than the people up there."

"So I am fated to die and float like foam upon the sea? Can I do nothing to win an immortal soul?"

"No," answered the old lady, "that could only happen if a human being held you so dear that you were more to him than father and mother. If he loved you with all his heart and soul and if his right hand were joined to yours by a monk, with the promise to be faithful to you here and in all eternity, then his soul would pass into your body and you would have a share in the happiness of mankind. He would give you a soul and yet retain his own. But that can never happen. The very thing that is considered beautiful here in the sea —your fish's tail—is considered ugly on the earth. People have very poor judgment indeed; they have two clumsy supports which they call 'legs,' and think them beautiful."

Then the little mermaid sighed, and looked sadly at her fish's tail.

"Come, let us be happy!" said her grandmother. "Let us leap and jump about during the three hundred years we have to live; that seems a fair enough amount of time. After that we can rest the more merrily. To-night we are giving a court ball."

Truly it was a magnificent affair such as one never sees on earth. The walls and ceiling of the great ball-room were made of thick, transparent glass. In rows on each side stood several hundred gigantic shells, rose-red and grass-green; a blue fire was burning in each—they lit up the entire room and, shining through the walls, lit up the sea as well. Innumerable fishes, great and small, could be seen swimming near the glass walls; some had scales gleaming scarlet, while others shone just like silver and gold. Down through the middle of the hall there flowed a broad stream on which the mermen and mermaids danced to their own beautiful singing. No voices such as theirs are ever heard among people of the earth. The little mermaid sang more beautifully than anyone else. Everyone applauded her, and for a moment her heart was filled with joy, for she knew she had the loveliest voice of all, on the earth or in the sea. But she could not forget the handsome Prince nor her sorrow at not having an immortal soul. So she stole out of her father's palace and, while everything within was joy and gaiety, sat sadly outside in her little garden.

Suddenly she heard bugles sounding down through the water and she thought: He is sailing up there, he whom I love more than my father or grandmother, he to whom my thoughts are clinging and in whose hand I would gladly place the happiness of my life. I will risk everything in my world to win him and an immortal soul. While my sisters are dancing in my father's palace, I shall go to see the old Sea Witch. She has always terrified me, but perhaps now she can advise and help me.

So she left her garden and set out toward the roaring whirlpools, for beyond them lived the witch. The little mermaid had never been that way before. No flowers grew there. Only the bare, gray sandy bottom stretched as far as the whirlpools which swirled around like roaring mill wheels, sweeping everything within reach down into the fathomless sea. She had to pass right through those crushing, whirling waters to enter the territory of the Sea Witch; then for a long way the only road went over a hot, bubbling morass—her peat bog, as the witch called it. Behind it lay her house, in the midst of a strange-looking forest. All the trees and bushes were polyps—half animal and half plant. They looked like hundred-headed snakes growing out of the ground. The branches were long slimy arms with slithery wormlike fingers, moving joint by joint from the root up to the very tip. They twined around anything they could reach, never loosening their grip. Terror-stricken, the little mermaid stopped on the edge of this forest. Her heart beat faster with fear and she almost turned back, but then she thought of the Prince and of the human soul, and her courage returned. She bound her long flowing hair tightly around her head so that the polyps might not seize her by it, she folded her arms closely across her breast and darted off as a fish darts through the water, in among the hideous polyps which stretched out their supple arms and fingers to catch her. She saw how each of them clung tightly to something it had caught.

People who had perished at sea and sunk deep down to the bottom were visible as white human bones among the arms of the polyps. The polyps also clutched ships' rudders, sea chests and skeletons of land animals, and, most horrible of all, she even saw a little mermaid whom they had caught and strangled.

She came next to a great slimy clearing in the forest, where big fat water snakes writhed and rolled, showing their ugly yellowish-white bellies. In the center of the clearing was a house built of the bones of ship-wrecked men; there sat the Sea Witch, letting a toad feed out of her mouth exactly as we let a canary eat sugar. She called the hideous, fat water snakes her little chickens and let them creep and crawl over her great spongy bosom.

"I know what you want," said the Sea Witch. "It is very foolish of you, for it will bring trouble upon you, my pretty one, but all the same you shall have your way. You want to get rid of your fish's tail and to have two bits of stumps to walk with instead, like the people of the earth, so that the young Prince will fall in love with you and you will win both him and an immortal soul."

Here the witch let out a laugh so loud and so ghastly that the toad and the snakes she had been fondling tumbled down to the ground, where they lay wallowing about.

"You have just come in time," said the witch. "Had you waited until sunrise tomorrow, I could not have helped you for a whole year. I am going to brew a potion for you. Before the sun rises, you must swim to land with it, sit down on the shore and drink it. Then your tail will part in two and shrink to what the people of the earth call 'pretty legs,' but it will hurt as if a sharp sword were cutting through you. Everybody who sees you will say that you are the prettiest human being they have ever seen. You are to keep your gliding motion, no dancer will be able to move as gracefully as you, but at every step it will feel as if you were treading on a sharp-edged knife, so sharp that your feet will seem to be bleeding."

She paused for a moment, then went on, "If you can bear all this, I shall be able to help you."

"I can," said the little mermaid in a quivering voice, and she thought of the Prince and of winning an immortal soul.

"But remember," said the witch, "once you have taken human shape, you can never become a mermaid again. You can never return to your father's palace, and if you do not win the love of the Prince, so that for your sake he forgets father and mother and clings to you with heart and soul and lets the monk join your hands, making you man and wife, then you will not win an immortal soul. On the very morning after he has married someone else, your heart will break and you will become foam on the sea."

"I am willing," said the little mermaid, who was as pale as death.

"But you will also have to pay me," said the witch, "and it is not a trifle that I require. You have the most beautiful voice of anyone down here in the depths of the sea. You think that you will be able to charm the Prince with it, but you must give that voice to me. I want the best thing you possess in exchange for my precious potion. I must drop some of my own blood into it so that the draught may be as sharp as a two-edged sword."

"But if you take my voice," said the little mermaid, "what shall I have left?"

"Your beautiful form," said the witch, "your gliding motion and your eloquent eyes—they will be enough for you to beguile any human heart.

"Well," she went on after a moment, "have you lost your courage? Put out your little tongue, and I will cut it out and take it as my payment, and you shall have the potent draught in return."

"So be it," said the little mermaid, and the witch put her caldron on the fire to brew the magic draught. "Cleanliness is a good thing," she said, and she scoured out the caldron with the snakes that she had tied up into a knot. Then she made a cut in her finger and let her black blood drip into the caldron. The witch kept on throwing in different ingredients, and when the mixture finally started to bubble it sounded like a crocodile sobbing. The steam coming from the caldron shaped itself into the most terrifying and horrible forms. When at last the potion was ready, it looked as clear as the clearest water.

"There you are," said the witch, and she cut out the tongue of the little mermaid. Now she had become mute and could neither sing nor speak.

"If the polyps should clutch you when you are on your way back through my forest," said the witch, "just throw one single drop of this draught upon each of them, and their arms and fingers will scatter into a thousand pieces."

But there was no need for the little mermaid to do that—the polyps shrank back in terror when they saw the shining potion gleaming in her hand like a twinkling star; thus she passed quickly through the forest, the bog and the roaring whirlpools.

She could see her father's palace. The torches had been extinguished in the great ballroom; her family were probably all asleep, but she had not the courage to approach them now that she was mute and was leaving them forever.

It seemed as if her heart was going to break with sorrow. She stole into the garden, picked one flower from each of her sisters' flower beds, blew a thousand kisses toward her home and rose up through the deep blue sea.

It was not yet sunrise when she saw the Prince's palace and went up the stately marble steps. The moon was still shining beautifully clear. The little mermaid drank the sharp, burning draught given her by the witch, and she felt as if a two-edged sword had cut through her delicate body; she swooned with agony and lay as if she were dead.

When the sun spread its rays over the sea she awoke and felt a stinging pain, but before her stood the handsome young Prince. He fixed his coal-black eyes upon her, and under his gaze she lowered her eyes and saw that her fish's tail had gone and that she had the prettiest pair of white legs any young girl could desire; but her body was naked, so she veiled herself with her long thick hair.

The Prince asked who she was and how she had come there, and she looked up at him with her dark blue eyes, so mild and yet so full of sadness, for she could not speak. Then he took her by the hand and led her into the palace.

As the witch had foretold, she seemed at each step to be treading on sharp knives and pointed daggers, but she bore the pain gladly. Led by the Prince, she moved lightly as a bubble, and he and everyone else marveled at her graceful gliding motion.

They clad her in costly robes of silk and muslin. She was the fairest of all in the palace, but she was mute and could neither speak nor sing. Beautiful slave girls, dressed in silk and gold, came before them and sang for the Prince and his royal parents. One of them sang more delightfully than any of the others, and the Prince clapped his hands and smiled at her, which saddened the little mermaid, for she knew that she herself used to sing far more beautifully; and she thought, Oh, if he only knew that I gave away my voice forever in order to be with him!

The slave girls now danced gracefully to the accompaniment of the loveliest music imaginable, and then the little mermaid lifted her pretty white arms and, rising on the tips of her toes, flitted across the floor, dancing as no one had ever danced before. With each of her movements her beauty became more and more evident, and her eyes spoke more deeply to the heart than the song of the slave girls.

Everyone was enchanted, especially the Prince, who called her his own little foundling. And she danced again and again, though every time her foot touched the ground it seemed to her as if she were treading on sharp knives.

The Prince said that she must always remain with him, and she was allowed to sleep on a velvet cushion outside his door.

He had a page's dress made for her, so that she might accompany him on horseback. They rode through the fragrant woods, where the green boughs brushed her shoulders and the little birds sang hidden among the leaves.

She climbed the highest mountains in the kingdom with the Prince, and though her delicate feet bled so that even the others in the group with them noticed it, she only laughed and followed him until they could see the clouds moving far below them like flocks of birds on their way to distant lands.

At night, when the others were asleep in the Prince's palace, she would go out onto the broad marble steps and cool her burning feet in the cold seawater, and then she would think of her dear ones in the depths of the sea.

One night her sisters appeared arm in arm, singing mournful songs as they swam along. She beckoned to them and they recognized her and told her how much she had grieved them all. They visited the little mermaid every night after that and once, in the far, far distance, she saw her old grandmother, who had not been above the water for many years, and the Sea King with his crown upon his head. They stretched out their hands toward her, but did not venture so near the land as her sisters.

Day by day she grew dearer to the Prince. He loved her as one loves a good child, but had no thought of making her his Queen. Yet his wife she must be, or she could never win an immortal soul, but would become merely a cloud of foam on the sea the morning after he wed another.

"Am I not dearer to you than anyone else?" her eyes seemed to ask, when he took her in his arms and kissed her fair brow.

"Yes, you are the dearest of all to me," said the Prince, "for you have the kindest heart of all. You are more devoted to me than anyone else, and you look like a young girl whom I once saw, but whom I shall probably never see again. I was on board a ship which was wrecked; the waves carried me ashore near a holy temple where a group of young maidens were serving.

The youngest of them found me and saved my life. I saw her but twice. She is the only one in the world I could ever love, but you look so much like her that you almost take the place of her image in my heart. She belongs to that holy temple, and therefore destiny sent you to me. We will never part."

Alas, he does not know that I saved his life, thought the little mermaid. It was I who carried him over the water to the forest where the temple stands. I stayed hidden in the foam to see if anyone would come. I saw the pretty maiden whom he loves better than me. And she gave a deep sigh—for as a mermaid she had no tears. The maiden belongs to the holy temple, he tells me, she will never come out into the world, so they will never meet again. I am with him, I see him every day. I will cherish him, love him and give up my life to him.

But soon it was rumored that the Prince was going to marry the beautiful daughter of a neighboring King, and that was why he was fitting out such a splendid ship. They said that the Prince was paying a state visit to the country of that King, but the real reason was to see the King's daughter. He was to have a great entourage with him.

The little mermaid shook her head and laughed, for she knew the Prince's thoughts far better than anyone else.

"I must go away," he had said to her. "I must go

and see the beautiful Princess—my parents insist upon it; but they will not compel me to bring her home as my bride. I cannot love her! She is not like the beautiful maiden in the temple or as you are. If I ever had to choose a bride, I would sooner choose you, my dear mute foundling with the speaking eyes." And he kissed her red lips, played with her long hair and laid his head on her heart, so that she dreamed of human happiness and an immortal soul.

"I hope you are not afraid of the sea, my poor mute child," he said, when they stood on the splendid ship which was to carry him to the country of the neighboring King. Then he told her of storm and calm at sea, of strange fishes in the depths of the ocean and what divers had seen down there, and she smiled at his description, for she knew more than anyone else about the bottom of the sea.

In the moonlit night, when all were asleep except the helmsman at the wheel, she sat by the rail and, gazing down through the water, she fancied she could see her father's palace. On the top stood her old grandmother with a silver crown on her head, gazing at the keel of the ship through the fast-flowing current. Then her sisters came up above the water and looked at her with deep sorrow in their eyes and wrung their white hands. She beckoned to them, smiling, and tried to make them understand that she was well and happy, but when the cabin boy came toward her, her sisters dived down again, so he felt quite certain that the gleam of white he had seen was nothing but foam.

Next morning the ship sailed into the harbor of the neighboring King's magnificent city. All the church bells rang, and from the tall towers trumpets were blown, while the soldiers stood at attention with flying colors and glittering bayonets. Each day brought new festivity, balls and parties were given all the time, but the Princess had not yet arrived. People said she was being brought up in a holy temple, where she was learning every royal accomplishment. At last she appeared on the scene.

The little mermaid waited anxiously to see her beauty, and she had to admit that she had never seen a more graceful form. The Princess' skin was fine and delicate, and behind the long dark eyelashes smiled a pair of dark blue eyes, full of devotion.

"It is you! You who saved me when I lay like a corpse on the shore!" said the Prince, and he clasped his blushing bride-to-be in his arms. "Oh, I am more than happy!" he said to the little mermaid. "My dearest wish, the thing I have never dared to hope for, has been granted me. You will rejoice in my happiness, for you are more devoted to me than anyone else." Then the little mermaid kissed his hand, and already her heart seemed to be breaking. The morning after his wedding would bring death to her and change her to foam on the sea.

All the church bells rang out; heralds rode about the streets and proclaimed the betrothal. On every altar fragrant oil was burning in costly silver lamps. The priests swung their censers, and bride and bridegroom joined hands and received the bishop's blessing. The little mermaid, clad all in silk and gold, was holding the bride's train, but her ears heard nothing of the festive music, her eyes saw nothing of the holy ceremony; she thought of the last night she had to live and of all she had lost in this world.

That very evening, bride and bridegroom went on board the ship. Cannons were fired, banners fluttered in the wind, and in the middle of the ship a royal tent of gold and purple was set up, furnished with great sumptuous cushions on which the bridal couple were to sleep in the calm, cool night.

The sails swelled out in the breeze, and the ship glided smoothly and without any perceptible motion over the limpid sea.

When it grew dark, colored lanterns were lighted, and the sailors danced merry dances on the deck. The little mermaid could not help thinking of the first time she rose to the surface of the sea and saw a similar sight of splendor and joy. Light as a swallow in full flight she joined in the dance, and to the sound of cheers and shouting danced as she had never danced before. Her delicate feet seemed to be cut by sharp knives, but the anguish of her heart was so great that she did not feel the pain. She knew only that this was the last evening she was ever to see the Prince, for whom she had forsaken her people and her home, had given up her beautiful voice to the Sea Witch and had daily suffered untold agony, while he remained unaware of it all.

The gaiety and merriment lasted until long past midnight, and the little mermaid laughed and danced like the others, but with the thought of death in her heart. The Prince kissed his beautiful bride, and she played with his black hair, and arm in arm they went to rest in the splendid tent.

A hushed silence fell upon the ship; only the helmsman stood at the wheel. The little mermaid laid her white arms on the rail and gazed toward the east, waiting to see the red tinge of the dawn—the first rays of the sun, she knew, would kill her. Then she saw her sisters rising out of the sea; they were pale like herself, their long, beautiful hair no longer fluttered in the wind—it had all been cut off.

"We have given it to the witch so that she may give you help and save you from dying before dawn. She has given us a knife, look, here it is! Do you see its sharp edge? Before the sun rises you must plunge it into the Prince's heart, and when his warm blood splashes over your feet, they will grow into a fish's tail, and you will become a mermaid again; you will be able to come down to us in the water and live your three hundred years before you turn into dead salt sea foam. Make haste! Either he or you must die before the sun rises. Our old grandmother has been mourning till her white hair has fallen out as ours fell under the witch's scissors. Kill the Prince and come back! Make haste! Do you see that red streak in the sky? In a few minutes the sun will rise and you must die!" Having said this, they uttered a strange deep sigh and disappeared in the waves.

The little mermaid drew back the purple curtains of the tent and saw the beautiful bride sleeping with her head on the Prince's breast. She bent down and kissed him on his fair brow, then she looked up at the sky where the first faint flush of dawn became brighter and brighter. She looked at the sharp knife and again fixed her eyes on the Prince, who in his sleep was murmuring the name of his bride. She and only she was in his thoughts. The knife quivered in the mermaid's hand, but then—she flung it far out into the waves! They gleamed red where it fell; it seemed as if drops of blood were bubbling up through the water. Once more she looked with dimming eyes upon the Prince. Then she threw herself from the ship into the water, and felt her body dissolving into foam.

The sun rose out of the sea. Its rays fell mild and warm upon the death-cold sea foam, and the little mermaid felt not the hand of Death. She saw the bright sun, and above her floated hundreds of beautiful ethereal beings, so transparent that through them she could see the white sails of the ship and the rosy clouds of the sky; their voices were music, but so unearthly that no human ear could grasp it, just as no human eye could see their forms. Without wings they floated by their own lightness through the air. The little mermaid saw that she too had a body like theirs, and that it was gradually freeing itself more and more from the foam.

"Toward whom am I floating?" she asked, and her voice sounded like that of the other beings, so ethereal that no earthly music could possibly render it.

"To the daughters of the air," answered the others. "The mermaid has no immortal soul and can never gain one unless she wins the love of a human being. Her eternal life depends upon a power outside herself. The daughters of the air have no immortal souls either, but they can gain one by their good deeds. We fly to the hot countries where the torrid air of pestilence kills men; we bring cool breezes to them, we spread the fragrance of flowers through the air and send to them solace and healing. When we have tried for three hundred years to do all the good we can, we receive an immortal soul and share in the everlasting happiness of mankind. You, poor little mermaid, have tried with your whole heart to do the same. By your sufferings and by your courage in enduring them, you have raised yourself into the world of the spirits of the air, and now you can gain an immortal soul by good deeds accomplished in the course of three hundred years."

The little mermaid raised her translucent arms toward God's sun, and for the first time she felt tears in her eyes.

Noise and bustle had started again on the ship. She saw the Prince and his beautiful wife searching for her; then they gazed with sorrow in their hearts at the bubbling foam, as if they knew that she had thrown herself into the waves.

Invisible by now, the little mermaid kissed the bride on her forehead, smiled at the Prince and soared with the other children of the air toward the rose-colored cloud floating through space.

"In this way we shall float into the Heavenly Kingdom in three hundred years."

"We may even reach it sooner," whispered one of them. "Invisibly we float into the houses of human beings where there are children, and for every day on which we find a good child who brings joy to his parents and deserves their love, our time of probation is shortened by God. The child is unaware of it when we float through the room, and if we smile at him in our joy, one year is taken from the three hundred. But if we see a bad and naughty child, then we must weep tears of sorrow over him, and every tear adds one day to our time of probation."

HANS CHRISTIAN ANDERSEN, TRANSLATED BY PAUL LEYSSAC

FIVE WISE WORDS

ONCE THERE lived a handsome young man named Ram Singh who, though a favorite with everyone, was unhappy because he had a sharp-tongued, nagging stepmother. All day long she went on talking, until the youth was so distracted he determined to go away and seek his fortune. No sooner had he decided to leave his home than he made his plans, and the very next morning he started off with a few clothes wrapped in a bundle and a little money in his pocket.

But there was one person in the village to whom the young man wished to say good-bye, and that was a wise old guru, or teacher, who had taught him a great deal. So he turned his face first of all toward his master's hut and, before the sun was well up, was knocking at his door.

The old man received his pupil affectionately; but he was wise in reading faces, and saw at once that the youth was troubled. "My son," he said quietly, "what is the matter?"

"Nothing, father," replied the young man, "but I

have determined to go out into the world and seek my fortune."

"Be advised," said the guru, "and remain in your father's house. It is better to have half a loaf at home than to seek a whole one in distant countries."

But Ram Singh was in no mood to heed such advice, and very soon the old man ceased to press him.

"Well," said he at last, "if your mind is made up, I suppose you must have your way. But listen carefully, and remember five parting counsels which I will give you; if you keep these no evil shall befall you. First, always obey without question the orders of him whose service you enter. Second, never speak harshly or unkindly to anyone. Third, never lie. Fourth, never try to appear the equal of those above you in station. And fifth, wherever you go, if you meet those who read or teach from the holy books, stay and listen, if but for a few minutes, that you may be strengthened in the path of duty."

Then Ram Singh started out upon his journey, promising to bear in mind the old man's words.

After some days he came to a great city. He had spent all the money he had brought with him, and therefore resolved to look for work, however humble it might be. Catching sight of a prosperous-looking merchant standing in front of a grain shop, Ram Singh asked whether he could give him anything to do.

The merchant gazed at him so long the young man

began to lose heart, but at length the merchant answered him, "Yes, of course; there is a place waiting for you."

"What do you mean?" asked Ram Singh.

"Why," replied the other, "yesterday our Rajah's chief Wazir dismissed his body servant and is looking for another. Now you are just the sort of person he needs, for you are young and tall and handsome. I advise you to apply there."

Thanking the merchant for this advice, the young man set out at once for the Wazir's house. On account of his good looks and appearance, he was engaged as the great man's servant.

One day, soon after this, the Rajah started on a journey, and his chief Wazir accompanied him. With them was an army of servants and attendants, soldiers, muleteers, camel drivers, merchants with grain and stores for man and beast, singers to make entertainment along the way and musicians to accompany them, besides elephants, camels, horses, mules, ponies, donkeys, goats and carts and wagons of every kind and description. The caravan seemed more like a large town on the march than anything else.

Thus they traveled till they entered a country that was like a sea of sand, where the swirling dust floated in clouds, and men and beasts were half choked by it. Toward the close of day they came to a village. The headmen hurried out to salute the Rajah and to pay him their respects, but they soon began, with very long and serious faces, to explain that, while they and all they had were of course at the disposal of the Rajah, the coming of so large a company had put them into dreadful difficulty. They had neither a well nor a spring in their country, and so they had no water to give drink to such an army of men and beasts!

Great fear fell upon the caravan at the words of the headmen, but the Rajah merely told the Wazir that he must get water somehow, and that settled the matter as far as he was concerned. The Wazir sent off in haste for all the oldest men in the town and began to question them as to whether there were any wells in the neighborhood.

The men all looked helplessly at each other and said nothing; but at length one old graybeard replied, "Truly, Sir Wazir, there is, within a mile or two of this village, a well which some former king made hundreds of years ago. It is, they say, great and inexhaustible, covered in by heavy stonework, with a long flight of steps leading down to the water in the very bowels of the earth. But no man ever dares to go near it because it is haunted by evil spirits, and it is known that whosoever disappears down the well shall never be seen again."

The Wazir stroked his beard and considered a moment. Then he turned to Ram Singh, who stood behind his chair. "There is a proverb," said he, "that no man

can be trusted until he has been tried. Go you and get
the Rajah and his people water from this well."

Then there flashed into Ram Singh's mind the first
counsel of the old guru: "Always obey without question the order of him whose service you enter." So he
replied at once that he was ready, and he left to prepare for his adventure. He fastened two great brass
vessels to a mule, two lesser ones he bound upon his
shoulders, and thus provided he set out with the old
villager for his guide.

In a short time they came within sight of a spot
where some big trees towered above the barren country, while in their shadow lay the dome of an ancient
building. This the guide pointed out as the well, but
he excused himself from going farther, saying he was
an old man and tired, and it was already sunset. So
Ram Singh bade him farewell and went on alone.

Arriving at the trees, Ram Singh tied up his mule,
lifted the two large vessels down and, having found the
opening of the well, descended a flight of steps into
the darkness. The steps were broad white slabs of ala-
baster which gleamed in the shadows as he went lower
and lower. All was very silent. Even the sound of his
bare feet upon the steps seemed to wake an echo in
that lonely place, and, when one of the vessels he was
carrying fell, it clanged so loudly that he jumped.

Still he went on, until at last he reached a wide pool
of sweet water, where he washed his jars with care,

then filled them and began to remount the steps, carrying the lighter vessels. The big ones were so heavy that he could only take up one at a time.

Suddenly, something moved, and above him he saw a great giant standing on the stairway! In one hand the giant held clasped to his heart a dreadful-looking mass of bones, in the other was a lamp which cast long shadows about the walls and made him seem even more terrible than he really was.

"What think you, O mortal," said the giant, "of my fair and lovely wife?" And he held the light toward the bones in his arms and looked lovingly at them.

Now this poor giant had had a very beautiful wife whom he loved dearly; but, when she died, he refused to believe in her death and always carried her about even long after she had become nothing but bones. Ram Singh of course did not know of this, but there came to his mind the second wise saying of the guru, which forbade him to speak harshly or inconsiderately to others; so he replied, "Truly, sir, I am sure you could nowhere find such another."

"Ah, what eyes you have!" cried the delighted giant. "You at least can see! I do not know how often I have slain those who insulted her by saying she was but dried bones! You are a fine young man, and I will help you."

So saying, he laid down the bones with great tenderness and, snatching up the huge brass vessels, carried them up and put them on the mule with such ease that it was all done by the time Ram Singh had reached the open air with the smaller jars.

"Now," said the giant, "you have pleased me, and you may ask of me one favor. Whatever you wish I will do for you. Perhaps you would like me to show you where lies buried the treasure of dead kings?" he added eagerly.

But Ram Singh shook his head at the mention of buried wealth. "The favor I would ask," said he, "is that you will leave off haunting this well, so men may freely go in and out to obtain water."

Perhaps the giant expected some favor more difficult to grant, for his face brightened and he promised to depart at once. As Ram Singh went off through the gathering darkness with his precious burden of water, he beheld the giant striding away with the bones of his dead wife in his arms.

Great was the wonder and rejoicing in the camp when Ram Singh returned with the water. He said nothing about his adventure with the giant, but merely told the Rajah there was nothing to prevent the well from being used. And used it was, and nobody ever saw any more of the giant.

The Rajah was so pleased with the bearing of Ram Singh that he ordered the Wazir to give the young man to him in exchange for one of his own servants. So Ram Singh became the Rajah's attendant; and as the days went by, the Rajah became more and more delighted with the youth because, being ever mindful of the old guru's third counsel, he was always honest and spoke the truth. He grew in favor rapidly, until at last the Rajah made him his treasurer, and thus he reached a high place in the court and had wealth and power in his hands.

Unluckily, the Rajah had a brother who was a very bad man. This brother thought that if he could win the young treasurer over to his side he might by this means manage to steal, little by little, as much of the Rajah's treasure as he needed. Then, with the money, he could bribe the soldiers and some of the Rajah's counselors to dethrone and kill his brother, and he would reign himself.

He was too wary, of course, to tell Ram Singh of these wicked plans, but he began by flattering him whenever he saw him and at last he offered him his daughter in marriage. But Ram Singh remembered the fourth counsel of the old guru—never to try to appear the equal of those above him in station—therefore he respectfully declined the great honor of marrying a princess. The Prince, thwarted at the very beginning of his enterprise, was furious. He determined to bring about Ram Singh's ruin and he told the Rajah that his treasurer had spoken insulting words about his sovereign and also about the Princess.

What these words were nobody knew, and as the

story was not true, the wicked Prince did not know either. But the Rajah grew very angry and red in the face as he listened, and declared that until Ram Singh's head was cut off neither he nor the Princess nor his brother would eat or drink.

"But," the Rajah added, "I do not wish anyone to know that this was done by my desire, and anyone who mentions the subject will be severely punished." And with this the Prince was forced to be content.

Then the Rajah sent for an officer of his guard and told him to take some soldiers and ride at once to a tower outside the town. If anyone came to inquire when the building was going to be finished or asked any other questions about it, the officer must chop his head off and bring it to him. As for the body, that should be buried on the spot. The old officer thought these instructions rather odd, but it was no business of his, so he saluted and went off to do his master's bidding.

Early in the morning, the Rajah, who had not slept all night, sent for Ram Singh. He bade him go to the new hunting tower and ask the people there how it was getting on and when it was going to be finished, and then to hurry back with the answer. Away went Ram Singh upon his errand but, on the road, as he was passing a little temple on the outskirts of the city, he heard someone inside reading aloud. Remembering the guru's fifth counsel, he stepped inside and sat down to listen. He did not mean to stay long, but became so interested in the wisdom of the teacher that he sat and sat, while the sun rose higher and higher.

In the meantime, the wicked Prince, who dared not disobey the Rajah's command, was feeling very hungry, and the Princess was quietly crying in a corner, waiting for the news of Ram Singh's death so that she might eat her breakfast.

Hours passed, and stare as he might from the window, the Prince could see no messenger. At last he could not bear it any longer and, hastily disguising himself so that no one should recognize him, he jumped on a horse and galloped out to the hunting tower where the Rajah had told him the execution was to take place. But, when he arrived, there were only some men engaged in building and a number of soldiers idly watching them.

He forgot that he had disguised himself and that no one would know him and he cried out, "Now then, you men, why are you idling about here instead of finishing what you came to do? When is it to be done?"

At his words the soldiers looked at the commanding officer, who was standing a little apart from the rest. Unnoticed by the Prince, he made a slight sign, a sword flashed in the sun, and off flew a head to the ground beneath!

As part of the Prince's disguise had been a thick beard, the men did not recognize the dead man as the

Rajah's brother. They wrapped the head in a cloth and buried the body as their commander bade them. When this was ended, the officer took the cloth and rode off in the direction of the palace.

Meanwhile the Rajah came home from his council and to his great surprise found neither head nor brother awaiting him. As time passed, he became uneasy and thought he had better go and see what the matter was. So, ordering his horse, he rode off alone.

Just as the Rajah came near the temple where Ram Singh still sat, the young treasurer, hearing the sound of a horse's hooves, looked over his shoulder and saw that the rider was the Rajah himself! Feeling much ashamed for having forgotten his errand, he jumped up and hurried out to meet his master, who reined in his horse and seemed very surprised (as indeed he was) to see him. At that moment the officer arrived, carrying his parcel. He saluted the Rajah gravely and, dismounting, laid the bundle in the road and began to undo the wrappings, while the Rajah watched him with wonder and amazement.

When the last string was undone, and the head of his brother was displayed to his view, the Rajah sprang from his horse and caught the officer by the arm. As soon as he could speak he questioned the man as to what had occurred, and little by little a dark suspicion grew. Then, telling the soldier he had done well, the Rajah drew Ram Singh to one side, and in a few minutes learned from him how, in attending to the guru's counsel, he had delayed in doing his ruler's bidding.

In the end the Rajah found proof of his dead brother's treachery, and Ram Singh established his innocence and integrity. He continued to serve the Rajah for many years with unswerving fidelity, married a maiden of his own rank, with whom he lived happily, and died honored and loved by all men. Sons were born to him; and, in time, to them also he taught the five wise sayings of the old guru.

OLD PUNJÂBI TALE, ANDREW LANG COLLECTION

THE GOOSE-GIRL

ONCE UPON a time there was an old Queen who had a beautiful daughter. When she grew up she was betrothed to a Prince who lived a great way off.

Now when the time drew near for the Princess to be married and to depart into the foreign kingdom, her old mother gave her much costly baggage and many ornaments, gold and silver, trinkets and knickknacks and, in fact, everything belonging to a royal trousseau, for she loved her daughter dearly. The Queen also sent a waiting-maid, who was to ride with the Princess and hand her over to the bridegroom, and she provided each of them with a horse for the journey. Now the Princess' horse, which was called Falada, was able to speak.

When the hour for departure drew near, the old mother went to her bedroom and, taking a small knife, she cut her fingers till they bled. Then she held a white cloth under them, and, letting three drops of blood fall into it, she gave it to her daughter, saying, "Dear child, take great care of this cloth. It may be of use to you on the journey."

So they took a sad farewell of each other. The Princess put the cloth in the front of her dress, mounted her horse and set forth on the journey to her bridegroom's kingdom.

After they had ridden for about an hour the Princess became thirsty and said to her waiting-maid, "Please dismount and fetch me some water in my golden cup from yonder stream. I would like a drink."

"If you are thirsty," said the maid, "dismount yourself, and lie down by the water and drink. I do not mean to be your servant any longer."

The Princess was so thirsty that she got down and bent over the stream, for the golden goblet had not been brought to her. As she drank she murmured,

"Oh, Heaven, what am I to do?" And the three drops of blood replied:

> If your mother only knew,
> Her heart would surely break in two.

But the Princess was meek and said nothing about her maid's rude behavior and quietly mounted her horse again. They rode on their way for several miles, but the day was hot, and the sun's rays beat fiercely on them. The Princess was soon overcome by thirst again. And as they passed another brook she called out once more to her waiting-maid, "Pray get me a drink in my golden cup," for she had long ago forgotten her maid's rude words.

But the waiting-maid answered her mistress more haughtily even than before, "If you want a drink, you can dismount and get it. I do not mean to be your servant."

Then the Princess was compelled by her thirst to dismount. Bending over the flowing water, she cried, "Oh, Heaven, what am I to do?" And the three drops of blood replied:

> If your mother only knew,
> Her heart would surely break in two.

And as she drank, leaning over the water, the cloth containing the three drops of blood fell from her bosom and floated down the stream. In her anxiety the

Princess never even noticed her loss, but the waiting-maid had observed it with delight. She knew that now she could do as she wished with the bride, for in losing the drops of blood the Princess had become weak and powerless.

When the Princess wished to get on her horse again, the waiting-maid called out, "I mean to ride Falada; you must mount my beast." And to this too the Princess had to submit. Then the waiting-maid commanded her harshly to take off her royal robes and to put on her common ones, and finally she made her swear by Heaven not to say a word about the matter when they reached the palace. If she did not do so, she would be killed on the spot. And Falada observed everything and took it all to heart.

The waiting-maid now mounted Falada, and the real bride the other horse, and so they continued their journey till at length they arrived at the palace. There was great rejoicing over the arrival, and the Prince sprang forward to meet them. Thinking that the waiting-maid was his bride, he lifted her down from her horse and led her upstairs to the royal chamber.

In the meantime the real Princess was left standing below in the courtyard.

The old King, who was looking out of his window, beheld her in this plight, and it struck him how sweet and gentle, even beautiful, she looked. He went at once to the royal chamber and asked the false bride who it was she had brought with her and left standing in the courtyard below.

"Oh," replied the bride, "I brought her with me to keep me company on the journey. Give the girl something to do, that she may not be idle."

But the old King had no work for her and could not think of anything, so he said, "I have a small boy who looks after the geese. She had better help him." The youth's name was Curdken, and the real bride was made to assist him in herding geese.

Soon after this, the false bride said to the Prince, "Dearest bridegroom, I pray you grant me a favor."

He answered, "That I will."

"Then have the horse I rode here killed, because it behaved very badly on the journey."

But the truth was she was afraid lest the horse should speak and tell how she had treated the Princess. When the news came to the ears of the real Princess she went to the slaughterer and secretly promised him a piece of gold if he would do something for her. There was in the town a large dark gate, through which she had to pass night and morning with the geese. Would he kindly hang up Falada's head there that she might see it again?

The man said he would do as the Princess desired, and the next day he chopped off the head and nailed it firmly over the gateway.

When she and Curdken drove their flock through

the gate early the next morning, she whispered as she passed under:

> Oh, Falada, 'tis you hang there,

and the head replied:

> 'Tis you; pass under, Princess fair:
> If your mother only knew,
> Her heart would surely break in two.

Then the real Princess and Curdken left the tower and drove the geese out into the country. And when they had reached the meadow where the geese fed she sat down and unloosed her hair, which was of pure gold. Curdken loved to see it glitter in the sun and wanted very much to pull out a few hairs.

Then the Princess spoke:

> Wind, wind, gently sway,
> Blow Curdken's hat away;
> Let him chase o'er field and wold
> Till my locks of ruddy gold,
> Now astray and hanging down,
> Be combed and plaited in a crown.

A gust of wind blew Curdken's hat away, and he had to chase it over hill and dale. When he returned from the pursuit she had finished combing and curling her hair, and his chance of getting a lock was gone. Curdken was very angry and would not speak to her.

They herded the geese in silence till evening and then went home.

The next morning, as they passed under the gate, driving the geese before them, the girl said:

> Oh, Falada, 'tis you hang there,

and the head replied:

> 'Tis you; pass under, Princess fair:
> If your mother only knew,
> Her heart would surely break in two.

Then she went on her way till she came to the meadow, where she sat down and began to comb out her hair.

Curdken ran up to her and wanted to pull a lock from her head, but she called out hastily:

> Wind, wind, gently sway,
> Blow Curdken's hat away;
> Let him chase o'er field and wold
> Till my locks of ruddy gold,
> Now astray and hanging down,
> Be combed and plaited in a crown.

Then a puff of wind came and blew Curdken's hat far away and he had to run after it. When he returned she had long finished putting up her golden locks, and he could not get one; so they watched the geese till it was dark.

But that evening when they came home Curdken went to the old King and said, "I refuse to herd geese any longer with that girl."

"For what reason?" asked the King.

"Because she does nothing but annoy me all day long," replied Curdken, and he proceeded to relate her strange behavior.

"Every morning as we drive the flock through the tower gate she says to a horse's head that is nailed on the wall:

> Oh, Falada, 'tis you hang there,

and the head replies:

> 'Tis you; pass under, Princess fair:
> If your mother only knew,
> Her heart would surely break in two."

And Curdken went on to tell what happened on the meadow where the geese fed, and how he had always to chase his hat.

The old King bade him go and drive forth his flock as usual next day. And when morning came he himself took up his position behind the dark gate and heard how the goose-girl greeted Falada. Then he followed her through the field and hid himself behind a bush on the meadow.

He soon saw with his own eyes how the goose-boy and the goose-girl looked after the geese, and how after a time the maiden sat down and loosened her hair, that glittered like gold, and repeated:

> Wind, wind, gently sway,
> Blow Curdken's hat away;
> Let him chase o'er field and wold
> Till my locks of ruddy gold,
> Now astray and hanging down,
> Be combed and plaited in a crown.

Then a gust of wind came and blew Curdken's hat away so he had to fly over hill and dale after it, and the girl in the meantime quietly combed and braided her hair. All this the old King observed and returned to the palace without anyone having noticed him. In the evening, when the goose-girl came home, he called her aside and asked her why she behaved as she did.

"I may not tell you why," she replied. "How dare I confide my woes to anyone? For I swore by Heaven not to, otherwise I should have lost my life."

The old King begged her to tell him, and left her no peace, but he could get nothing out of her. At last he said, "Well, if you will not tell me, confide your trouble to the iron stove there." And he went away, leaving her alone.

Then she crept to the stove, and began to sob and to pour out her sad little heart, and said, "Here I sit, deserted by the whole world—I who am a King's daughter, and a false waiting-maid has forced me to remove my own clothes and has taken my place with my bridegroom, while I fulfill the lowly task of goose-girl.

> If my mother only knew,
> Her heart would surely break in two."

But the old King stood outside at the stove chimney and listened to her words. Then he entered the room again, and he ordered royal apparel to be put on her, in which she looked amazingly lovely. Next he summoned his son and revealed to him that he had a false bride who was nothing but a waiting-maid, while the real bride, in the guise of the goose-girl, was now standing at his side.

The young Prince rejoiced with all his heart when he saw her beauty and learned how good she was, and a great banquet was prepared, to which everyone was bidden. The bridegroom sat at the head of the table, the real Princess on one side of him and the waiting-maid on the other. The waiting-maid was so dazzled she did not recognize the Princess in her glittering garments. When they had eaten and were merry, the King asked the false bride to solve a problem for him.

"What," said he, "should be done to a certain person who has deceived everyone?" And he proceeded to relate the whole story, ending up with: "Now what sentence should be passed?" Then the false bride answered, "She deserves to be put naked into a barrel lined with sharp nails, which should be dragged by two white horses up and down the street till she is dead."

"You are the person," said the King, "and you have passed sentence on yourself. And even so it shall be done to you."

The young Prince was married to his real bride, and both reigned over the kingdom in peace and happiness.

JAKOB AND WILHELM GRIMM, TRANSLATED BY MAY SELLAR

BEAUTY AND THE BEAST

ONCE UPON a time, in a far-off country, there lived a merchant who was enormously rich. He had six sons and six daughters, however, who were accustomed to having everything they fancied, and he did not find he had a penny too much. But a series of misfortunes befell them. One day their house caught fire and speedily burned to the ground, with all the splendid furniture, books, pictures, gold, silver and precious goods it contained. Then the father suddenly lost every ship he had upon the sea, because of pirates, shipwreck or fire. As though that were not enough, he heard that his clerks in distant countries, whom he had trusted, had proved dishonest. And at last from great wealth he fell into the direst poverty.

All that he had left was a little house in a desolate place a long distance from the town. The daughters at first hoped their friends, who had been so numerous while they were rich, would insist that they stay in their houses, but they soon found they were left alone. These former friends even attributed the family's misfortunes to the daughters' extravagance and showed no intention of offering any help.

So nothing was left for them but to take their departure to the cottage, which stood in the midst of a dark forest. They were too poor to have any servants, and the girls had to work hard; the sons, for their part, cultivated the fields to earn their living. Roughly clothed, and living in the simplest way, the girls never ceased to yearn for the luxuries and amusements of their former life. Only the youngest daughter tried to be brave and cheerful.

She had been as sad as anyone when misfortune first overtook her father, but soon recovered her natural gaiety. She set to work to make the best of things, to amuse her father and brothers as well as she could and to persuade her sisters to join her in dancing and singing. But they would do nothing of the sort and, because she was not as gloomy as themselves, they declared their miserable life was all she was fit for. But she was really far prettier and cleverer than they were. Indeed, she was so lovely she was always called Beauty.

After two years, their father received news that one of his ships, which he had believed lost, had come safely into port with a rich cargo. All the sons and daughters at once thought that their poverty was at an end and wanted to set out directly for the town; but their father, who was more prudent, begged them to wait a little.

Only the youngest daughter had any doubt but that they would soon again be as rich as they were before. They all loaded their father with demands for jewels and dresses which it would have taken a fortune to buy; only Beauty did not ask for anything. Her father, noticing her silence, said, "And what shall I bring for you, Beauty?"

"The one thing I wish for is to see you come home safely," she answered.

But this reply annoyed her sisters, who fancied she was blaming them for having asked for such costly things. Her father, however, was pleased, and he urged her to choose something.

"Well, dear Father," she said, "as you insist upon it, I beg that you will bring me a rose. I have not seen one since we came here, and I love them so much."

The merchant set out, only to find that his former companions, believing him to be dead, had divided his cargo among themselves. After six months of trouble and expense he found himself as poor as when he started on his journey. To make matters worse, he returned during a terrible snowstorm. By the time he was within a few miles of his home he was almost exhausted with cold and fatigue. Though he knew it would take some hours to get through the forest, he resolved to go on. But night overtook him, and the deep snow and bitter frost made it impossible for his horse to carry him any farther.

The only shelter he could find was the hollow trunk of a great tree, and there he crouched all night. The howling of the wolves kept him awake, and when at last day broke, the falling snow had covered every path, and he did not know which way to turn.

At length he made out some sort of way, but it was so rough and slippery that he fell more than once. Presently it led him into an avenue of orange trees which ended in a splendid castle. It seemed to the merchant very strange that no snow had fallen in the avenue of trees, which were covered with flowers and fruit. When he reached the first courtyard he saw before him a flight of agate steps. He went up and passed through several splendidly furnished rooms.

The pleasant warmth of the air revived him, and he felt very hungry; but there seemed to be nobody in all this vast and splendid palace. Deep silence reigned everywhere, and at last, tired of roaming through empty rooms and galleries, he stopped in a room

smaller than the rest, where a cheerful fire was burning and a couch was drawn up before it. Thinking this
must be prepared for someone who was expected, he
sat down to wait till he should come, and very soon fell
into a sweet sleep.

When extreme hunger wakened him after several
hours, he was still alone; but a little table, with a good
dinner on it, had been drawn up close to him. He lost
no time in beginning his meal, hoping he might soon
thank his considerate host, whoever he might be. But
no one appeared, and even after another long sleep,
from which he awoke completely refreshed, there was
no sign of anybody, though a fresh meal of dainty cakes
and fruit was on the little table at his elbow.

Being naturally timid, he grew terrified of the silence, and he resolved to search once more through all
the rooms; but it was of no use, there was no sign of
life in the palace! Then he went down into the garden,
and though it was winter everywhere else, here the sun
shone, the birds sang, the flowers bloomed and the air
was soft and sweet. The merchant, in ecstasies at all
he saw and heard, said to himself, "All this must be
meant for me. I will go this minute and bring my children to share all these delights."

In spite of being so cold and weary when he reached
the castle, he had taken his horse to the stable and fed
it. Now he thought he would saddle it for his homeward journey, and he turned down the path which led

to the stable. This path had a hedge of roses on each side of it, and the merchant thought he had never seen such exquisite flowers. They reminded him of his promise to Beauty, and he stopped and had just gathered one to take to her when he was startled by a strange noise behind him. Turning around, he saw a frightful Beast.

"Who told you you might gather my roses?" cried the Beast in a terrible voice. "Was it not enough that I sheltered you in my palace and was kind to you? This is the way you show your gratitude, by stealing my flowers! But your insolence shall not go unpunished."

The merchant, terrified by these furious words, dropped the fatal rose and, throwing himself on his knees, cried, "Pardon me, noble sir. I am truly grateful for your hospitality. It was so magnificent I could not imagine you would be offended by my taking such a little thing as a rose."

But the Beast's anger was not lessened by his speech. "You are very ready with excuses and flattery," he cried. "But that will not save you from the death you deserve."

Alas, thought the merchant, if my daughter Beauty could only know to what danger her rose has brought me! And in despair he began to tell the Beast all his misfortunes and the reason for his journey, not forgetting to mention Beauty's request. "A king's ransom would hardly have procured all that my other daughters asked for," he said. "But I thought I might at least take Beauty her rose. I beg you to forgive me, for you see I meant no harm."

The Beast said, in a less furious tone, "I will forgive you on one condition—that you will give me one of your daughters."

"Ah," cried the merchant, "if I were cruel enough to buy my own life at the expense of one of my children's, what excuse could I invent to bring her here?"

"None," answered the Beast. "If she comes at all she must come willingly. On no other condition will I have her. See if any one of them is courageous enough, and loves you enough, to come and save your life. You seem to be an honest man, so I will trust you to go home. I give you a month to see if any of your daughters will come back with you and stay here, so that you may go free. If none of them is willing, you must come alone, for then you will belong to me. And do not imagine that you can hide from me, for if you fail to keep your word I will come and fetch you!" added the Beast grimly.

The merchant accepted this proposal. He promised to return at the time appointed, and then, anxious to escape from the presence of the Beast, he asked permission to set off at once. But the Beast answered that he could not go until the next day. "Then you will find a horse ready for you," he said. "Now go and eat your supper and await my orders."

The poor merchant, more dead than alive, went back to his room, where the most delicious supper was already served on the little table drawn up before a blazing fire. But he was too terrified to eat and only tasted a few of the dishes, for fear the Beast should be angry if he did not obey his orders. When he had finished, the Beast warned him to remember their agreement and to prepare his daughter for exactly what she had to expect.

"Do not get up tomorrow," he added, "until you see the sun rise and hear a golden bell ring. Then you will find your breakfast waiting for you, and the horse you are to ride will be ready in the courtyard. He will also bring you back again when you come with your daughter a month from now. Farewell. Take a rose to Beauty, and remember your promise!"

The merchant lay down until dawn. Then, after breakfast, he went to gather Beauty's flower and mounted his horse, which carried him off so swiftly that in an instant he had lost sight of the palace. He was still wrapped in gloomy thoughts when it stopped before the door of his cottage.

His sons and daughters, who had been uneasy at his long absence, rushed to meet him, eager to know the result of his journey which, seeing him mounted upon a splendid horse and wrapped in a rich mantle, they supposed to be favorable. But he hid the truth from them at first, only saying sadly to Beauty as he gave her the rose: "Here is what you asked me to bring you. Little you know what it has cost."

Presently he told them his adventures from beginning to end, and then they were all very unhappy. The girls lamented loudly over their lost hopes, and the sons declared their father should not return to the terrible castle. But he reminded them he had promised to go back. Then the girls were very angry with Beauty and said it was all her fault. If she had asked for something sensible this would never have happened.

Poor Beauty, much distressed, said to them, "I have indeed caused this misfortune, but who could have guessed that to ask for a rose would cause so much misery? But as I did the mischief it is only just that I should suffer for it. I will therefore go back with my father to keep his promise."

At first nobody would hear of it. Her father and brothers, who loved her dearly, declared nothing should make them let her go. But Beauty was firm. As the time drew near she divided her little possessions among her sisters and said good-bye to everything she loved. When the fatal day came she and her father both mounted the horse which had brought him back. It seemed to fly rather than gallop, but so smoothly that Beauty was not frightened. Indeed, she would have enjoyed the journey if she had not feared what might happen at the end of it. Her father tried to persuade her to go back home with him, but in vain.

While they were riding the night fell. Then, to their great surprise, splendid fireworks blazed out before them and all the forest was illuminated. They even felt pleasantly warm, though it had been bitterly cold before. They reached the avenue of orange trees and saw that the palace was brilliantly lighted from roof to ground, and music sounded softly from the courtyard.

"The Beast must be very hungry," said Beauty, trying to laugh, "if he makes all this rejoicing over the arrival of his prey." But, in spite of her anxiety, she admired all the wonderful things she saw.

When they had dismounted, her father led her to the little room. Here they found a crackling fire and the table spread with a delicious supper.

Beauty, who was less frightened now that she had passed through so many rooms and seen nothing of the Beast, was quite willing to begin, for her long ride had made her very hungry. But they had hardly finished their meal when the noise of the Beast's footsteps was heard approaching, and Beauty clung to her father in terror, which became all the greater when she saw how frightened he was. But when the Beast appeared, though she trembled at the sight of him, she made a great effort to hide her horror, and faced him respectfully.

This evidently pleased the Beast. After looking at her he said, in a tone that might have struck terror into the boldest heart, though he did not seem to be angry, "Good evening, old man. Good evening, Beauty."

The merchant was too terrified to reply, but Beauty answered sweetly, "Good evening, Beast."

"Have you come willingly?" asked the Beast. "Will you be content to stay here when your father has gone away?"

Beauty answered bravely that she was quite prepared to stay.

"I am pleased with you," said the Beast. "You have come of your own accord, so you may remain. As for you, old man," he added, turning to the merchant, "at sunrise tomorrow take your departure. When the bell rings, get up quickly and eat your breakfast, and you will find the same horse waiting to take you home."

Then turning to Beauty, he said, "Take your father into the next room, and help him choose gifts for your brothers and sisters. You will find two traveling trunks there; fill them as full as you can. It is only just that you should send them something very precious as a remembrance." Then he went away.

Beauty was beginning to think with great dismay of her father's departure, but they went into the next room and were greatly surprised at the riches they found. There were splendid dresses fit for a queen, and when Beauty opened the chests she was dazzled by the gorgeous jewels lying in heaps upon every shelf. After choosing a vast quantity for each of her sisters, she opened the last chest and discovered that it was full of gold.

"I think, Father," she said, "that, as the gold will be more useful to you, we had better take out the other things and fill the trunks with it."

So they did this, but the more they put in, the more room there seemed to be, and at last they put back all the jewels and dresses they had taken out, and Beauty even added as many more of the jewels as she could carry. Even then the trunks were not too full, but they were so heavy an elephant could not have carried them!

"The Beast was mocking us!" cried the merchant. "He pretended to give us all these things, knowing that I could not carry them away."

"Let us wait and see," answered Beauty. "I cannot believe he meant to deceive us. All we can do is to fasten them and have them ready."

So they did this and returned to the little room, where they found breakfast prepared. The merchant ate with a good appetite, as the Beast's generosity made him believe he might perhaps venture to come back soon and see Beauty. But she felt sure her father was leaving her forever, so she was very sad when the bell rang sharply.

They went down into the courtyard, where two horses were waiting, one loaded with the two trunks, the other for him to ride. They were pawing the ground in their impatience to start, and the merchant bade Beauty a hasty farewell. As soon as he was mounted, the horses went off at such a pace that she lost sight of him in an instant. Then Beauty began to cry and wandered sadly back to her own room.

But she soon found she was very sleepy, and as she had nothing better to do she lay down and instantly fell asleep. And then she dreamed she was walking by a brook bordered with trees, and lamenting her sad fate, when a young Prince, handsomer than anyone she had ever seen and with a voice that went straight to her heart, came and said to her, "Ah, Beauty, you are not so unfortunate as you suppose. Here you will be rewarded for all you have suffered elsewhere. Your every wish shall be gratified. Only try to learn who I am, no matter how I may be disguised, for I love you dearly, and in making me happy you will find your own happiness. Be as truehearted as you are beautiful, and we shall have nothing left to wish for."

"What can I do, Prince, to make you happy?" said Beauty.

"Only be grateful," he answered, "and do not trust too much to your eyes. Above all, do not desert me until you have saved me from my cruel misery."

As her dream continued she found herself in a room with a stately and beautiful lady, who said to her, "Dear Beauty, try not to regret all you have left behind you; you are destined for a better fate. Only do not let yourself be deceived by appearances."

Beauty found her dream so interesting that she was in no hurry to awake, but presently the clock roused her by calling her name softly twelve times. Then she rose and found her dressing table set out with everything she could possibly want, and when she was dressed, she found dinner waiting in the room next to hers. But dinner does not take very long when one is alone, and soon she sat down cozily in the corner of a sofa and began to think about the charming Prince she had seen in her dream.

"He said I could make him happy," said Beauty to herself. "It seems, then, that this horrible Beast keeps him a prisoner. How can I set him free? I wonder why they both told me not to trust to appearances? But, after all, it was only a dream, so why should I trouble myself about it? I had better find something to do to amuse myself."

So she began to explore some of the rooms in the palace. The first she entered was lined with mirrors. Beauty saw herself reflected on every side and thought she had never seen such a charming room. Then a bracelet which was hanging from a chandelier caught her eye, and on taking it down she was greatly surprised to find that it held a portrait of her unknown admirer, just as she had seen him in her dream. With great delight she slipped the bracelet on her arm and went on into a gallery of pictures, where she soon found a portrait of the same handsome Prince, as large as life, and so well painted that as she studied it he seemed to smile kindly at her.

Tearing herself away from the portrait at last, she passed into a room which contained every musical instrument under the sun, and here she amused herself for a long while in trying them. By this time it was growing dusk, and wax candles in diamond and ruby candlesticks lit themselves in every room.

Beauty found her supper served just at the time she liked to have it, but she did not see anyone or hear a sound and, though her father had warned her she would be alone, she began to find it rather dull.

Presently she heard the Beast coming and wondered tremblingly if he meant to eat her now. However, he did not seem at all ferocious, and only said gruffly: "Good evening, Beauty."

She answered cheerfully and managed to conceal her terror. The Beast asked how she had been amusing herself, and she told him all the rooms she had seen. Then he asked if she thought she could be happy in his palace; and Beauty answered that everything was so beautiful she would be very hard to please if she could not be happy. After an hour's talk Beauty began to think the Beast was not nearly so terrible as she had supposed. Then he rose to leave and said in his gruff voice: "Do you love me, Beauty? Will you marry me?"

"Oh, what shall I say?" cried Beauty, for she was afraid to make the Beast angry by refusing.

"Say yes or no without fear," he replied.

"Oh, no, Beast," said Beauty hastily.

"Since you will not, good night, Beauty," he said.

And she answered, "Good night, Beast," very glad to find her refusal had not provoked him. After he was gone she was very soon in bed and dreaming of her unknown Prince.

She thought he came and said, "Ah, Beauty! Why are you so unkind to me? I fear I am fated to be unhappy for many a long day still."

Then her dreams changed, but the charming Prince figured in them all. When morning came she decided to amuse herself in the garden. She was astonished to find that every place was familiar to her, and presently she came to the very brook and the myrtle trees where she had first met the Prince in her dream. That made her think more than ever that he must be kept a prisoner by the Beast.

When she was tired she went back to the palace and found a new room full of materials for every kind of work—ribbons to make into bows and silks to work into flowers. There was also an aviary full of rare birds, which were so tame that they flew to Beauty as soon as they saw her and perched upon her shoulders and her head.

"Pretty little creatures," she said, "how I wish your cage was nearer my room that I might often hear you sing!" So saying, she opened a door and found to her delight that it led into her own room, though she had thought it was on the other side of the palace.

There were more birds in a room farther on, parrots and cockatoos that could talk, and they greeted Beauty by name. Indeed, she found them so entertaining that she took one or two back to her room, and they talked to her while she was at supper. The Beast paid her his usual visit and put to her the same questions he had asked before, and then with a gruff good-night he took his departure, and Beauty went to bed to dream of her mysterious Prince.

The days passed swiftly in different amusements, and after a while Beauty found another strange thing which often pleased her when she was tired of being alone. There was one room which she had not noticed particularly; it was empty, except that under each of the windows stood a very comfortable chair. The first time she had looked out of a window, it seemed a black curtain prevented her from seeing anything outside. But the second time she went into the room she happened to be tired and sat down in one of the chairs. Instantly the curtain was rolled aside, and a most amusing pantomime was acted before her. There were dances and colored lights, music and pretty dresses, and it was all so gay that Beauty was in ecstasies. After that she tried the other seven windows in turn, and there was some new and surprising entertainment to be seen from each of them, so Beauty never could feel lonely anymore. Every evening after supper the Beast came to see her, and always before saying good-night he would ask her in his terrible voice: "Beauty, will you marry me?"

It occurred to Beauty, now that she understood him better, that when she said, "No, Beast," he went away quite sad. Her happy dreams of the handsome young Prince soon made her forget the poor Beast, and the only thing that disturbed her was being told to distrust appearances, to let her heart guide her and not her eyes. Think about this as she would, she could not understand.

So everything went on for a long time, until at last, happy as she was, Beauty began to yearn for the sight of her father and her brothers and sisters. One night, seeing her looking very sad, the Beast asked what was the matter. Beauty had quite ceased to be afraid of him. Now she knew he was really gentle in spite of his ferocious looks and his dreadful voice. So she answered that she wished to see her home once more. Upon hearing this the Beast seemed distressed and cried out miserably, "Ah, Beauty, have you the heart to desert an unhappy Beast like this? What more do you want to make you happy? Is it because you hate me that you want to escape?"

"No, dear Beast," answered Beauty softly, "I do not hate you, and I should be very sorry never to see you anymore, but I long to see my father again. Only let me go for two months, and I promise to come back to you and stay for the rest of my life."

The Beast, who had been sighing unhappily while she spoke, now replied, "I cannot refuse you anything you ask, even though it should cost me my life. Take the four boxes you will find in the room next to your own and fill them with everything you wish to take with you. But remember your promise and come back when the two months are over, for if you do not return in good time you will find your faithful Beast dead. You will not need any chariot to bring you back. Only say good-bye to your father and brothers and sisters the night before you come away and, when you have gone to bed, turn this ring around upon your finger and say firmly, 'I wish to go back to my palace and see my Beast again.' Good night, Beauty. Fear nothing, sleep peacefully, and before long you shall see your family once more."

As soon as Beauty was alone she hastened to fill the boxes with all the rare and precious things she saw about her, and only when she was tired of heaping things into them did they seem to be full. Then she went to bed, but could hardly sleep for joy. When at last she began to dream of her beloved Prince she was grieved to see him stretched upon a grassy bank, sad and weary, and hardly like himself.

"What is the matter?" she cried.

But he looked at her reproachfully and said, "How can you ask me, cruel one? Are you not leaving me to my death perhaps?"

"Ah, don't be sorrowful!" cried Beauty. "I am only going to assure my father that I am safe and happy. I have promised the Beast faithfully I will come back, and I know that he would die of grief if I did not keep my word!"

"What would that matter to you?" asked the Prince. "Surely you would not care?"

"Indeed I should be ungrateful if I did not care for such a kind Beast," cried Beauty indignantly. "I would die to save him from pain. I assure you it is not his fault he is so ugly."

Just then a strange sound woke her—someone was speaking not very far away. Opening her eyes she found herself in a room she had never seen before, which was certainly not as splendid as those she had seen in the Beast's palace. Where could she be? She rose and dressed hastily and then saw that the boxes she had packed the night before were all in the room. Suddenly she heard her father's voice and rushed out to greet him joyfully. Her brothers and sisters were astonished at her appearance, for they had never expected to see her again. Beauty asked her father what he thought her strange dreams meant and why the Prince in them constantly begged her not to trust to appearances. After much consideration he answered, "You tell me yourself that the Beast, frightful as he is, loves you dearly and deserves your love and gratitude for his gentleness and kindness. I think the Prince must mean you to understand that you ought to reward the Beast by doing as he wishes you to, in spite of his ugliness."

Beauty could not help seeing that this seemed likely; still, when she thought of her dear Prince who was so handsome, she did not feel at all inclined to marry the Beast. At any rate, for two months she need not decide but could enjoy herself with her family. Though they were rich now, and lived in a town again and had plenty of acquaintances, Beauty found that nothing amused her very much. She often thought of the palace, where she was so happy, especially as at home she never once dreamed of her beloved Prince, and she felt quite sad without him.

And her sisters seemed quite used to being without her, and even found her rather in the way. So she would not have been sorry when the two months were over but for her father and brothers. She did not have the courage to say good-bye to them. Every day when she rose she meant to say it at night, and when night came she put it off again, until at last she had a dismal dream which helped her to make up her mind.

She thought she was wandering in a lonely path in the palace gardens, when she heard groans. Running quickly to see what could be the matter, she found the Beast stretched out upon his side, apparently dying. He reproached her faintly with being the cause of his distress, and at the same moment a stately lady appeared and said very gravely: "Ah, Beauty, see what happens when people do not keep their promises! If you had delayed one day more, you would have found him dead."

Beauty was so terrified by this dream that the very next evening she said good-bye to her father and her brothers and sisters, and as soon as she was in bed she turned around upon her finger the ring which the Beast had given her, and said firmly, "I wish to go back to my palace and see my Beast again."

Then she fell asleep instantly, and only woke up to hear the clock saying, "Beauty, Beauty," twelve times in its musical voice, which told her she was really in the palace once more. Everything was just as before, and her birds were very glad to see her, but Beauty thought she had never known such a long day. She was so anxious to see the Beast again that she felt as if supper-time would never come.

But when it came no Beast appeared. After listening and waiting for a long time, she ran down into the garden to search for him. Up and down the paths and avenues ran poor Beauty, calling him. No one answered, and not a trace of him could she find. At last, Beauty saw that she was standing opposite the shady path she had seen in her dream. She rushed down it and, sure enough, there was the Beast—asleep, so Beauty thought. Quite glad to have found him, she ran up and stroked his head, but to her horror he did not move or open his eyes. "Oh, he is dead, and it is all my fault!" cried Beauty, weeping bitterly.

But then, looking at him again, she fancied he still breathed. Hastily fetching some water from the nearest fountain, she sprinkled it over his face, and to her great delight he began to revive. "Oh, Beast, how you frightened me!" she cried. "I never knew how much I loved you until just now, when I feared I was too late to save your life."

"Can you really love such an ugly creature as I am?" asked the Beast faintly. "Ah, Beauty, you came only just in time. I was dying because I thought you had forgotten your promise. But go back now and rest, and I shall see you again by and by."

Beauty, who had half expected he would be angry with her, was reassured by his gentle voice and went back to the palace. And after a while the Beast came in to visit her and talked about the time she had spent with her father, asking if she had enjoyed herself and if they had all been glad to see her.

Beauty quite enjoyed telling him all that had happened to her. When at last the time came for him to leave, he asked, as he had so often asked before: "Beauty, will you marry me?"

She answered softly, "Yes, dear Beast."

As she spoke, a blaze of light sprang up before the windows of the palace; fireworks crackled and guns boomed, and across the avenue of orange trees, in letters all made of fireflies, was written: "Long live the Prince and his bride."

Turning to ask the Beast what it could all mean, Beauty found he had disappeared, and in his place stood her long-loved Prince! At the same moment the wheels of a chariot were heard upon the terrace, and two ladies entered the room. One of them, Beauty realized, was the stately lady she had seen in her dreams; the other was so queenly that Beauty hardly knew which to greet first. But the one she recognized said to her companion: "Well, my Queen, this is Beauty, who has had the courage to rescue your son from the terrible enchantment. They love each other, and only your consent to their marriage is wanting to make them perfectly happy."

"I consent with all my heart," cried the Queen. "How can I ever thank you enough, charming girl, for having restored my dear son to his natural form?" And then she tenderly embraced Beauty and the Prince, who had meanwhile been greeting the other lady, who was a fairy, and receiving her congratulations.

"Now," said the fairy to Beauty, "I suppose you would like me to send for your father and all your brothers and sisters to dance at your wedding?"

And so she did, and the marriage was celebrated the very next day with the utmost splendor, and Beauty and the Prince lived happily ever after.

MADAME DE VILLENEUVE, ANDREW LANG COLLECTION

THE TOWN MOUSE AND
THE COUNTRY MOUSE

O NCE UPON a time a
Town Mouse met a Country Mouse on the outskirts of
a wood. The Country Mouse was sitting under a hazel
thicket plucking nuts.

"Busy harvesting, I see," said the Town Mouse.
"Who would think of our meeting in this out-of-the-
way part of the world?"

"Just so," said the Country Mouse.

"You are gathering nuts for your winter store?"
asked the Town Mouse.

"I am obliged to do so if we intend having anything
to live upon during the winter," said the Country
Mouse.

"The husk is big and the nut full this year, enough
to satisfy any hungry body," said the Town Mouse.

"Yes, you are right there," said the Country Mouse,
and then she related how well she lived and how comfortable she was at home.

The Town Mouse maintained that she was the better
off, but the Country Mouse said that nowhere could

one be so well off as in the woods and hills. And as they could not agree on this point they promised to visit each other at Christmas; then they could see for themselves which was really the more comfortable.

The first visit was to be paid by the Town Mouse.

Now, although the Country Mouse had moved down from the mountains for the winter, the road to her house was long and tiring, and one had to travel up hill and down dale. The snow lay thick and deep, so the Town Mouse found it hard work to get on, and she became tired and hungry before she reached the end of her journey. How nice it will be to get some food, she thought.

The Country Mouse had scraped together the best she had. There were nut kernels, polypody and all sorts of roots and many other good things which grow in woods and fields. She kept everything in a hole far underground so the frost could not reach it, and close by was a running spring which was free of ice all winter long, so she could drink as much water as she liked. There was an abundance of all she had, and they ate well and heartily; but the Town Mouse thought it was very poor fare indeed. "One can, of course, keep body and soul together on this," said she, "but I don't think much of it. Now you must be good enough to visit me and taste what we have."

Yes, that her hostess would, and before long she set out. The Town Mouse had gathered together all the scraps from the Christmas fare which the woman of the house had dropped on the floor during the holidays —bits of cheese and butter, candle ends, cake crumbs, pastry and many other good things. In the dish under a beer tap she had drink enough; in fact, the place was full of all kinds of dainties. They ate and fared well. The Country Mouse seemed never to have enough; she had never tasted such delicacies. But then she became thirsty, for she found the food both strong and rich, and so she wanted something to drink.

"We haven't far to go for the beer we shall drink," said the Town Mouse, and jumped upon the edge of the dish and drank till she was no longer thirsty. She did not drink too much, for she knew the Christmas beer was strong. The Country Mouse, however, thought the beer a splendid drink; she had never tasted anything but water, so she took one sip after another, but as she could not stand strong drink she became dizzy before she left the dish. The drink got into her head and down into her toes, and she began running from one beer barrel to the other and dancing about on the shelves among the cups and mugs. She squeaked and squealed as if she were intoxicated.

"You must not carry on as if you had just come from the backwoods and make such a row and noise," said the Town Mouse. "The master of the house is a bailiff, and he is very strict indeed."

The Country Mouse said she didn't care either for

See page 304

303

bailiffs or beggars. But the Cat sat at the top of the cellar steps, lying in wait, and heard all the chatter and noise. When the woman of the house went down to draw some beer and lifted the trapdoor the Cat slipped by into the cellar and struck its claws into the Country Mouse. Then there was quite another sort of dance.

The Town Mouse slid back into her hole and sat in safety looking on, while the Country Mouse suddenly became sober when she felt the Cat's claws in her back.

"Oh, my dearest bailiff, be merciful and spare my life and I will tell you a fairy tale," she said.

"Well, go on," said the Cat.

"Once upon a time there were two little mice," said the Country Mouse, squeaking slowly and pitifully, for she wanted to make the story last as long as she possibly could.

"Then they were not lonely," said the Cat dryly and curtly.

"And they had a steak they were going to fry."

"Then they could not starve," said the Cat.

"And they put it out on the roof to cool," said the Country Mouse.

"Then they did not burn themselves," said the Cat.

"But there came a fox and a crow and they ate it all up," said the Country Mouse.

"Then I'll eat you," said the Cat. But just at that moment the woman shut the trapdoor with a slam, which so startled the Cat that she let go her hold of the

Mouse. One bound, and the Country Mouse found her-self in the hole with the Town Mouse.

From there a passage led out into the snow, and you may be sure the Country Mouse did not wait long before she set out homeward.

"And this is what you call living at ease and being well off," she said to the Town Mouse. "Heaven pre-serve me from having such a fine place and such a master! Why, I only just got away with my life!"

OLD SCANDINAVIAN TALE, COLLECTION OF
KATE DOUGLAS WIGGIN AND NORA ARCHIBALD SMITH

SNOW WHITE AND THE
SEVEN DWARFS

ONCE UPON a time in the middle of winter, when the snowflakes were falling like feathers on the earth, a Queen sat at a window framed in black ebony and sewed. And as she sewed and gazed out on the white landscape, she pricked her finger with the needle, and three drops of blood fell on the snow outside.

Because the red showed up so well against the white, the Queen said to herself, "Oh, what would I not give to have a child as white as snow, as red as blood and as black as ebony!"

And her wish was granted, for not long afterward a little daughter was born to her, with a skin as white as snow, lips and cheeks as red as blood and hair as black as ebony. They called her Snow White, and not long after her birth the Queen died.

After a year, the King married again. His new wife was a beautiful woman, but so proud and overbearing that she could not stand any rival to her beauty.

The new Queen possessed a magic mirror, and when she stood before it, gazing at her own reflection, she asked:

> Mirror, mirror, on the wall,
> Who is fairest of us all?

and it always replied:

> Thou, Queen, art the fairest of all.

Then she was quite happy, for she knew the mirror always spoke the truth.

But Snow White was growing prettier and prettier every day, and when she was seven years old she was as beautiful as she could be, and fairer than even the Queen herself. One day when the Queen asked her mirror the usual question, it replied:

Thou art fair, my Queen, 'tis true.
But Snow White is fairer far than you.

Then the Queen flew into the most awful passion and turned every shade of green in her jealousy. From this hour she hated poor Snow White, and every day her envy, hatred and malice grew, for envy and jealousy are like evil weeds which spring up and choke the heart.

At last she could endure Snow White's presence no longer and, calling a huntsman to her, she said, "Take the child out into the wood and never let me see her face again. You must kill her and bring me back her lungs and heart, so that I may know for certain she is dead."

The huntsman did as he was told and led Snow White out into the wood, but as he was in the act of drawing out his knife to slay her, she said, "Oh, dear huntsman, spare my life. I promise you that I will disappear into the forest and never return home again."

Because she was so young and pretty the huntsman had pity on her and said, "Well, run along, poor child." For he thought the wild beasts would soon find her and eat her up.

And his heart felt lighter because he hadn't had to do the deed himself. As he turned away, a young boar came running past, so he shot it and brought its lungs and heart home to the Queen as a proof that Snow

White was really dead. And the wicked woman had them stewed in salt, and ate them, thinking she had made an end of Snow White forever.

Now when the poor child found herself alone in the big wood the very trees seemed to take strange shapes, and she felt so frightened she didn't know what to do. Over the sharp stones and through the bramble bushes she stumbled, and the wild beasts ran past her, but they did her no harm. She ran as far as her legs would carry her, and as evening drew in she saw a little house and stepped inside to rest.

Everything was very small in the house, but very clean and neat. In the middle of the room there stood a little table, covered with a white tablecloth and seven little plates and forks and spoons and knives and tumblers. Side by side against the wall there were seven little beds, covered with immaculate white counterpanes.

Snow White felt so hungry and so thirsty she ate a bit of bread and a morsel of porridge from each plate and drank a drop of wine out of each tumbler. Then, feeling tired and sleepy, she lay down on one of the beds, but it wasn't comfortable. Then she tried all the others in turn, but one was too long, another too short, and it was only when she tried the seventh that she found one to suit her exactly. So she lay down upon it, said her prayers like a good child and soon fell fast asleep.

When it was quite dark the masters of the little house returned. They were seven dwarfs who worked in the mines, deep down in the heart of the mountain. They lighted their seven little candles, and as soon as their eyes were accustomed to the glare they saw that someone had been in the room, for all was not in the same order as they had left it.

The first said, "Who has been sitting on my chair?"

The second said, "Who has been eating my loaf?"

The third said, "Who has been tasting my porridge?"

The fourth said, "Who has been eating out of my plate?"

The fifth said, "Who has been using my fork?"

The sixth said, "Who has been cutting with my knife?"

The seventh said, "Who has been drinking out of my tumbler?"

Then the first dwarf looked around and saw a hollow in his bed, and he asked, "Who has been lying on my bed?" The others came running around, and cried when they saw their beds, "Somebody has lain on ours, too."

But when the seventh came to his bed, he started back in amazement, for there he beheld Snow White fast asleep. Then he called the others, who turned their little candles full on the bed, and when they saw Snow White lying there they nearly fell down with surprise.

"Goodness gracious," they cried, "what a beautiful child she is!"

They were so enchanted by her beauty that they did not wake her but let her sleep on in the little bed. The seventh dwarf slept with his companions one hour in each bed, and in this way he managed to pass the night.

In the morning Snow White awoke, and when she saw the seven little dwarfs she felt frightened. But they were so friendly, and asked her what her name was in such a kind way, that she replied, "I am Snow White."

"Why did you come to our house?" continued the seven dwarfs.

Then she told them how her stepmother had wished her put to death, and how the Queen's huntsman had spared her life, and how she had run all day till she had come to their little house. The dwarfs, when they had heard her sad story, asked her, "Will you stay and keep house for us, cook, make the beds, do the washing, sew and knit? If you keep everything neat and clean, you shall want for nothing."

"Yes," answered Snow White, "I will gladly do all you ask."

And so she lived happily with them. Every morning the dwarfs went into the mountain to dig for gold, and in the evening when they returned home, Snow White always had their supper ready for them. But during the day she was left quite alone, so the

good dwarfs warned her, saying, "Beware of your step-mother. She will soon find out you are here, and what-ever you do don't let anyone into the house."

Now the Queen never dreamed but that she was once more the most beautiful woman in the world; so, stepping before her mirror one day, she said:

> Mirror, mirror, on the wall,
> Who is fairest of us all?

and the mirror replied:

> You are fair, my Queen, 'tis true,
> But Snow White is fairer far than you.
> Snow White, who dwells with the seven little men,
> Is as fair as you and as fair again.

When the Queen heard these words she was nearly struck dumb with horror, for the mirror always spoke the truth. She knew now that the huntsman must have deceived her and that Snow White was still alive. She pondered day and night how she might destroy her, for her jealous heart left her no rest. At last she hit upon a plan. She stained her face and dressed herself up as an old peddler woman, so that she was quite unrecognizable. In this guise she went over the seven hills till she came to the house of the seven dwarfs. There she knocked at the door, calling out at the same time: "Fine wares to sell, fine wares to sell!"

Snow White peeped out of the window and spoke

to her, "Good day, kind lady, what have you to sell?"

"Good wares, fine wares," she answered, "laces of every shade and description." And she held one up that was made of some gaily colored silk.

"Surely I can let the honest woman in," said Snow White, and she unbarred the door and bought the pretty lace.

"Good gracious, child," said the old woman, "what a figure you have! Come! I'll lace you up properly for once."

Snow White, suspecting no evil, stood before her and let her lace up her bodice; but the old woman laced her so quickly and so tightly that it took Snow White's breath away, and she fell down as though she were dead.

"Now you are no longer the fairest," said the wicked old woman, and then she hastened away.

In the evening the seven dwarfs came home, and what a fright they had when they saw their dear Snow White lying on the floor, as still and motionless as a dead person. They lifted her up tenderly, and when they saw how tightly laced she was they cut the lacing, and she began to breathe a little and gradually came back to life. When the dwarfs heard what had happened, they said, "Depend upon it, the old peddler woman was none other than the Queen. In the future you must be sure to let no one inside if we are not at home."

As soon as the wicked old Queen reached home she went straight to her mirror and said:

> Mirror, mirror, on the wall,
> Who is fairest of us all?

and the mirror answered as before:

> You are fair, my Queen, 'tis true,
> But Snow White is fairer far than you.
> Snow White, who dwells with the seven little men,
> Is as fair as you, and as fair again.

When she heard this, the Queen became as pale as death, because she knew at once that Snow White must still be alive. "This time," she said to herself, "I will think of something that will make an end of her once and for all."

And by the witchcraft which she understood so well she made a poisonous comb. Then she dressed herself up in the form of another old woman. So she went over the seven hills till she reached the house of the seven dwarfs, and knocking at the door she called out, "Fine wares for sale."

Snow White looked out of the window and said, "You must go away, for I may not let anyone in."

"But surely you are not forbidden to look out?" asked the old woman and she held up the poisonous comb for her to see.

It pleased the girl so much that she opened the

door. When they had settled their bargain, the old woman said, "Come, I'll comb your hair properly."

Poor Snow White suspected no evil, but hardly had the comb touched her hair than the poison worked, and she fell down unconscious.

"Now, my fine lady, you're really done for this time," said the wicked woman and she made her way home as fast as she could.

Fortunately it was near evening and the seven dwarfs came home. When they saw Snow White lying there as if dead on the ground, they at once suspected that the wicked Queen had been at work again. So they searched till they found the poisonous comb, and the moment they pulled it out of her hair Snow White came to herself again and told them what had happened. So once more they warned her to open the door to no one.

As soon as the Queen was home she went straight to her mirror, and asked:

> Mirror, mirror, on the wall,
> Who is fairest of us all?

and it replied as before:

> You are fair, my Queen, 'tis true,
> But Snow White is fairer far than you.
> Snow White, who dwells with the seven little men,
> Is as fair as you and as fair again.

When she heard these words she literally shook with rage.

"Snow White shall die!" she cried. "Yes, though it cost me my own life."

Then she went to a secret chamber, which no one knew of but herself, and there she made a poisonous apple. Outwardly it looked beautiful, half white and half red—anyone who saw it would long to eat it. When the apple was finished, she stained her face and dressed herself up as a peasant and went over the seven hills to the house of the seven dwarfs. She knocked at the door, but Snow White put her head out of the window and called, "I may not let anyone in. The seven dwarfs have forbidden me to do so."

"Are you afraid of being poisoned?" asked the old woman. "See, I will cut this apple in half. I'll eat the white cheek and you can eat the red."

The apple was so cunningly made that only the red cheek was poisonous. Snow White longed to eat the tempting fruit, and when she saw that the peasant woman was eating it herself, she couldn't resist the temptation any longer and, stretching out her hand, she took the poisonous half. But hardly had the first bite passed her lips than she fell down dead on the ground. Then the eyes of the cruel Queen sparkled and, laughing aloud, she cried, "As white as snow, as red as blood and as black as ebony, this time the dwarfs won't be able to bring you back to life."

When she reached home she asked the mirror:

> Mirror, mirror, on the wall,
> Who is fairest of us all?

and this time it replied:

> Thou, Queen, art the fairest one of all.

Then her jealous heart was at rest—at least, as much at rest as a jealous heart can ever be.

When the little dwarfs came home in the evening they found Snow White lying on the ground, and she neither breathed nor stirred. They lifted her up and looked everywhere to see if they could find anything poisonous about. They unlaced her bodice, combed her hair, washed her with water and wine, but it was in vain: the child was dead and remained dead. Then they placed her on a bier, and the seven dwarfs sat around it, weeping and sobbing for three whole days. At last they made up their minds to bury her, but she looked as blooming as a living being, and her cheeks were still such a lovely color that they said, "We cannot hide her away in the dark ground."

So they had a coffin made of transparent glass, and they laid her in it and wrote on the lid in golden letters that she was a royal princess. Then they put the coffin on the top of the mountain, and one of the dwarfs always remained beside it and kept watch over it. And the very birds of the air came and bewailed Snow

White's death, first an owl, and then a raven, and then a little dove.

Snow White lay a long time in the coffin, and she always looked the same, just as if she were fast asleep, remaining as white as snow, as red as blood and her hair as black as ebony.

Now it happened one day that a Prince came to the wood and passed by the dwarfs' house. He saw the coffin on the hill with the beautiful Snow White inside, and when he had read the golden letters that were written there, he said to the dwarf, "Give me the coffin. You shall have whatever you ask."

But the dwarf said, "No, we wouldn't part with it for all the gold in the world."

"Well, then," he replied, "give it to me only because I cannot live without Snow White. I will cherish and love her as my dearest possession."

He spoke so sadly that the good dwarfs had pity on him and gave him the coffin, and the Prince made his servants bear it away on their shoulders. As they were going down the hill they stumbled over a bush and jolted the coffin so violently that the poisonous bit of apple fell out of Snow White's mouth. She opened her eyes, lifted up the lid of the coffin and sat up alive and well.

"Oh, dear me, where am I?" she cried.

The Prince answered joyfully, "You are with me." He told her what had happened, adding, "Snow

White, I love you better than anyone in the whole wide world. Will you come with me to my father's palace and be my wife?"

Snow White consented and went with him, and the marriage was celebrated with great pomp and splendor.

Now Snow White's wicked stepmother was one of the guests invited to the wedding feast. When she had dressed herself very splendidly for the occasion, she went to the mirror, and said:

> Mirror, mirror, on the wall,
> Who is fairest of us all?

and the mirror answered:

> You are fair, my Queen, 'tis true,
> But the Prince's bride is fairer far than you.

When the wicked woman heard these words she was beside herself with rage and mortification. At first she didn't want to go to the wedding, but at the same time she felt she would never be happy till she had seen the young Queen.

As she entered, Snow White recognized her and nearly fainted with fear. But red-hot iron shoes had been prepared especially for the wicked old Queen, and she was made to get into them and dance till she fell down dead.

JAKOB AND WILHELM GRIMM, TRANSLATED BY MAY SELLAR

THE TINDERBOX

A SOLDIER CAME marching along the highroad—Left, right! Left, right! He had his knapsack on his back and a sword by his side, for he had been to the wars and was now returning home. An old witch met him on the road. She was very ugly to look at, for her underlip hung down close to her chest.

"Good evening, soldier!" she said. "What a fine sword and knapsack you are wearing! You are quite a soldier! You ought to have as much money as you are able to carry!"

"Thank you, old witch," said the soldier.

"Do you see that great tree?" said the witch, pointing to a tree beside them. "It is hollow within. You must climb up to the top, and then you will see a hole through which you can let yourself down into the tree. I will tie a rope around your waist so I can pull you up again when you call."

"What shall I do down there?" asked the soldier.

"Get money!" answered the witch. "Listen! When you reach the bottom of the tree you will find yourself

in a large hall. It is light, for there are more than three hundred lamps burning there. Then you will see three doors, which you can open—the keys are in the locks. If you go into the first room, you will see a great chest in the middle of the floor with a dog sitting upon it; he has eyes as large as saucers, but you needn't trouble about him. I will give you my blue-checked apron, which you must spread out on the floor. Then go back quickly and pick up the dog and set him upon it. Open the chest and take as much money as you like. It is all copper there. If you would rather have silver, you must go into the next room, where there is a dog with eyes as large as mill wheels. But don't take any notice of him. Just set him upon my apron and help yourself to the money. If you prefer gold, you can get that too, as much as you can carry, if you go into the third room. But the dog that guards the chest there has eyes as large as the Round Tower at Copenhagen! He is a savage dog, I can tell you. But you needn't be afraid of him, either. Put him on my apron and he won't touch you. Then you can take as much gold out of the chest as you like!''

"Come, this is not bad!" said the soldier. "But what am I to give you, old witch, for surely you are not doing this for nothing?"

"Yes, I am!" replied the witch. "For me you shall bring nothing but an old tinderbox which my grandmother forgot last time she was down there."

"Well then, tie the rope around my waist right now!" said the soldier.

"Here it is," said the witch, "and here is my blue-checked apron."

Then the soldier climbed up the tree, let himself down through the hole and found himself standing, as the witch had said, in the large hall where more than three hundred lamps were burning.

Well, he opened the first door. There sat the dog glaring at him with eyes as big as saucers. "You are a fine fellow!" said the soldier and, putting him on the witch's apron, took as much copper as his pockets could hold.

Then he shut the chest, put the dog on it again and went into the second room. Sure enough, there sat the dog with eyes as large as mill wheels. "You had better not look at me so hard!" said the soldier. "Your eyes will pop out of their sockets!"

He set the dog on the apron. When he saw all the silver in the chest, he threw away the copper he had taken and filled his pockets and knapsack with nothing but silver.

Then he went into the third room. Horrors! The dog had two eyes as large as the Round Tower at Copenhagen, spinning around in his head like wheels.

"Good evening!" said the soldier and saluted, for he had never seen a dog like this before. But when he had examined him more closely, he thought: Now then,

I've had enough of this, and put him down on the floor on the apron and opened the chest. What a heap of gold there was! With that he could buy up the whole town and all the sugar pigs, all the tin soldiers, whips and rocking horses in the entire world. So he threw away the silver with which he had filled his pockets and knapsack, and filled them with gold instead—yes, his pockets, his knapsack, cap and boots even, so that he could hardly walk. Now he was rich indeed. He put the dog back on the chest, shut the door and called through the tree, "Pull me up again, old witch!"

"Have you the tinderbox also?" asked the witch.

"Botheration!" said the soldier. "I had clean forgotten it!" And he went back and fetched it.

The witch pulled him up, and there he stood again on the highroad, with pockets, knapsack, cap and boots filled with gold. "What do you want to do with the tinderbox?" asked the soldier.

"That doesn't matter to you," replied the witch. "You have your money. Give me my tinderbox."

"We'll see!" said the soldier. "Tell me at once what you want to do with it, or I will cut off your head!"

"No!" screamed the witch.

The soldier immediately cut off her head. That was the end of her! But he tied up his gold in her apron, slung the bundle over his shoulder, put the tinderbox in his pocket and set out toward the town.

It was a splendid town! He went straight to the

finest inn and ordered the best room and his favorite dinner, for he had so much money he really was rich.

It certainly occurred to the servant who had to clean his boots that they were astonishingly old for such a rich man. But that was because he had not yet bought new ones. The next day he appeared in a respectable pair and fine clothes. Instead of a soldier he had become a noble lord, and people told him about the grand doings of the town and about the King and what a beautiful princess his daughter was.

"How can one see her?" asked the soldier.

"She is never to be seen at all!" they told him. "She lives in a great copper castle, surrounded by many walls and towers! No one except the King and Queen may go in or out, for it is prophesied that she will marry a common soldier, and the King is not happy with the idea."

I should very much like to see her, thought the soldier; but he could not get permission.

Now he lived most gaily, went to the theater, drove in the King's garden and gave the poor a great deal of money, which was quite nice of him. He remembered so well how hard it is not to have a penny in the world. Being so rich, he wore fine clothes and made many friends, who said that he was an excellent man, a real nobleman. The soldier liked that. But as he was always spending money and never made any more, at last the day came when he had nothing left but two shillings, and he had to leave the beautiful rooms in which he had been living and move into a little attic under the roof, clean his own boots and mend them with a darning needle. None of his friends came to visit him there, for there were too many stairs to climb.

It was a dark evening and he could not even buy a light. But all at once it came to him that there was a little end of tinder in the tinderbox which he had taken from the hollow tree. He found the box with the tinder in it; but just as he struck a spark out of the tinderbox, the door burst open, and the dog he had seen down in the tree—with eyes as large as saucers—stood before him and said, "What does my lord command?"

"Do you mean what you say?" exclaimed the soldier. "This is a pretty fine tinderbox, if I can get whatever I want. Get me money!" he cried to the dog, and presto! he was off and back, holding a great purse of money in his mouth.

Now the soldier knew what a precious tinderbox he had. If he rubbed once, the dog that sat on the chest of copper appeared. If he rubbed twice, there came the dog that watched over the silver chest. If he rubbed three times, the one that guarded the gold appeared. So the soldier moved back to his beautiful rooms and appeared again in splendid clothes. All his friends immediately came to see him and paid him great court.

One night he thought: It is very strange that no person can see the Princess. They say she is very pretty, but what's the use of that if she has to sit forever in the great copper castle with all the towers? I must manage to see her somehow. Where is my tinderbox? He struck a spark, and presto! there appeared the dog with eyes as large as saucers.

"It is the middle of the night, I know," said the soldier, "but I should very much like to see the Princess for a moment."

The dog was already outside the door, and before the soldier could look around, in he came with the Princess. She was lying asleep on the dog's back, and was so beautiful that anyone could see she was a real princess. The soldier could not refrain from kissing her—he was such a true soldier. Then the dog ran back with the Princess. When it was morning, and the King and Queen were drinking tea, the Princess said she had had such a very strange dream about a dog and a soldier. She had ridden on the dog's back, and the soldier had kissed her.

"That is certainly a fine story," said the Queen. But the next night one of the ladies-in-waiting was sent to watch at the Princess' bed, to see if it was only a dream or if it had actually happened.

The soldier had an overpowering longing to see the Princess again, so the dog went to the castle in the middle of the night, picked her up and ran back as fast as he could. But the lady-in-waiting followed them. When she saw them disappear into a large house, she made a great cross on the door with a piece of chalk. Then she went home to bed, and the dog went back also with the Princess. But when he saw that a cross had been made on the door where the soldier lived, he took a piece of chalk and cleverly made crosses on all the doors in the town, so that the lady-in-waiting would not find the right house.

Early next morning, the King, Queen, ladies-in-waiting and officers came to see where the Princess had been. "There it is!" said the King, when he saw the first door with a cross on it.

"No, there it is, my dear!" said the Queen, when she saw a door with a cross.

"But here is one, and there is another!" they exclaimed, for wherever they looked there were crosses on the doors. Then they realized that the sign would not help them in their search.

But the Queen was a very clever woman who could do a great deal more than just drive about in a coach. She took her large golden scissors, cut up a piece of silk and made a pretty little bag of it. This she filled with the finest buckwheat grains and tied it around the Princess' neck. When this was done she cut a little hole in the bag so the grains would trickle along the road wherever the Princess went.

That night, the dog came again, took the Princess on his back and ran with her to the soldier, who had fallen so much in love with her that he would have given anything to be a prince so that he might have her for his wife.

The dog did not notice that the grains left a trail right from the castle to the soldier's window, where he ran up the wall with the Princess.

Next morning the King and the Queen saw plainly where their daughter had been and they arrested the soldier and put him into prison.

There he sat. Oh, how dark and dull it was there! And, besides, they had told him, "Tomorrow you are to be hanged." Hearing that did not exactly cheer him, and he had left his tinderbox at the inn.

Next morning he could see, through the iron grating in front of his little window, the people hurrying out of the town to see him hanged. He heard the drums and saw the soldiers marching. All the people were running to and fro. Just below his window there appeared a shoemaker's apprentice, wearing a leather apron and shoes. He was skipping along so merrily that one of his shoes flew off and fell against the wall just at the place where the soldier was peeping through the iron grating.

"Oh, shoemaker's boy, you needn't be in such a hurry!" said the soldier to him. "There's nothing going on till I arrive. If you will run back to the house where I lived, and fetch me my tinderbox, I will give you four shillings. But you must run like the wind."

The shoemaker's boy was very eager to earn four shillings, so he ran and brought the tinderbox to the soldier quickly.

Outside the town a great scaffold had been erected, and all around it were standing soldiers and hundreds of thousands of people. The King and Queen were sitting on a magnificent throne opposite the judges and the whole council.

When the soldier was standing on the top of the ladder and they wanted to put the rope around his neck, he said that one innocent request was always granted to a poor criminal before he died. He would so much like to smoke a small pipe of tobacco. It would be his last pipe in this world.

The King could not refuse him this, and so he took out his tinderbox and rubbed it once, twice and three times. And lo and behold! There stood the three dogs —the first with eyes as large as saucers, the second with eyes as large as mill wheels and the third with eyes as large as the Round Tower at Copenhagen.

"Save me! Don't let them hang me!" cried the soldier. Thereupon the dogs fell upon the judges and the entire council, seized some by the legs, others by their noses, and threw them high into the air.

"I won't stand this!" said the King. But the largest dog seized him, too, and the Queen as well, and threw them up in the air after the others. This frightened the soldiers, and the people cried, "Good soldier, you shall be our King, and marry the beautiful Princess!"

Then they put the soldier into the King's coach, and the three dogs danced in front, crying "Hurrah!" And boys whistled and soldiers presented arms.

The Princess came out of the copper castle and became Queen and that pleased her very much. The wedding festivities lasted for eight days, and the dogs sat at the table and made eyes at everyone.

HANS CHRISTIAN ANDERSEN, ANDREW LANG COLLECTION

LITTLE FIR TREE

THERE WAS once a pretty little fir tree in a forest. It grew in an excellent spot, for it could get sun and plenty of air, and all around it grew many tall companions, pines as well as firs. The little fir tree's greatest desire was to grow up. It did not care about the warm sun and the fresh air or notice the peasant children who ran about chattering when they came out to gather wild strawberries and raspberries. Often they could fill a whole basketful and would string them up on a straw. Sometimes they would sit down by the little fir tree and exclaim, "What a sweet little one this is!" The tree did not like that at all.

By the next year it had grown a whole ring wider and the year after that another ring more, for you can always tell a fir tree's age from its rings.

"Oh, if I were only as tall as the others," sighed the little fir tree, "then I could stretch my branches far and wide and look out upon the great world! The birds would build their nests in my branches, and when the wind blew I would bow politely just like the others!"

The fir tree took no pleasure in the sunshine nor in the birds nor in the rosy clouds that sailed over it at dawn and at sunset. Then the winter came and the ground was covered with sparkling white snow. Sometimes a hare would come and leap right over the little fir tree. This annoyed it very much. But when two more winters had passed, the fir tree was so tall that the hare had to run around it. "Ah, to grow and grow, and become big and old! That is the only pleasure in life," thought the tree.

In the autumn, woodcutters used to come and chop down some of the tallest trees. This happened every year, and the young fir tree would shiver as the magnificent trees fell crashing to the ground, their branches hewn off and the great trunks left bare, so that they were almost unrecognizable. Then they were loaded onto wagons and dragged out of the forest by horses.

"Where are they going? What will happen to them?" thought the fir tree.

In the spring, when the swallows and storks came, the fir tree asked them, "Do you know where they were taken? Have you met them?"

The swallows knew nothing about them, but a stork nodded his head thoughtfully, saying, "I think I know. I saw many new ships with splendid masts as I flew from Egypt. I imagine those must be the trees you mean! They had the scent of fir about them. Ah, they were grand, grand!"

"Oh, if I were only big enough to sail over the sea too! What sort of thing is the sea? What does it look like?" asked the fir tree.

"It would take much too long to tell you all that," said the stork, and off he went.

"Rejoice in your youth," said the sunbeams, "rejoice in the sweet growing time, in the young life within you." And the wind kissed it and the dew wept tears over it, but the fir tree did not understand.

Toward Christmastime, quite a few of the little trees were cut down, some not as big as the young fir tree or just the same age, and now it had no peace or rest for longing to be away. These young trees, which were chosen for their beauty, did not have their branches chopped off. They were stacked onto carts and dragged out of the forest by horses.

"Where are those going?" asked the fir tree. "They

are no bigger than I, and one was even much smaller! Why do they keep their branches? Where are they being taken?"

"We know! We know!" twittered the sparrows. "Down there in the city we have peeked in at windows, we know where they go! They are set up in the greatest splendor and magnificence you can imagine! We have looked in windows and seen them planted in the middle of a warm room and adorned with the most beautiful things—golden apples, sweets, toys and hundreds of candles."

"And then?" asked the fir tree, trembling in every limb with eagerness. "What happens then?"

"Oh, we haven't seen anything more than that. But that was simply wonderful!"

"Am I, too, destined for the same brilliant future?" wondered the fir tree excitedly. "That is even better than sailing over the sea! I am sick with longing. If it were only Christmas! I am as tall and grown up now as the ones that were taken away last year. If I were only in that warm room with all that splendor and magnificence! Oh! I am pining away! I really don't know what's the matter with me!"

"Rejoice in us," said the air and sunshine, "rejoice in your fresh youth out here in the open!"

But the fir tree took no notice, and just grew and grew. There it stood fresh and green in winter and in summer, and those who saw it said, "What a beautiful tree!" And the following Christmas it was the first to be cut down. The axe went deep into the core and the tree fell to the ground with a sigh. It felt bruised and faint. It could not think of happiness, it was sad at leaving its home, the place where it had grown up. It knew, too, that it would never again see its dear companions or the shrubs and flowers, perhaps not even the birds. Altogether the parting was not pleasant.

When the tree came to, it found itself packed in a yard with other trees, and a man was saying, "This one is perfect. This is the one we will take."

Then came two footmen in livery who carried the fir tree into a beautiful big room. There were pictures hanging upon the walls, and near the Dutch stove stood great Chinese vases with lions on their lids; there were armchairs, silk-covered sofas, large tables laden with picture books and toys worth lots and lots of money—at least so the children said. The fir tree was placed in a great tub filled with sand, but no one could see that it was a tub, for it was covered with greenery and stood on a gaily colored carpet.

How the tree trembled! What was coming now? Young ladies and men servants began to decorate it. On its branches they hung little baskets cut out of bright paper, each full of sugarplums. Gilded apples and nuts hung down as if they grew there, and over a hundred red, blue and white candles were fastened among the branches. Dolls as lifelike as human beings

—the fir tree had never seen any before—were suspended among the branches, and at the top was fixed a gold tinsel star. It was gorgeous, quite gorgeous! "Tonight," they all said, "tonight it will be lighted!"

"Ah," thought the tree, "if only it were evening! If only the candles were already lit! What will happen then? I wonder whether the trees will come from the forest to see me, or if the sparrows will peek in at the windows? Am I to stand here decked out thus through winter and summer?"

It was not a bad guess, but the fir tree had real barkache from sheer longing, and barkache in trees is just as bad as headache in human beings.

At last the candles were lighted. What glittering splendor! The tree quivered so much in all its branches that one of the candles singed a twig. "Take care!" cried one of the young ladies, and they extinguished that candle.

Now the tree did not even dare to quiver. It was really terrible! It was so afraid of losing any of its ornaments and it was quite bewildered by the radiance.

Then the folding doors were opened, and a crowd of children rushed in, so excitedly it seemed as if they would overturn the whole tree, while the older people followed more calmly. The children stood perfectly still, but only for a moment, and then they started to shout with excitement and dance around the tree, and snatch off one present after another.

"What are they doing?" thought the tree. "What is going to happen?" The candles burned low on the branches, and were put out one by one, and then the children were given permission to plunder the tree. They rushed at it so that all its branches creaked. If it had not been fastened to the ceiling by the gold star, it would have toppled over.

The children danced around with all their splendid toys, and no one looked at the tree except the old nurse, who came and poked among the branches just to see if by chance a fig or an apple had been forgotten.

"A story! A story!" cried the children, and dragged a stout little man to the tree. He sat down beneath it, saying, "Here we are in the greenwood, and the tree will be delighted to listen! But I am only going to tell one story. Shall it be Chicken Little or Humpty Dumpty, who fell downstairs and yet won great honors and married a princess?"

"Chicken Little!" cried some. "Humpty Dumpty!" cried others. There was absolute bedlam! Only the fir tree kept silent, and thought, "Am I not to be in it? Am I to have nothing to do with it?"

But it had already been in it and played out its part. And the man told them about Humpty Dumpty, who fell downstairs and married a princess. The children clapped their hands and cried, "Another, another!" They wanted the story of Chicken Little too, but they had to be satisfied with Humpty Dumpty. The fir tree stood quite astonished and thoughtful. The birds in the forest had never related anything like that. "Humpty Dumpty fell downstairs and yet married a princess! Yes, that is the way of the world!" thought the tree, and was sure it must be true, because such a nice man had told the story. "Well, who knows? Perhaps I shall fall downstairs and marry a princess." And it rejoiced, thinking that next day it would be decked out again with candles and toys, tinsel and fruit. "Tomorrow I shall quiver again with excitement. I shall enjoy all my splendor. Tomorrow I shall hear Humpty Dumpty again, and perhaps Chicken Little, too." And the tree stood silent and thoughtful through the night.

Next morning the servants came in. "Now the decorating will begin again," thought the tree. But they dragged it out of the room and up the stairs to the attic. There they put it in a dark corner where no ray of light could penetrate. "What does this mean?" said the tree. "What am I to do here? What am I to hear?" And it leaned against the wall and thought and thought. There was time enough for that, for days and nights went by, and no one came up. At last when someone did come, it was only to put some big boxes into the corner. Now the tree was so hidden it seemed as if it had been completely forgotten.

"It is winter outdoors now," thought the fir tree. "The ground is hard and covered with snow. They cannot plant me at this time, and that is why I am staying here under cover till the spring. How thoughtful they are! Only I wish it were not so terribly dark and lonely here; not even a little hare! It was so nice out in the forest when the snow lay on the ground and the hare raced past me; yes, even when he leaped over me, but I didn't like it then. The loneliness up here is more than I can stand."

"Squeak, squeak!" said a little mouse, scampering out, followed by a second. They sniffed at the fir tree and then crept between its boughs. "It's frightfully cold," said the little mice. "How nice it is to be here! Don't you think so too, you old fir tree?"

"I'm not at all old," said the tree. "There are many much older than I am."

"Where do you come from?" asked the mice, "and what do you know?" They were extremely inquisitive. "Do tell us about the most beautiful place in the world. Is that where you come from? Have you been in the storeroom, where cheeses lie on the shelves and hams hang from the ceiling, where one dances on tallow candles and where one goes in thin and comes out fat?"

"I know nothing about that," said the tree. "But I know the forest, where the sun shines and the birds sing." And then it told them about its young days, and the little mice had never heard anything like that before. "Oh," they said, "how much you have seen! How happy you must have been!"

"I?" said the fir tree and then thought it over.

"Yes, on the whole those were very happy times."
But it went on to tell them about Christmas Eve, when
it had been adorned with sweets and candles.

"Oh," said the little mice, "how lucky you have
been, you old fir tree!"

"I'm not at all old," said the tree. "I just came out
of the forest this winter. I am just a little backward,
perhaps, in my growth."

"How beautifully you tell stories!" said the little
mice. And the next evening they came with four
others, who wanted to hear the tree's story, and it told
still more, for it remembered everything so clearly and
said, "Those were happy times! But they may come
again. Humpty Dumpty fell downstairs, and yet he
married a princess. Perhaps I shall also marry a princess!" And then it thought of a pretty little birch tree
that grew out in the forest and it seemed to the fir tree
that it was a real princess, and a very beautiful one, too.

"Who is Humpty Dumpty?" asked the little mice.

And then the tree told the whole story. It could
remember every single word, and the little mice were
ready to leap to the topmost branch out of sheer joy!
The next night many more mice came, and on Sunday
even two rats appeared; but they did not care about
the story, and that troubled the little mice, for now
they thought less of it too.

"Is that the only story you know?" asked the rats.

"The only one," answered the tree. "I heard that on

my happiest evening, but I did not realize then how happy I was."

"That's a very dull story. Don't you know one about bacon or tallow candles? A storeroom story?"

"No," said the tree.

"Then we are much obliged to you," said the rats, and they went back to their friends.

At last the little mice went also, and the tree said, sighing, "Really it was very pleasant when the lively little mice sat around and listened while I told them stories. But now that's over too. Perhaps I should think of the time when I shall be taken out of here."

But when would that happen? Well, it happened one morning when the servants came to tidy up the attic. The boxes were set aside. The tree was brought out and thrown rather roughly on the floor. Then a servant dragged it off downstairs, where there was daylight once more.

"Now life begins again!" exclaimed the tree. It felt the fresh air, the first sunbeams, and there it was out in the yard! Everything happened so quickly that the tree forgot to think of itself, there was so much to see all around. The yard opened on a garden full of flowers; the roses were so fragrant and pretty, hanging over a little trellis, the lime trees were in blossom, and the swallows flew about, saying, "Quirre-virre-vit, my love has come home." But it was not the fir tree they meant.

"Now I am really going to live," said the tree

joyfully, stretching out its branches wide. Alas! they
were dry, withered and yellow, and it was lying in a
corner among weeds and nettles. The golden star was
still fastened to its top, and it glittered in the bright
sunlight. Some of the merry children who had danced
so gaily around the tree at Christmas were playing in
the yard. One of the little ones ran up and tore off the
gold star. "Look what was left on the ugly old fir tree!"
he cried, and stamped on the branches so that they
crackled under his feet.

And the tree looked at all the splendor and beauty
of the flowers in the garden, and then looked at itself,
and wished that it had been left lying in the dark corner of the attic. It thought of its fresh green youth in
the woods, of the merry Christmas Eve and of the little
mice who had listened so happily to the story of
Humpty Dumpty. "Too late! Too late!" thought the
discarded tree. "If only I had enjoyed them while I
could. Now all is over and gone."

And a servant came and cut the tree into small
pieces; there was quite a stack of them. A huge fire
blazed up, and the logs flickered brightly under a great
copper vat. The tree sighed deeply, and each sigh was
like a pistol shot. The children who were playing there
ran up and sat in front of the fire, gazing at it and crying, "Piff! Puff! Bang!" But for each crack, which was
really a sigh, the tree was thinking of a summer's day
in the forest, or of a star-filled winter's night there;

it thought of Christmas Eve and of Humpty Dumpty, which was the only story it had heard, or could tell, and then the tree became a heap of ashes.

The children played on in the garden, and the youngest had on his breast the golden star which the tree had worn on the happiest evening of its life. Now that was past—and the tree had passed away—and the story too, ended and done with.

And that's the way with all stories!

HANS CHRISTIAN ANDERSEN, ANDREW LANG COLLECTION

THE BRONZE RING

ONCE UPON a time in a certain country there lived a King whose palace was surrounded by a spacious garden. And though the gardeners were many and the soil was good, this garden yielded neither flowers nor fruits, not even grass nor shady trees.

The King was in despair about it when a wise old man said to him: "Your gardeners do not understand their business. But what can you expect of men whose fathers were cobblers and carpenters? How could they have learned to garden?"

"You are quite right," cried the King.

"Therefore," continued the old man, "send for a gardener whose father and grandfather have been gardeners before him. Soon your garden will be full of green grass and gay flowers, and you will enjoy its delicious fruit."

So the King sent messengers to every town, village and hamlet in his dominions to look for a gardener whose forefathers had been gardeners also. And, after forty days, one was found.

"Come with us and be gardener to the King," the messengers said to him.

"How can I go to the King," asked the gardener, "a poor wretch like me?"

"That is of no consequence," they answered. "Here are new clothes for you and your family."

"But I owe money to several people."

"We will pay your debts," they said.

So he allowed himself to be persuaded and he went away with the messengers, taking his wife and his son with him. The King, delighted to have found a real gardener, entrusted him with the care of his grounds. The man found no difficulty in making the royal garden produce flowers and fruit, and at the end of a year the park was a mass of glowing colors. In gratitude, the King showered gifts upon his new servant.

The gardener's son was a very handsome young man with most agreeable manners. Every day, he carried the best fruit from the garden to the King and all the loveliest flowers to his daughter. Now this Princess, who was wonderfully pretty, was just sixteen years old, and the King was beginning to think it was time she should be married.

"My dear child," said he, "you are of an age to take a husband, therefore I am thinking of marrying you to the son of my prime minister."

"Father," replied the Princess, "I will never marry the son of the minister."

"Why not?" asked the King.

"Because I love the gardener's son," answered the Princess.

On hearing this the King was at first very angry, and then he wept and sighed and declared that a gardener's son was not worthy of his daughter. But the young Princess was not to be persuaded to change her mind. So the King consulted his ministers.

"This is what you must do," they said. "To get rid of the gardener you must send both suitors to a far distant country. The one who returns first shall marry your daughter."

The King followed this advice. The minister's son was presented with a splendid horse and a purse full of gold pieces, while the gardener's son had only an old lame horse and a purse full of copper money, and everyone thought he would never come back from his hopeless journey.

The day before they started, the Princess met the gardener's son and said to him, "Be brave, and remember always that I love you. Take this purse full of jewels and make the best use you can of them for love of me. Then come home again quickly and ask my father for my hand."

The two suitors left the town together, but the minister's son went off at a gallop on his good horse and very soon was lost to sight behind the distant hills. He traveled on for some days and presently reached a fountain beside which an old woman all in rags sat upon a stone.

"Good day to you, young traveler," said she.

But the minister's son made no reply.

"Have pity upon me, traveler," she said again. "I am dying of hunger, as you see. Three days have I been here, and no one has given me anything."

"Let me alone, old witch," cried the young man, "I can do nothing for you." And so saying he went on his way.

That same evening, the gardener's son rode up to the fountain upon his lame gray horse.

"Good day to you, young traveler," said the beggar woman.

"Good day, good woman," answered he.

"Young traveler, have pity upon me."

"Take my purse, good woman," said he, "and if you wish, ride behind me on my horse, for your legs cannot be very strong."

The old woman did not wait to be asked twice but mounted behind him, and in this style they reached the chief city of a powerful kingdom.

The minister's son was lodged in a grand inn, but the gardener's son and the old woman dismounted at the inn for beggars.

The next day, the gardener's son heard a great noise in the street, and the King's heralds passed, blowing all kinds of instruments and crying: "The King, our master, is old and infirm. He will give a great reward to whosoever will cure him and give him back the strength of his youth."

Then the old beggar woman said to her benefactor, "This is what you must do to obtain the reward which the King promises. Go out of the town by the south gate and there you will find three little dogs of different colors. The first will be white, the second, black, the third, red. You must kill them, burn them separately and gather up the ashes.

"Put the ashes of each dog into a bag of its own color, then go before the door of the palace and cry out, 'A celebrated physician has come from Janina in Albania! He alone can cure the King and give him back the strength of his youth.' The King's physicians will say, 'This is an impostor and not a learned man,' and they will make all sorts of difficulties. But you will over-come them at last and will present yourself before the King.

"You must then demand as much wood as three mules can carry and a great caldron and shut yourself up in a room with the King. When the caldron boils, throw him into it and leave him there until his flesh is completely separated from his bones. Then arrange the bones in their proper places and throw over them the ashes out of the three bags. The King will come back to life and will be just as he was when he was twenty years old.

"For your reward, demand the bronze ring which has the power to grant everything you desire. Go, my son, and do not forget any of my instructions."

The young man followed the old woman's direc-tions. On going out of the town, he found the white, red and black dogs, just as she had said, and he killed and burned them, gathering the ashes into three bags —white, red and black. Then he ran to the palace and cried: "A celebrated physician has just come from Janina in Albania! He alone can cure the King and give him back the strength of his youth."

The physicians at first laughed at the unknown way-farer, but the King ordered that the stranger be ad-mitted. The gardener's son asked the servants to bring a great caldron and three loads of wood, and very soon the King was boiling away.

Toward midday, the youth arranged the bones in their places and had hardly scattered the dogs' ashes over them before the old King revived and found himself once more young and hearty.

"How can I reward you, young man?" he cried. "Will you take half my treasures?"

"No," said the gardener's son.

"My daughter's hand?"

"No."

"Take half my kingdom!"

"No. Give me only the bronze ring which can instantly grant me anything I wish for."

"Alas!" said the King, "I set great store by that marvelous ring. Nevertheless, you shall have it." And he gave it to him.

The gardener's son went back to say good-bye to the old beggar woman. Then he said, "Bronze ring, obey thy master. Prepare a splendid ship for my journey. Let the hull be of fine gold, the masts of silver and the sails of brocade. Let the crew consist of twelve young men of noble appearance, dressed like kings. St. Nicholas will be at the helm. As for the cargo, let it be diamonds, rubies, emeralds and garnets."

And immediately such a ship appeared upon the sea. Stepping on board, he set forth on his journey. Presently he arrived at a great town and established himself in a splendid palace. After several days, he met his rival, the minister's son, who had spent all his money

and was reduced to being a carrier of dust and rubbish. The gardener's son said to him: "Tell me, what is your name, what is your family and from what country do you come?"

"I am the son of the prime minister of a great nation, and yet you see to what a degrading occupation I am reduced."

"Listen to me. Though I don't know anything more than that about you, I am willing to help you. I will give you a ship to take you back to your own country, but only upon one condition," said the son of the gardener.

"Whatever it may be, I accept it willingly."

"Follow me to my palace."

The minister's son followed the rich stranger, whom he had not recognized. When they reached the palace, the gardener's son made a sign to his slaves, who completely undressed the newcomer.

"Make this ring red hot," commanded the master, "and mark the man with it upon his back."

The slaves obeyed him.

"Now, young man," said the rich stranger, "I am going to give you a vessel which will take you back to your own country." And, going out, he took the bronze ring and said: "Bronze ring, obey thy master. Prepare for me a ship of which the half-rotten timbers shall be painted black. Let the sails be rags and the sailors infirm and sickly. One shall have lost a leg, another an arm, and most of them shall be covered with scars. Go, and let my orders be executed."

The minister's son embarked in this old vessel and, thanks to favorable winds, at length reached his own country. In spite of the pitiable condition in which he returned he was received joyfully.

"I am the first to come back," said he to the King. "Now fulfill your promise and give me the Princess in marriage."

So they began to prepare the wedding festivities. And the poor Princess was sorrowful and angry enough about it.

The next morning, at daybreak, a wonderful ship with every sail set came to anchor before the town. The King happened that moment to be at the palace window.

"What strange ship is this," he cried, "that has a golden hull, silver masts and silken sails, and who are the young men like princes who man it? Do I not see St. Nicholas at the helm? Go at once and invite the captain of the ship to come to the palace." Very soon, in came an enchantingly handsome young man, dressed with rich silk ornamented with pearls and diamonds.

"Young man," said the King, "you are welcome, whoever you may be. Do me the favor to be my guest as long as you remain in my capital."

"Many thanks, sire," replied the captain. "I accept your offer."

"My daughter is about to be married," said the King. "Will you give her away?"

"I shall be charmed, sire."

Soon after, in came the Princess and her betrothed.

"Why, how is this?" cried the young captain. "Would you marry this charming Princess to such a man?"

"But he is my prime minister's son!"

"What does that matter? I cannot give your daughter away. The man she is betrothed to is one of my servants."

"Your servant?"

"Certainly! I met him in a distant town working as a dustman and rubbish collector. I had pity on him and engaged him as one of my servants."

"It is impossible!" cried the King.

"Do you wish me to prove what I say? This young man returned in a vessel which I fitted out for him, an unseaworthy ship with a black battered hull. The sailors were infirm and crippled."

"It is quite true," said the King.

"It is false!" cried the minister's son. "I do not know this man."

"Sire," said the young captain, "order him to be stripped and see if the mark of my ring is not branded upon his back."

The minister's son, to save himself from such an indignity, admitted the story was true.

"And now, sire," said the young captain, "guess who I am."

"I recognize you," said the Princess. "You are the gardener's son whom I have always loved, and it is you I wish to marry."

"Young man, you shall be my son-in-law and no one else," cried the King. "The marriage festivities are already begun."

And that very day the gardener's son married the beautiful Princess.

Several months passed. The young couple were as happy as the day was long, and the King was more and more pleased with himself for having acquired such a son-in-law.

But, presently, the gardener's son found it necessary to take a long voyage on his golden ship, and, after embracing his wife tenderly, he embarked.

Now in the outskirts of the capital there lived a wicked man who had spent his entire life in studying the black arts—alchemy, astrology, enchantment and magic. This magician found out one day that the gardener's son had succeeded in marrying the young Princess only through the help of the genies who obeyed the bronze ring.

"I will have that ring," said he to himself. So he went down to the seashore and caught some little red fishes that were wonderfully pretty. Then he went back and, passing before the Princess' window, he began to cry out: "Who wants some pretty little red fishes?"

The Princess heard him and sent out one of her slaves, who said to the old man, "What will you take for your fishes?"

"A bronze ring."

"A bronze ring, old simpleton! And where shall I find one?"

"Under the cushion in the Princess' room."

The slave went back to her mistress. "The old madman will take neither gold nor silver," said she.

"What does he want, then?"

"A bronze ring that is hidden under a cushion in your room."

"Then find the bronze ring and give it to him," said the Princess.

The slave found the bronze ring which the Princess' husband had accidentally left behind. She carried it to the magician, who made off with it at once.

Hardly had he reached his own house when, taking the ring, he said, "Bronze ring, obey thy master. I desire that the golden ship shall turn to black wood and the crew to hideous old men. St. Nicholas shall leave the helm, and the only cargo that it shall carry will be black cats."

And the genies of the bronze ring obeyed him.

Finding himself upon the sea in this miserable condition, the young captain understood someone must have stolen the bronze ring and he lamented his misfortune loudly. But that did him no good. "Alas," he said to himself, "whoever has taken my ring has probably taken my dear wife also. What good will it do to go back to my own country?"

And he sailed about from island to island and from shore to shore. Soon his poverty was so great that he and his crew and the poor black cats had nothing to eat but herbs and roots. After wandering about a long time, they reached an island inhabited by mice. There were mice everywhere—nothing but mice. The black cats, not having been fed for several days, were fearfully hungry and made terrible havoc among the little creatures.

Then the Queen of the Mice held a council. "These cats will certainly eat every one of us," she said, "if the captain of the ship does not shut the ferocious animals up. Let us send the bravest among us to him to ask him this."

Several mice offered themselves for this mission and set out to find the young captain.

"Captain," said they, "go away quickly from our island with your black cats or we shall perish, every mouse of us."

"Willingly," replied the young captain, "upon one condition. Bring me back the bronze ring which some clever magician has stolen from me."

The mice withdrew in great dismay.

"What is to be done?" said the Queen. "How can we find this bronze ring?"

She held a new council, calling in mice from every quarter of the globe, but nobody knew where the bronze ring was.

Suddenly three mice arrived from a far distant country. One was blind; the second, lame; and the third had had her ears cropped.

"Ho, ho, ho!" said the newcomers. "We come from a far distant country."

"Do you know where the bronze ring is which the genies obey?"

"Ho, ho, ho! We know. A wicked man has it. He keeps it in his pocket by day and in his mouth by night."

"Go and take it from him, and bring it back to us as soon as possible," the Queen of the Mice instructed them.

So the three mice made themselves a boat and set sail for the magician's country. When they reached the capital, they landed and ran to the palace, leaving only the blind mouse on the shore to take care of the boat. Then they waited till it was night. The man lay down in bed and put the bronze ring into his mouth, and very soon he was asleep.

"Now, what shall we do?" said the two little mice to each other.

The mouse with the cropped ears found a lamp full

of oil and a bottle full of pepper; so she dipped her tail first in the oil and then in the pepper and held it to the man's nose.

"Achoo! Achoo!" sneezed the man. He did not awaken, but the shock made the bronze ring jump out of his mouth. Quick as a wink, the lame mouse snatched up the precious talisman and carried it off to the boat.

Imagine the despair of the magician when he awoke and the bronze ring was nowhere to be found! But by that time the three mice had set sail with their prize. A favoring breeze was carrying them toward the island where the Queen of the Mice was awaiting them. Naturally they began to talk about their daring rescue of the bronze ring.

"Which of us deserves the most credit?" each cried, all at once.

"I do," said the blind mouse. "Without my watchfulness, our boat certainly would have drifted away to the open sea."

"No, indeed," cried the mouse with the cropped ears, "the credit is mine. Did I not cause the ring to jump out of the magician's mouth?"

"No, it is mine," cried the lame mouse, "for I ran off with the ring."

And from high words they soon came to blows and, alas, while the quarrel was raging, the bronze ring fell into the sea.

THE WORLD'S BEST FAIRY TALES

"How are we to face our Queen," said the three mice, "when by our folly we have lost the talisman and condemned our people to death by the cats? We cannot go back to our country; let us land on this desert island and there end our miserable lives."

No sooner said than done: the boat reached the island, and the mice landed.

As the blind mouse wandered sadly along the shore, she found a dead fish and was eating it when she felt something very hard. At her cries the other two mice ran up.

"It is the bronze ring! It is the talisman!" they cried joyfully, and, getting into their boat again, they soon reached the mouse island and returned the ring to the captain.

"Bronze ring," commanded the young man, "obey thy master once again. Let my ship appear as it was before."

Immediately the genies of the ring set to work, and the old black vessel became once more the wonderful golden ship with sails of brocade. The sailors, young and handsome again, swiftly ran to the silver masts and the silken ropes, and very soon they set sail for the capital.

Ah! How merrily the sailors sang as they flew over the glassy sea! At last the port was reached.

The captain landed and ran to the palace, where he found the magician asleep. The Princess clasped her husband in a long embrace. The magician tried to escape, but he was seized and bound with the strongest of cords.

The next day the magician was tied to the tail of a mule loaded with nuts and broken into as many pieces as there were nuts upon the mule's back.

HENRI CARNOY, ANDREW LANG COLLECTION

THREE BILLY GOATS GRUFF

ONCE UPON a time there were three Billy Goats and their name was Gruff.

They were going up the mountain to get fat. On their way up, they had to cross a bridge, and under this bridge there lived a Troll, with eyes as big as saucers and a nose as long as a broomstick.

The Billy Goats did not know that the Troll lived there.

First of all came Little Billy Goat Gruff. He went trip-trap, trip-trap, trip-trap over the bridge.

The Troll poked up his head and said, "Who goes trip-trap, trip-trap, trip-trap over my bridge?"

The Little Billy Goat said, "It is I, Little Billy Goat Gruff, and I'm going up the mountain to get fat."

"Oh, no, you're not," said the Troll, "because I'm going to eat you."

"Oh," said Little Billy Goat Gruff, "you wouldn't eat me, would you?—I am so small. Just wait for my brother, Second Billy Goat Gruff, and you eat him. He is much larger than I."

"Very well then," said the Troll, "be off with you." And trip-trap, trip-trap, trip-trap went Little Billy Goat Gruff.

Presently along came Second Billy Goat Gruff, and he went TRIP-TRAP! TRIP-TRAP! TRIP-TRAP! over the bridge.

The Troll poked up his head and said, "Who goes TRIP-TRAP! TRIP-TRAP! TRIP-TRAP! over my bridge?"

The Second Billy Goat Gruff tried to make his voice sound very weak, and he said, "It is I, Second Billy Goat Gruff, and I'm going up the mountain to get fat."

"Oh, no, you're not," said the Troll, "because I'm going to eat you." Then the Second Billy Goat said, "Oh, you wouldn't eat me, would you?—I am so small. You wait for my brother, Great Billy Goat Gruff, and you eat him. He is much larger than I."

"Very well then," said the Troll, "be off with you." And TRIP-TRAP! TRIP-TRAP! TRIP-TRAP! went Second Billy Goat Gruff.

Last of all came Great Billy Goat Gruff. Oh, he was

a great, large fellow. His great shaggy fur hung down to his feet, he had two large horns coming out of his forehead. When he walked, the bridge shook. He went TRIP-TROP! TRIP-TROP! TRIP-TROP! "Oh!" went the bridge—he was so heavy.

The Troll poked up his head and said, "Who goes TRIP-TROP! TRIP-TROP! TRIP-TROP! over my bridge?"

The Great Billy Goat stood there and said, "It is I, Great Billy Goat Gruff, and I'm going up the mountain to get fat."

"Oh, no, you're not," said the Troll, "because I am going to eat you."

"Come along, then," said Great Billy Goat Gruff, and up came the Troll. The Great Billy Goat caught him with his two horns and tossed him way up into the sky.

That was the end of the Troll; and TRIP-TROP! TRIP-TROP! TRIP-TROP! away went Great Billy Goat Gruff over the bridge.

By this time the three Billy Goats are so fat that they couldn't come back across the bridge even if they wanted to. So—

> Snip, snap, snout
> My tale is out.

PETER C. ASBJÖRNSEN AND JÖRGEN E. MOE,
RETOLD BY VERONICA S. HUTCHINSON

THE BOY WHO KEPT A SECRET

Once upon a time there lived a poor widow who had one son. At first sight you would not have thought that he was different from a thousand other little boys. Then you noticed that by his side hung a scabbard, and as the boy grew bigger the scabbard was growing bigger, too. The sword which belonged in the scabbard was found sticking out of the ground in the garden, and every day the boy pulled it up to see if it would go into the scabbard. But though the scabbard was plainly becoming longer, it would be some time before the two fitted together.

However, there came a day finally when the sword slipped into the scabbard quite easily. The child was so delighted he could hardly believe his eyes, but, pleased though he was, he determined not to tell anyone about it, particularly not his mother, who never could keep anything from her neighbors.

Still, in spite of his resolutions, he could not hide altogether that something had happened. When he went in to breakfast later his mother asked him what was the matter. "Oh, Mother, I had such a nice dream

See page 368

last night," he said, "but I can't tell it to anybody."

"You can tell it to me," she answered.

"No, Mother, I can't tell it to anybody," returned the boy, "till it comes true."

"I want to know what it was, and know it I will," she cried. "I will beat you till you tell me."

But it was no use; neither words nor blows would get the secret out of the boy. When she stopped beating him, the child ran into the garden and knelt weeping beside his sword. It was working around and around all by itself, and anyone except the boy trying to catch hold of it would have been badly cut. But the moment he stretched out his hand it stopped turning and slid quietly into the scabbard.

For a long time the child sat sobbing, and the noise was heard by the King as he was driving by. "Go and see who is crying so," he said to one of his servants.

The servant returned saying, "Your Majesty, a young boy is sobbing because his mother has beaten him."

"Bring him to me at once," commanded the monarch, "and tell him that it is the King who sends for him. Tell him the King has never cried in all his life and cannot bear anyone else to do so." On receiving this message, the boy dried his tears and went with the servant to the royal carriage.

"Will you be my son?" asked the King.

"Yes, if my mother will let me," answered the boy. And the King sent his servant for the mother and told her that if she gave her boy to him, he would live in the palace and marry the King's prettiest daughter as soon as he was a man.

The widow's anger now turned to joy, and she kissed the King's hand. "I hope you will be more obedient to His Majesty than you were to me," she said, and the boy shrank from her half-frightened. But when she had gone back to her cottage, he asked the King if he might fetch something that he had left in the garden. Given the permission, he pulled up his sword, which he slid into the scabbard. Then he climbed into the coach and was driven away.

After they had gone some distance the King said, "Why were you crying so bitterly in the garden when we came along?"

"Because my mother had been beating me," replied the boy.

"And why did she do that?" asked the King.

"Because I would not tell her my dream."

"And why wouldn't you tell it to her?"

"Because I will never tell it to anyone till it comes true," answered the boy.

"And won't you tell it to me either?" asked the King in surprise.

"No, not even to you, Your Majesty."

"Oh, I am sure you will when we get home," said the King, smiling, and he talked to him about other things till they came to the palace.

"I have brought you such a nice present," he said to his daughters. And as the boy was very charming, they were delighted to see him and gave him all their best toys.

"You must not spoil him," observed the King one day, when he had been watching the children playing together. "He has a secret which he won't tell to anyone."

"He will tell me," answered the eldest Princess. But the boy only shook his head.

"He will tell me," said the second girl.

"Not I," replied the boy.

"He will tell me," cried the youngest, who was the prettiest, too.

"I will tell nobody till it comes true," said the boy, as he had said before, "and I will beat anybody who asks me."

The King was very sorry when he heard this. He loved the boy dearly, but he thought it would never do to keep anyone near him who would not do as he was bidden. So he commanded his servants to take him away and not let him enter the palace until he had come to his right senses.

The sword clanked loudly as the boy was led off, but the child said nothing, though he was very unhappy at being treated so when he had done nothing wrong. However, the servants were very kind to him, and their children brought him fruit and all sorts of nice things. Soon he grew cheerful again and lived among them for many years till he reached his seventeenth birthday.

Meanwhile, the two eldest Princesses had become women and had married powerful kings who ruled over great countries across the sea. The youngest one was also old enough to be married, but she was very particular and turned up her nose at every young prince who sought her hand.

One day she was sitting in the palace, feeling rather bored and lonely, and suddenly she began to wonder what the servants were doing and whether it was not more amusing down in their quarters. The King was at his council and the Queen was ill in bed, so there was no one to stop the Princess, and she hastily ran across the gardens to the houses where the servants lived. Outside one of them she noticed a youth who was handsomer than any prince she had ever seen, and in a moment she knew him to be the little boy she had once played with.

"Tell me your secret and I will marry you," she said to him, but the boy only gave her the beating he had promised her long ago, when she asked him the same question.

The girl was very angry, besides being hurt, and ran home to complain to her father.

"If he had a thousand lives, I would take them all," swore the King.

That very day a gallows was built outside the town. The people crowded around to see the execution of the young man who had dared to beat the King's daughter.

The prisoner, his hands tied behind his back, was brought to the scene by the hangman. His sentence was being read by the judge, amid deathly silence, when the sword clanked against his side.

Suddenly a great noise was heard and a golden coach with a white flag waving from the window rumbled over the stones. It stopped underneath the gallows, and from it stepped the King of the Magyars, the ruler of Hungary. He begged that the life of the boy might be spared.

"Sir, he has beaten my daughter, who merely asked him to tell her his secret. I cannot pardon that," answered the Princess' father.

"Give him to me. I'm sure he will tell me the secret. If not, I have a daughter who is like the Morning Star, and he is sure to tell it to her."

The sword clanked again, and the King said angrily, "Well, if you want him so much you can have him; only never let me see his face again." And he made a sign to the hangman.

The cords were removed from the young man's wrists, and he took his seat in the golden coach beside the King of the Magyars. Then the coachman whipped up his horses, and they set out for Buda.

The King talked very pleasantly for a few miles, and when he thought that his new companion was quite at ease with him, he asked him what was the secret which had brought him into such trouble. "That I cannot tell you," answered the youth, "until the day it comes true."

"You will tell my daughter, I am sure," said the King, smiling.

"I will tell nobody," replied the youth, and as he spoke the sword clanked loudly.

The King said not another word, but he was confident that his daughter's beauty would get the secret from him.

The journey to Buda was long, and it was several days before they arrived there. The beautiful Princess happened to be picking roses in the garden when her father's coach drove up.

"Oh, what a handsome youth! Have you brought him from Fairyland?" she cried, when they all stood upon the marble steps in front of the castle.

"I have brought him from the gallows," answered the King, rather vexed at his daughter's words, as never before had she consented to give attention to any man.

"I don't care where you brought him from," said the spoiled girl. "I shall marry him and nobody else, and we will live together till we die."

"You may tell another tale," replied the King,

"when you ask him his secret. After all, he is no better than a servant."

"That is nothing to me," said the Princess, "for I love him. He will tell his secret to me and will always have a place in my heart."

But the King shook his head and gave orders that the lad was to be lodged in the summer house.

One day, about a week later, the Princess put on her finest dress and went to pay him a visit. She looked so beautiful that, at the sight of her, the book he held dropped from his hand, and he stood up speechless with wonder.

"Tell me," she said, coaxingly, "what is this wonderful secret? Just whisper it in my ear, and I will give you a kiss."

"My angel," he answered, "be wise and ask no questions, if you wish to get safely back to your father's palace. I have kept my secret all these years and do not mean to give it up now."

However, the girl would not listen and went on pressing him, till at last he slapped her face so hard that her nose bled. She shrieked with pain and rage, and ran screaming back to the palace where her father was waiting to hear if she had succeeded.

"I will starve him to death, the son of a dragon," cried he, when he saw her streaming with blood. Then he ordered all the masons and bricklayers in the town to come before him.

"Build me a tower as fast as you can," he said, "and see that there is room inside for a stool and a small table and for nothing else."

The men set to work and in two hours the tower was built. Then they started for the palace to inform the King that his orders had been followed. On the way, they met the Princess, who began to talk to one of the masons. When the rest were out of hearing she asked if he could manage to make a hole in the tower which nobody could see, large enough for a bottle of wine and food to pass through.

"To be sure I can," said the mason, turning back, and in a few minutes the hole was bored.

At sunset a large crowd assembled to watch the youth being led to the tower and, after his misdeeds had been proclaimed, he was solemnly walled up. But every morning the Princess passed food to him through the hole. Every third day the King sent his secretary to climb up the tower on a ladder and look down through a little window to see if the boy was dead, but the secretary always came back with the report that he was fat and rosy.

"There is some magic about this," said the King.

This state of affairs lasted a long time, till one day a messenger arrived from the Sultan of Turkey bearing a letter for the King, and also three canes. "My master bids me say," said the messenger, bowing low, "that if you cannot tell him which of these three canes grows nearest the root, which in the middle and which at the top, he will declare war against you."

The King was very much frightened when he heard this, and, though he took the canes and examined them closely, he could see no difference between one or the other. He looked so sad that his daughter noticed it and inquired the reason.

"Alas, my daughter," he answered, "how can I help being sad? The Sultan has sent me three canes and says that if I cannot tell him which of them grows near the root, which in the middle and which at the top, he will make war upon me. And you know that his army is far greater than mine."

"Oh, do not despair, my father," said she. "We shall be sure to find out the answer," and she quickly ran away to the tower and told the young man what had occurred.

"Go to bed as usual," he replied, "and, when you wake, tell your father you have dreamed that the canes must be placed in warm water. After a little while, one of them will sink to the bottom; that is the one which grows nearest the root. The one which neither sinks nor comes to the surface is the cane that is cut from the middle; and the one that floats is cut from the top."

The next morning the Princess told her father of her dream, and on her advice he cut tiny notches in each of the canes when he took them out of the water, so he might make no mistake when he handed them back to the messenger.

The Sultan, who could not imagine how the King had found out the answer to the puzzle, did not declare war against Buda.

The following year, the Sultan again wanted to pick a quarrel with the King of the Magyars, so he sent another messenger, this one bearing a letter and three foals. The letter required the King to say which of the animals was born in the morning, which at noon and which in the evening. If an answer was not ready in three days, war would be declared at once.

The King's heart sank when he read the letter. He could not expect his daughter to be lucky enough to dream rightly a second time. To add to his troubles, a plague which was raging through the country had killed off many of his soldiers and his army was even weaker than before. At this thought his face became so gloomy that his daughter noticed it and inquired what was the matter.

"I have had another letter from the Sultan," replied the King, "and he says that if I cannot tell him which of three foals he has sent was born in the morning, which at noon and which in the evening, he will declare war at once."

"Oh, don't be downcast," she said, "something is sure to happen." And she ran down to the tower to consult the youth.

"Go home, idol of my heart, and when night comes, pretend to scream out in your sleep, so your father hears you. Then tell him that you dreamed he was just being carried off by the Turks—because he could not answer the question about the foals—when the lad whom he had walled in the tower ran up and told them which had been born in the morning, which at noon and which in the evening."

So the Princess did exactly as the youth had bidden her. No sooner had she spoken than the King ordered the tower to be pulled down and the prisoner brought before him.

"I did not think that you could have lived so long without food," said he, "and as you have had plenty of time to repent your wicked conduct, I will grant you pardon, on condition that you help me solve a terrible problem. Read this letter from the Sultan; you will see that if I fail to answer his question about the foals, a dreadful war will be the result."

The youth took the letter and read it through. "Yes, I can help you," he replied. "But first you must bring me three troughs, all exactly alike. Into one you must put oats, into another, wheat, and into the third, barley. The foal which eats the oats is the one which was foaled in the morning; the foal which eats the wheat is the one which was foaled at noon; and the foal which eats the barley is the one which was foaled at night."

The King followed the youth's directions and, marking the foals, sent them back to Turkey, and there was no war that year. Now the Sultan became very angry that both of his plots to get possession of Hungary had been such total failures, so he sent for his aunt, who was a witch, to consult her about what he should do next.

"It is not the King who has answered your questions," observed the aunt, when he had told his story. "He is far too stupid ever to have done that! The person who has solved the puzzle is the son of a poor woman. If he lives, he will become King of Hungary. Therefore, if you want the crown yourself, you must get him here and kill him."

After this conversation, another letter was written to the King of Hungary, saying that if the youth in the palace was not sent to Turkey within three days, a large army would cross the border. The King's heart was sorrowful as he read, because he was grateful to the lad for what he had done to help him. The boy only laughed, bade the King fear nothing and to search the town instantly for two youths who looked exactly alike. Then he would paint himself a mask that would make him a replica of them. And the sword at his side clanked loudly.

After a long search, twin brothers were found, so identical that even their own mother could not tell the difference between them. The youth painted a mask that was a precise copy of their faces and, after he had put it on, no one would have known one boy from the other two.

They set out for the Sultan's palace, and as soon as they reached it, they were taken straight into his presence. He made a sign for them to come near; they all bowed low in greeting. He asked them about their journey; they answered his questions all together, and in the same words. If one sat down to supper, the others sat down at the same instant. When one got up, the others got up too, as if there had been one body instead of three. The Sultan could not detect any difference between them and told his aunt that he could not be so cruel as to kill the three of them.

"Well, you will see a difference tomorrow," replied the witch, "for one will have a cut on his sleeve. That is the youth you must kill." And one hour before midnight, when witches are invisible, she glided into the room where the three lads were sleeping in the same bed. She took out a pair of scissors and cut a small piece out of the boy's coat sleeve and then crept silently from the room. But in the morning the youth saw the slit and marked the sleeves of his two companions in the same way, and all three went down to breakfast with the Sultan.

The old witch was standing in the window and pretended not to see them, but witches have eyes in the backs of their heads, and she knew at once that not one sleeve but three were cut, and they were alike as before. After breakfast, the Sultan, who was getting tired of the whole affair and wanted to be alone to invent some other plan, told them they might return home. So, bowing together, they went.

The Princess welcomed the boy back joyfully, but the poor youth was not allowed to rest long in peace, for one day another letter arrived from the Sultan, saying that he had discovered that the young man was a very dangerous person—and he must be sent to Turkey at once. The girl burst into tears when the boy told her what was in the letter which her father had bade her carry to him.

"Do not weep, love of my heart," said the boy, "all will be well. I will start at sunrise tomorrow."

So next morning at sunrise, the youth set forth; and in a few days he reached the Sultan's palace. The old witch was waiting for him at the gate and whispered as he passed, "This is the last time you will ever enter it." But the sword clanked, and the lad did not even look at her.

As he crossed the threshold, fifteen armed Turks barred his way, with the Sultan in the lead. Instantly, the sword darted forth and cut off the heads of everyone but the Sultan and then went quietly back into its scabbard. The witch, who was looking on, saw that as long as the youth had possession of the sword her schemes would be in vain. She tried to steal the sword that night, but it jumped out of its scabbard and sliced off her nose, which was made of iron. And in the morning, when the Sultan brought a great army to capture the lad and take away his sword, they were all cut to pieces, while the boy remained without a scratch.

Meanwhile the Princess was in despair because the days slipped by and the young man did not return. She never rested until her father let her lead some troops against the Sultan. Dressed in uniform, she rode proudly before them, but they had just left the town when they met the lad and his sword.

When he told them what he had done, they shouted for joy and carried him back in triumph to the palace. There the King declared that the youth had shown himself worthy to become his son-in-law, and that he should marry the Princess and succeed to the throne at once, because he himself was getting old and the cares of government were becoming too much for him. But the young man said he must first go and see his mother, and the King sent him in state, with a troop of soldiers as his bodyguard.

The old woman was quite frightened at the array which drew up before her little house. She was still more surprised when a handsome young man, whom she did not know, dismounted and kissed her hand, saying: "Now, dear Mother, you shall hear my secret at last! I dreamed that I should become King of Hungary, and my dream has come true. When I was a child and you begged me to tell you, I had to keep silence or the Magyar King would have killed me. And if you had not beaten me, nothing would have happened that has happened, and I should not now be King of Hungary." FROM FOLK TALES OF THE MAGYARS, ANDREW LANG COLLECTION

THE MAGIC KETTLE

RIGHT IN the middle of Japan, high in the mountains, an old man lived in his little house. He was very proud of his home and never tired of admiring the whiteness of his straw mats and the pretty papered walls, which in warm weather slid back to allow the fragrance of the trees and flowers to come in.

One day he was standing looking at the mountain opposite his home, when he heard a rumbling noise in the room behind him. He turned around and in the corner he beheld a rusty old iron kettle, which could not have seen the light of day for many years. How the kettle got there the old man did not know, but he took it up and looked it over carefully, and when he found that it was quite whole he cleaned off the dust and took it into his kitchen. "That was a piece of luck," he said, smiling to himself. "A good kettle costs money, and it is always well to have a second one at hand in case of need. My kettle is nearly worn out now, and the water is already beginning to leak through its bottom."

Then he took the old kettle off the fire, filled the new one with water and put it in its place.

No sooner was the water in the kettle getting warm than a strange thing happened, and the man, who was standing nearby, thought he must be dreaming. First the handle of the kettle gradually changed its shape and became a head, and the spout grew into a tail, while out of the body sprang four paws, and in a few minutes the man found himself watching—not a kettle, but a living creature which the people of Japan called a *tanuki*.

It jumped off the fire and bounded about the room like a kitten, running up the walls and over the ceiling, till the old man was in an agony lest his pretty room be spoiled. He cried to a neighbor for help, and between them they managed to catch the *tanuki* and shut it up safely in a wooden chest.

Then, quite exhausted, they sat down and consulted together about what they should do with this troublesome beast. At length they decided to sell it and asked a child who was passing by to send them a certain tradesman called Jimmu.

When Jimmu arrived, the old man told him that he had something which he wished to get rid of, and he lifted the lid of the wooden chest where he had shut up the *tanuki*. But, to his surprise, no *tanuki* was there, nothing but the kettle he had found in the corner. It was certainly very odd, but the man remembered what had taken place on the fire and did not want to keep the kettle in his house anymore, so, after a little bargaining about the price, Jimmu went away carrying the kettle with him.

Now Jimmu had not gone very far before he felt that the kettle was getting heavier and heavier. By the time he reached home he was so tired that he was thankful to put it down in the corner of his room and then forgot all about it.

In the middle of the night, however, he was awakened by a loud noise in the corner where the kettle stood and raised himself up in bed to see what it was. But nothing was there except the kettle, which seemed quiet enough. He thought he must have been dreaming and fell asleep again, only to be roused a second time by the same disturbance. He jumped up and went to the corner and, by the light of the lamp that he always kept burning, he saw that the kettle had become the *tanuki*, which was running around after its tail. After it grew weary of that, the *tanuki* turned several somersaults on the balcony from pure gladness of heart.

The tradesman was much troubled as to what to do with the creature, and it was almost morning before he managed to get any sleep. But when he opened his eyes, there was no *tanuki*, only the old kettle he had left in the corner the night before.

As soon as he had tidied his house, Jimmu set off to tell his story to a friend next door. The man listened quietly and did not appear so surprised as Jimmu expected, for he recollected having heard, in his youth, something about a wonder-working kettle.

"Go and travel with it; display it," said he, "and you will become a rich man. But be careful first to ask the *tanuki*'s permission. It would be wise also to perform some magic ceremonies to prevent it from running away at the sight of people."

Jimmu thanked his friend for his counsel, which he followed exactly. The *tanuki*'s consent was obtained, a booth was built and a notice was hung up outside inviting the people to come and witness the most wonderful transformation that ever was seen.

They came in crowds, and the kettle was passed from hand to hand. They were allowed to examine it all over and even to look inside. Then Jimmu took it back and, setting it on the platform, commanded it to become a *tanuki*. In an instant the handle began to change into a head and the spout into a tail, while the four paws appeared at the sides.

"Dance," said Jimmu, and the *tanuki* did its steps, moving first on one side and then on the other, till the people could not stand still any longer and began to dance too. Gracefully the *tanuki* led a fan dance and glided without a pause into a shadow dance and an umbrella dance, and it seemed as if it might go on dancing forever. And very likely it would have, if Jimmu had not declared that the *tanuki* had danced enough and the booth must now be closed.

Day after day the booth was so full it was hardly possible to enter it, and what the neighbor foretold came to pass and Jimmu was a rich man. Yet he did not feel happy. He was an honest man and thought that he owed some of his wealth to the man from whom he had bought the kettle.

One morning, he put a hundred gold pieces into the kettle and, hanging it on his arm, he returned to the old man who had sold it to him. "I have no right to keep it any longer," he added when he had told his story, "so I have brought it back to you, and inside you will find a hundred gold pieces I have put there as the price of its hire."

The man thanked Jimmu, saying that few people would have been as honest. And the kettle brought them both luck; everything went well with them till they died, which they did when they were very, very old and respected by everyone.

FROM JAPANESE TALES, ANDREW LANG COLLECTION

See page 384

JORINDA AND JORINGEL

ONCE UPON a time there was a castle in the middle of a deep forest where an old woman lived quite alone, for she was an enchantress. In the daytime she changed herself into a cat or an owl, but in the evening she became an ordinary woman again. She was able to entice animals and birds to come to her castle, and then she would kill and cook them.

If any youth found himself within a hundred paces of the castle, he became rooted to the spot and could not stir till the woman set him free. If a pretty girl came inside the magic circle, the old enchantress changed her into a bird and locked her up in a wicker cage. She had seven thousand such cages in the castle, each containing a rare bird that had been a happy, carefree young girl.

Now, there was once a maiden called Jorinda, who was very beautiful. She was betrothed to a youth named Joringel, and their greatest delight was to be together. One summer evening, the two went for a walk in the forest. It was calm and peaceful under the trees, and the fading sunlight glinted on the dark green leaves.

"How beautiful this place is!" sighed Joringel. "But we must take care not to come too close to the witch's castle."

They wandered on, hand in hand, and, without knowing why, they began to feel sad and forlorn. In a nearby tree a turtledove sang its plaintive lament. They looked around, quite confused, for they did not remember their way home. Jorinda began to weep and sob, overcome by a strange fear. Joringel tried to comfort her, but he, too, felt something ominous in the air around them.

Half the sun was still above the mountain and half had dropped behind it when Joringel looked through the trees and saw the old wall of the witch's castle near them. He was terrified.

In the last rays of the setting sun, Jorinda sank to the ground and began to sing:

> My little bird with throat so red
>   Sings sorrow, sorrow, sorrow;
> He sings to the little dove that's dead,
>   Sings sorrow, sor——jug, jug, jug.

Joringel looked at Jorinda. Right before his eyes she had been changed into a nightingale and was singing "Jug, jug, jug."

An owl with glowing eyes flew three times around

her and screeched three times, "Tu-whit, tu-whit, tu-whoo." Joringel could not stir. He stood like a stone—he could not weep nor speak nor move hand or foot.

Now the sun had disappeared. The owl flew into a bush, and immediately an old, bent woman came out of it. She was yellow-skinned and thin and had large red eyes and a hooked nose which met her chin. She muttered to herself, caught the nightingale that had once been Jorinda and carried it away in her hand.

Joringel stood speechless and motionless until at last the woman returned and said in a gruff voice, "Good evening, young man. When the moon shines on the basket in my castle you will be freed."

And suddenly the moon broke through a cloud and Joringel was free. He fell on his knees before the old woman and implored her to give him back his Jorinda. She said he would never see Jorinda again, and then she went away. He called after her, he wept, but all in vain. "What is to become of me?" he cried.

After a while he found a way out of the forest and came to a strange village. There he took employment as a shepherd and stayed on herding sheep for a long time. He often went back to the castle, but never too close. Then one night he dreamed that he found a blood-red flower, in the center of which lay a beautiful pearl. He plucked it, and in the castle everything he touched with the flower was freed from the enchantment and thus he rescued his lovely Jorinda.

When Joringel awoke he set out to find such a flower. He roamed through woods and valleys and crossed steep mountains in his search. For eight days he did not give up hope, and on the ninth, early in the morning, he found it. In the center of this flower was a large dewdrop, as big as the most lovely pearl.

He traveled day and night with the flower till he arrived at the castle. This time, when he came within a hundred paces, he was still able to move, and he continued on till he reached the gate. Delighted at his success, he touched the great gate with the flower, and it sprang open. He entered, passed through the courtyard and then stopped to listen for the singing of the birds. At last Joringel heard the melodious chirping and followed the sounds until he found himself in the great hall of the castle. And there was the enchantress, with her thousands of birds in their wicker cages.

When she saw Joringel, she went into a rage and breathed out poison and gall at him, but she could not move a step toward him. He took no notice of her and looked at the thousands of cages filled with birds. How was he to find Jorinda among them? While he was considering, he saw the old witch pick up a cage and steal toward the door—but he sprang after her and touched her and the cage with his flower, making her powerless to work enchantment ever again. And the little nightingale stepped out of the wicker cage and became Jorinda, more beautiful than before.

Then Joringel walked all around the room, touching each cage with his magic flower. One by one the birds were released and turned back into lovely maidens. When they were all freed, Joringel went home with his Jorinda, and they lived a long and happy life.

JAKOB AND WILHELM GRIMM, TRANSLATED BY MAY SELLAR

PUSS IN BOOTS

ACERTAIN MILLER had three sons, and when he died the sole worldly goods which he bequeathed to them were his mill, his donkey and his Cat. This little legacy was very quickly divided up, and you may be quite sure that neither notary nor attorney were called in to help, for they would speedily have grabbed it all for themselves.

The eldest son took the mill, and the second son took the donkey. Consequently, all that remained for the youngest son was the Cat, and he was not a little disappointed at receiving such a miserable portion.

"My brothers," said he, "will be able to get a decent

living by joining forces, but for my part, as soon as I have eaten my Cat and made a muff out of his skin, I am sure to die of hunger."

These remarks were overheard by Puss, who pretended not to have been listening, and said very soberly and seriously, "There is not the least need for you to worry about your share, Master. All you have to do is to give me a pouch and have a pair of boots made for me so that I can walk in the woods."

Now this Cat had often shown himself capable of performing cunning tricks. When catching rats and mice, for example, he would hide himself among the grain and hang downward by the feet as though he were dead. Therefore his new master felt some hope of being assisted in his miserable plight.

On receiving the boots which he had asked for, Puss gaily pulled them on. Then he hung the pouch around his neck and, holding the cords that tied it in front of him with his paws, he sallied forth to a warren where rabbits abounded. Placing some bran and lettuce in the pouch, he stretched out and lay as if dead. His plan was to wait until some young rabbit, unlearned in worldly wisdom, should come and rummage in the pouch for the eatables he had placed there.

Hardly had he lain himself down when things happened as he wished. A stupid young rabbit went into the pouch, and Master Puss, pulling the cords tight, killed him on the instant.

Well satisfied with his capture, Puss departed to the King's palace. There he demanded an audience and was ushered upstairs. He entered the royal apartment and bowed profoundly to the King. "I bring you, sire," said he, "a rabbit from the warren of the Marquis of Carabas (such was the title he invented for his master), which I am bidden to present to you on his behalf."

"Tell your master," replied the King, "that I thank him and am pleased by his attention."

Another time the Cat hid himself in a wheat field, keeping the mouth of his pouch wide open. Two partridges ventured in, and by pulling the cords tight he captured both of them. Off he went and presented them to the King, just as he had done with the rabbit. His Majesty was not less gratified by the brace of partridges, and handed the Cat a present for himself.

For two or three months Puss went on in this way, every now and again taking to the King, as a present from his master, some game which he had caught. There came a day when he learned that the King intended to take his daughter, who was the most beautiful princess in the world, for an excursion along the riverbank.

"If you will do as I tell you," said Puss to his master, "your fortune is made. You have only to go and bathe in the river at the spot which I shall point out to you. Leave the rest to me."

The so-called Marquis of Carabas had no idea what plan was afoot, but did as the Cat directed.

While he was bathing, the King drew near, and Puss began to cry out at the top of his voice: "Help! help! The Marquis of Carabas is drowning!"

At these shouts the King stopped the carriage. He recognized the Cat who had so often brought him game, and bade his escort go speedily to the help of the Marquis of Carabas.

While they were pulling the poor Marquis out of the river, Puss approached the carriage and explained to the King that while his master was bathing robbers had come and taken away his clothes, though he had cried "Stop, thief!" at the top of his voice. As a matter of fact, the rascal Puss had hidden them under a big stone. The King at once commanded the keepers of his wardrobe to go and select a suit of his finest clothes for the Marquis of Carabas.

The King received the Marquis with many compliments, and, as the fine clothes which the latter had just put on set off his good looks, for he was handsome and comely in appearance, the King's daughter found him very much to her liking. Indeed, the Marquis of Carabas had not bestowed more than two or three respectful but sentimental glances upon her when she fell madly in love with him. The King invited him to enter the coach and join the party.

Delighted to see his plan so successfully launched,

the Cat went on ahead and presently came upon some peasants who were mowing a field. "Listen, my good fellows," said he, "if you do not tell the King that the field which you are mowing belongs to the Marquis of Carabas, you will all be chopped up into little pieces like mincemeat."

In due course the King came along and asked the mowers to whom the field on which they were at work belonged. "It is the property of the Marquis of Carabas," they all cried with one voice, for the threat from Puss had frightened them.

"You have inherited a fine estate," the King remarked to Carabas.

"As you see for yourself, sire," replied the Marquis, "this is a meadow which never fails to yield an abundant crop each year."

Still traveling ahead, the Cat came upon some harvesters. "Listen, my good fellows," said he, "if you do not declare that every one of these fields belongs to the Marquis of Carabas, you will all be chopped up into little bits like mincemeat."

The King came by a moment later and wished to know who was the owner of the fields in sight.

"It is the Marquis of Carabas," cried the harvesters.

At this the King was more pleased than ever with the Marquis.

Preceding the coach on its journey, the Cat made the same threat to all whom he met, and the King grew astonished at the great wealth of the Marquis of Carabas.

Finally Master Puss reached a splendid castle, which belonged to an ogre. He was the richest ogre that had ever been known, for all the lands through which the King had passed were part of the castle domain.

The Cat had taken care to find out who this ogre was and what powers he possessed. He now asked for an interview, declaring that he was unwilling to pass so close to the castle without having the honor of paying his respects to the owner. The ogre received him as politely as an ogre can and bade him sit down.

"I have been told," said Puss, "that you have the power to change yourself into any kind of animal—for example, that you can transform yourself into a lion or an elephant."

"That is perfectly true," said the ogre, curtly, "and just to prove it you shall see me turn into a lion."

Puss was so frightened on seeing a lion before him that he sprang onto the roof—not without difficulty and danger, for his boots were not meant for walking on tiles.

Perceiving presently that the ogre had abandoned his transformation, Puss descended and admitted having been thoroughly frightened. "I have also been told," he added, "but I can scarcely believe it, that you have the further power to take the shape of even the smallest animals—for example, that you can change yourself into a rat or a mouse. I confess that to me it seems quite impossible."

"Impossible?" cried the ogre. "You shall see!" And in the same moment he changed himself into a mouse, which began to run about the floor. No sooner did Puss see it than he pounced on it and ate it.

Presently the King came along and, noticing the ogre's beautiful mansion, desired to visit it. The Cat heard the rumble of the coach as it crossed the castle drawbridge and, running out to the courtyard, he cried, "Welcome, Your Majesty, to the castle of the Marquis of Carabas!"

"What's that?" cried the King. "Is this castle also yours, Marquis? Nothing could be finer than this courtyard and the buildings which I see all about. With your permission we will go inside and look around."

The Marquis gave his hand to the young Princess and followed the King as he led the way up the staircase. Entering a great hall they found a magnificent banquet there. This had been prepared by the ogre for some friends who were to pay him a visit that very day. These friends had not dared to enter when they learned that the King was there.

The King was now quite as charmed with the excellent qualities of the Marquis of Carabas as his daughter. The latter was completely captivated by him. Noting the great wealth of which the Marquis was evidently possessed, and having quaffed several cups of wine, the King turned to the Marquis, saying, "It rests with you, whether you will be my son-in-law."

The Marquis, bowing very low, accepted the honor which the King bestowed upon him. The very same day he married the Princess.

Puss became a personage of great importance and gave up hunting mice, except for amusement.

CHARLES PERRAULT, TRANSLATED BY A. E. JOHNSON

THE EMPEROR'S NEW CLOTHES

MANY YEARS ago there lived an Emperor who was so fond of new clothes that he spent all his money for them. He did not care about his soldiers, he did not care about the theater; he only liked to go out walking to show off his new clothes. He had a costume for every hour of the day; and just as they say of a king, "He is in the council chamber," they always said of him, "The Emperor is in his dressing room."

Life was very gay in the great city in which the Emperor lived. There was always something going on and every day many strangers came to visit. One day two swindlers arrived who announced that they were weavers and knew how to manufacture the most beautiful cloth imaginable. Not only were the texture and pattern uncommonly beautiful, but the clothes which were made from it had the wonderful quality of becoming invisible to anyone who was not fit for his office or who was unpardonably stupid.

"My, oh, my," said the people. "Think of that!"

"Those must indeed be splendid clothes," said the Emperor to himself. "If I wore them I could find out which men in my kingdom are unfit for the offices they hold. I could distinguish the wise men from the fools! Yes, this cloth must be woven for me at once." And he gave both the weavers money so that they could begin their work.

They set up two weaving looms and pretended they were working, but actually the looms had nothing on them. They also demanded the finest silk and the best gold thread, which they put into their bags, and worked at the empty looms till late into the night.

"I would certainly like to know how much cloth they have woven," said the Emperor. But he remembered, when he thought about it, that whoever was a fool or unfit for his office would not be able to see the material. Now he certainly believed that he had nothing to fear for himself, but he wanted first to send somebody else in order to see how he stood with regard to his office. Everybody in the whole town knew what a wonderful power the cloth had, and all were curious to see how incompetent or stupid their neighbors were.

"I will send my old and honored minister to the weavers," said the Emperor. "He can judge best what the cloth is like, for he has great intellect and no one understands his office better than he."

Now the good old minister went into the hall where the two men sat working at the empty looms. Dear me! thought he, opening his eyes wide, I can see nothing! But he did not say so.

Both the weavers begged him to be good enough to step closer, and asked him if the cloth were not of beautiful texture and lovely colors. They pointed to the empty loom, and the poor old minister went forward rubbing his eyes. But he could see nothing, for there was nothing to see.

"Dear, dear," he said to himself, "can I be stupid? I have never thought that, and nobody must know it! Can I be unfit for my office? No, I must certainly not say I cannot see the cloth!"

"Have you nothing to say about it?" asked one of the weavers.

"Oh, it is lovely, most lovely!" answered the old minister, looking through his spectacles. "What a texture! What colors! Yes, I will certainly tell the Emperor that it pleases me very much."

"We are delighted to hear that," said both the weavers, and thereupon they named the colors and explained the making of the pattern. The old minister paid great attention so he could tell it all to the Emperor when he went back to him, which he did.

The deceitful pair now wanted more money, more silk and more gold thread to use in their weaving. They put it in their own pockets and went on as they had before, working at the empty looms. The Emperor soon sent another worthy old statesman to see how the weaving was progressing and whether the cloth would soon be finished. It was the same with this gentleman as with the other old minister; he looked and looked, but because there was nothing on the looms he could see nothing.

"Is it not a beautiful piece of cloth?" asked the two men, as they described the splendid material which was not there.

Stupid I am not, thought the man, so it must be that I am not fitted for my good office. It is strange, certainly, but no one must be allowed to notice it. And he praised the cloth which he did not see, and expressed his delight at the beautiful colors and the splendid texture.

"Yes, it is quite beautiful," he said to the Emperor.

Everybody in the town was talking of the magnificent cloth.

Now the Emperor wanted to see it himself while it

was still on the loom. With a great crowd of select followers, including the two worthy statesmen who had
been there before, he went to the cunning workmen
now weaving more busily than before, but without
fiber or thread, of course.

"Is it not splendid!" said both the old statesmen.
"See, Your Majesty, what a texture! What colors!"
And they pointed to the empty looms, for they be-
lieved that the others could see the cloth quite well.

What! thought the Emperor, I can see nothing!
This is indeed horrible! Am I a fool? Am I not fit to
be Emperor?

"Oh, very beautiful," he said aloud. "It has my
gracious approval." And he nodded pleasantly and
examined the empty looms, for he would not say he
could see nothing.

His whole court around him looked and looked and
saw no more than the others, but they said like the
Emperor, "Oh, it is beautiful!" And they advised him
to wear the new and magnificent clothes to be made of
it for the first time at the great procession which was
soon to take place. "Splendid! Lovely! Most beautiful!" went from mouth to mouth.

Everyone seemed delighted, and the Emperor gave
the two impostors the title of Court Weavers to the
Emperor.

Throughout the night before the procession was to
take place, the weavers were up and working by the

light of more than sixteen candles. People could see that they were very busy finishing the Emperor's new clothes. They pretended they were taking the cloth from the loom, jabbed the air with huge scissors and sewed with needles without thread. At last they said, "Now the clothes are finished!"

The Emperor came himself with his most distinguished courtiers, and each weaver lifted up his arms as if he were holding something, and said, "See, here are the breeches! Here is the coat! Here is the cloak!" and so on. "These clothes are so comfortable that one would imagine one had nothing on at all. But that is the beauty of it!"

"Yes," said all the courtiers, but they could see nothing, for there was nothing there.

"Will it please Your Majesty to take off your clothes," said the weavers, "then we will dress you in the new clothes, here before the mirror."

The Emperor removed his clothes, and the weavers placed themselves before him as if they were putting on each part of his new clothing which was ready, and the Emperor turned and examined himself in front of the mirror. "How beautifully they fit! How well they are made!" said everybody. "What material! What colors! Such a gorgeous suit!"

"They are waiting outside with the canopy which is held over Your Majesty in the processions," announced the Master of Ceremonies.

"Look, I am ready," said the Emperor. "Doesn't it fit well!" And he turned again to the mirror to see if his finery was on properly.

The courtiers groped on the floor as if they were lifting up the train. Then they pretended that they were holding something in the air. They would not have it said that they could see nothing.

So the Emperor went along in the procession under the splendid canopy, and all the people in the streets and at the windows said, "How gorgeous are the Emperor's new clothes! The train fastened to his dress, how beautifully it hangs!"

No one wished to admit that he could see nothing, for then he would have been unfit for his office or else a fool. Never before had the Emperor's clothes met with such approval as had these.

"But he has nothing on!" said a little child.

"Just listen to the innocent child!" said the father, and each one whispered to his neighbor what the child had said.

"But he has nothing on!" the whole town shouted at last.

The Emperor could not help but hear, and he began to realize that the people were right. But I must go on with the procession now, he thought. And the courtiers walked along still more uprightly, holding up the train which was not there at all.

HANS CHRISTIAN ANDERSEN, ANDREW LANG COLLECTION

BILLY BEG AND HIS BULL

O NCE UPON a time there was in Ireland a King and Queen, and they had one son, Billy Beg. The Queen gave Billy a Bull that he was very fond of, and it was just as fond of him.

After some time the Queen died, and she put it as her last request to the King that he never part Billy and the Bull; and the King promised that, come what might, come what may, he would not. After his wife died, the King married again, and the new Queen didn't take to Billy Beg, and no more did she like the Bull, seeing himself and Billy so thick. But she couldn't get the King on any account to part Billy and the Bull, so she consulted with a hen-wife—a woman who raises chickens—to see what they could do about separating the two.

"What will you give me," says the hen-wife, "and I'll very soon part them?"

"Whatever you ask," says the Queen.

"Well and good then," says the hen-wife. "You are to take to your bed, making pretend that you are sick with a complaint, and I'll do the rest of it."

And, well and good, to her bed she took, and none of the doctors could do anything for her or make out what was her complaint. So the Queen asked for the hen-wife to be sent for. And sent for she was, and when she came in and examined the sick Queen, she said there was one thing, and one thing only, which could cure her.

The King asked what was that, and the hen-wife said it was three mouthfuls of the blood of Billy Beg's Bull. But the King would on no account hear of this, and the next day the Queen was worse, and the third day she was worse still and told the King she was dying and he'd have her death on his head. So, rather than that, the King had to consent to Billy Beg's Bull being killed.

When Billy heard this, he got very down in the heart and he went doithering about, and the Bull saw him and asked what was wrong that he was so mournful. So Billy told the Bull what was wrong with him, and the Bull told him to never mind but to keep up his heart, for the Queen would never taste a drop of his blood.

The next day, then, the Bull was to be killed, and the Queen got up and went out to have the delight of seeing his death. But as the Bull was being led up, says he to Billy, "Jump up on my back till we see what kind of a horseman you are."

Up Billy jumped on his back, and with that the Bull

leaped nine miles high, nine miles deep and nine miles broad and came down to earth with Billy sticking between his horns.

Hundreds were looking on, dazed at the sight, and through them the Bull rushed and over the top of the Queen, killing her dead, and away he galloped to where you wouldn't know day from night or night from day, over high hills, low hills, sheepwalks and ox trails, the Cove of Cork and old Tom Fox with his bugle horn.

When at last they stopped, the Bull says to Billy, "Put your hand in my left ear, and you'll get a napkin that, when you spread it out, will be covered with eats and drinks of all sorts, fit for the King himself."

Billy did this and, when he spread out the napkin, ate and drank to his heart's content. When he was finished, he rolled up the napkin and put it back into the Bull's ear.

"Now," says the Bull, "put your hand into my right ear and you'll find a bit of a stick. If you wind it over your head three times it will be turned into a sword and give you the strength of a thousand men besides your own, and when you have no more need of it as a sword, it will change back into a stick again."

Billy did all this, and the Bull said, "At twelve o'clock tomorrow I'll have to meet and fight a great bull."

Billy then got up again on the Bull's back, and they

started off and away to where you wouldn't know day from night or night from day, over high hills, low hills, sheepwalks and ox trails, the Cove of Cork and old Tom Fox with his bugle horn.

There, Billy's Bull met the other bull, and both of them fought, and the like of their fight was never seen before or since. They knocked the soft ground into hard and the hard into soft, the soft into spring-wells, the spring-wells into rocks and the rocks into high hills. They fought long, and Billy Beg's Bull killed the other and drank his blood.

After the fight, Billy took the napkin out of the Bull's ear again and spread it out and ate a hearty good dinner.

Then says the Bull to Billy, says he, "At twelve o'clock tomorrow, I'm to meet the brother of the bull that I killed today, and we'll have a hard fight."

Billy got up on the Bull's back again, and the Bull started off and away to where you wouldn't know day from night or night from day, over high hills, low hills, sheepwalks and ox trails, the Cove of Cork and old Tom Fox with his bugle horn.

There he met the brother of the bull that he killed the day before, and they set to and they fought, and the like of the fight was never seen before or since. They knocked the soft ground into hard, the hard into soft, the soft into spring-wells, the spring-wells into rocks and the rocks into high hills. They fought long, and at last Billy's Bull killed the other and drank his blood.

And then Billy took the napkin out of the Bull's ear once again and spread it out and ate another good, hearty dinner.

Then says the Bull to Billy, says he, "At twelve o'clock tomorrow I'm to fight the brother of the two bulls I killed—he's a mighty, great bull, the strongest of them all. He's called the Black Bull of the Forest, and he'll be a match for me. When I'm dead," says the Bull, "you, Billy, will take with you the napkin, and you'll never be hungry; and the stick, and you'll be able to overcome everything that comes in your way; and take out your knife and cut a strip of the hide off my back and make a belt of it, and as long as you wear it you cannot be killed."

Billy was very sorry to hear this, but he got up on the Bull's back again, and they started off and away to where you wouldn't know day from night or night from day, over high hills, low hills, sheepwalks and ox trails, the Cove of Cork and old Tom Fox with his bugle horn.

And sure enough, at twelve o'clock the next day they met the great Black Bull of the Forest, and both of the bulls commenced to fight, and the like of the fight was never seen before or since. They knocked the soft ground into hard ground, and the hard ground into soft, and the soft into spring-wells, and spring-wells

into rocks, and the rocks into high hills. And they fought long, but at length the Black Bull of the Forest killed Billy Beg's Bull and drank his blood.

Billy Beg was so vexed at this that for two days he sat over his Bull, neither eating nor drinking but crying salt tears all the time.

Then he got up, and he spread out the napkin and ate a hearty dinner, for he was very hungry from his long fast. After that, he cut a strip of the hide off the Bull's back and made a belt for himself and, taking it, the bit of stick and the napkin, he set out to seek his fortune.

He traveled for three days and three nights till at last he came to a great gentleman's place.

Billy asked the gentleman if he could give him employment, and the gentleman said he wanted just such a boy for herding cattle. Billy asked what cattle would he have to herd and what wages would he get. The gentleman said that he had three goats, three cows, three horses and three donkeys that he fed in an orchard, but no boy who went with them ever came back alive, for there were three giants—brothers—who came to milk the cows and goats every day and always killed the boy who was herding. If Billy wanted to try, they wouldn't fix the wages till they'd seen if he came back alive.

"Agreed, then," said Billy. So the next morning he got up and drove out the three goats, the three cows, the three horses and the three donkeys to the orchard, and commenced to feed them.

About the middle of the day, Billy heard three terrible roars that shook the apples off the trees, shook the horns on the cows and made the hair stand up on Billy's head, and in comes a frightful big giant with three heads who begins to threaten Billy.

"You're too big for one bite," says the giant, "and too small for two. What will I do with you?"

"I'll fight you," says Billy, says he, stepping out to him and swinging the bit of stick three times over his head; whereupon it changed into a sword and gave him the strength of a thousand men besides his own, and he up and killed the giant.

When it was evening, Billy drove home the three goats, three cows, three horses and three donkeys, and all the vessels in the house weren't able to hold all the milk the cows gave that night.

"Well," says the gentleman, "this beats me, for I never saw anyone come back alive out of there before, nor the cows with a drop of milk. Did you see anything in the orchard?" says he.

"Nothing worse than myself," says Billy. "What about my wages now?"

"Well," says the gentleman, "you'll hardly come out of the orchard alive tomorrow. So we'll wait till after that."

Next morning his master told Billy that something

must have happened to one of the giants, for he used to hear the cries of three every night, but the night before he had heard only two crying.

That morning after breakfast, Billy drove the three goats, three cows, three horses and three donkeys into the orchard again and began to feed them. About twelve o'clock he heard three terrible roars that shook the apples off the trees, shook the horns on the cows and made the hair stand up on Billy's head, and in comes a frightful big giant with six heads, and he accuses Billy of killing his brother.

"You're too big for one bite," says he, "and too small for two. What will I do with you?"

"I'll fight you," says Billy, swinging his stick three times over his head and turning it into the sword which gave him the strength of a thousand men besides his own, and he up and killed the giant.

When it was evening, Billy drove home the three goats, three cows, three horses and three donkeys, and what milk the cows gave that night overflowed all the vessels in the house and, running out, turned a rusty wheel in a mill that hadn't been turned for more than thirty years.

If the master was surprised at seeing Billy come back the night before, he was ten times more surprised at seeing him now.

"Did you see anything in the orchard today?" says the gentleman.

"Nothing worse than myself," says Billy. "What about my wages now?"

"Never mind about your wages," says the gentleman, "till tomorrow, for I think you'll hardly come back alive again," says he.

Well and good. Billy went to his bed, and, when the gentleman rose in the morning, says he to Billy, "I don't know what's wrong with two of the giants; I heard only one crying last night."

When Billy had had his breakfast that day, he set out to the orchard, driving before him the three goats, three cows, three horses and three donkeys; and sure enough about the middle of the day he hears three terrible roars, and then in comes the last giant, this one with twelve heads on him; and if the other two giants were frightful, surely this one was ten times more so.

"You villain, you," says he to Billy, "you've killed my two brothers, and I'll have my revenge on you now. You're too big for one bite and too small for two. What will I do with you?"

"I'll fight you," says Billy and, waving the bit of stick three times over his head, he up and killed the third giant.

That evening he drove home the three goats, three cows, three horses and three donkeys, and the milk of the cows had to be turned into a valley, where it made a lake three miles long, three miles broad and three miles deep, and that lake has been filled with salmon and white trout ever since.

The gentleman wondered now more than ever at seeing Billy back the third day alive. "You saw nothing in the orchard today, Billy?" says he.

"No, nothing worse than myself," says Billy.

"Well, you're a good, mindful boy and I couldn't do easy without you," says the gentleman. "I'll give you any wages you ask for in the future."

The next morning, says the gentleman to Billy, "I heard none of the giants crying last night. I don't know what has happened to them."

"I don't know," says Billy, "they must be sick."

"Now, Billy," says the gentleman, "you must look after the cattle today again, while I go see the fight."

"What fight?" says Billy.

"It's the King's daughter is going to be devoured by a fiery dragon if the greatest fighter in the land, whom they have been feeding specially for the last three months, isn't able to kill the dragon first. And, if he's able to kill the dragon, the King is to give him his daughter in marriage."

"That will be fine," says Billy.

Billy drove out the three goats, three cows, three horses and three donkeys to the orchard that day again; and the like of the people who passed him on their way to the fight between the man and the fiery dragon Billy never witnessed before. They were in coaches and carriages, on horses and donkeys, riding and walking, crawling and creeping.

"My good little fellow," says a man that was passing to Billy, "why don't you come to see the great fight?"

"What would take the likes of me there?" says Billy.

But when Billy found them all gone, he saddled and bridled the best black horse his master had, put on the best suit of clothes he could find in his master's house and rode off to the fight after the rest.

When Billy arrived, he saw the King's daughter with the whole court about her on a platform before the castle, and he thought he had never seen anything half so beautiful. The great warrior who was to fight the dragon was walking up and down on the lawn before the Princess, with three men carrying his sword and everyone in the whole country gathered there looking at him.

But when the fiery dragon came up, with twelve heads on him, and every mouth of them spitting fire, and let twelve roars out of him, the warrior ran away and hid himself up to the neck in a well of water, and they couldn't get him to face the dragon.

Then the King's daughter asked if there was no one who could save her from the dragon and win her in marriage. And not a person stirred.

When Billy saw this, he tied the belt of the Bull's

hide around him, swung his stick over his head and, after a terrible fight, killed the dragon.

Everyone then gathered about to find out who the stranger was. Billy jumped on his horse and darted off rather than let them know, but just as he was getting away, the King's daughter pulled a shoe off his foot. The warrior who had hidden in the well of water came out and, cutting the heads off the dragon, he brought them to the King and said that it was he, in disguise, who had killed the dragon. And he claimed the King's daughter.

But the Princess tried the shoe on the warrior and found it didn't fit him, so she said that he wasn't the right man and that she would marry no one, only the one the shoe fitted.

When Billy got home, he changed his clothes and had the horse in the stable and the animals all in before his master arrived.

The master began telling Billy about the wonderful day, and about the warrior hiding in the well of water, and about the grand stranger who had come down out of the sky in a cloud, riding on a black horse, and had killed the fiery dragon and then vanished into a cloud again.

"And," says he, "Billy, wasn't that wonderful?"

"It was, indeed," says Billy, "very wonderful."

After that, it was given over the whole country that all the men were to come to the King's castle on a certain day so that the Princess could try the shoe on each one of them; and whoever it fitted she was to marry.

When the day arrived, Billy was in the orchard with the three goats, three cows, three horses and three donkeys, as usual, and the like of all the crowd that passed that day going to the King's castle to get the shoe tried on, he never saw before. They went in coaches and carriages, on horses and donkeys, riding and walking, crawling and creeping.

They asked Billy was he not going to the King's castle, but Billy said, "Arrah, what would be bringing the likes of me there?"

At last, when all the others had gone, there passed an old man with a very scarecrow suit of rags on his back, and Billy stopped him and asked if he would swap clothes.

"Just take care of yourself, now," says the old man to Billy, "and don't be playing your jokes in my clothes, or maybe I'd make you feel the weight of this stick."

But Billy soon let him see it was in earnest he was, and both of them swapped suits.

Then off to the castle started Billy, with the suit of rags on his back and an old stick in his hand, and when he got there he found all in great commotion trying on the shoe. But it was of no use—the shoe did not fit any of them.

The King's daughter was going to give up in despair, when a ragged boy, who was Billy, elbowed his way through the crowd and said, "Let me try it on; maybe it will fit me."

The people, when they saw him, began to laugh at the sight of him, and "Go along out of that," says they, shoving and pushing him back.

But the King's daughter saw him and called on them by all manner of means to let him come up and try on the shoe.

So Billy went up to the Princess, and the people looked on, almost breaking their hearts laughing at the conceit of it.

But to the dumbfounding of them, the shoe fitted Billy as nicely as if it had been made with his foot for the form. So the King's daughter claimed Billy as her husband.

He then confessed that it was he who had killed the fiery dragon; and when the King had him dressed in a silk and satin suit, with plenty of gold and silver ornaments on the front, everyone gave out that his like they never saw before.

Billy was married to the King's daughter, and the wedding lasted nine days, nine hours, nine minutes, nine half-minutes and nine quarter-minutes, and the two of them have lived happily and well from that day to this.

OLD IRISH TALE,
RETOLD BY VERONICA S. HUTCHINSON

LITTLE ONE EYE, LITTLE TWO EYES AND LITTLE THREE EYES

THERE WAS once upon a time a one-eyed woman who had three daughters. The eldest was called Little One Eye, because she had only one eye in the middle of her forehead; the second was called Little Two Eyes, because she had two eyes like other people; and the youngest was called Little Three Eyes, because she had three eyes, and her third eye was also in the middle of her forehead.

But because Little Two Eyes did not look any different from other children, her sisters and mother would say to her, "You, with your two eyes, are no better than common folk. You don't belong to our family." They pushed her here, threw her wretched clothes there and gave her to eat only the little that they left. They were about as unkind to her as ever they could be.

It happened one day that Little Two Eyes had to go out into the fields to take care of her goat. She was still hungry because her sisters had given her so little to eat, and she sat down in the meadow and began to cry. She cried so much that two little brooks were running out of her eyes.

When she looked up, there stood a woman beside her, who smiled and asked: "Little Two Eyes, why are you crying?"

Little Two Eyes answered, "Have I not reason to cry? Because I have two eyes like other people, my sisters and my mother cannot bear me. They push me from one corner to another and give me nothing to eat except what they leave. Today they gave me so little I am still very hungry."

Then the wise woman said, "Little Two Eyes, dry your eyes. I will tell you something so you need never be hungry again. Only say to your goat:

> Little goat, bleat,
> Little table, appear,

and a beautifully spread table will stand before you with the most delicious food on it, and you can eat as much as you want.

"When you have had enough to eat, you have only to say:

> Little goat, bleat,
> Little table, away,

and it will vanish." After telling the little girl this, the wise woman went away.

Little Two Eyes thought, I must try at once to see

if what she has told me is true, for I am hungrier than ever. She said:

> Little goat, bleat,
> Little table, appear.

And scarcely had she uttered the words when a little table stood before her, covered with a white cloth, on which were arranged a plate, a silver knife, fork and spoon and the most beautiful dishes, which were smoking hot, as if they had just come out of the kitchen. Then Little Two Eyes said a short prayer of thanks and ate a good dinner. When she had eaten enough, she said, as the wise woman had told her:

> Little goat, bleat,
> Little table, away,

and immediately the table and all that was on it disappeared. "That is a splendid way to keep house," said Little Two Eyes, and she was quite happy.

In the evening, when she went home with her goat, she found a small earthenware dish with the food her sisters had left for her, but she did not touch it. The next day she went out again with her goat and left the few scraps given her. At first her sisters did not notice this, but finally they said, "Something is the matter with Little Two Eyes. She always leaves her food now and she used to gobble up all she was given. She must be getting food elsewhere." So Little One Eye was told to go along with Little Two Eyes when she drove the goat to pasture, to see whether anyone brought her food and drink.

Now when Little Two Eyes was setting out, Little One Eye came up to her and said, "I will go into the field with you and see if you take good care of the goat and if you drive him properly to get grass." But Little Two Eyes knew what Little One Eye had in her mind, and she drove the goat into the long grass and said, "Come, Little One Eye, we will sit down here and I will sing you something."

Little One Eye sat down. She was tired by the long walk to which she was not accustomed and by the hot day, and when Little Two Eyes began to sing:

> Little One Eye, are you awake?
> Little One Eye, are you asleep?

she shut her one eye and fell asleep. When Little Two Eyes saw Little One Eye was asleep, she said:

> Little goat, bleat,
> Little table, appear,

and sat down at her table and ate and drank as much as she wanted. Then she said again:

> Little goat, bleat,
> Little table, away,

and in the twinkling of an eye everything had vanished.

Little Two Eyes then woke Little One Eye, and said, "Little One Eye, you meant to watch and, instead, you went to sleep. In the meantime the goat might have run far and wide. Come, we will go home." So they went home. Little Two Eyes again left her dinner untouched. Little One Eye could not tell her mother why, and said as an excuse, "The fresh air made me so tired I fell asleep."

The next day the mother said to Little Three Eyes, "This time you shall go with Little Two Eyes and watch what she does out in the fields and whether anyone brings her food or drink."

So Little Three Eyes went to Little Two Eyes and said, "I will go with you and see if you take good care of the goat and if you drive him properly to get grass."

But Little Two Eyes knew what Little Three Eyes had in mind. She drove the goat into the tall grass and said to Little Three Eyes, "Sit down here, I will sing something for you." Little Three Eyes sat down; she was tired by the walk and the hot day. And Little Two Eyes sang the same song again, but instead of singing as she should have:

> Little Three Eyes, are you asleep?

she sang, without thinking:

> Little Two Eyes, are you asleep?

And she went on singing it.

428

The two eyes of Little Three Eyes fell asleep, but the third, which was not spoken to in the little rhyme, did not fall asleep. Of course Little Three Eyes shut that eye also, to make it seem as if she really was asleep, but her third eye kept blinking and could see everything quite well.

When Little Two Eyes thought Little Three Eyes was sound asleep, she said her rhyme:

> Little goat, bleat,
> Little table, appear,

and ate and drank to her heart's content. Then she made the table go away again by saying:

> Little goat, bleat,
> Little table, away.

But Little Three Eyes had seen everything. Then Little Two Eyes came to her, woke her and said, "Well, Little Three Eyes, have you been asleep? You watch well! Come, we will go home."

When they reached home, Little Two Eyes did not eat again, and Little Three Eyes said to their mother, "I know now why that proud thing eats nothing. When she says to the goat in the field:

> Little goat, bleat,
> Little table, appear,

a table stands before her, spread with food much better

than what we have. When she has had enough, she says:

> Little goat, bleat,
> Little table, away,

and everything disappears. I saw it all. She made two of my eyes go to sleep with a little rhyme, but the one in my forehead remained awake, luckily!"

Then the envious mother cried out to Little Two Eyes, "Will you fare better than we do? You shall not have the chance to do so again!" She fetched a knife and killed the goat.

When Little Two Eyes saw what her mother had done, she went out full of grief and sat down in the meadow weeping bitter tears. Again the wise woman stood before her and said, "Little Two Eyes, why are you crying?"

"Have I not reason to cry?" she answered. "My mother has killed the goat which spread the table so beautifully before me when I said the rhyme. Now I must suffer hunger again."

The wise woman said, "Little Two Eyes, I will give you a good piece of advice. Ask your sisters to give you the heart of the dead goat. Bury it in the earth before the house door. That will bring you good luck."

Then she disappeared, and Little Two Eyes went back home and said to her sisters, "Dear sisters, do give me something of my goat. I ask nothing more than its heart."

They laughed and said, "You may have that if you want nothing more."

Little Two Eyes took the heart and in the evening, when all was quiet, buried it before the house door as the wise woman had told her. The next morning, when they all awoke, there stood a most wonderful tree, which had leaves of silver and fruit of gold growing on it—more lovely and gorgeous than anything they had ever seen in their lives.

But only Little Two Eyes knew that the marvelous gold and silver tree had sprung from the heart of the goat, for it was standing just where she had buried it in the ground.

Then the mother said to Little One Eye, "Climb up, my child, and break us off some fruit from the tree." Little One Eye climbed up, but just when she was going to take hold of one of the golden apples, the bough sprang out of her hands. And this happened every time, so she could not break off a single apple, however hard she tried.

Then the mother said, "Little Three Eyes, do you climb up. With your three eyes you can see much better than Little One Eye." So Little One Eye slid down, and Little Three Eyes climbed up. She was no more successful than her sister. Try as she might, the branches of golden apples sprang out of her hands. And at last the mother grew impatient and climbed up herself, but she was even less successful than Little

One Eye and Little Three Eyes in catching hold of the fruit and only grasped at the empty air.

Then Little Two Eyes said, "I will try just once; perhaps I shall do better."

The sisters called out, "You with your two eyes will no doubt succeed!"

Little Two Eyes climbed up, and the golden apples did not jump away from her. They behaved properly so that she could pluck them off, one after the other, and brought a whole apronful down with her. The mother took them from her. But instead of treating poor Little Two Eyes better, as they should have, they were jealous that only she could reach the fruit and were still more unkind.

One day, when the three were standing together by the tree, a young knight came riding along. "Be quick, Little Two Eyes," cried the two sisters. "Creep under this so you shall not disgrace us."

They put poor Little Two Eyes beneath an empty cask and pushed under with her the golden apples which she had plucked.

When the knight, who was a very handsome young man, rode up, he was amazed to see the marvelous tree of gold and silver and said to the two sisters, "Whose is this beautiful tree? Whoever will give me a twig of it shall have whatever she wants." Then Little One Eye and Little Three Eyes answered that the tree belonged to them and they would certainly break off a twig for him. They went to a great deal of trouble, but in vain. The twigs and fruit bent away from their hands every time.

Then the knight said, "It is very strange that the tree should belong to you and yet you cannot break anything from it!"

But they insisted the tree was theirs. While they were saying this, Little Two Eyes rolled a couple of golden apples from under the cask so they lay at the knight's feet. She was angry with Little One Eye and Little Three Eyes for not speaking the truth.

When the knight saw the apples he was astonished and asked where they had come from.

Little One Eye and Little Three Eyes answered that they had another sister, but she had been hidden away and could not be seen because she had only two eyes, like ordinary people.

But the knight demanded to see her and called out, "Little Two Eyes, come forth."

Little Two Eyes came out quite happily from beneath the cask.

The knight was astonished at her great beauty and said, "Little Two Eyes, I am sure you can break off a twig for me from the tree."

"Yes," answered Little Two Eyes, "I can, for the tree is mine."

So she climbed up and broke off a small branch with its silver leaves and golden fruit without any trouble at all and, leaning forward, she gave it to the knight.

Then he said, "Little Two Eyes, what shall I give you for this?"

"Ah," answered Little Two Eyes, "I suffer hunger and thirst, neglect and sorrow, from early morning till late in the evening. If you would take me with you and free me from this, I should be happy!"

Then the knight lifted Little Two Eyes onto his horse and took her home to his father's castle. There he gave her beautiful clothes and food and drink, and because he loved her so much he married her.

When the handsome knight carried Little Two Eyes away with him, the two sisters at first envied her good luck. "But the wonderful tree is still with us, after all," they said. "Although we cannot break any fruit from it, everyone will stop and look at it and will come to us and praise it. Who knows whether we may not reap a harvest from it?"

But next morning the tree had vanished and their hopes were gone. When Little Two Eyes looked out of her window there the tree stood, to her great delight.

Once two poor women came to the castle to beg alms. Little Two Eyes looked at them and recognized both her sisters, who had become so poor they had to beg bread at her door. But Little Two Eyes bade them welcome and was so good to them they both repented of having been so unkind to their sister.

JAKOB AND WILHELM GRIMM, TRANSLATED BY MAY SELLAR

THE RED SHOES

THERE WAS once a little girl, a dainty and pretty little girl, but because she was very poor she always went barefoot in summer, and in winter wore heavy wooden shoes which made her insteps very red, dreadfully red.

In the heart of the village lived an old shoemaker's widow. She sewed a pair of shoes as well as she possibly could out of strips of old red cloth. They were rather clumsy, but she meant well, and she wanted them to be a present for the little girl. The little girl's name was Karen.

On the very day her mother was buried, Karen was given the red shoes and wore them for the first time. They were not really suitable for mourning, but as she had no others she walked in them, bare-legged, behind the poor pine coffin.

Suddenly a large old carriage drove up with a large old lady in it. She looked at the little girl and, feeling very sorry for her, she said to the parson, "Let me take the little girl and I'll look after her."

Karen thought that it was all because of the red

shoes, but the old lady said they were hideous and had them burned. However, she gave her some neat new clothes and had her taught to read and sew. People said she was pretty, but her mirror said, "You are more than pretty, you are lovely."

Now the Queen happened to travel through the country, and she had her little daughter with her—naturally she was a princess. People soon flocked to the palace to see them, and Karen was among the crowd. The little Princess stood at the window in a snow-white dress to let herself be admired. She was wearing neither a train nor a golden crown, but she had on a pair of beautiful red morocco shoes. Of course they were far nicer than the ones the shoemaker's widow had made for little Karen. There could be nothing in the world like a pair of red shoes!

When Karen was old enough to be confirmed, she had new clothes and was to have new shoes as well. The fashionable shoemaker in town took the measure of her little feet. He fitted her in his own house, where lovely shoes and shiny leather boots were arranged in great glass cases. The display was very attractive, but it gave no pleasure to the old lady, whose eyesight was rather weak. Among all the shoes was a pair of red leather ones exactly like those the little Princess had worn. How beautiful they were! In fact, the shoemaker said that they had been made for a nobleman's daughter but they had not fitted very well.

"I suppose they are patent leather, they're so shiny," said the old lady.

"Yes, they are shiny," said Karen. The shoes fitted her and they were bought, but the old lady did not know they were red, or she would never have allowed Karen to wear them for her confirmation. However, that's what happened.

Everybody looked at Karen's feet when she walked up the aisle of the church toward the chancel. It seemed to her as if those old pictures on the wall, those portraits of clergymen and their wives with ruffs and long black garments, fixed their eyes upon her red shoes. She thought of nothing else when the rector laid his hand upon her head and spoke to her of Holy Baptism, the Covenant with God, and told her that she was now a grown-up Christian.

The organ played a solemn melody, the children sang with their lovely voices, and the old choirmaster sang, but Karen could think of nothing but her new red shoes.

By the afternoon everybody had informed the old lady that Karen had worn red shoes, so she told Karen that it was very naughty of her and not at all the proper thing to do, and that thereafter whenever she went to church she must wear black shoes, even if they were her oldest pair.

The following Sunday there was Holy Communion, and Karen looked at the black shoes and she looked at the red ones—she looked at the red ones again, and finally put them on.

It was beautiful sunny weather. Karen and the old lady followed the dusty path through the cornfield. At the church door stood an old soldier with a crutch and a funny long beard that was more red than white; in fact, it was practically red. He bowed right down to the ground and asked the old lady if he might dust her shoes. Karen also put out her little foot. "My, what beautiful dancing shoes!" said the soldier. "Stick on tightly when you dance!" and he slapped the soles with his hand.

The old lady gave the soldier a penny and went into the church with Karen.

Everyone stared at Karen's red shoes, and all the portraits stared, and when Karen knelt at the altar and put her lips to the gold chalice, she thought only of the red shoes—it seemed to her as if they were floating before her eyes. She forgot to sing the hymn and she forgot to say the Lord's Prayer.

Then everyone left the church, and the old lady got into her carriage. Karen was about to step in after her when the old soldier said, "Look at the pretty dancing shoes!" And Karen could not keep her feet still. She just could not resist dancing a few steps, and when once she had begun, her feet continued to dance—it was as if the shoes had gained control over them. She danced around the corner of the church—she could not help herself. The coachman had to run after the girl, take hold of her and lift her into the carriage, but her dancing feet kicked the nice old lady violently. Finally they took her shoes off and her legs were still.

At home the shoes were put away in a cupboard, but Karen could not resist looking at them now and then.

Soon after this, the old lady lay ill and the doctors said that she could not live. She needed constant attention and careful nursing, and this was naturally Karen's duty. But a big ball was being given in town and Karen was invited. The little girl looked at the old lady, who in any case could not live, and then she looked at the red shoes—for she thought there could be no sin in doing that—and she put on the red shoes, thinking there was no sin in doing that, either. Then she went off to the ball and started dancing.

When she wanted to turn to the right, the shoes danced to the left; when she wanted to dance up to one end of the room, the shoes danced down to the other; they danced down the stairs, through the streets and out of the town gate. Dance she did, and dance she must, straight out into the dark forest.

She saw something shining between the trees, and because of its face she thought it was the moon, but it was the old soldier with the red beard, who nodded to her and said, "Look at the pretty dancing shoes!"

Filled with terror, Karen tried to kick off the red shoes, but they stuck to her feet. She tore off her stockings, but the shoes had grown fast to her feet, and so dance she did, and dance she must, over field and meadow, in rain and sunshine, by day and by night. It was most horrible at night. She danced through the gate of the churchyard, but the dead did not dance in there; they had something far more sensible to do. She tried to sit down on the grave of a pauper where bitter tansy grew, but for Karen there was neither rest nor peace, and as she danced toward the open church door, she saw an angel standing there with long white robes and white wings reaching from his shoulders right to the ground; his face was grave and severe, and in his hand he held a broad and shining sword.

"Dance thou shalt!" he said. "Dance in thy red shoes till thou art pale and cold, till thy body shrivels to a skeleton! Dance from door to door, and wherever proud, conceited children live, thou shalt knock at the door till they hear thee and fear thee! Dance, I command thee, dance!"

"Have mercy!" shrieked Karen. But she did not hear what the angel answered, for the shoes carried her through the gate, into the fields, along the highway and byway, dancing, ever and ever dancing.

One morning she danced past a door she knew well. Inside, a hymn was being sung and a coffin was carried out covered with flowers. Then she realized that the old lady was dead, and she felt that she herself was forsaken by all and accursed by the angel of God.

Dance she did, and dance she must, dance through the dark night. The shoes carried her on over stump and thorn; she was scratched till she bled; she danced across the heath to a lonely little house. She knew that the executioner lived there, and she tapped with her finger on the windowpane and cried, "Come out! Come out! I can't come in, for I'm dancing!"

And the executioner said, "You don't seem to know who I am. I chop off the heads of wicked people, and I can feel my axe beginning to quiver."

"Don't chop off my head," said Karen, "for then I can never repent of my sin, but chop off my feet with the red shoes on!"

Then she confessed her sin, and the executioner chopped off her feet with the red shoes on, and the shoes danced away with the little feet still in them over the fields into the depths of the forest.

Then he made her a pair of crutches and taught her a hymn—the one that penitents always sing. She kissed the hand which had wielded the axe, and went away across the heath.

"I have suffered enough because of the red shoes," she said. "Now I will go to church and show myself to everyone." And she went quickly to the church door, but when she arrived there the red shoes were dancing in front of her so that she became very frightened and turned back.

The whole week through she was very sad and shed

many bitter tears, but when Sunday came she said, "There, now, I have suffered and struggled long enough. I think I am just as good as many of the people who sit in church and hold their heads high." She set forth confidently, but no sooner did she reach the churchyard gate than she saw the red shoes dancing in front of her again, and she was terrified. She turned back, away from the church, and repented of her sin with all her heart.

Then she went to the rectory and begged to be taken into service there. She would be hardworking and do all she could—the wages were not important if only she might have a roof over her head and be with good people. The rector's wife felt sorry for Karen and took her into her service. Karen was serious and industrious. She sat quietly and listened in the evening when the rector read aloud from the Bible. The little children were very fond of her, but when they spoke of frills and finery and of being as beautiful as a queen, she would shake her head.

The following Sunday when they went to church they asked her to go with them, but with tears in her eyes she looked sadly at her crutches. The others went to hear the Word of God. Left alone, she went into her tiny room. It was just big enough for a bed and a chair. She sat down with her hymnbook in her hand, and while she was reading it devoutly, the wind carried the organ notes from the church straight into her room.

She raised her face, all wet with tears, and said, "Lord, help me!"

Then the sun shone brightly, and the angel of God in white robes, the same one whom she had seen that other night at the church door, stood before her. Instead of the sharp sword, he held a beautiful green branch covered with roses. He touched the ceiling with it, raising it high up, and a golden star appeared; then he touched the walls and they opened wide. She saw the organ, she saw the old pictures of the clergymen and their wives and she saw the congregation seated in their flower-decorated pews, singing from their hymnbooks. For the church itself had come to the poor girl in her narrow little room, or was it she who had been brought to the church? She sat in the pew with the people from the rectory, and when they had sung the hymn, they looked up and nodded to her, saying, "It was right of you to come, Karen."

"It was by God's mercy that I came," she said.

The music of the organ pealed forth, and the voices of the children's choir rang out in mellow and lovely tones. The bright rays of the sun streamed warmly through the window to the pew where Karen sat. Her heart was so filled with the sunshine of peace and joy that it broke, and the sunbeams carried her soul to Heaven. And no one there questioned her about the red shoes.

HANS CHRISTIAN ANDERSEN, TRANSLATED BY PAUL LEYSSAC

THE STEADFAST TIN SOLDIER

THERE WERE once upon a time five-and-twenty tin soldiers—all brothers, for they were made out of the same old tin spoon. Their uniforms were red and yellow; they shouldered arms and looked straight ahead. The first words they heard in this world, when the lid was taken off their box, were, "Hurrah! Tin soldiers!" This was shouted by a little boy as he clapped his hands. They had been given to him because it was his birthday, and he began setting them out on the table. Each soldier was exactly like the next, except one, who had been made last when the tin was running short. There he stood as firmly on his one leg as the rest did on two and he is the one who became famous.

There were many other playthings on the table. But the nicest of all was a pretty little castle made of cardboard, with windows through which one could see into the room. In front of the castle stood some little trees surrounding a tiny mirror which looked like a lake. Wax swans were floating about, and were reflected in the glass. That was all very pretty, but the prettiest was a little lady who stood in the open doorway of the castle. She, too, was cut out of paper, but she had on a dress of the finest gauze, with a scarf of narrow blue ribbon around her shoulders. The ribbon scarf was fastened in the middle by a glittering paper rose almost as large as her head. The lady had both her arms outstretched, for she was a dancer, and one leg was raised so high behind her that the tin soldier couldn't see it and he thought that she, too, had only one leg.

That's the wife for me! he thought; but she is so grand and lives in a castle, while I have only a box with four-and-twenty others. This is no place for her! But I must make her acquaintance. Then he stationed himself next to a snuffbox on the table. From there he could watch the dainty lady, who continued to stand on one leg without losing her balance.

When night came all the other tin soldiers were put into their box, and the people of the house went to bed. Then the toys began to play at visiting, dancing and fighting. The tin soldiers rattled in their box, for they wanted to be out, too, but they could not raise the lid. The nutcrackers played at leapfrog and the slate pencil ran about the slate. There was so much noise that the canary woke up and began to talk to them—in poetry, if you please! The only two who did not stir from their places were the tin soldier and the little dancer. She remained on tiptoe, with both arms outstretched. He stood steadfastly on his one leg, never moving his eyes from her face.

The clock struck twelve, and crack! Off flew the lid of the snuffbox. But there was no snuff inside, only a little black imp—that was the charm of it. "Hello, tin soldier!" said the imp. "Don't look at things that aren't intended for the likes of you!"

But the tin soldier took no notice and seemed not to hear him.

"Very well, very well! Wait till tomorrow!" said the imp, peevishly.

When it was morning and the children were up, the tin soldier was put on the windowsill. Whether it was the wind or the little black imp, I don't know, but all at once the window flew open and out fell the little soldier, head over heels, from the third story window! That was a terrible fall, I can tell you! He landed on his head with his leg in the air, his gun wedged between two paving stones.

The nursery maid and the little boy rushed down to look for him but, though they were so near they almost stepped on him, they did not see him. If the tin soldier had only shouted, "Here I am!" they would certainly have found him, but he did not think it right to shout, when he was in uniform.

Then it began to drizzle. Soon the drops came faster, and there was a regular downpour. When it was over, two little boys came along.

"Just look!" cried one. "Here is a tin soldier! Let's send him sailing."

So they made a little boat out of newspaper, put the tin soldier in it and made him sail up and down the gutter. Both the boys ran along beside him, clapping their hands. What great waves there were in the gutter and what a swift current! The paper boat tossed up and down, and in the middle of the stream it went so fast that the tin soldier trembled. But he remained steadfast, showing no emotion and looking straight in front of him, shouldering his gun. Suddenly the boat passed into a long tunnel that was as dark as his box had been. "Where can I be now?" he wondered. "Oh, dear! This is the black imp's fault! Ah, if only the little lady were sitting beside me in the boat, it could be twice as dark for all I'd care!"

Then there came along a great water rat that lived in the tunnel.

"Where's your passport?" asked the rat. "Out with your passport!"

But the tin soldier was silent and grasped his gun more firmly. The boat sped on and the rat behind it. Ugh! How he gnashed his teeth as he cried to chips of wood and straw: "Catch him, catch him! He hasn't paid the toll! He hasn't shown his passport!"

The current became swifter and stronger. The tin soldier could already see daylight where the tunnel ended. In his ears there sounded a roaring enough to frighten any brave man. Just imagine! At the end of the tunnel the gutter emptied into a great canal that was just as dangerous for him as it would be for us to go down a waterfall.

It came nearer and nearer; on went the boat, the poor tin soldier keeping himself as stiff as he could. No one could say of him afterwards that he had flinched. The boat whirled three, four times and became filled to the brim with water. It began to sink! The tin soldier was standing up to his neck in water. Deeper and deeper sank the boat. Softer and softer grew the paper. Now the water was over his head. He was thinking of the pretty little dancer, whose face he would never see again, and there sounded in his ears, over and over:

> Forward, forward, soldier bold,
> Death's before thee, grim and cold!

The paper came apart, and the soldier fell right through—but at that moment he was swallowed by a great fish! Inside it was even darker than in the tunnel. It was really very close quarters! But the steadfast little tin soldier lay full length, shouldering his gun.

Up and down swam the fish, then it made the most dreadful contortions and suddenly became quite still. It was as if lightning had passed through it; the daylight streamed in and a voice exclaimed, "Why, here is the little tin soldier!" The fish had been caught and taken to market, then sold and brought into the kitchen,

See page 448

451

where the cook had cut it open with a great knife.

She picked up the soldier between her fingers and carried him into the room, where everyone wanted to see the hero who had been found inside a fish. The tin soldier was not at all proud. They put him on the table and—what strange things do happen in this world— the tin soldier was in the same room in which he had been before! He saw the same children and the same toys on the table. There was the same grand castle with the pretty little dancer. She was still standing on one leg with the other high behind her. She too was steadfast. That touched the tin soldier. He was nearly ready to shed tin tears, and that would not have been fitting for a soldier. He looked at her, but she said nothing.

Suddenly one of the little boys picked up the tin soldier and, for no reason, threw him into the stove. Doubtless the little black imp in the snuffbox was at the bottom of that, too.

There the tin soldier lay and felt a truly terrible heat. Whether he was suffering from real fire or from love he did not know. All his color had disappeared. Whether this had happened on his travels or whether it was the result of trouble, who can say? He looked at the little lady, she looked at him, and he felt that he was melting. He remained steadfast with his gun at his shoulder.

Then a door opened, the draft caught up the little dancer, and off she flew like a sylph to the tin sol-

dier in the stove, burst into flames—and that was the
end of her! The tin soldier melted down into a small
lump, and next morning when the maid was taking
out the ashes, she found him in the shape of a heart.
There was nothing left of the little dancer but her gilt
rose, burned as black as a cinder.

HANS CHRISTIAN ANDERSEN, ANDREW LANG COLLECTION

SNEGOURKA, THE SNOW MAIDEN

ONCE UPON a time a peas-
ant named Ivan had a wife called Marousha. They had
been married many years, but they had no children.
This was a great sorrow to them. Their only pleasure
was watching the children of their neighbors.

One winter day, when fresh white snow lay deep
everywhere, Ivan and his wife watched the children
playing in it, laughing loudly as they played. The children began to make a beautiful snowman, and Ivan
and Marousha enjoyed seeing it grow. Suddenly Ivan
said, "Wife, let us go out and make a snowman, too!"

Marousha was ready. "Why not?" she said. "We may as well amuse ourselves a little. But why should we make a big snowman? Let us make a snow child, since God has not given us a living one."

"You are right," said Ivan, and he led his wife outdoors.

There in the garden by their house they set to work to make a child of snow. They made a little body, and little hands, and little feet. When all that was done, they rolled a snowball and shaped it into a head.

"Heaven bless you!" cried a passerby.

"Thank you," replied Ivan.

"The help of Heaven is always good," said Marousha.

"What are you doing?" asked the passerby.

"We are making a snow girl," said Marousha.

On the ball of snow which stood for a head they put a nose and a chin, and they made two little holes for eyes.

Just as they finished their work—oh, wonder of wonders!—the little snow maiden moved! Ivan felt a warm breath come from her lips. He drew back and looked: the snow maiden's sparkling eyes were blue, and her lips, rosy now, curved in a lovely smile.

"What is this?" cried Ivan, making the sign of the cross.

The snow maiden bent her head and the snow fell from now golden hair, which curled about her soft round cheeks. She moved her little arms and legs in the snow as if she were a real child.

"Ivan! Ivan!" cried Marousha. "Heaven has heard our prayers." She threw herself on the child and covered her with kisses.

"Ah, Snegourka, my own dear snow maiden," she cried, and she carried her into the house.

Ivan had much to do to recover from his surprise, and Marousha became foolish with joy.

Hour by hour, Snegourka, the snow maiden, grew both in size and in beauty. Ivan and Marousha could not take their eyes away from her.

The little house, which had held such sadness, now was full of life and merriment. The neighboring children came to play with the snow maiden. They chattered with her and sang songs to her, teaching her all they knew.

The snow maiden was very clever. She observed everything and learned quickly. When she spoke, her voice was so sweet that one could have gone on listening to it forever. She was gentle, obedient and loving. In turn, everyone loved her. She played in the snow with the other children and they saw how well her little hands could model things of snow and ice.

Marousha said, "See what joy Heaven has given us after these many years."

"Heaven be thanked," replied Ivan.

At last the winter came to an end, and the spring

sun shone down and warmed the earth. The snow melted, green grass sprang up in the fields, and the lark sang high in the sky. The village girls went about singing:

> Sweet spring, how did you come to us?
> How did you come?
> Did you come on a plow, or on a harrow?

Although the other children were gay with spring, and full of song and dance, the snow maiden sat by the window looking sadder and sadder.

"What is the matter with you, my dear child?" asked Marousha, drawing her close and caressing her. "Are you not well? Why aren't you happy?"

"It is nothing, Mother," answered the snow maiden. "I am quite well."

The last snow of the winter had now melted and disappeared. Flowers bloomed in every field and garden. In the forest, the nightingale poured out its song and all the world seemed glad, except the snow maiden, who became sadder still.

She would run away from her friends and hide from the sun in dark corners, like a timid flower under the trees. She liked best to play by the water, under shady willow trees. She was happiest at night and during a storm, even a fierce hailstorm. When the hail melted and the sun broke forth again—she began to weep.

Summer came, with ripening fields, and the Feast

of St. John was soon to be celebrated. The snow maiden's friends begged her to go with them to the forest, to pick berries and flowers.

The snow maiden did not want to go, but her mother urged her, even though she, too, felt afraid.

"Go, my darling, and play. And you, children, look after her well. You know how much I love her."

In the forest the children picked wild flowers and made themselves wreaths. It was warm, and they ran about singing, each wearing a crown of flowers.

"Look at us!" they shouted. "Come play with us," they urged the snow maiden. "Follow us."

They went on, dancing and singing. Then all of a sudden they heard, behind them, a sigh.

They turned and looked. There was nothing to be seen but a fast-melting little heap of snow. The snow maiden was no longer among them.

They called and called and shouted her name, but there was no answer.

"Where can she be? She must have gone home," they said.

Back they ran to the village, but no one there had seen her either.

During the next day and the day following, everyone searched. They went through the woods and looked through every thicket, but no trace of the little snow maiden was to be found.

Ivan and Marousha felt that their hearts would

break, and for a long time Marousha cried, "Sne-gourka, my sweet snow maiden, come to me!"

Sometimes Ivan and Marousha thought they could hear the voice of their child. Perhaps, when the snow returned, she would come back to them.

TRADITIONAL RUSSIAN TALE, RETOLD BY VIRGINIA HAVILAND

THE THREE LITTLE PIGS

THERE WAS an old Sow with three little Pigs, and as she had not enough to keep them, she sent them out into the world to seek their fortune.

The first that went off met a man with a bundle of straw and said to him, "Please, man, give me that straw to build me a house."

Which the man did, and the little Pig built a house with it.

Presently along came a Wolf, who knocked at the door, and said, "Little Pig, little Pig, let me come in."

To which the Pig answered: "No, no, by the hair of my chinny chin chin."

The Wolf answered to that: "Then I'll huff, and I'll puff, and I'll blow your house in."

So he huffed, and he puffed, and he blew the house in, and ate up the little Pig.

The second little Pig met a man with a bundle of twigs and said, "Please, man, give me those twigs to build a house."

Which the man did, and the Pig built his house. Then along came the Wolf and said, "Little Pig, little Pig, let me come in."

"No, no, by the hair of my chinny chin chin."

"Then I'll puff, and I'll huff, and I'll blow your house in."

So he huffed, and he puffed, and he puffed, and he huffed, and at last he blew the house down, and he ate up the little Pig.

The third little Pig met a man with a load of bricks and said, "Please, man, give me those bricks to build a house with."

The man gave him the bricks, and he built his house with them. So the Wolf came, as he did to the other little Pigs, and said, "Little Pig, little Pig, let me come in."

"No, no, by the hair on my chinny chin chin."

"Then I'll huff, and I'll puff, and I'll blow your house in."

Well, he huffed, and he puffed, and he huffed, and he puffed, and he puffed; but he could not get the house down. When he found that he could not, with all his huffing and puffing and huffing, blow it down, he said, "Little Pig, I know where there is a nice patch of turnips."

"Where?" said the little Pig.

"In Mr. Smith's home field, and if you will be ready tomorrow morning I will call for you, and we will go together and get some for dinner."

"Very well," said the little Pig, "I will be ready. What time do you mean to go?"

"Oh, at six o'clock."

Well, the little Pig woke up at five and got the turnips before the Wolf came—which he did about six—and said, "Little Pig, are you ready?"

The little Pig said, "Ready! I have been and come back again, and got a nice potful for dinner."

The Wolf felt very angry at this, but thought that he would catch the little Pig somehow or other, so he said, "Little Pig, I know where there is a nice apple tree."

"Where?" said the Pig.

"Down in the big park," replied the Wolf, "and if you will not deceive me I will come for you at five o'clock tomorrow, and we will get some apples."

Well, the little Pig bustled out the next morning at four o'clock, and went off for the apples, hoping to get back before the Wolf came; but he had farther to go and had to climb the tree, so that just as he was

climbing down from it, he saw the Wolf coming, which, as you may suppose, frightened him very much.

When the Wolf came up he said, "What! Little Pig, are you here before me? Are they nice apples?"

"Yes, very," said the little Pig. "I will throw you down one." And he threw it so far that, while the Wolf had gone to pick it up, the little Pig jumped down and ran all the way home.

The next day the Wolf came again and said to the little Pig, "Little Pig, there is a fair in the town this afternoon. Will you go?"

"Oh yes," said the Pig, "I will go. What time shall you be ready?"

"At three," said the Wolf. The little Pig went off before the time, as usual, and arrived at the fair. He bought a butter churn, which he was going home with when he saw the Wolf coming. Then he could not tell what to do. He got into the churn to hide, and by so doing turned it around, and it rolled down the hill with the Pig in it, which frightened the Wolf so much that he ran home without going to the fair. He went to the little Pig's house and told him how frightened he had been by a great round thing which came down the hill past him.

Then the little Pig said, "Hah, I frightened you, did I? I had been to the fair and bought myself a butter churn, and when I saw you, I got into it and rolled down the hill."

Then the Wolf was very angry indeed and declared that he would eat up the little Pig and he would come down the chimney after him. When the little Pig saw what he was about, he hung up a pot full of water and made a blazing fire, and, just as the Wolf was coming down, took off the cover of the pot, and in fell the Wolf. So the little Pig put on the cover again in an instant, boiled the Wolf up and ate him for supper, and lived happily ever afterwards.

OLD ENGLISH TALE, RETOLD BY JOSEPH JACOBS

THE SHOEMAKER AND THE ELVES

THERE WAS once a shoe-maker who, through no fault of his own, had become so poor that at last he had only enough leather left for one pair of shoes. That evening he cut out the shoes which he intended to begin upon the next morning and, since he had a good conscience, he lay down quietly, said his prayers and fell asleep.

In the morning when he had prayed as usual and

was preparing to sit down to work, he found the pair of shoes standing finished on his table. He was amazed, and could not understand it in the least.

He took the shoes in his hand to examine them more closely. They were so neatly sewn that not a stitch was out of place, and were as good as the work of a master.

Soon after, a purchaser came into the shop. He was very pleased with the shoes and paid more than the ordinary price for them, so that the shoemaker was able to buy leather for two pairs with the money.

He cut them out that evening, and the next day with fresh courage was about to go to work; but he had no need to, for when he got up, the shoes were finished, and buyers were not lacking. These gave him so much money that he was able to buy leather for four pairs of shoes.

Early next morning he found the four pairs finished, and so it went on; what he cut out at night was finished in the morning, so that he was soon again in comfortable circumstances and became a well-to-do man.

Now it happened one evening not long before Christmas, when he had cut out shoes as usual, that he said to his wife, "How would it be if we were to sit up tonight to see who it is that comes to lend us such a helping hand?"

The wife agreed, and so they lit a candle and hid themselves in the corner of the room behind the clothes which were hanging there.

At midnight came two little naked men who sat down at the shoemaker's table, took up the cut-out work and began with their tiny fingers to stitch, sew and hammer so neatly and quickly that the shoemaker could not believe his eyes. They did not stop till everything was quite finished and stood complete on the table; then they ran swiftly away.

The next day the wife said to the shoemaker, "The little men have made us rich, and we ought to show our gratitude. They run about with nothing on and must freeze with cold. Now I will make them shirts, coats and vests, and will even knit them some thick stockings, and you shall make them each a pair of shoes."

The husband agreed, and in the evening when they had everything ready they laid out the presents on the table and hid themselves to see how the little men would behave.

At midnight they came skipping in and were about to set to work. But instead of the leather already cut out they found the charming clothes. At first they were surprised, then excessively delighted. With the greatest speed they put on and smoothed down the pretty clothes, singing:

> Now we're dressed so fine and neat,
> Why cobble more for others' feet?

Then they hopped and danced about, and leaped

466

over chairs and tables and out of the door. From that time on, the little men came back no more, but the shoemaker fared well as long as he lived and had good luck in all his undertakings.

OLD GERMAN TALE, COLLECTION OF
KATE DOUGLAS WIGGIN AND NORA ARCHIBALD SMITH

DOCTOR KNOW-IT-ALL

ONCE THERE was a peasant and he was very poor. All he had in the world was a patch of woodland, a two-wheeled cart and a pair of oxen to pull it. From time to time he chopped down some of his trees, cut them up into logs and carted them into the village. If he was lucky enough to find a buyer for the wood, he would sell it for two dollars a load.

One day, this peasant Fish—for that was his name —took his oxcart full of wood to the village and sold it to a doctor. While Fish was standing at the open door waiting for his two dollars, a powerful smell of rich, savory food reached his nostrils. He peeped in at the door. There was the doctor's dinner laid out on the table, all steaming and ready to eat: soup and roast, juicy vegetables, a frosted cake and a dish of luscious fruit such as peasant Fish had never even laid eyes upon before.

Oh! thought the poor man. If I could only be a doctor too, and eat such heavenly dinners.

This set him thinking. After the doctor had given him his two dollars for the wood, the peasant lingered in the doorway, twirling his cap this way and that; and at last he asked whether he might not learn to be a doctor also.

"Well, and why not?" the doctor said to him. "It's easy enough."

"And how would one go about doing that, now?" asked Fish.

"First of all," said the doctor, "you must sell your two oxen and the cart. With that money you must buy some fine clothes. You must also buy a few medicine bottles, pills and capsules, salts, salves and so on. Next you must get yourself a book—one of those ABC books will do, the kind with the picture of a rooster inside. And last of all, you must get a board with the words I AM DOCTOR KNOW-IT-ALL painted on it, and you must nail it over your door."

Fish did all this. Over his door hung the newly painted sign, in his room was a shelf full of medicine bottles and on his table was the ABC book. He himself

was so fine and grand he felt like someone new. With his spectacles, his long-tailed coat, his watch and his pointed beard, he really looked as if he knew it all. He was ready to start, but day after day went by and nothing happened: there he sat among his salves and pills with not a thing to do.

At last someone came, and a lord, no less. This lord had been robbed of a big sum of money, and when he saw the sign I AM DOCTOR KNOW-IT-ALL, he said to himself, "That's just the fellow I want. If he really knows it all, he will surely know who has stolen my money."

He knocked at the door, and when Fish heard him he straightened his spectacles, gave a pull at his watch chain, put on his tall hat, but took it off again and at last opened the door.

"So you are Doctor Know-It-All," said the rich lord.

"Oh, yes," said Fish.

"I want you to find my stolen money," said the lord. "Can you come with me now to my palace?"

"Yes, indeed," said Fish. "And my wife, Gretl— may she come, too?"

"Certainly," said the lord; so they all stepped into his coach and drove off.

It was the dinner hour when they reached the lord's palace, and he invited Fish and Gretl to join him at the table. They all sat down, and when the first servant came in with a dish of soup, Fish whispered to his wife, "Look, Gretl, that is the first."

He meant that this was the first course being served, but the servant, who had overheard him, thought he meant this was the first thief who had stolen the lord's money. As he really was one of the thieves, he became worried, and when he reached the kitchen he said to his fellow servants, "Things will go ill with us, now that this Doctor Know-It-All is around here. Just think! As soon as he set eyes on me, he told his wife I was the first thief!"

The other servants gasped in alarm, and when the bell tinkled for the next course, the second servant hardly had the courage to go into the dining room. But what could he do? It was his turn to serve. He tried to look innocent as he entered with a dish of steaming food, but Fish leaned over to his wife and whispered, "See, Gretl, that's the second."

He meant this was the second course, but the servant thought that he himself was meant, and his knees knocked together as he rushed back to the kitchen.

When the third servant came in with still another dish, it was the same. Fish nudged his wife, whispering, "And that, Gretl, is the third."

The third servant, his hair standing on end, set the dish on the table and dashed into the kitchen as fast as he could. Luckily for the thieves, the lord had noticed nothing, for he had been too busy thinking up some way of putting Doctor Know-It-All to the test, and now he said, "Doctor, here is the fourth servant with a covered dish. If you really know it all, you should be able to guess what is in the dish."

Poor peasant Fish! How should he know what was in it? He looked and looked at the covered dish; and at last, seeing he was caught, he said, "Oh, you poor Fish. You're done for!"

As luck would have it, there was a fish in the dish! And the lord cried, "Well, well, Doctor, you've guessed it! Now I know you can find my stolen money."

He was in a fix, the peasant Fish, and no mistake about it. He was still racking his brains for something to say when the fourth servant, who was just leaving the room, winked meaningly at him. Fish excused himself from the table and followed the man into the kitchen. The servants, looking greatly frightened, said, "Oh, Doctor, you told your wife we were the thieves who stole my lord's money, and it's true. But we'll give it all back to him and we'll reward you besides, if you'll only promise not to tell on us."

Fish promised to keep their secret, and they showed him where the stolen money was hidden. When he returned to the dining room, he cleared his throat and stroked his beard, saying, "Hm, hm! So you want to know what's become of your money, my lord. Hm, hm! Well! I'll have to consult my book about that."

He sat down and spread the ABC book on his knees.

Then he put his spectacles on his nose and, with an important air, began to look for the picture of the rooster. Meanwhile, the servants were curious to know whether Doctor Know-It-All would really keep their secret, so the fifth servant was sent in to listen. He sneaked in on tiptoe and hid in the oven.

All this time, peasant Fish or Doctor Know-It-All— whichever you wish to call him—was still flipping pages back and forth in his ABC book, but he couldn't find the picture of the rooster. At last he lost his temper and shouted, "You rascal! I know you're in there, and I'll find you yet!"

The servant who was in hiding thought that he was the "rascal." He jumped out of the oven, yelling, "Hulla! The man knows everything!"

Doctor Know-It-All, who had found the rooster at last, looked pleased, closed his ABC book and cleared his throat again. "Hm, hm!" he said. "Yes. Well, well! And now as to your stolen money, my lord, I can show you just where it is."

He led the lord to the place where the servants had hidden the money, saying, "You see, my lord. Here it is, every penny of it."

The lord was pleased—so very pleased, in fact, that he grabbed a great handful of gold, pressed it into Fish's hands and said, "Well done, my good Doctor, and my undying thanks to you. I will spread your fame far and wide."

This he did, too; and from that time on, Fish and his good wife Gretl lived in wealth and ease, had plenty of good food to eat and rode about town in a fine carriage.

JAKOB AND WILHELM GRIMM, TRANSLATED BY WANDA GÁG

THE SIX SWANS

A KING WAS once hunting in a great wood, and he hunted the game so eagerly that none of his courtiers were able to keep up with him. When evening came on he saw that he had lost his way and was quite alone. He sought a way out of the forest, but could not find one. Then he saw an old woman with a shaking head coming toward him.

"Good woman," he said to her, "can you not show me the way out of the wood?"

"Oh, certainly, Sir King," she replied, "I can do that, but only on one condition. If you do not fulfill my request, you will never get out of the wood and will die of hunger."

"What is the condition?" asked the King.

"I have a daughter," said the old woman, "who is so beautiful that she has not her equal in the world and she is well worthy of being your wife. If you will make her Queen, I will show you how to get out of the wood."

The King, in his anguish of mind, consented, and the old woman, who was indeed a witch, led him to her little house where her daughter was sitting by the fire. She received the King as if she were expecting him, and he saw that she was certainly beautiful.

But somehow the girl did not please the King, and he could not look at her without a secret feeling of horror. As soon as he had lifted the maiden onto his horse, the old woman showed him the way. Soon the King reached his palace, and the wedding was celebrated there.

Now, the King had already been married once and had by his first wife seven children, six boys and one girl, whom he loved more than anything in the world. But because he was afraid that their new stepmother might not treat them well, he put them all in a lonely castle that stood in the middle of a wood. It lay so hidden, and the way to it was so hard to find, that he himself could not have reached it had not a wise woman given him a spool of thread which possessed a marvelous property: when he threw it before him it unwound itself and showed him the way.

But the King went so often to visit his dear children

476

that the Queen became annoyed with his absences. She grew more and more curious, and decided to discover what he did alone in the wood. So she gave his servants a great deal of money, and they betrayed his secret to her and also told her of the spool of thread which alone could point out the way. She did not rest till she found out where the King guarded the spool. Then she made some little white shirts and, as she had learned from her witch mother, sewed an enchantment in each of them.

And one day, when the King had ridden off, she took the little shirts and went into the wood, and the spool showed her the way. The boys, who saw someone in the distance, thought it was their dear father coming to see them and they rushed out to meet him joyfully. Then she threw a white shirt over each one, which changed them all into swans, and they flew away over the forest.

The Queen went home quite satisfied and thought she was well rid of her stepchildren. But of the King's daughter she knew nothing, because fortunately the child had not run out of the castle to meet her.

The next day the King went to visit his children and he found no one but his daughter.

"Where are your brothers?" he asked her.

"Alas, dear Father!" she answered. "They have gone away and left me all alone." And she told him that, looking out of her window, she had seen all of

THE WORLD'S BEST FAIRY TALES

her brothers flying over the wood in the shape of swans.

The King mourned for his sons and, since he was afraid of losing his daughter also, he decided to take her with him. But she was afraid of the stepmother and begged the King to let her stay just one night more in the castle in the wood.

The poor girl thought: My home is no longer here. I will go and seek my brothers. And when night came she went deep into the forest. She walked all through the night and the next day, till she could go no farther for weariness.

Then she saw a hut, went in and found a room with six little beds. She crept under one of them, lay down on the hard floor and was going to spend the night there.

Just before sunset she heard a rustling sound and saw six swans flying in the window. They stood on the floor and blew all their feathers off, and then they stripped off their swan skins like shirts. Overjoyed as she recognized her brothers, the girl crept out from under the bed.

And her brothers were no less delighted to see their little sister again, but their joy did not last very long.

"You cannot stay here," they said to her. "This is a den of robbers."

"Could you not protect me?" asked the sister.

"No," they answered. "For just a quarter of an hour

after sunset do we regain our human forms. After that, we are changed into swans again."

Then the little sister cried and said, "Can you not be freed?"

"Oh, no," they said, "the conditions are too hard. You, our dear little sister, could not speak or laugh for six years and in that time must make six shirts for us out of starflowers. If a single word comes out of your mouth, all your labor would be in vain, and we would remain under the spell."

When the brothers had said this, the quarter of an hour came to an end, and they flew away through the window as swans.

The maiden determined to free her brothers even if it should cost her her life. She left the hut, went into the forest, climbed a tree and spent the night there. The next morning she came down, collected star-flowers and, returning to the tree, began to sew. She could speak to no one and she had no wish to laugh, so she sat there, looking only at her work.

When she had lived there some time, it happened that the King of another country was hunting in that forest, and his hunters came to the tree in which the maiden sat. They called out to her and asked, "Who are you?"

But she gave no answer.

"Come down to us," they called, "we will do you no harm."

She shook her head silently. As they pressed her further with questions, she threw them a golden chain from her neck. But they would not leave off, and she threw them her belt, and when this was no use, her garters and then her dress. The huntsmen would still not leave her alone, but climbed the tree, lifted the maiden down and led her to the King.

The King asked, "Why are you in that tree?"

But she answered nothing.

He asked her in all the languages he knew, but she was as silent as a fish. Because she was so beautiful, however, the King's heart was touched and he was overcome with a great love for her. He wrapped her up in his cloak, placed her before him on his horse and brought her to his castle. There he had her dressed in rich clothes, but not a word could be drawn from her. He seated her by his side, and her modest ways and behavior pleased him so much that he said: "I will marry this maiden and none other in the world."

And after some days he married her. Now the King had a wicked mother who was displeased with the marriage and said terrible things of the young Queen.

"This girl is not worthy of a King," she said.

After a year, when the Queen had her first child, the old mother took it away from her. Then she told the King that the Queen had killed their baby. The King could not believe it and would not allow any harm to be done her. And his wife sat quietly sewing at the

shirts, apparently not troubling herself about anything.

The next time she had a child the wicked mother did the same thing, but the King would not believe her. He said, "She is too sweet and good to do that."

But when the third child was taken away, and his wife was again accused and could not utter a word in her own behalf, the King was obliged to give her over to the law, which decreed that she be burned to death.

When the day came on which the sentence was to be executed, it was the last day of the six years in which she could not speak or laugh. The six shirts were done, except for the left sleeve of the last. As she was being led to the stake, the Queen laid the shirts on her arm and, when she stood on the pile of sticks and the fire was about to be lighted, she looked around her and saw six swans flying through the air. Then she knew that her release was at hand and that she could free her dear brothers from enchantment. Her heart danced for joy.

The swans fluttered around her and hovered so low that she could throw the shirts over them. The swan skins fell off, and her brothers stood before her—living, well and handsome. Only the youngest had a swan's wing instead of his left arm because his shirt-sleeve had not been finished. They embraced and kissed each other, and the Queen went to the King, who was standing by in great astonishment.

"Dearest husband, now I can speak and tell you that I am innocent and have been falsely accused."

She told him of his old mother's deceit and how she had taken the three children away and hidden them. Then the children were fetched, to the great joy of the King, but the wicked old woman came to no good end.

And the King and the Queen, their children and her brothers lived for many years in happiness and peace.

OLD GERMAN TALE, ANDREW LANG COLLECTION

DICK WHITTINGTON
AND HIS CAT

ICK WHITTINGTON was a very little boy when his father and mother died; so little, indeed, that he never knew them nor the place where he was born. He strolled about the country as ragged as a colt till he met with a wagoner who was going to London. He gave Dick leave to walk all the way by the side of his wagon without paying anything for his passage. This pleased little Whittington very much, as he wanted to see London.

He had heard the streets were paved with gold and he was more than willing to get a bushel of it. But how great was his disappointment, poor boy, when he saw the streets covered with mud instead of gold and found himself in a strange place without a friend, without food and without money.

Though the wagoner had the charity to let him walk by the side of the wagon for nothing, he parted hastily from Dick when they came to town, and the poor boy was, in a short time, so cold and so hungry that he wished himself in a good kitchen and by a warm fire in the country.

In his distress he asked charity of several people, and one of them with a sneer bade him, "Go to work for an idle rogue."

"That I will," said Whittington, "with all my heart. I will work for you if you will let me."

The man, who thought this savored of impertinence —though the poor lad intended only to show his readiness to work—gave him such a blow with a stick that he cut his head so the blood ran down. In this situation, and fainting for want of food, he lay down at the door of Mr. Fitzwarren, a merchant, where the cook saw him. Being an ill-natured woman, she ordered him to go about his business or, she declared, she would scald him. At this moment, Mr. Fitzwarren came from the Exchange and began also to scold the poor boy, bidding him to work.

Whittington answered that he should be glad to work if anybody would employ him, and he would be able to if he could get some food, for he had eaten nothing for three days, and he was a poor country boy who knew nobody.

He then endeavored to get up, but he was so weak he fell down again, which aroused such compassion in the merchant that he ordered the servants to take Dick in and give him meat and drink and let him help the cook to do any work she had to give him. People are often too apt to reproach beggars for being idle but give themselves no concern to find them work or to consider whether they are able to do it, which is not true charity.

Whittington would have been happy in this worthy family had he not been bumped about by the cross cook, who was always roasting or basting; and when the grill was idle she employed her hands upon poor Whittington! At last, Miss Alice, his master's daughter, was informed of this and took compassion on the boy and made the servants treat him kindly.

Besides the crossness of the cook, whose name was Cicely, Whittington had another difficulty to overcome before he could be happy. There was, by order of his master, a lumpy bed placed for him in a garret, but rats and mice often ran over the poor boy's nose and disturbed him in his sleep. After some time, however, a gentleman who came to his master's house gave Whittington a penny for brushing his shoes. This he put into his pocket, and the next day, seeing a woman in the street with a cat under her arm, he ran up to ask the price of it. Because the cat was a good mouser, the woman wanted a great deal of money for it, but on Whittington's telling her he had but a penny in the world and wanted a cat badly, she let him have it.

Whittington concealed his cat in the garret, for fear she should be beaten by his enemy the cook. Puss soon killed or frightened away the rats and mice so the poor lad could now sleep as soundly as a top.

Soon after this, the merchant, who had a ship ready to sail, called for his servants, as his custom was, that they might offer something they had to sell on the voyage. Whatever they sent was to pay neither freight nor custom, for he thought justly that God Almighty would bless him the more for his readiness to let the poor partake of his fortune.

All the servants appeared except poor Whittington, who had neither money nor goods to try his luck. But his good friend Miss Alice, thinking his poverty kept him away, ordered him to be called. She then offered to lay down something for him, but the merchant said that would not do—it must be something of his own— upon which Whittington said he had nothing in the world but a cat which he had bought for a penny that was given to him.

"Fetch the cat, boy," said the merchant, "and send her along."

Whittington brought poor Puss and delivered her

to the captain with tears in his eyes, for he said he should now be disturbed by the rats and mice as much as ever. All the company laughed at this but Miss Alice, who pitied the boy and gave him some coins to buy another cat.

While Miss Puss was being tossed by the billows at sea, poor Whittington was being severely beaten at home by his tyrannical mistress the cook, who used Dick cruelly and made such mockery of him for sending his cat to sea that at last the unhappy boy determined to run away from his place and, having packed up the few things he had, he set out very early on the morning of Halloween. He traveled as far as Cheapside, and there sat down on a stone to consider what course he should take. While he was thus ruminating, the Bow Bells, of which there were six, began to ring, and he thought their sounds addressed him in this manner:

> Turn again, Whittington,
> Thrice Lord Mayor of London.

"Lord Mayor of London!" said he to himself. "What would one not endure to be Lord Mayor of London and ride in such a fine coach? Well, I will go back again and bear all the pummeling and ill-usage of Cicely rather than miss the opportunity of being Lord Mayor!" So home he went, and happily got into the merchant's house and about his work before Cicely made her appearance.

The ship which had the cat on board was a long time at sea and, at last, by contrary winds, was driven onto a part of the coast of Barbary inhabited by Moors unknown to the English. The people received the voyagers with civility; therefore, the captain sent some of his goods to the King.

The King was so pleased that he asked the captain and Mr. Fitzwarren's business agent, who always traveled with the boat, to come to his palace, which was about a mile from the sea.

Here they were placed, according to the custom of the country, on rich carpets flowered with gold and silver, with the King and Queen seated at the upper end of the room. Dinner was brought in, which consisted of many courses; but no sooner were the dishes put down than an amazing number of rats and mice came from all quarters and devoured everything in an instant. The agent, in surprise, turned around to the notables and asked if these vermin were not offensive to them.

"Oh, yes," they said, "very offensive. The King would give half his treasure to be freed of them, for they not only destroy his dinner, as you can see, but they also assault him in his chamber, and even in bed. He has to have a guard in his room while he is sleeping for fear of them."

The agent jumped for joy. He remembered Dick Whittington and his cat; and he told the King he had a creature on board the ship that would dispatch all these rats and mice immediately. The King's heart heaved so high at the joy this news gave him that his turban dropped off his head.

"Bring this creature to me," said he. "If she will do what you say I will load your ship with gold and jewels in exchange for her."

The agent, who knew his business, set forth the merits of Miss Puss. He told His Majesty that it would be inconvenient to part with her, for, without her, rats and mice might destroy the goods in the ship—but to oblige His Majesty he would fetch her.

"Run, run," said the Queen. "I am impatient to see the dear thing."

Away flew the agent, and another dinner was prepared in his absence. He returned with the cat just as the rats and mice were devouring that also. He immediately put down Miss Puss, who killed a great number of them.

The King rejoiced greatly to see his old enemies destroyed by so small a creature, and the Queen was highly pleased and desired the cat to be brought near that she might look at her. The agent called, "Pussy, pussy, pussy!" and she came to him. He then presented her to the Queen, who started back. She was afraid to touch an animal who had made such havoc among the rats and mice. However, when the agent stroked the cat and said, "Pussy, pussy," the Queen

also touched her and cried, "Putty, putty," for she had not learned English.

He then put the cat down on the Queen's lap, where, purring, she played with Her Majesty's hand and then sang herself to sleep.

The King, having seen the exploits of Miss Puss, and being informed that her kittens would stock the whole country, bargained with the captain and agent for the ship's whole cargo, and then gave them ten times as much for the cat as for all the rest—on which, taking leave of Their Majesties and other personages at court, they sailed with a fair wind for England.

In London, morning had scarcely dawned when Mr. Fitzwarren rose to count over the cash and settle the business for that day. He had just entered the counting house and seated himself at the desk, when somebody came, tap, tap, at the door. "Who is there?" said Mr. Fitzwarren.

"A friend."

"What friend comes at this unseasonable time?"

"A real friend is never unseasonable," answered the caller. "I come to bring you good news of your ship *Unicorn*."

The merchant instantly opened the door, and who should be there but the captain and agent, with a cabinet of jewels and a bill of lading, for which the merchant lifted up his eyes and thanked Heaven for sending him such a prosperous voyage. Then they told him the adventures of the cat, and showed him the cabinet of jewels which they had brought for young Dick Whittington. Upon which he cried out:

> Go, send him in, and tell him of his fame,
> And call him Mr. Whittington by name.

When some who were present told Mr. Fitzwarren this treasure was too much for such a poor boy as Whittington, he said: "God forbid that I should deprive him of his due; it is his own and he shall have it to a penny."

He then sent for Mr. Whittington, who was cleaning the kitchen and would have excused himself from going into the counting house, saying his master's room was swept and his shoes were dirty and full of hobnails. The merchant, however, made him come in and ordered a chair to be set for him. Upon which, thinking they intended to make sport of him, as had been too often the case in the kitchen, he besought his master not to mock a poor simple fellow who intended no harm, but let him go about his work.

The merchant, taking him by the hand, said, "Indeed, Mr. Whittington, I am in earnest with you and wish to congratulate you on your great success. Your cat has procured you more money than I am worth in the world, and may you enjoy it long and be happy!"

At length, being shown the treasure and convinced that all of it belonged to him, he fell upon his knees and thanked the Almighty for his providential care of such a poor and miserable creature. He then laid all the treasure at his master's feet, but Mr. Fitzwarren refused to take any part of it and told Dick he heartily rejoiced at his prosperity and hoped the wealth he had acquired would be a comfort to him and would make him happy.

Dick Whittington then applied to his mistress and to his friend Miss Alice, who both refused to take any part of the money, but Miss Alice told him she was gladdened by his good success and wished him all felicity. He then gave gifts to the ship's captain, the agent and the ship's crew for the care they had taken of his cargo. He likewise distributed presents to all the servants in the house, not forgetting even his old enemy the cook, though she little deserved it.

After this, Mr. Fitzwarren suggested Mr. Whittington send for the necessary people to advise him how best to dress himself like a gentleman, and made him the offer of his house to live in till he could provide himself with a better one.

Now it came to pass, when Mr. Whittington's face was washed, his hair curled and he was dressed in a rich suit of clothes, that he turned out a genteel young fellow. Since wealth contributes much to give a man confidence, he soon grew to be a sprightly and good companion, so much so that Miss Alice, who had formerly pitied him, now fell in love with him.

When her father perceived the two young people had this good liking for each other he proposed a match between them, to which both cheerfully consented, and the Lord Mayor, aldermen, sheriffs, the Company of Stationers, the Royal Academy of Arts and a number of eminent merchants attended the ceremony and were elegantly treated at an entertainment made for that purpose.

History further relates that they lived very happily, had several children and died at a fine old age. Mr. Whittington served as Sheriff of London and, as the Bow Bells had told him many years before, was three times Lord Mayor.

The last year of his mayoralty he entertained King Henry V and his Queen, after his conquest of France, upon which occasion the King, in consideration of Mr. Whittington's merit, said, "Never had king such a subject." On hearing this, Mr. Whittington replied, "Never had subject such a king." His Majesty, out of respect for his host's good character, conferred the honor of knighthood on him soon after.

For many years before his death, Sir Richard constantly fed a great number of poor citizens and built a church and a college, to which he gave a yearly allowance for poor scholars. He also gave liberally to St. Bartholomew's Hospital and other public charities to help the people of London.

OLD ENGLISH TALE, ANDREW LANG COLLECTION

RAPUNZEL

ONCE UPON a time a man and his wife were very unhappy because they had no children. These good people had a little window at the back of their house which looked into the most lovely garden full of all manner of beautiful flowers and vegetables; but the garden was surrounded by a high wall, and no one dared to enter it, for it belonged to a witch who possessed great power and who was feared by the whole world.

One day the woman stood at the window overlooking the garden and saw there a bed full of the finest salad greens called rampion. The leaves looked so fresh and green that she longed to eat them. The desire grew day by day, and just because she knew she couldn't possibly get any, she pined away and became pale and wretched. Then her husband grew alarmed and said, "What ails you, dear wife?"

"Oh," she answered, "if I don't get some rampion to eat from the garden behind the house, I know I shall die."

The man, who loved her dearly, said to himself,

THE WORLD'S BEST FAIRY TALES

"Come! Rather than let your wife die you shall pick her some rampion, no matter the cost." So at dusk he climbed over the wall into the witch's garden and, hastily gathering a handful of rampion leaves, he returned with them to his wife. She made them into a salad, which tasted so good that her longing for the forbidden food was greater than ever. If she were to know any peace of mind, there was nothing for it but that her husband must climb over the garden wall again and fetch her some more. Again at dusk over he went, but when he reached the other side he drew back in terror, for there, standing before him, was the old witch.

"How dare you," she said, with a wrathful glance, "climb into my garden and steal my rampion like a common thief? You shall suffer greatly for your rashness."

"Oh," he implored, "please forgive my boldness; necessity alone drove me to the deed. My wife saw your rampion from her window and had such a desire for it that she would certainly have died if her wish had not been gratified."

Then the witch's anger was a little appeased, and she said, "If it's as you say, you may take as much rampion away with you as you like, but on one condition only—that you give me the child your wife will shortly bring into the world. All shall go well with it, and I will look after it like a mother."

The man in his terror agreed to everything she asked. As soon as the child was born, the witch appeared and, having given it the name of Rapunzel, which in that country means the same as rampion, she carried it off with her.

Rapunzel was the most beautiful child under the sun. When she was twelve years old the witch shut her up in a tower, in the middle of a great forest, and the tower had neither stairs nor doors, only high up at the very top a small window. When the old witch wanted to visit the girl she stood underneath and called out:

> Rapunzel, Rapunzel,
> Let down your golden hair.

For Rapunzel had wonderful long hair, and it was as fine as spun gold. Whenever she heard the witch's voice she loosened her braids and let her hair fall down out of the window. This became a ladder for the old witch to climb straight up to the top of the tower.

After they lived like this for a few years, it happened one day that a Prince was riding through the woods and passed by the tower. As he drew near it he heard someone singing so sweetly that he stood spellbound and listened. It was Rapunzel, in her loneliness trying to while away the time by letting her sweet voice fill her solitude. The Prince longed to

see the owner of the voice, but he sought in vain for a door in the tower. He rode home, but he was so haunted by the song he had heard that he returned every day to the woods and listened. One day, when he was standing thus behind a tree, he saw the old witch approach and heard her call out:

Rapunzel, Rapunzel,
Let down your golden hair.

Then Rapunzel let down her braids, and the witch climbed up by them.

"So that's the staircase, is it?" said the Prince. "Then I, too, will climb it and try my luck."

On the following day, at dusk, he went to the foot of the tower and cried:

Rapunzel, Rapunzel,
Let down your golden hair.

And as soon as she had let down the marvelous golden ladder the Prince climbed up.

At first Rapunzel was terribly frightened when a man came in, for she had never seen one before. But the Prince spoke to her kindly and told her at once that his heart had been so touched by her singing he felt he should know no peace of mind till he had seen her. Very soon Rapunzel forgot her fear, and when he asked her to marry him she consented at once.

For, she thought, he is young and handsome, and

I'll certainly be happier with him than with the old witch. So she put her hand in his and said: "Yes, I will gladly go with you, only how am I to get down out of the tower? Every time you come to see me you must bring a skein of silk with you, and I will braid it into a ladder. When it is finished I will climb down by it, and you will take me away on your horse."

They arranged that, till the ladder was ready, he was to come to her every evening, because the old woman was with her during the day. Each time the Prince came he brought some silk.

The old witch, of course, knew nothing of what was going on, till one day Rapunzel, not thinking of what she was about, turned to the witch and said, "How is it, good mother, that you are so much harder to pull up than the young Prince? He is always with me in a moment."

"Oh, you wicked child," cried the witch. "What is this I hear? I thought I had hidden you from the whole world and in spite of it you have managed to deceive me."

In her wrath she seized Rapunzel's beautiful hair, wound it around and around her left hand and then, grasping a pair of scissors in her right, snip, snap, off it came, and the golden braids lay on the ground. And, worse than this, she was so hardhearted that she took Rapunzel to a lonely desert place and there left her to live in loneliness and misery.

But on the evening of the day in which she had taken poor Rapunzel away, the witch fastened the braids onto a hook in the window, and when the Prince came and called out:

> Rapunzel, Rapunzel,
> Let down your golden hair,

she let them down, and the Prince climbed up as usual.

Instead of his beloved Rapunzel he found the old witch, who fixed her evil, glittering eyes on him and cried mockingly, "Ah, ah! You thought to find your lady love, but the pretty bird has flown and its song is mute. The cat caught it and will scratch out your eyes, too. Rapunzel is lost to you forever—you will never see her again."

The Prince was beside himself with grief, and in his despair he jumped right down from the tower and, though he escaped with his life, the thorns among which he fell pierced his eyes. Then he wandered, blind and miserable, through the forest, eating nothing but roots and berries and weeping and lamenting the loss of his lovely bride.

So he wandered about for a year, as wretched and unhappy as he could be, and at last he came to the desert place where Rapunzel was living. Suddenly he heard a voice which seemed strangely familiar to him. He walked eagerly in the direction of the sound, and, when he was quite close, Rapunzel recognized him and fell on his neck and wept. Two of her tears touched his eyes, and in a moment they were healed, and he could see as well as ever before. Then he led her to his kingdom, where they were welcomed with great joy, and they lived happily ever after.

JAKOB AND WILHELM GRIMM, TRANSLATED BY MAY SELLAR

ALADDIN AND
THE WONDERFUL LAMP

THERE ONCE lived a poor tailor who had a son called Aladdin, a careless, idle boy who would do nothing but play all day in the streets with other idle little boys. This so grieved the father that he died; yet, in spite of his mother's tears and prayers, Aladdin did not mend his ways.

One day, when he was playing in the streets as usual, a stranger asked him his age and if he were not the son of Mustapha the tailor.

"I am, sir," replied Aladdin. "But he died a long while ago."

On this, the stranger, who was a famous African

magician, fell on his neck and kissed him, saying, "I am your uncle and I knew you from your likeness to my brother. Go to your mother and tell her I am coming."

Aladdin ran home and told his mother of his newly found uncle. "Indeed, child," she said, "you have no uncle by your father's side or mine."

However, she prepared supper and bade Aladdin bring home the man who called himself his uncle. He came laden with wine and fruit and presently he knelt and kissed the place where Mustapha used to sit. He told Aladdin's mother not to be surprised at never having seen him before, as he had been forty years out of the country.

The African magician then turned to Aladdin and asked him his trade, at which the boy hung his head, while his mother burst into tears. On learning that Aladdin was idle and would learn no trade, he offered to take a shop for him and stock it with merchandise. The next morning he bought Aladdin a fine suit of clothes and took him all over the city, showing him the sights, and brought him home at nightfall to his mother, who was overjoyed to see her son so finely dressed.

Next day the magician led Aladdin into some beautiful gardens a long way outside the city gates. They sat down by a fountain, and the magician pulled a cake from his pocket, which he divided between them. They then journeyed onward till they had almost reached the mountains. Aladdin was so tired that he begged to go back, but the magician beguiled him with pleasant stories and led the boy on in spite of himself.

At last they came to two mountains divided by a narrow valley. "We will go no farther," said the false uncle. "I will show you something wonderful; but first you gather up sticks while I kindle a fire."

When the fire was lit the magician threw on it a powder he had with him, at the same time saying some magical words. The earth trembled a little and opened in front of them, disclosing a square, flat stone with a brass ring in the middle to raise it by. Aladdin became so frightened that he tried to run away, but the magician caught him and gave him such a blow that it knocked him to the ground.

"What have I done, Uncle?" he asked piteously.

Whereupon the magician said more kindly, "Fear nothing, but obey me. Beneath this stone lies a treasure which is to be yours, and no one else may touch it, so you must do exactly as I tell you."

At the word "treasure," Aladdin forgot his fears and grasped the ring as he was told, saying the names of his father and grandfather. The stone came up quite easily and steps appeared.

"Go down," said the magician. "At the foot of those steps you will find an open doorway leading into three large halls. Tuck up your trousers and go through them without touching anything, or you will die instantly. These halls lead into a garden of fine fruit trees. If you should wish any of the fruit you may gather as much as you please. Walk on till you come to a niche in a terrace where stands a lighted lamp. Pour out the oil it contains and bring it to me."

He then drew a ring from his finger and gave it to Aladdin, telling him that it would protect him from any evil he might meet.

Aladdin found everything as the magician had said. He gathered some fruit off the trees and, having got the lamp, arrived at the mouth of the cave.

The magician cried out in a great hurry, "Make haste and give me the lamp." This Aladdin refused to do until he was out of the cave. The magician flew into a terrible passion and, throwing some more powder on the fire, muttered something, and the stone rolled back into its place, sealing Aladdin inside.

The magician instantly left Persia for Africa, which plainly showed that he was no uncle of Aladdin's but a cunning sorcerer who had read in his magic books of a wonderful lamp which would make him the most powerful man in the world. Though he alone knew where to find it, he could only receive it from the hand of another. He had picked out the foolish Aladdin for this purpose, intending to get the lamp and kill him afterward.

For two days Aladdin remained in the dark, crying and lamenting. At last he clasped his hands in prayer,

and in so doing rubbed the ring, which the magician had forgotten to take from him.

Immediately an enormous and frightful genie rose out of the earth, saying, "What wouldst thou with me? I am the slave of the ring and will obey thee in all things."

Aladdin fearlessly replied, "Deliver me from this place," whereupon the earth opened, and he found himself outside. As soon as his eyes could bear the light he went home, but fainted on the threshold. When he came to himself he told his mother what had passed, and showed her the lamp and the fruits—in reality precious stones—which he had gathered in the garden. He then asked for some food.

"Alas, child," his mother said, "I have nothing in the house, but I have spun a little cotton and will go and sell it."

Aladdin bade her keep her cotton, for he would sell the lamp instead. As it was very dirty she began to rub it, that it might fetch a higher price. Instantly a hideous genie appeared and asked what she would have.

She fainted away, but Aladdin, snatching the lamp, said boldly, "Bring me something to eat!"

The genie returned with a silver bowl, twelve silver plates containing rich meats, two silver cups and a bottle of wine.

Aladdin's mother, when she came to herself, said, "Whence comes this splendid feast?"

"Ask not, but eat," replied Aladdin. So they sat at breakfast till it was dinner time, and Aladdin told his mother what had happened when he had rubbed the lamp. She begged him to sell it and have nothing to do with genies.

"No," said Aladdin, "since chance has made us aware of its virtues, we will use it and the ring likewise, which I shall always wear on my finger." When they had eaten all the genie had brought, Aladdin sold one of the silver plates, then another and another. When none were left, he had recourse to the genie, who gave him another set of plates, and thus he and his mother lived for many years.

One day Aladdin heard an order from the Sultan proclaiming that everyone was to stay at home and close his shutters while the Princess, his daughter, went to and from the bath. Aladdin was seized by a desire to see her face, which was very difficult as she was veiled. He hid himself behind the door of the bath and peeped through a chink.

The Princess lifted her veil as she went in, and looked so beautiful that Aladdin fell in love with her at first sight. He went home quite changed and his mother became frightened. He told her he loved the Princess and could not live without her and meant to ask for her in marriage. His mother, on hearing this, burst out laughing, but Aladdin at last prevailed upon her to go before the Sultan and carry his request. She fetched a napkin and laid in it the magic fruits from the enchanted garden, which sparkled and shone like the most beautiful jewels. She took these with her to please the Sultan and set out, trusting in the lamp.

The Grand Vizier and the lords of council had just gone into the hall as she entered and placed herself in front of the Sultan. He, however, took no notice of her. She went every day for a week and stood in the same place. When the council broke up on the sixth day the Sultan said to his Vizier, "I see a certain woman in the audience chamber day after day, carrying something in a napkin. Call her tomorrow that I may find out what she wants."

Next day, at a sign from the Vizier, she went up to the foot of the throne and remained kneeling till the Sultan said to her, "Rise, good woman, and tell me what you want." She hesitated, so the Sultan sent away all but the Vizier and bade her speak freely, promising beforehand to forgive her for anything she might say.

She then told him about her son's violent love for the Princess.

"I prayed him to forget her," she said, "but in vain; he threatened to do some desperate deed if I refused to go and ask Your Majesty for the hand of the Princess. Now I pray you to forgive not me alone but my son Aladdin."

The Sultan asked her kindly what she had in the

napkin, whereupon she unfolded the jewels and presented them.

He was thunderstruck, and turning to the Vizier, said, "What sayest thou? Ought I not to bestow the Princess on one who values her at such a price?"

The Vizier, who wanted her for his own son, begged the Sultan to withhold her for three months, in the course of which he hoped his son would contrive to make him a richer present. The Sultan granted this and told Aladdin's mother that, though he consented to the marriage, she must not appear before him again for three months.

Aladdin waited patiently for quite a while, but after two months had elapsed, his mother, going into the city to buy oil, found everyone rejoicing and asked what was going on.

"Do you not know," was the answer, "that the son of the Grand Vizier is to marry the Sultan's daughter tonight?"

Breathless, she ran and told Aladdin, who was overwhelmed at first, but presently bethought him of the lamp. He rubbed it, and the genie appeared, saying, "What is thy will?"

Aladdin replied, "The Sultan, as thou knowest, has broken his promise to me, and the Vizier's son is to have the Princess. My command is that tonight you bring hither the bride and bridegroom."

"Master, I obey," said the genie.

Aladdin then went to his chamber where, sure enough, at midnight, the genie transported the bed containing the Vizier's son and the Princess.

"Take this new-married man," Aladdin said, "and put him outside in the cold and return at daybreak."

Whereupon the genie took the Vizier's son out of bed, leaving Aladdin with the Princess.

"Fear nothing," Aladdin said to her. "You are my wife, promised to me by your unjust father, and no harm shall come to you."

The Princess was too frightened to speak and passed the most miserable night of her life, while Aladdin lay down beside her and slept soundly. At the appointed hour the genie fetched in the shivering bridegroom, laid him in his place and transported the bed back to the palace.

Presently the Sultan came into the chamber to wish his daughter good morning. The Vizier's unhappy son jumped up and hid himself, while the Princess would not say a word and was very sorrowful.

The Sultan sent her mother to her, who said, "How comes it, child, that you will not speak to your father? What has happened?"

The Princess sighed deeply, and at last told her mother how, during the night, the bed had been carried into some strange house, and what had happened there. Her mother did not believe her in the least but bade her rise and consider it an idle dream.

The following night exactly the same thing happened, and next morning, on the Princess' refusing to speak, the Sultan threatened to cut off her head. She then confessed, bidding him ask the Vizier's son if it were not so. The Sultan told the Vizier to ask his son, who admitted the truth, adding that, dearly as he loved the Princess, he would rather die than go through another such fearful night, and he wished to be separated from her. His wish was granted, and there was an end of feasting and rejoicing.

When the three months were over, Aladdin sent his mother to remind the Sultan of his promise. She stood waiting to see the Sultan, and he, who had forgotten Aladdin, at once remembered him and summoned his mother. On seeing her poverty, the Sultan felt less inclined than ever to keep his word and asked advice from the Vizier, who told him to set so high a value on the Princess that no man could come up to it.

The Sultan then turned to Aladdin's mother, saying, "Good woman, a Sultan must remember his promises and I will remember mine, but your son must first give me forty basins of gold brimful of jewels, carried by forty black slaves, led by as many white ones, splendidly dressed. Tell him that I await his answer."

The mother of Aladdin bowed low and went home, thinking all was lost. She gave Aladdin the Sultan's message, then said, "He may wait long enough for your answer!"

"Not so long, Mother, as you think," her son replied. "I would do a great deal more than that for the Princess." He summoned the genie, and in a few moments the eighty slaves arrived and filled up the small house and garden.

Aladdin made them set out to the palace, two and two, followed by his mother. They were so richly dressed, with such splendid jewels in their belts, that everyone crowded to see them and the basins of gold they carried on their heads.

The procession entered the palace and, after kneeling before the Sultan, stood in a half-circle around the throne, each man with his arms crossed, while Aladdin's mother presented them to the Sultan.

"Good woman," said the Sultan, "return and tell your son I wait for him with open arms."

She lost no time in telling Aladdin, bidding him make haste. But he first called the genie. "I want a scented bath," he ordered, "and a richly embroidered robe, a horse surpassing the Sultan's and twenty slaves to attend me. Besides these I desire six slaves, beautifully dressed, to wait on my mother; and lastly, ten thousand pieces of gold in ten purses."

No sooner said than done. Aladdin mounted his horse and passed through the streets, the slaves strewing gold as they went. Those who had played with him in his childhood knew him not, he had grown so handsome.

When the Sultan saw him, he came down from his throne, embraced him and led him into a hall where a feast was spread, intending to marry him to the Princess that very day. But Aladdin refused, saying, "I must build a palace fit for her," and took his leave.

Once home, he said to the genie, "Build me a palace of the finest marble, set with jasper, agate and other precious stones. In the middle you shall build me a large room with a dome, its four walls of massive gold and silver, each side having six windows whose lattices—except for one, which is to be left unfinished— must be set with diamonds, emeralds and rubies. There must be stables and horses and grooms and slaves. Go and see about it!"

The palace was finished by the next day, and the genie transported him there and showed him all his orders faithfully carried out, even to the laying of a velvet carpet from Aladdin's palace to the Sultan's. Aladdin's mother then dressed herself carefully and walked to the palace with her slaves. The Sultan sent musicians with trumpets and cymbals to meet them, and the air resounded with music and cheers.

Aladdin's mother was taken to the Princess, who saluted her and treated her with great honor. That night the Princess said good-bye to her father and set out on the carpet for Aladdin's palace, his mother beside her, and followed by one hundred slaves. She was charmed at the sight of Aladdin, who ran to receive her.

"Princess," he said, "blame your beauty for my boldness if I have displeased you."

She told him that, having seen him, she willingly obeyed her father in this matter. After the wedding had taken place, Aladdin led her into the hall where a feast was spread, and she supped with him, after which they danced till midnight.

Next day Aladdin invited the Sultan to see the palace. On entering the hall with the four-and-twenty windows, with their rubies, diamonds and emeralds, he cried, "It is a world's wonder! There is only one thing that surprises me. Was it by accident that one window was left unfinished?"

"No, sir, it was by design," returned Aladdin. "I wished Your Majesty to have the glory of finishing this palace."

The Sultan was pleased and sent for the best jewelers in the city. He showed them the unfinished window and bade them fit it up like the others.

"Sir," replied their spokesman, "we cannot find jewels enough."

The Sultan had his own gems fetched, which they soon used, but to no purpose, for in a month's time the work was not half done. Aladdin, knowing that their task was in vain, bade them undo their work and carry the jewels back, and the genie finished the window at his command. The Sultan was surprised to receive his gems again and visited Aladdin, who

showed him the window finished. The Sultan embraced him, the envious Vizier meanwhile hinting that
it was the work of enchantment.

Aladdin had won the hearts of the people by his
gentle bearing. He was made captain of the Sultan's
armies and won several battles for him, but remained
modest and courteous as before and lived thus in peace
and contentment for many years.

But far away in Africa the magician remembered
Aladdin, and by his magic arts discovered that Aladdin,
instead of perishing miserably in the cave, had escaped
and had married a Princess, with whom he was living
in great honor and wealth. He knew that the poor
tailor's son could only have accomplished this by
means of the lamp. So he traveled night and day till he
reached the capital of Persia, bent on Aladdin's ruin.
As he passed through the town he heard people talking
about a marvelous palace. "Forgive my ignorance," he
said, "what is this palace you speak of?"

"Have you not heard of Prince Aladdin's palace,"
was one man's reply, "the greatest wonder of the
world? I will direct you if you have a mind to see it."

The magician thanked the man and, having seen the
palace, knew that it had been raised by the genie of the
lamp, and he became half mad with rage. He determined to get hold of the lamp and again plunge Aladdin into the deepest poverty.

Unluckily, Aladdin had gone hunting for eight days,

which gave the magician plenty of time. He bought a dozen copper lamps, put them into a basket and went to the palace, crying, "New lamps for old!" and followed by a jeering crowd.

The Princess, sitting in the hall of four-and-twenty windows, sent a slave to find out what the noise was about. The slave came back laughing, so the Princess scolded her.

"Madam," replied the slave, "who can help laughing to see an old fool offering to exchange fine new lamps for old ones?"

Another slave, hearing this, said, "There is an old one on the cornice there which he can have."

Now this was the magic lamp, which Aladdin had left there, as he could not take it hunting with him. The Princess, not knowing its value, laughingly bade the slave take it and make the exchange. She went and said to the magician, "Give me a new lamp for this."

He snatched it and bade the slave take her choice, amid the jeers of the crowd. Little he cared, but left off crying his lamps and went beyond the city gates to a lonely place, where he remained till nightfall, when he pulled out the magic lamp and rubbed it. The genie appeared and at the magician's command carried him, together with the palace and the Princess in it, to a lonely place in Africa.

Next morning the Sultan looked from the window toward Aladdin's palace and rubbed his eyes, for it was gone. He sent for the Vizier and asked what had become of the palace. The Vizier was lost in astonishment. He again put it down to enchantment; and this time the Sultan believed him, sending thirty men on horseback to fetch Aladdin in chains. They met him as he was riding home, bound him and forced him to go with them on foot.

The people, however, who loved him, followed, armed, to see that he came to no harm. He was carried before the Sultan, who ordered the executioner to cut off his head. The executioner made Aladdin kneel, bandaged his eyes and raised his scimitar to strike. At that instant the Vizier, who saw that the crowds had forced their way into the courtyard and were scaling the walls to rescue Aladdin, called to the executioner to stay his hand. The people, indeed, looked so threatening that the Sultan gave way and ordered Aladdin to be unbound, and pardoned him in the sight of the crowd.

Aladdin begged to know what he had done.

"False wretch!" said the Sultan, "come hither," and showed him from the window the place where his palace had stood. Aladdin was so amazed that he could not say a word.

"Where is the palace and my daughter?" demanded the Sultan. "For the first I am not so deeply concerned, but my daughter I must have and you must find her or lose your head."

Aladdin begged for forty days in which to find her, promising, if he failed, to return and suffer death at the Sultan's pleasure. The Sultan granted his request, and Aladdin went forth sadly from the palace. For three days he wandered about like a madman, asking everyone what had become of his palace, but they only pitied him. He came to the banks of a river and knelt down to say his prayers before throwing himself in. In so doing he rubbed the magic ring he still wore. The genie he had seen in the cave appeared and asked his will.

"Save my life, genie," said Aladdin, "and bring my palace back."

"That is not in my power," said the genie. "I am only the slave of the ring; for that you must ask the slave of the lamp."

"Even so," said Aladdin, "but thou canst take me to the palace and set me down under my dear wife's window." He at once found himself in Africa, under the window of the Princess, where he fell asleep from sheer weariness.

He was awakened by the singing of the birds, and his heart was lighter. He saw plainly that all his misfortunes were owing to the loss of the lamp and vainly wondered who had robbed him of it.

That morning the Princess rose earlier than she had since she had been carried into Africa by the magician, whose company she was forced to endure once a day. She, however, treated him so harshly that he dared not live there altogether. As she was dressing, one of her women looked out and saw Aladdin. The Princess ran to open the window. Hearing her there, Aladdin looked up. She called him to come to her, and great was their joy at seeing each other again.

After he had kissed her, Aladdin said, "I beg of you, Princess, before we speak of anything else, for your own sake and mine, tell me what has become of an old lamp I left on the cornice in the hall of four-and-twenty windows, when I went hunting."

"Alas," she said, "I am the innocent cause of our sorrows," and told him of the exchange of the lamp.

"Now I know," cried Aladdin, "that we have to thank the African magician for all this! Where is the lamp?"

"He carries it about with him," said the Princess. "I know, for he pulled it out of his robe to show me. He wishes me to break my faith with you and marry him, saying that you were beheaded by my father's command. He is forever speaking ill of you, but I only reply by my tears. If I persist, I doubt not that he will use violence."

Aladdin comforted her and left her for a while. He changed clothes with the first person he met in the town, and after buying a certain powder returned to the Princess, who let him in by a little side door.

"Put on your most beautiful dress," he said to her, "and receive the magician with smiles. Lead him to believe that you have forgotten me. Invite him to sup with you and say you wish to taste the wine of his country. Now listen while I tell you what else to do."

She listened carefully to Aladdin and, when he left her, arrayed herself gaily for the first time since leaving Persia. She put on a belt and headdress of diamonds, and seeing in a glass that she looked more beautiful than ever, received the magician, saying to his great amazement, "I have made up my mind that Aladdin is dead and that all my tears will not bring him back to me, so I am resolved to mourn no more and therefore invite you to sup with me. But I am tired of the wines of Persia and therefore desire to taste those of Africa."

The magician flew to his cellar, and the Princess put the powder Aladdin had given her in her cup. When he returned she asked him to drink her health in the wine of Africa, handing him her cup in exchange for his as a sign she was reconciled to him.

Before drinking, the magician made a speech in praise of her beauty, but the Princess cut him short, saying, "Let us drink first, and you shall say what you will afterward." She set her cup only to her lips, while the magician drained his to the dregs and thereupon fell back, lifeless.

The Princess then opened the door to Aladdin and flung her arms around his neck, but Aladdin held her off, bidding her to leave him, as he had more to do. He then went to the dead magician, took the lamp out of his vest and bade the genie carry the palace back to Persia. This was done, and the Princess in her chamber felt only two slight shocks and little thought she was at home again.

The Sultan, who was sitting in his bedchamber mourning for his lost daughter, happened to look up and rubbed his eyes, for there stood the palace as before! He hastened forth, and Aladdin received him in the hall of the four-and-twenty windows, with the Princess at his side. Aladdin told him what had happened and showed him the dead body of the magician, that he might believe. A ten days' feast was proclaimed, and it seemed as if Aladdin might now live the rest of his life in peace, but it was not to be.

The African magician had a younger brother, who was, if possible, more wicked and cunning than the elder. He traveled to Persia to avenge his brother's death and went to visit a pious woman called Fatima, thinking she might be of use to him. He entered her cell and clapped a dagger to her breast, telling her to rise and do his bidding on pain of death. He changed clothes with her, colored his face like hers, covered it with her own veil and murdered her that she might tell no tales.

Then he went toward the palace of Aladdin, and all the people, thinking he was the holy woman, gathered around him, kissing his hands and begging his blessing.

When he reached the palace there was such a noise that the Princess bade her slave look out the window and ask what was the matter. The slave said it was the holy woman, curing people of their ailments by her touch, whereupon the Princess, who had long desired to see Fatima, sent for her.

On coming to the Princess, the magician offered up a prayer for her health and prosperity. When he had finished, the Princess made him sit by her and begged him to stay with her always. The false Fatima, who wished for nothing better, consented, but kept his veil down for fear of discovery.

The Princess showed him the hall and asked him what he thought of it.

"It is truly beautiful," said the false Fatima. "In my mind it wants but one thing."

"And what is that?" said the Princess.

"If only a roc's egg," replied he, "were hung up from the middle of this dome, it would be the wonder of the world."

After this the Princess could think of nothing but a roc's egg, and when Aladdin returned from hunting he found her in a very ill humor. He begged to know what was amiss, but she told him that all her pleasure in the hall was spoiled for the want of a roc's egg hanging from the dome.

"If that is all," replied Aladdin, "you shall soon be happy."

He left her and rubbed the lamp, and when the genie appeared, commanded him to bring a roc's egg.

The genie gave such a loud and terrible shriek that the hall shook. "Wretch," he cried, "is it not enough that I have done everything for you, but you must command me to bring my master and hang him up in the midst of this dome? You and your wife and your palace deserve to be burned to ashes for this request, but I know it does not come from you but from the brother of the African magician whom you destroyed. He is now in your palace disguised as the holy woman Fatima—whom he murdered. He it was who put that wish into your wife's head. Take care of yourself, for that man means to kill you." So saying, the genie disappeared.

Aladdin went back to the Princess, saying his head ached and requesting that the holy Fatima should be fetched to lay her hands on it. But when the magician came near, Aladdin, seizing his dagger, pierced him to the heart.

"What have you done?" cried the Princess. "You have killed the holy woman!"

"Not so," replied Aladdin, "but a wicked magician," and told her of how she had been deceived.

After this Aladdin and his wife lived in peace. He succeeded the Sultan when he died, and reigned for many years, leaving behind him a long line of kings.

ARABIAN NIGHTS, TRANSLATED BY ANTOINE GALLAND

THE THREE BEARS

ONCE UPON a time there were three Bears who lived together in a house of their own in a wood. One of them was a little, small, wee Bear; and one was a middle-sized Bear; and the other was a great, huge Bear. Each of the Bears had a porridge pot: a little pot for the little, small, wee Bear; and a middle-sized pot for the middle Bear; and a great pot for the great, huge Bear.

Each of the Bears had a chair to sit in: a little chair for the little, small, wee Bear; and a middle-sized chair for the middle Bear; and a great chair for the great, huge Bear. And they each had a bed to sleep in: a little bed for the little, small, wee Bear; and a middle-sized bed for the middle Bear; and a great bed for the great, huge Bear.

One day, after they had made the porridge for their breakfast and poured it into their porridge pots, they walked out into the wood while the porridge was cooling, so that they might not burn their mouths by beginning to eat it too soon. And while they were walking, a little girl called Goldilocks came to the house. First she looked in at the window and then she peeped in at the keyhole; and, seeing nobody in the house, she turned the handle of the door. The door was not fastened, because the Bears were good bears who never did anybody any harm, and never suspected that anybody would harm them. So Goldilocks opened the door and went in; and well pleased she was when she saw the porridge on the table. If she had been a thoughtful little girl, she would have waited till the Bears came home and then, perhaps, they would have asked her to breakfast; for they were good bears—a little rough, as the manner of bears is, but for all that very good-natured and hospitable. The porridge looked tempting, and little Goldilocks set about helping herself.

So first she tasted the porridge of the great, huge Bear, and that was too hot for her. And then she tasted the porridge of the middle Bear, and that was too cold for her. And then she went to the porridge of the little, small, wee Bear and tasted that; and that was neither too hot nor too cold, but just right, and she liked it so well that she ate it up.

Then Goldilocks sat down in the chair of the great, huge Bear, and that was too hard for her. And then she sat down in the chair of the middle Bear, and that was too soft for her. And then she sat down in the chair of the little, small, wee Bear, and that was neither too hard nor too soft, but just right. So she seated herself in it, and there she sat till the bottom of the chair fell out, and down she went plump onto the ground.

Then Goldilocks went upstairs into the bedchamber in which the Three Bears slept. And first she lay down upon the bed of the great, huge Bear, but that was too high at the head for her. And next she lay down upon the bed of the middle Bear, but that was too high at the foot for her. And then she lay down upon the bed of the little, small, wee Bear; and that was neither too high at the head nor at the foot, but just right. So Goldilocks covered herself up comfortably and lay there till she fell fast asleep.

By this time, the Three Bears thought their porridge would be cool enough; so they had come home to breakfast. Now Goldilocks had left the spoon of the great, huge Bear standing in his porridge.

SOMEBODY HAS BEEN AT MY PORRIDGE!

said the great, huge Bear, in his great, rough, gruff voice.

And when the middle Bear looked at hers, she saw that the spoon was standing in it, too.

SOMEBODY HAS BEEN AT MY PORRIDGE!

said the middle Bear, in her middle voice.

Then the little, small, wee Bear looked at his, and there was the spoon in the porridge pot, but the porridge was all gone.

SOMEBODY HAS BEEN AT MY PORRIDGE, AND HAS EATEN IT ALL UP!

said the little, small, wee Bear, in his little, small, wee voice.

At this, the Three Bears, seeing that someone had entered their house and had eaten up the little, small, wee Bear's breakfast, began to look about the room. Now Goldilocks had forgotten to put the hard cushion straight when she rose from the chair of the great, huge Bear.

SOMEBODY HAS BEEN SITTING IN MY CHAIR!

said the great, huge Bear, in his great, rough, gruff voice.

And Goldilocks had flattened down the soft cushion of the middle Bear.

SOMEBODY HAS BEEN SITTING IN MY CHAIR!

said the middle Bear, in her middle voice.

And you know what Goldilocks had done to the third chair.

SOMEBODY HAS BEEN SITTING IN MY CHAIR, AND HAS SAT THE BOTTOM OUT OF IT!

said the little, small, wee Bear, in his little, small, wee voice.

Then the Three Bears thought it necessary that they should make further search; so they went upstairs into their bedchamber. Now Goldilocks had pulled the pillow of the great, huge Bear out of its place—

See page 530

529

SOMEBODY HAS BEEN LYING IN MY BED!

said the great, huge Bear, in his great, rough, gruff voice.

And Goldilocks had pulled the bolster of the middle Bear's bed out of its place.

SOMEBODY HAS BEEN LYING IN MY BED!

said the middle Bear, in her middle voice.

And when the little, small, wee Bear came to look at his bed, there was the bolster in its place; and the pillow in its place upon the bolster; and upon the pillow was the head of Goldilocks—which was not in its place at all, for she had no business there.

SOMEBODY HAS BEEN LYING IN MY BED—AND HERE SHE IS!

said the little, small, wee Bear, in his little, small, wee voice.

Goldilocks had heard in her sleep the great, rough, gruff voice of the great, huge Bear, and the middle voice of the middle Bear, but only as if she had heard someone speaking in a dream. But when she heard the little, small, wee voice of the little, small, wee Bear, it was so sharp and so shrill that it awakened her at once. Up she started; and when she saw the Three Bears on one side of the bed she tumbled herself out at the other, and ran to the window.

Now the window was open, because the Bears, like

the good, tidy bears that they were, always opened their bedchamber window when they got up in the morning. Out Goldilocks jumped, and ran through the woods as fast as she could run—never looking behind her; and what happened to her afterward I cannot tell you. But the Three Bears never saw anything more of her again.

ROBERT SOUTHEY,
L. LESLIE BROOKE COLLECTION

RUMPELSTILTZKIN

THERE WAS once upon a time a poor miller who had a very beautiful daughter. It happened one day that he had an audience with the King, and in order to appear a person of some importance he told His Majesty that he had a daughter who could spin straw into gold. "Now that is certainly a talent worth having," said the King to the miller. "If your daughter is as clever as you say she is, bring her to my palace tomorrow morning."

When the girl arrived the next day, the King led her into a room full of straw, gave her a spinning wheel and spindle and said, "Set to work and spin all night till early dawn, and if by that time you have not spun the straw into gold you shall die."

Then he closed the door behind him and left her alone inside.

So the poor miller's daughter sat down and did not know what in the world she was to do. She had not the least idea of how to spin straw into gold and at last became so miserable that she began to cry.

Suddenly the door opened, and in stepped a tiny little man who said: "Good evening, Miss Miller-Maid. Why are you crying so bitterly?"

"Oh," answered the girl, "I have to spin straw into gold for the King and I haven't a notion how it is done."

"What will you give me if I spin it for you?" asked the manikin.

"My necklace," replied the girl.

The little man took the necklace, sat himself down at the wheel, and whir, whir, whir, the wheel went around three times, and the bobbin was full. Then he put on another, and whir, whir, whir, the wheel went around three times, and the second too was full. And so it went on till the morning, when the whole room full of straw was spun away, and all the bobbins were full of gold.

As soon as the sun rose, the King came, and when he perceived the gold he was astonished and delighted, but seeing it only made him more greedy than ever for the precious metal. He had the miller's daughter put into another room full of straw, much bigger than the first, and bade her, if she valued her life, to spin it all into gold before the following morning.

The girl did not know what to do and began to cry. Then the door opened as before, and the tiny little man appeared, and said: "What will you give me if I spin the straw into gold for you?"

"The ring from my finger," answered the girl.

The manikin took the ring, and whir, around went the spinning wheel again, and when the sun rose he had spun all the straw into glittering gold. The King was pleased beyond measure at the sight, but he was still not satisfied, and he had the miller's daughter brought into a yet bigger room full of straw.

"You must spin all this away in the night," he said, "but if you succeed this time you shall become my wife." She's only a miller's daughter, he thought, but I could not find a richer wife if I were to search the whole world over.

When the girl was alone the little man appeared for the third time and said, "What will you give me if I spin the straw for you once again?"

"I've nothing more to give," answered the girl.

"Then promise me when you are Queen to give me your first child."

Who knows what may happen before that? thought

the miller's daughter, and, besides, she saw no other way out. So she promised the manikin what he demanded, and he set to work once more and spun the straw into gold. When the King came in the morning and found everything as he had desired, he straightway made her his wife, and the miller's daughter became a queen.

When a year had passed, a beautiful son was born to her. She had forgotten about the little man, till one day he suddenly stepped into her room and said, "Now give me what you promised."

The Queen was terribly upset, and offered the little man all the riches in her kingdom if he would only leave her the child.

But the manikin said, "No, a living creature is dearer to me than the finest treasures in the world." The poor Queen began to cry and sob so bitterly that the little man was sorry for her, and said: "I'll give you three days to guess my name, and if you discover it in that time you may keep your child."

Then the Queen pondered the whole night over all of the names she had ever heard and sent a messenger to scour the land to pick up far and near any names he should come across. When the little man arrived on the following day she began with Caspar, Melchior, Balthazar and every other name she had ever heard, but at each one the manikin called out, "That is not my name."

See page 536

535

The next day she sent to inquire the names of all the people in the neighborhood and had a long list of the most uncommon and extraordinary ready to ask the little man.

"Is your name, perhaps, Sheepshanks, Cruickshanks, Spindleshanks?"

But he always replied, "That is not my name."

On the third day the messenger returned and announced: "I have not been able to find any new names; but as I came upon a high hill around the corner of the wood, where the foxes and hares bid each other good night, I saw a little house, and in front of the house burned a fire, and around the fire danced the most grotesque little man, hopping on one leg and crying:

> Tomorrow I brew, today I bake,
> And then the child away I'll take;
> For little deems my royal dame
> That Rumpelstiltzkin is my name!"

Imagine the Queen's delight at hearing the name— and when the little man stepped in shortly afterward and asked, "Now, my Lady Queen, what is my name?" she asked first: "Is your name Conrad?"

"No."

"Is your name Harry?"

"No."

"Is your name, perhaps, Rumpelstiltzkin?"

"Some demon has told you that! Some demon has told you that!" screamed the little man, and in his rage he drove his right foot so far into the ground that his leg sank in up to his waist. Then in a passion he seized his left foot with both of his hands and tore himself in two.

JAKOB AND WILHELM GRIMM, TRANSLATED BY MAY SELLAR

THE GOLDEN-HEADED FISH

ONCE UPON a time there lived in Egypt a King who had lost his sight from a bad illness. Of course he was very unhappy, and became more so as months passed and all the best doctors in the land were unable to cure him. The poor man grew so thin from misery that everyone thought he was going to die, and the Prince, his only son, thought so too. Great, therefore, was the rejoicing throughout Egypt when a traveler down the river Nile declared he was court physician to the king of a far country and would gladly, if he was allowed, examine the eyes of the blind man.

He was at once admitted into the royal presence and, after a few minutes of careful study, announced that the King's case, though very serious, was not entirely hopeless.

"Somewhere in the Great Sea," he said to the King, "there exists a golden-headed fish. If you can manage to catch this creature and bring it to me, I will prepare an ointment from its blood which will restore your sight. For a hundred days I will wait here, but if at the end of that time the fish should still not be caught, I must return to my own master."

The next morning the young Prince set forth in quest of the fish, taking with him a hundred men, each carrying a net. A little fleet of boats was awaiting them, and in these they sailed to the middle of the Great Sea.

For three months and more, they labored diligently from sunrise to sunset, but though they caught large multitudes of fishes not one of them possessed a golden head.

"It is quite useless now," said the Prince on the very last night, "for even if we find it this evening, the hundred days will be over in an hour, and long before we could reach the Egyptian capital the doctor will be on his way home. Still, I will go out and cast the net once more myself."

And the Prince did this, and at the very moment that the hundred days given him were up, he drew in his net and found the golden-headed fish entangled in its meshes.

"Success has come, but as often happens, it is too late," murmured the young man, who had studied in the schools of philosophy. "All the same, put the fish in that vessel full of water, and we will take it back. Then my father will know that we have done what we could." But when he drew near the fish, it looked up at him with such piteous eyes that he could not make up his mind to condemn it to death. For he knew well that, though the doctors of his own country were ignorant of the secret of the ointment, they would do everything in their power to extract something from the fish's blood.

He picked up the prize of so much labor and threw it back into the sea and then began his journey home to the palace. When at last the Prince reached it, he found the King in a high fever, caused by his disappointment, and he refused to believe the story told him by his son.

"Your head shall pay for it! Your head shall pay for it!" cried he, and bade his courtiers instantly summon the executioner to the palace.

Somebody ran at once to the Queen and told her of the King's order. She put common clothes on the Prince, filled his pockets with gold and hurried him on board a ship which was sailing that very night for a distant island.

"Your father will repent of this some day, and then he will be thankful to know that you are still alive," said she to her son. "But one last counsel will I give you: take no man into your service who desires to be paid every month."

The young Prince thought this advice rather odd. If a servant had to be paid anyhow, he did not understand what difference it could make whether it was by the year or by the month. However, he had many times learned that his mother was wiser than he, so he promised obedience.

After a voyage of several weeks, the Prince arrived at the island of which his mother had spoken. It was full of hills and woods and flowers, and beautiful white houses stood everywhere in gardens.

What a charming spot to live in, thought the Prince, and he lost no time in buying one of the prettiest of the dwellings.

Then servants came pressing to offer their services; but as they all declared that they must have payment at the end of every month, the young man declined to hire them.

At length, an Arab appeared one morning, begging the Prince to engage him.

"And what wages do you ask?" inquired the Prince, when he had questioned the newcomer and found him suitable.

"I do not want money," answered the Arab. "At

the end of a year you can see what my services are worth to you and can pay me in whatever way you like." The young man was pleased and took the Arab for his servant.

Now, although no one would have guessed it from the look of the part of the island where the Prince had landed, the other side was a complete desert, owing to the ravages of a horrible sea monster which devoured all the corn and cattle. The Governor had sent bands of soldiers to lie in wait for the creature in order to kill it, but, somehow, none ever happened to be awake at the moment that the ravages were committed. It was in vain that the sleepy soldiers had been punished severely—the same thing invariably occurred next time a group went on watch. At last, heralds went throughout the island to offer a great reward to the man who could slay the sea-beast.

As soon as the Arab heard the news he went straight to the Governor's palace. "If my master can succeed in killing the monster, what reward will you give him?" asked he.

"My daughter and anything besides that he chooses," answered the Governor.

The Arab shook his head.

"Give him your daughter and keep your wealth," said he. "But, henceforth, let her share in your gains, whatever they are."

"It is well," replied the Governor, and ordered a

deed to be prepared, which was signed by both of the men.

That night the Arab stole down to the shore to watch, but before setting out, he had rubbed himself with an oil which made his skin smart so badly that there was no chance of his going to sleep as the soldiers had done. Then he hid himself behind a large rock and waited. By and by a swell seemed to rise on the water and, after a few minutes, a hideous monster—part bird, part beast and part serpent—stepped noiselessly onto the rocks. It walked stealthily up toward the fields, but the Arab was ready for it and, when it passed, plunged his dagger into the soft flesh behind one ear. The creature staggered, gave a loud cry and then rolled over dead.

The Arab watched for a little while, in order to make sure there was no life left in his enemy. Since the huge body remained quite still, he quit his hiding place and cut off its ears. These he carried to his master, bidding him show them to the Governor and declare that he himself, and no other, had killed the monster.

"But it was you, and not I, who slew him," objected the Prince.

"Never mind; do what I bid you. I have a reason for it," answered the Arab. And, although the young man did not like taking credit for what he had not done, he finally gave in.

The Governor was so delighted at the news that he begged the Prince to marry his daughter that very day; but the Prince refused, saying that all he desired was a ship which would carry him to see the world. Of course this was granted him at once, and when he and his faithful Arab embarked, they found, heaped up in the vessel, stores of diamonds and many other precious stones which the grateful Governor had placed there for him.

So they sailed and they sailed and they sailed, and at length they reached the shores of a great kingdom. Leaving the Prince on board, the Arab went into the town to find out what sort of place it was. After some hours he returned, saying he had heard that the King's daughter was the most beautiful princess in the world and that the Prince would do well to ask for her hand in marriage.

The Prince listened to this advice and, taking some of the finest necklaces given him by the Governor, he mounted a splendid horse which the Arab had bought for him. He rode up to the palace, closely followed by his faithful attendant.

The strange King happened to be in a good humor, and they were readily admitted to his presence. Laying down his offerings on the steps of the throne, the Prince requested the King to grant him his daughter in marriage.

The monarch listened to him in silence, but finally

answered, "Young man, I will give you my daughter to wed, if that is your wish; but first I must tell you that she has already gone through the marriage ceremony with a hundred and ninety young men, and not one of them lived more than twelve hours. I advise you to think, while there is yet time."

The Prince was so frightened that he very nearly went back to his ship without any more words. But just as he was about to withdraw his proposal, the Arab whispered to him: "Fear nothing the King says, but take her."

"The luck must change some time," he said at last, "and who would not risk his head for the hand of the peerless Princess?"

"As you will," replied the King. "Since you wish it, I will give orders for the marriage to be celebrated tonight."

And so it was done. After the ceremony was performed the bride and bridegroom retired to their own apartment to sup by themselves, for such was the custom of the country. The moon shone bright, and the Prince walked to the window to look over the river and upon the distant hills, when his gaze suddenly fell on a silken shroud neatly laid out on a couch, with his name embroidered in gold thread across the front; for this was the pleasure of the King.

Horrified at the spectacle, he turned his head away, and this time his glance rested on a group of men digging busily beneath the window. It was a strange hour for anyone to be at work, and what was the hole for? It was a curious shape, so long and narrow, almost like——Ah, yes, that was what it was! It was his grave they were digging!

The shock of the discovery rendered him speechless, yet he stood fascinated and unable to move. At this moment a small black snake darted from the mouth of the Princess, who was seated at the table, and wriggled quickly toward him. But the Arab had hidden himself in the room and was secretly watching for something of the sort to happen. Seizing the serpent with a pair of pincers he had been holding in his left hand, he cut off its head with a sharp dagger.

The King could hardly believe his eyes when, early the next morning, his new son-in-law craved an audience with His Majesty.

"What, you?" he cried, as the young man entered his presence.

"Yes, I. Why not?" asked the bridegroom, who thought it best to pretend not to know anything that had occurred. "You remember I told you that the luck must turn at last, and so it has. But I came to ask whether you would be so kind as to bid the gardeners fill up a great hole right underneath my window; it spoils the view."

"Oh, certainly. Yes, of course it shall be done!" stammered the King. "Is there anything else?"

"No, nothing, thank you," replied the Prince, as he bowed and withdrew.

Now, from the moment the Arab cut off the snake's head, the spell, or enchantment—whatever it was— seemed to have been taken off the Princess, and she lived very happily with her husband. The days passed swiftly in hunting in the forests or sailing on the broad river that flowed past the palace, and when night fell she would sing to her harp, or the Prince would tell tales of his own country.

One evening, a man in strange garb, with a face burned brown by the sun, arrived at court. He asked to see the bridegroom and, falling on his face before the Prince, announced that he was a messenger sent by the Queen of Egypt, proclaiming him King in succession to his father, who was dead.

"Her Majesty begs you to set forth without delay, and your bride also, as the affairs of the kingdom are somewhat in disorder," ended the messenger.

Then the young man hastened to seek an audience with his father-in-law, who was delighted to find that his daughter's husband was not merely the Governor of a province, as he had supposed, but the King of a powerful country. He at once ordered a splendid ship to be made ready for the young couple, and in a week's time rode down to the harbor to bid farewell to the new ruler and his bride.

In spite of her grief for the dead King, the Queen

was overjoyed to welcome her son home, and commanded the palace to be hung with colorful banners to honor his bride. The people expected great things from their new sovereign, for they had suffered much under the harsh rule of the old one, and crowds presented themselves every morning with petitions which they hoped to persuade the King to grant.

Truly, the new King had enough to keep him busy; but he was very happy for all that, till one night the Arab came to him and begged permission to return to his own land.

Filled with dismay, the young man said, "Leave me? Do you really wish to leave me?"

Sadly, the Arab bowed his head. "No, my master, never could I wish to leave you! But I have received a summons, and I dare not disobey it."

The young King was silent, trying to choke down the grief which he felt at the thought of losing his faithful servant.

"Well, I must not try to keep you," he faltered at last. "That would be a poor return for everything you have done for me! Everything I have is yours; take what you will, for without you I should long ago have been dead!"

"And without you, I too should long ago have been dead," answered the Arab. "For I am the golden-headed fish."

ADAPTED BY FRÉDÉRIC MACLER, ANDREW LANG COLLECTION

HANSEL AND GRETEL

ONCE UPON a time there dwelt on the outskirts of a large forest a poor wood-cutter with his wife and two children; the boy was called Hansel and the girl Gretel. They had always little enough to live on, and once, when there was a great famine in the land, the woodcutter could not even provide them with daily bread.

One night, as he was tossing about in bed, full of cares and worry, he sighed and said to his wife, "What is to become of us? How are we to support our poor children, now that we have nothing more left even for ourselves?"

"Early tomorrow morning," answered the woman, who was the children's stepmother, "we will take Hansel and Gretel out into the thickest part of the woods. There we shall light a fire for them, give them each a piece of bread and go on to our work, leaving them alone. They will not be able to find their way home, and we shall thus be rid of them."

"No, wife," said her husband, "that I won't do. How could I find it in my heart to leave my children alone in the woods? The wild beasts would come and tear them to pieces."

"Oh," said she, "then we must all four die of hunger, and you may just as well go and prepare the boards for our coffins." And she left him no peace till he had consented.

"But I feel very sorry for the poor children just the same," said the husband.

The children, too, had not been able to sleep for hunger, and they overheard what their stepmother and father had said. Gretel wept bitterly, but Hansel whispered, "Don't fret, little Gretel. I will find a way to save us."

When the old people had fallen asleep he got up, slipped on his coat, opened the back door and stole out. The moon was shining brightly, and the white pebbles in front of the house glittered like bits of silver.

Hansel bent down and filled his pocket with as many of the stones as he could. Then he went back and said to Gretel, "Be comforted, dear sister, and go to sleep. God will not desert us." And he lay down in bed again.

At daybreak, even before the sun was up, the woman came and woke the two children. "Get up, you lazy things. We are going to the forest this morning to gather wood."

She gave them each a bit of bread and said, "There's

something for your luncheon, but do not eat it before, for it is all you will get."

Gretel put the bread into her apron pocket, as Hansel had the stones in his pocket. Then they set out together on the way to the forest.

After they had walked for a little while, Hansel stood still and looked back at the house, and this he did again and again.

His father observed him, and asked, "Hansel, what are you gazing at, and why do you always lag behind? Take care, and do not lose your footing."

"Oh, Father," said Hansel, "I am looking back at my white kitten, which is sitting on the roof, waving me a farewell."

The woman exclaimed, "What a donkey you are! That isn't your kitten, that is the morning sun shining on the chimney."

But Hansel had not been looking back at his kitten; he had been dropping the white pebbles out of his pocket onto the path.

When they reached the middle of the forest the father said, "Now, children, go and find some wood, and I will light a fire."

Hansel and Gretel heaped up brushwood till they had made a pile nearly the size of a small hill. The brushwood was set alight, and when the flames leaped high the woman said: "Now lie down by the fire, children, and rest yourselves. We are going into the forest to cut wood; when we have finished we will come back and fetch you."

Hansel and Gretel sat down beside the fire, and at midday ate their little bits of bread. They thought they heard the strokes of their father's axe close by. It was no axe they heard, however, but a bough on a dead tree blown about by the wind. And when they had sat for a long time their eyes closed with fatigue and they fell fast asleep. When they awoke at last they found it was pitch dark.

Gretel began to cry, and said, "How are we ever to get out of the wood?"

But Hansel comforted her. "Wait a bit," he said, "till the moon is up, and then we will find our way."

And when the full moon had risen he took his sister by the hand and followed the pebbles, which shone like silver and showed them the path. They walked all through the night, and at daybreak reached their father's house again. They knocked at the door and, when the woman opened it, she exclaimed, "You naughty children, what a long time you have slept in the forest! We thought you were never coming back." But the father rejoiced, for his conscience had tormented him for leaving his children.

Not long afterward there was again great scarcity in the land, and the children heard the woman say, "Everything is eaten up once more; we have only half a loaf of bread in the house. We shall lead them deeper into the woods this time so they cannot find their way out again."

The father's heart was filled with sadness as he pleaded with the woman, "Surely it would be better to share the last bite with one's children!" But if a man yields once he's done for.

When the old people were asleep Hansel wanted to go out and pick up pebbles again, as he had done the first time. The woman had barred the door, though, and he could not get out. But he consoled his little sister, and said, "Don't cry, Gretel. Sleep peacefully, for God is sure to help us."

At early dawn the woman came and made the children get up. They received their bit of bread, but it was even smaller than the time before. On the way to the woods Hansel crumbled it in his pocket, and every few minutes he stood still and dropped a crumb on the ground.

"Hansel, why are you stopping and looking about you?" said the father.

"I'm looking back at my little pigeon, which is sitting on the roof waving me a farewell," answered Hansel.

"That isn't your pigeon," said the woman, "it is the morning sun glittering on the chimney."

But Hansel gradually made a trail of crumbs to guide them home.

The woman led the children still deeper into the

forest, farther than they had ever been in their lives. Then a big fire was lit again, and she said, "Just sit down, children, and if you are tired you can sleep a bit. Your father and I are going into the forest to cut some wood and when evening comes we shall come back to fetch you."

At midday Gretel divided her bread with Hansel, for he had strewn his all along their path. Then they fell asleep, and it was evening, but nobody came for the poor children. They did not awake till it was pitch dark, and Hansel comforted his sister, saying, "Only wait, Gretel. When the moon rises, we shall see the crumbs I scattered along the path. They will show us the way back to the house."

When the moon rose they searched but found no crumbs, for the thousands of birds that fly about the woods and fields had picked them up. "Never mind," said Hansel, "we shall find a way out."

They wandered about the whole night, and the next day, from morning till evening, but they could not find a path out of the wood. They were very hungry, for they had eaten nothing but a few berries. And at last they were so tired they lay down under a tree and fell sound asleep.

On the third morning after they had left their father's house they were still wandering, and now they felt that if help did not come soon they must perish. At midday they saw a beautiful little snow-white bird sitting on a branch, which was singing so sweetly that they stopped to listen. When its song was finished it flapped its wings and flew on in front of them. They followed it and came to a little house, on the roof of which the bird perched. When they were quite near they saw that the cottage was made of gingerbread and covered with cakes, while the windows were made of transparent sugar.

"Now we can have a real feast," said Hansel. He reached up and broke off a bit of the roof to see what it was like, and Gretel went to a window and began to nibble at it. Thereupon a shrill voice called out from the room inside:

> Nibble, nibble, little mouse,
> Who is nibbling at my house?

The children answered:

> 'Tis Heaven's own child,
> The tempest wild,

and went on eating. Hansel, who thoroughly enjoyed the roof, tore down a big bit of it, while Gretel pushed out a whole round windowpane and sat down, the better to enjoy it. Suddenly the door opened, and an old woman leaning on a staff hobbled out. Hansel and Gretel were so terrified that they dropped what they had in their hands. But the old woman shook her head and said, "Oh, ho, you dear children! What has

brought you here? Just come in and stay with me; no harm shall befall you." She led them into the house and laid a sumptuous dinner before them—milk and sugared pancakes, pears, apples and nuts. After they had eaten, two beautiful little white beds were prepared for them, and when Hansel and Gretel lay down in them they felt as if they were in Heaven.

The old woman had appeared to be most friendly, but she was really an old witch. When anyone came into her power she cooked and ate him and held a regular feast day. Now witches have red eyes and cannot see far, but, like beasts, they have a keen sense of smell and know when human beings are nearby. When Hansel and Gretel fell into this witch's hands, she laughed maliciously and said, "I have them now. They cannot escape me."

Early in the morning, before the children were awake, she rose, and when she saw them both sleeping so peacefully, with their round, rosy cheeks, she muttered to herself, "They will make a dainty dish." Then she seized Hansel, carried him into a little stable and barred the door on him. He might scream as much as he liked; it would do him no good.

Then she went to Gretel, shook her awake roughly and cried, "Get up, you lazybones, fetch water and cook something for your brother. When he is fat I shall eat him." Gretel began to cry bitterly, but it was no use; she had to do what the witch bade her.

So the best food was cooked for poor Hansel, but Gretel got nothing but crab shells. Every morning the old woman hobbled out to the stable and cried, "Hansel, put out your finger that I may feel if you are getting fat or not."

But Hansel always stretched out a bone, and the old woman, because of her red eyes, never knew the difference and, always thinking it was Hansel's finger, wondered why he fattened so slowly.

When four weeks passed and Hansel still remained thin, she lost patience and determined to wait no longer. "Here! Gretel," she called to the girl, "be quick and get some water. Hansel may be fat or thin, I'm going to cook him tomorrow."

Oh, how the poor little sister sobbed as she carried the water, and how the tears rolled down her cheeks! "Kind Heaven, help us now!" she cried. "If only the wild beasts in the forest had eaten us, then at least we should have died together."

"Keep quiet," said the old witch, "crying won't help you."

That morning Gretel, as usual, had to hang up the kettle full of water and light the fire. "First we shall bake," said the old woman. "I have heated the oven and kneaded the dough." She pushed Gretel toward the oven. "Look in," said the witch, "and see if it is properly heated so we can shove in the bread." For when she had Gretel near the oven she meant to push her in and close the door and let the girl bake, that she might eat her up too.

But Gretel knew what the old witch was up to, and said, "I do not know how I am to do it. How do I get my head in the oven?"

"You silly goose," said the witch, "the opening is big enough. See, I could get in myself," and she crawled toward it and poked her head into the oven. Then Gretel gave her a shove that sent her right in. She shut the iron door and drew the bolt. Gracious! How the witch yelled! It was quite horrible, but Gretel fled, and the wretched old woman was left there to perish miserably.

Gretel flew straight to Hansel, opened the little stable door and cried, "Hansel, we are free. The old witch is dead." How they rejoiced and fell on each other's necks and jumped for joy and kissed one another! As they no longer had any cause for fear, they went into the witch's house and there they found, in every corner of the room, boxes with pearls and precious stones.

"These are even better than pebbles," said Hansel, and crammed his pockets full of them.

"I, too, will bring something home." And Gretel filled her apron.

"But now," said Hansel, "let us go well away from the witch's forest."

When they had wandered about for some hours they

came to a big lake. "We cannot get over," said Hansel. "I see no bridge of any sort or kind."

"Yes, and there is no ferryboat either," answered Gretel. "But look, there swims a white duck; if I ask her she will help us." And she called out:

> Here are two children, mournful very,
> Seeing neither bridge nor ferry;
> Take us upon your downy white back,
> And row us over, quack, quack, quack!

The duck swam toward them, and Hansel got on her back and bade his sister sit beside him. "No," answered Gretel, "we should be too heavy a load for the duck. She shall carry us across separately." The good bird did this, and when they were landed safely on the other side and had gone on for a while, the wood became more and more familiar to them, and at length they saw their father's house in the distance. Then they set off at a run and, bounding into the front room, fell on their father's neck. The man had not passed a happy hour since he left them in the woods, and the woman had died. Gretel shook out her apron, and the pearls and precious stones rolled about the room, and Hansel threw down one handful after another from his pocket.

Thus all their troubles were ended, and they all lived happily ever afterward.

JAKOB AND WILHELM GRIMM, TRANSLATED BY MAY SELLAR

THE BRAVE LITTLE TAILOR

A TAILOR SAT in his work-
room one morning, stitching away busily at a coat for
the Lord Mayor. He whistled and sang so gaily that all
the little boys who passed the shop on their way to
school thought what a fine thing it was to be a tailor,
and told one another that when they grew up they
would be tailors, too.

"How hungry I feel, to be sure!" cried the little
man at last. "But I'm far too busy to trouble about
eating. I must finish His Lordship's coat before I touch
a morsel of food," and he broke once more into a
merry song.

"Fine new jam for sale!" sang out an old woman
as she walked along the street.

"Jam! I can't resist such a treat," said the tailor,
and, running to the door, he shouted: "This way,
please! Show me a pot of your very finest jam."

The woman handed him jar after jar, but the tailor
found fault with them all. At last he hit upon some
jam to his liking.

"And how many pounds will you take, sir?"

"I'll take four ounces," he replied in a solemn tone, "and mind you give me a good weight."

The old woman was very angry, for she had expected to sell several pounds, at least; and she went off grumbling after she had weighed out the four ounces.

"Now for some food!" cried the little man, taking a loaf of bread from the cupboard as he spoke. He cut a huge slice and spread the jam on half an inch thick; then he suddenly remembered his work.

"It will never do to get jam on the Lord Mayor's fine coat," said he, "so I'll finish it before I take even one bite."

He picked up his work again, and his needle flew in and out like lightning.

I am afraid that the Lord Mayor later found some stitches in his garment that were almost a quarter of an inch long.

The tailor glanced at his slice of bread and jam once or twice, but when he looked the third time it was covered with flies, and a fine feast they were having from it.

This was too much for the little fellow. Up he jumped, crying, "So you think I provide bread and jam for you? Well, we'll soon see! Take that!" and he struck the flies such a heavy blow with a duster that no fewer than seven lay dead upon the table, while the others flew up hastily to the ceiling.

"Seven at one blow!" said the little man with great

pride. "Such a brave deed ought to be known all over the town, and it won't be my fault if folks fail to hear about it."

So he cut out a wide belt, and stitched on it in big golden letters the words "Seven at one blow." When this was done he put it on, crying, "I'm destined to be something better than a tailor, it's quite clear. I'm one of the world's great heroes, and I'll be off at once to seek my fortune."

He glanced around the cottage, but there was nothing of value to take with him. The only thing he possessed in the world was a small cheese. "You may as well come, too," said he, stowing away the cheese in his pocket, "and now I'll be on my way."

When he got into the street the neighbors all crowded around him to read the words on his belt. "Seven at one blow!" said they to one another. "What a blessing he's going! It wouldn't be safe to have a man about who could kill seven of us at one stroke."

You see, they didn't know that the tailor had only killed flies; they took it to mean men.

He jogged along for some miles until he came to a hedge where a little bird was caught in the branches. "Come with me," said the tailor. "I'll have you to keep my cheese company." So he caught the bird and put it carefully into his pocket with the cheese.

Soon he reached a lofty mountain, and he made up his mind to climb it and see what was happening on the other side. When he reached the top, there stood a huge giant, gazing down into the valley below.

"Good day," said the tailor.

The giant turned around, and seeing nobody but the little tailor there, he cried with scorn, "And what might you be doing here, might I ask? You'd best move along at once."

"Not so fast, my friend," said the little man, showing the giant his belt. "Read this."

"Seven at one blow," read the giant, and he began to wish he'd been more civil.

"Well, I'm sure nobody would think it to look at you," he replied. "But since you are so clever, do this," and he picked up a stone and squeezed it until water ran out.

"Do that! Why, it's mere child's play to me," and the tailor produced his cheese and squeezed it until the whey ran from it. "Now who is cleverer?" he asked. "You see, I can squeeze milk from a stone, while you get only water."

The giant was too surprised to utter a word for a few minutes. Then, taking up another stone, he threw it so high into the air that for a moment they weren't able to see where it went; then down it fell to the ground.

"Good!" said the tailor. "But I'll throw a stone that won't come back at all."

Taking the little bird from his pocket, he threw it

into the air, and the bird, glad to get away, flew right off and never returned.

This sort of thing didn't suit the giant at all, for he wasn't used to being beaten by anyone. "Here's something you'll never manage," said he. "Just come and help me to carry this fallen oak tree for a few miles."

"Delighted!" said the tailor. "I'll take the end with the branches, for it's sure to be heavier."

"Agreed," replied the giant, and he lifted the heavy trunk onto his shoulder, while the tailor climbed up among the branches at the other end and he sang as loud as he could, as though carrying a tree was but nothing to him.

The poor giant, who was holding the tree trunk and the little tailor as well, soon grew tired. "I'm going to drop it!" he shouted, and the tailor jumped down from the branches and pretended he had been helping all the time.

"The idea of a man your size finding a tree too heavy to carry!" laughed the little tailor.

"You are a clever fellow, and no mistake," replied the giant, "and if you'll only come and spend the night in our cave, we shall be delighted to have you."

"I shall have great pleasure in coming, my friend," answered the little tailor, and together they set off for the giant's home.

There were seven other giants in the cave, and each one of them was eating a roasted pig for his supper.

They gave the little man some food, and then showed him a bed in which he might pass the night. It was so big that after tossing about in it for half an hour the tailor thought he would be more comfortable if he slept in the corner, so he crept out of bed without being noticed.

In the middle of the night the giant stole up to the bed where he thought the little man was fast asleep. Taking a big bar of iron, he struck such a heavy blow at it that he roused all the other giants. "Keep quiet, friends," said he. "I've just killed the little scamp."

The tailor made his escape as soon as possible, and he journeyed on for many miles until he began to feel very tired. So he lay down under a tree and fell fast asleep. When he awoke, he found a big crowd of people standing around him. Up walked one very wise-looking old man, who was really the prime minister of the kingdom there. "Is it true that you have killed seven at one blow?" he asked.

"It is a fact," answered the little tailor.

"Then come with me to the King, my friend, for he's been searching for a brave man like you for some time past. You will be made captain of his army, and the King will give you a fine house to live in."

"That I will," replied the little man. "It is just the sort of thing that will suit me, and I'll come at once."

He hadn't been in the King's service long before everyone grew jealous of him. The soldiers were afraid that if they offended him he would make short work of them all, while the members of the King's household didn't fancy the idea of making such a fuss over a stranger.

So the soldiers went in a body to the King and asked that another captain be assigned to them, for they were afraid of this one. The King did not like to refuse, lest they would desert, and yet he did not dare get rid of the captain, in case such a strong and brave man should try to have his revenge.

At last the King hit upon a plan. In some woods close by, there lived two giants who were the terror of the countryside. They robbed travelers who were passing through, and if any resistance was offered they killed the men on the spot.

Sending for the little tailor, the King said, "Knowing you to be the bravest man in my kingdom, I want to ask a favor of you. If you will kill these two giants and bring me back proof that they are dead, you shall marry the Princess, my daughter, and have half my kingdom. You shall take one hundred men to help you, and you are to set off at once."

"One hundred men, Your Majesty! Pray, what do I want with one hundred men? If I can kill seven at one blow, I needn't be afraid of two. I'll kill them fast enough, never fear."

The tailor chose ten strong men and told them to await him on the border of the woods, while he went on alone. He could hear the giants snoring for half an hour before he reached them, so he knew in which direction to go.

He found the pair fast asleep under a tree, so he filled his pockets with stones and climbed up into the branches above their heads. He began to pelt one of the giants with the missiles, until after a few minutes he awoke. Giving the other a rough push, the giant cried, "If you dare to strike me like that again, I'll know the reason why."

"I didn't touch you," said the other giant crossly, and they were soon fast asleep once more.

Then the tailor threw stones at the other giant, and soon he awoke as the first one had done. "What did you throw that at me for?" said he.

"You are dreaming," answered the other, "I didn't throw anything."

No sooner were they fast asleep again, than the little man began to pelt the two of them afresh.

Up they both sprang and, seizing each other, they began to fight in earnest. Not content with using their fists, they tore up nearby trees by the roots and beat each other with these until very soon the pair lay dead on the ground.

Down climbed the little tailor, and taking his sword in his hand he plunged it into each giant, and then he went back to the edge of the forest where the ten men were waiting for him.

"They are as dead as two doornails," shouted the little man. "I don't say that I had an easy task, for they tore up trees by the roots to try to protect themselves, but of course it was no good. What are two giants to a man who has slain seven at one blow?"

The men wouldn't believe it until they went into the forest and saw the two dead bodies each lying in a pool of blood, while the ground was covered with up-rooted trees. So they all told the King. But instead of handing over half his kingdom, as he had promised, His Majesty told the little tailor that there was still another brave deed for him to do before he got the Princess for his bride.

"Just name it, then; I'm more than ready," was the man's reply.

"You are to kill the famous unicorn that is running wild in the forest and doing so much damage. When this is done you shall have your reward at once."

"No trouble at all, Your Majesty. I'll get rid of him in a twinkling."

The tailor made the ten men wait for him at the entrance to the woods as they had done the first time and, taking a stout rope and a saw, he entered the forest alone once again.

Up came the unicorn, but just as it was about to rush at the man he darted behind a big tree. The unicorn dashed with such force against the tree that its horn was stuck quite fast in the trunk.

Taking his rope, the tailor tied it tightly around the animal, and, after sawing off the horn, back he went to the palace, leading the unicorn at his side.

But even then the King was not satisfied, and he demanded that the little man catch a wild boar that had been seen wandering in the woods. He took a party of huntsmen with him, but again he made them wait on the outskirts of the forest while he went on by himself.

The wild boar dashed at the little tailor, but the man was too quick for it. He slipped into a building close by, with the animal at his heels. Then, through a small window, he crawled out into the forest, while the boar inside the cabin was too big and clumsy to follow him. It stood gazing at the window where the man had disappeared, and the tailor ran around and closed the door, locking the animal inside. Then he called the hunters, who shot the boar and carried its body back to the palace.

This time the King was obliged to keep his promise. So the little tailor became a prince, and a grand wedding it was, too.

When they had been married for a few years, the Princess overheard her husband talking in his sleep one night. "Boy, take the Lord Mayor's coat to his home at once, or I'll box your ears," he said.

"Oh dear," cried the Princess, "to think that I've married a common tailor! Whatever can I do to get rid of him?"

See page 568

571

So she told her father the story, and the King said she need not worry, for he knew a way out of the difficulty. She was to leave the door open that night, and while the tailor was sleeping, the King's servants would steal into the room, bind the tailor and take him away to be killed. The Princess promised to see that everything was in readiness, and she tripped about all day with a light heart. She little knew that one of the tailor's servants had overheard their cruel plot and had carried the news straight to his master.

That night, when the Princess thought her husband was fast asleep, she crept to the door and opened it.

To her great terror, her husband began to speak. "Boy, take the Lord Mayor's coat to his home, or I'll box your ears. Haven't I killed seven at one blow? Haven't I slain two giants, a unicorn and a wild boar? What do I care for the men who are standing outside my door at this moment?"

At these words, off flew the men as though they had been shot from a gun, and no more attempts were ever made on the tailor's life. So the Princess had to make the best of a bad job.

He lived on, and when the old King died he ascended the throne in his stead. So the brave little tailor became ruler over the whole kingdom, and his motto throughout his whole life was, "Seven at one blow."

TRADITIONAL GERMAN TALE, COLLECTION OF
KATE DOUGLAS WIGGIN AND NORA ARCHIBALD SMITH

THE GINGERBREAD MAN

ONCE UPON a time there was a little old woman and a little old man, and they lived alone in a little old house. They didn't have any little girls or any little boys at all. So, one day, the little old woman made a boy out of gingerbread and she made a chocolate jacket and put cinnamon seeds in it for buttons. His eyes were made of fine, fat currants; his mouth was made of rose-colored sugar; and he had a gay cap of orange sugar-candy. When the little old woman had rolled him out, and dressed him up, and pinched his gingerbread shoes into shape, she put him in a pan. Then she put the pan in the oven and shut the door. Sitting there, she thought: Now I shall have a little boy of my own.

When it was time for the Gingerbread Boy to be done she opened the oven door and pulled out the pan. Out jumped the little Gingerbread Boy onto the floor and away he ran, out of the door and down the street! The little old woman and the little old man ran after him as fast as they could, but he just laughed and shouted:

Run! run! as fast as you can!
You can't catch me, I'm the Gingerbread Man!

And they couldn't catch him.

The little Gingerbread Boy ran on and on, until he came to a Cow by the roadside. "Stop, little Gingerbread Boy," said the Cow. "I want to eat you."

The little Gingerbread Boy laughed and said:

I have run away from a little old woman,
And a little old man,
And I can run away from you, I can!

And, as the Cow chased him, he looked over his shoulder and cried:

Run! run! as fast as you can!
You can't catch me, I'm the Gingerbread Man!

And the Cow couldn't catch him.

The little Gingerbread Boy ran on and on and on, until he came to a Horse in the pasture. "Please stop, little Gingerbread Boy," said the Horse, "you look very good to eat."

But the little Gingerbread Boy laughed out loud. "Oho! oho!" he said:

I have run away from a little old woman,
A little old man,
A cow,
And I can run away from you, I can!

574

And, as the Horse chased him, he looked over his shoulder and cried:

Run! run! as fast as you can!
You can't catch me, I'm the Gingerbread Man!

And the Horse couldn't catch him.

By and by the little Gingerbread Boy came to a barn full of threshers. When the threshers smelled the Gingerbread Boy, they tried to pick him up and said, "Don't run so fast, little Gingerbread Boy; you look very good to eat."

But the little Gingerbread Boy ran harder than ever and as he ran he cried out:

I have run away from a little old woman,
A little old man,
A cow,
A horse,
And I can run away from you, I can!

And, when he found that he was ahead of the threshers, he turned and shouted back to them:

Run! run! as fast as you can!
You can't catch me, I'm the Gingerbread Man!

And the threshers couldn't catch him.

Then the little Gingerbread Boy ran faster than ever. He ran and ran until he came to a field full of mowers.

When the mowers saw how fine he looked, they ran after him, calling out, "Wait a bit! Wait a bit, little Gingerbread Boy, we wish to eat you!"

But the little Gingerbread Boy laughed harder than ever, and ran like the wind. "Oho! oho!" he said:

> I have run away from a little old woman,
> A little old man,
> A cow,
> A horse,
> A barn full of threshers,
> And I can run away from you, I can!

And when he found that he was ahead of the mowers, he turned and shouted back to them:

> Run! run! as fast as you can!
> You can't catch me, I'm the Gingerbread Man!

And the mowers couldn't catch him.

By this time the little Gingerbread Boy was so proud that he didn't think there was anybody at all who could catch him.

Pretty soon he saw a Fox coming across a field toward him. The Fox looked at the Gingerbread Boy and began to run.

But the little Gingerbread Boy shouted across to him: "You can't catch me!"

The Fox began to run faster, and the little Gingerbread Boy ran faster, and as he ran he chuckled:

See page 578

577

I have run away from a little old woman,
A little old man,
A cow,
A horse,
A barn full of threshers,
A field full of mowers,
And I can run away from you, I can!
Run! run! as fast as you can!
You can't catch me, I'm the Gingerbread Man!

"Why," said the Fox, "I would not catch you if I could. I would not think of disturbing you."

Just then, the little Gingerbread Boy came to a river. He could not swim across, and he wanted to keep running away from the Cow and the Horse and the people.

"Jump on my tail, and I will take you across," said the Fox.

So the little Gingerbread Boy jumped on the Fox's tail, and the Fox swam into the river. When he was a little way from shore he turned his head and said, "You are too heavy on my tail, little Gingerbread Boy, I fear I shall let you get wet; jump on my back."

The little Gingerbread Boy jumped on his back.

A little farther out, the Fox said, "I am afraid the water will cover you there. Jump on my shoulder."

The little Gingerbread Boy jumped on his shoulder.

In the middle of the stream the Fox said, "Oh, dear! Little Gingerbread Boy, my shoulder is sinking. Jump on my nose, so that I can hold you out of the water."

So the little Gingerbread Boy jumped on his nose.

The minute the Fox got on shore he threw back his head and gave a snap!

"Dear me!" said the little Gingerbread Boy, "I am a quarter gone!" The next minute he said, "Why, I am half gone!" The next minute he said, "My goodness gracious, I am three quarters gone!" And after that, the little Gingerbread Boy never said anything more at all.

TRADITIONAL ENGLISH TALE, RETOLD BY SARA CONE BRYANT

A HORNED GOAT

THERE WAS once a Goat, a wicked, horned Goat. She was at war with everyone, did mischief to all, butted with her horns, stamped her feet and threatened: "I, a hairy, horned Goat! Whoever touches me will fare badly! I will stamp him with my feet, I will beat him with my tail and I'll eat him up!"

All feared her because she threatened them terribly.

She grew bold, minded nobody and pillaged every garden. What she couldn't eat, she broke, stamped on and damaged. All suffered because all were afraid. One day she went into a tailor's garden where the tailor sat sewing at the window. When he spied the Goat among his cabbages, he jumped up shouting, but the Goat minded him not, just as if she hadn't heard him cry out.

"Oh, your hour has come! Do you think a tailor is afraid of a Goat?" shouted the master.

He caught up his big tailor's shears, jumped through the window and ran toward the Goat, opening and shutting his shears. The Goat saw a tailor for the first time; for the first time, also, she saw shears, and she became frightened at the brave tailor. She ran, and yet he followed her, opening and shutting his shears all the while.

The tailor was thin, lean and light, and he had long legs, but still the Goat ran faster on her four feet than the tailor could on his two. She escaped him, and the tailor fell on the grass, puffing.

"I am a hero. There is none braver than I," he said, and he went home a proud and haughty man.

The Goat kept on running. Leaving the road, she ran through a thick forest until, almost ready to drop from exhaustion, she fell into a Fox's den.

"I shall remain here; the tailor won't be able to find me," she said.

So she stayed, but she was so frightened that she trembled all over.

By this time Mrs. Fox had come home, but she could not get into her den because it was occupied by the Goat.

"Who's in there?" she called angrily.

The Goat was afraid, but she shouted loudly: "I, a hairy, horned Goat! Whoever touches me will fare badly! I will stamp him with my feet, I will beat him with my tail and I'll eat him up!"

Mrs. Fox almost fainted from fear. She went aside and sat, crying that she had no place to go. Soon Mr. Fox came home and, seeing his wife in distress, he asked her: "What has happened to you, Mother? Why do you cry?"

She answered: "A terrible misfortune has befallen us! Somebody went into our den, does not want to come out and threatens to eat us up!"

"Oh, who can it be?" said the Fox. "I will make him come out."

Together they went to the den. The Fox, knowing he was in the right, asked boldly in a deep voice: "Who is in there?"

The Goat was very much frightened, but she shouted with all her might: "I, a hairy, horned Goat! Whoever touches me will fare badly! I will stamp him with my feet, I will beat him with my tail and I'll eat him up!"

The Fox lowered his head, hung his tail between his hind legs and whispered: "I am not strong enough to make the creature come out. I can't help us!"

They went away into the forest, crying bitterly. A Hare met them and said, wonderingly: "This is news, this is news! Mr. Fox crying?"

"Oh, it's nothing! I have just tasted some strong tobacco," explained the Fox, wiping his eyes with shame.

"Tobacco? A Goat, and not tobacco! A Goat went into our den and will not come out. Where shall we go now, poor orphans?" cried Mrs. Fox.

The Hare, being kindhearted, felt sorry for Mr. and Mrs. Fox. He cried with them a little and then said: "Am I, a Hare of Hares, afraid of a foolish Goat? We shall see!"

He whisked past the Foxes to their den so fast that they could barely follow him and he called: "Who is in there? Come right out!"

The Goat became more and more frightened, because she knew there were many animals in the forest and, although some were afraid of her, there might come one that would chase her out of the den. And she thought that the tailor with his big shears waited outside the den. She stamped her feet and cried in a fearful voice: "I, a hairy, horned Goat! Whoever touches me will fare badly! I will stamp him with my feet, I will beat him with my tail and I'll eat him up!"

The Hare jumped aside and fled, as if a whole pack of greyhounds pursued him. When he saw that no one was after him, however, he felt ashamed and went back to the Foxes.

Now the Foxes were asking the Wolf to help them. Mrs. Fox sat under a bush, adding a word or two to the gentlemen's conversation. Mr. Fox, arm in arm with the Wolf, paced to and fro, putting the whole matter up to the Wolf.

"What shall we do now?" the Fox kept saying. "It is of no use looking for a new place, as all the dens, small holes and even last year's nests are occupied. Everything has its own corner and a roof over its head except us, poor orphans! We, Foxes of Foxes, that used to live comfortably, what shall we do when the little cubs come? Help us, Mr. Wolf, as you are our relative, friend and godfather, and I am helpless."

The Wolf listened patiently and said, gnashing his teeth: "You will be sleeping on that Goat's skin yet, you'll see. Lead me to your den; it is time to end this evil thing."

They went to the den, the Hare scampering after them. The Goat heard them coming and closed her eyes, thinking her last hour had come. The Wolf gnashed his teeth again, shouting: "Who is in there?"

The Goat, awaiting her death, at first could not make a sound, but then, in her terrible fright, she screamed in a voice she could not recognize as her own:

THE WORLD'S BEST FAIRY TALES

"I, a hairy, horned Goat!" and threatened as she had before.

When the Wolf heard that the Goat would stamp him with her feet and beat him with her tail, he became so frightened that he flattened his ears, stepped aside from the den and whispered to the Fox: "I can't help it; it is too much for me."

"Well, didn't I say so?" groaned the Fox. "Such is my misfortune to die without a home because of a horned Goat!"

They all wept and cried aloud. Going farther into the forest, they met a Bear, very much satisfied with himself, having just eaten a lot of sweet honey. He had been somewhat bitten by the bees who guarded their property; one part of his face was swollen, but he did not care, the hairy beast. Hearing so much lamentation, he stopped and asked what had happened.

They all began talking at the same time, making so much noise that the Bear covered up his ears and shouted to them to speak one at a time; otherwise, he said, he could not understand them and they would make him deaf.

Mrs. Fox had a greater ability for talking than the rest, so she described their sad affliction, saying unpleasant things about each and every helper. The Bear laughed heartily, repeating time after time: "They're afraid of a Goat, they're afraid of a horned Goat!"

The Fox and the Wolf resented the Bear's belittling

remarks, but they said nothing, as they wished him to help them. When the Bear had stopped laughing, he said: "All right, now. Let us go to the Goat. But I must take along my two helpers."

His two helpers were a Crab and a Porcupine. The Crab walked along slowly, moved his claws and threatened: "I am a Crab, and this is the way I pinch!"

The Porcupine rolled on his short feet, stuck out his needles and kept on saying: "I am a Porcupine, and this is the way I prick!"

The Bear called his helpers, and the whole crowd went to the den. The Bear asked the Goat: "How fare you in the den, my Nanny Goat?"

The Goat was terror-stricken, because she had never heard such a gruff voice, but she threatened as usual: "I will stamp you with my feet, I will beat you with my tail and I'll eat you up!"

"Oh, dear me!" laughed the Bear. "Eat up fast, don't delay! I'll send you down two!" Turning to those around him, he said to them: "The Crab and the Porcupine will go in to chase the Goat. The Wolf and I will wait at the mouth of the den to catch her. Mr. and Mrs. Fox had better wait on top of the hill to get her in case she should slip from our hands. The Hare, being the fastest, had better run to the other side of the hill. Should she pass us all, he won't let her go."

So the Crab pinched the Goat with all his strength and the Porcupine rolled with his needles over her

See page 590

586

back, and the Goat whisked away from the den immediately, dashed past the Bear and the Wolf and ran up the hill so fast that the Foxes stepped aside. The Hare watched better than the rest; he jumped straight on her back and did not let her go. The whole crowd came running to mete out justice to the Goat.

"Well," said the Bear, "you got what you asked for. Your end has now come. Let the Foxes judge you, for they are the ones you wronged."

The Goat saw she was in trouble and that no one was afraid of her. So she began from a different angle. She stamped her feet, held her sides and mocked them: "What heroes you are! All of you together to get one Goat! A Bear and a Wolf, two Foxes and a Hare, and those other two have not reached me yet! Now you're so anxious to get to my skin! Hasten with my end; otherwise I'll make you known throughout the forest!"

They were ashamed and afraid that the other animals might hear the Goat shouting, and so the Wolf said: "All right, we will not go against you, a crowd against one. If you wish, we can have a proper war. Let us each gather an army and meet again in three days. Agreed?"

"Agreed!" shouted everybody. Even the Goat agreed, for what could she do? Just the same, she was glad that she gained three days' time. They parted to gather their armies. The Goat's enemies did not even try to find any allies, laughing at the thought of her army. The Bear, the Wolf and the Fox, just the three of them, were ready to fight the Goat, as it would not be becoming for Mrs. Fox to fight. The Crab and the Porcupine could not be found, and they were all ashamed to ask the Hare, for he had caught the Goat.

It went worse with the Goat. She was afraid of the tailor and she had accounts with other people. Where could she look for an army? She went hither and thither, but from each that she asked, a Dog or a Horse, she received the same answer: "You brewed the beer, drink it yourself!"

Besides, they were afraid to fight a Bear and a Wolf.

The Goat was desperate. She thought to herself: I will surely pay with my head, for I must keep my word and I cannot find anybody to help me.

But on the third day she came across Latek, a Dog with a scalded side, who was willing to help her.

He licked his side, saying: "I may just as well fight as not. I had one war with my master for killing his lamb and another war with my mistress for the lard she did not lock up in time. I may as well have a third war in the forest—I don't mind. Let us go!"

"There are not enough of us; we need at least one more," said the Goat.

"I'll bring along two more," promised the Dog. Soon he brought a dark gray Cat and a swaggering Rooster who was not afraid of anything.

"There are four of us now, and that makes a whole army," said the Dog. "Let us go." And they went into the forest.

The three left in the forest had grown tired of waiting so long for the Goat's army. The Fox at last begged the Bear: "Oh, brother, you know how to climb trees. Go up a pine, and you may be able to see them from that height."

The Bear climbed the pine, looked around and called down: "They're coming, they're coming! But—do you know?—it is a fierce-looking army! One shouts: 'Let me have him! Let me have him!' The second one crawls along the ground, scenting our tracks. The third one has a glistening sword hanging down his side. And this terrible Goat, to make matters worse! Well, my dears, you better look out for yourselves, for I am not coming down from this pine!"

At once the Wolf leaped aside and ran away. The Fox dug into the moss so that only the tip of his tail was seen. The Goat came with her army, looking for her enemies, but she found nobody. After a while the Cat spied the Fox's tail and grabbed it with his sharp claws. The Fox jumped out, shouting dreadfully, and in a fright the Goat's army ran in different directions. The Cat was frightened the most, and he ran up the tree to where the Bear sat.

They're after me! thought the terrified Bear. He let go of the branch where he sat and fell down to the ground with such a shock that the earth around trembled.

"Well, well," grumbled the Bear. "Now I may wander for three days and not meet anyone. My sides ache so I will not last without a massage. If I could only catch sight of the Hare! He would save me."

Somehow he got up and went along, moaning, when suddenly he heard nearby the Goat's doleful bleating.

If I could only get hold of you, I'd make your sides ache, too! thought the Bear to himself.

Just then the Goat appeared in front of him. The Hare sat on her back, holding her fast by her horns and threatening: "I will not let you go! You must be punished; you lost the war, since I caught you fleeing. Let the Fox judge you!"

"Oh, Mr. Hare!" called the delighted Bear. "Run, brother, bring me some mosquito fat, as I must be massaged after the war. My sides are so badly beaten that I can hardly stand. All my hope is in you, that you will save me, because I cannot go far by myself."

The Hare did not hesitate a moment; he jumped off the Goat's back and scuttled away for the mosquito fat. This was all the Goat needed. She knew the Bear could not chase her, so she leaped off and ran away. She ran one day, two, three; she ran six weeks and a year; and maybe she runs to this very day.

OLD POLISH TALE, TRANSLATED BY
LUCIA MERECKA BORSKI AND KATE B. MILLER

SEVEN SIMONS

FAR, FAR AWAY, beyond all the countries, seas and rivers, there stood a splendid city where lived King Archidej, who was as good as he was rich and handsome. His great army was made up of men ready to obey his slightest wish. He owned forty times forty cities, and in each city he had ten palaces with silver doors, golden roofs and crystal windows. His council consisted of the twelve wisest men in the country, each of whom was as learned as a whole college, and whose long white beards flowed down over their breasts. This council always told the King the exact truth.

Now the King had everything to make him happy, but he did not enjoy anything because he could not find a bride to suit him.

One day, as he sat in his palace looking out to sea, a great ship sailed into the harbor and several merchants came on shore. Said the King to himself, "These people have traveled far and beheld many lands. I will ask them if they have seen any princess who is as clever and as handsome as I am."

So he ordered the merchants to be brought before him. When they came, he said, "You have traveled much and visited many wonders. I wish to ask you a question and I beg you to answer truthfully.

"Have you anywhere seen or heard of the daughter of an emperor, king or prince, who is as clever and as handsome as I am and who would be worthy to be my wife and the Queen of my country?"

The merchants considered for some time.

At last the eldest of them said, "I have heard that across many seas, on the Island of Busan, there is a mighty King whose daughter, the Princess Helena, is so lovely that she can certainly not be plainer than Your Majesty and so clever that the wisest graybeard cannot guess her riddles."

"Is the island far off and which is the way to it?"

"It is not near," was the answer. "The journey would take ten years and we do not know the way. But even if we did, what use would that be? The Princess is no bride for you."

"How dare you say so?" cried the King angrily.

"Your Majesty must pardon us. Just think for a moment. Should you send an envoy to the island it will take him ten years to get there and ten more to return —twenty years altogether. Will not the Princess have grown old during that time and have lost all her beauty?"

The King reflected gravely. Then he thanked the

merchants, gave them leave to trade in his country without paying any duties and dismissed them.

After they were gone the King remained deep in thought. He felt puzzled and anxious, so he decided to ride into the country to distract his mind, and sent for his huntsmen and falconers.

The huntsmen blew their horns, the falconers took their hawks on their wrists, and they set out across country till they came to a green hedge. On the other side of the hedge stretched a great field of grain as far as the eye could see; the yellow tips swayed to and fro in the breeze like a rippling sea of gold.

The King drew rein and admired the field. "Upon my word," said he, "whoever dug and planted it must be good workmen. If every field in my kingdom were as well cared for as this, there would be more bread than my people could eat." And he wished to know to whom the field belonged.

Off rushed all his followers at once to do his bidding and found a nice, tidy farmhouse, in front of which sat seven peasants lunching on rye bread and water. They wore red shirts bound with gold braid, and were so much alike that one could hardly be told from another. The messengers asked, "Who owns this field of golden grain?"

The seven brothers answered, "The field is ours."

"And who are you?"

"We are King Archidej's laborers."

These answers were repeated to the King, who ordered the brothers to be brought before him at once. On being asked who they were, the eldest said, bowing low: "We, King Archidej, are your laborers, children of one father and mother, and we all have the same name—each of us is called Simon. Our father taught us to be true to our King, to till the ground and to be kind to our neighbors. He also taught each of us a different trade which he thought might be useful to us, and he bade us not to neglect Mother Earth, which would surely reward our labor."

The King was pleased with the honest peasant and said, "You have done well, good people, in planting your field and now you have a golden harvest. But I should like each of you to tell me what special trade your father taught you."

"My trade, O King," said the first Simon, "is not an easy one. If you will give me some workmen and materials I will build you a great white pillar that shall reach far above the clouds."

"Very good," replied the King. "And you, Simon the second, what is your trade?"

"Mine, Your Majesty," said the second Simon, "needs no great cleverness. When my brother has built the pillar I can climb it and, from the top, far above the clouds, I can see what is happening in every country under the sun."

"Good," said the King. "And Simon the third?"

"My work is very simple, sire. You have many ships built by learned men, with all sorts of new and clever improvements. If you wish it, I will build you quite a simple boat—one, two, three, and it's done! My plain little ship does not look grand enough for a king, but, where other ships take a year, mine makes the voyage in a day, and where they would require ten years, mine will do the distance in a week."

"Good," said the King again. "What has Simon the fourth learned?"

"My trade, O King, is really of no importance. Should my brother build you a ship, then let me embark in it. If we should be pursued by an enemy I can seize our boat by the prow and sink it to the bottom of the sea. When the enemy has sailed off I can draw it up to the top again."

"That is very clever of you," answered the King. "What does Simon the fifth do?"

"My work, Your Majesty, is mere blacksmith's work. Order me to build a smithy and I will make you a crossbow from which neither the eagle in the sky nor the wild beast in the forest is safe. The bolt hits whatever the eye sees."

"That sounds very useful," said the King. "And now, Simon the sixth, tell me your trade."

"Sire, it is so simple, I am almost ashamed to mention it. If my brother hits any creature I catch it quicker than any dog can. If it falls into the water I can pick it up out of the greatest depths; if it is in a dark forest I can find it even at midnight."

The King was much pleased with the trades and talk of the six brothers and said, "Thank you, good people. Your father did well to teach you all these things. Now follow me to the town, for I want to see what you can do. I need skillful people such as you about me, and when harvesttime comes I will send you home with royal presents."

The brothers bowed and said, "As the King wills."

Suddenly the King remembered that he had not questioned the seventh Simon, so he turned to him and said, "Why are you silent? What is your handicraft?"

And the seventh Simon answered, "I have no handicraft, O King: I have learned nothing; I could not manage it. And if I do know how to do anything it is not what might properly be called a real trade. It is, rather, a sort of performance which no one—not even the King himself—must watch me doing, and I doubt whether this performance of mine would please Your Majesty."

"Come, come," cried the King, "I will have no excuses! What is this trade?"

"First, sire, give me your royal word that you will not kill me when I have told you. Then you shall hear what it is."

"So be it, then. I give you my royal word."

Then the seventh Simon stepped back a little,

cleared his throat and said, "My trade, King Archidej, is such that a man who follows it in your kingdom generally loses his life and has no hope of pardon. There is only one thing I can do really well—that is to steal and to hide the smallest scrap of anything I have stolen. Not the deepest vault, even if its lock were enchanted, could prevent my stealing anything out of it that I wished to have."

When the King heard this he fell into a passion. "I will not pardon you, you rascal," he cried. "I will shut you up in my deepest dungeon, on bread and water, till you have forgotten such a trade. Indeed, it would be better to put you to death at once, and I've a good mind to do so."

"Don't kill me, O King! I am really not as bad as you think. Why, had I chosen, I could have robbed the royal treasury, bribed your judges to let me off and built a white marble palace with what was left. But though I know how to steal I don't do it. You yourself asked me my trade. If you kill me you will break your royal word."

"Very well," said the King, "I will not kill you. I pardon you. But from this hour you shall be shut up in a dark dungeon. Here, guards! Away with him to the prison! But you six Simons follow me and be assured of my royal favor."

So the six Simons followed the King. The seventh Simon was seized by the guards, who put him in chains and threw him into prison with only bread and water for food. Next day the King gave the first Simon carpenters, masons, blacksmiths and laborers, with great amounts of iron, mortar and the like. Simon began to build, and he built his great white pillar far, far up into the sky, as high as the nearest stars.

Then the second Simon climbed up the pillar and saw and heard all that was going on throughout the whole world. When he came down he had all sorts of wonderful things to tell. How one king was marching in battle against another and which was likely to be the victor. How, in another place, great rejoicings were going on, while in a third, people were dying of famine. In fact, there was not the smallest event going on over the earth that was hidden from him.

Next the third Simon began. He stretched out his arms, once, twice, thrice, and the wonder-ship was ready. At a sign from the King it was launched and floated like a bird on the waves. Instead of ropes it had wires for rigging, and musicians played on the wires with fiddle bows and made lovely music.

As the ship sailed about, the fourth Simon seized the prow with his strong hand and in a moment it was gone—sunk to the bottom of the sea. An hour passed, and then the ship was on top of the water again, drawn up by Simon's left hand, while in his right hand he carried a gigantic fish from the depths of the ocean for the royal table.

While this was going on, the fifth Simon had built his forge and hammered out his iron, and when the King returned from the harbor the magic crossbow was finished.

His Majesty went out into an open field at once, looked up into the sky and saw, far, far away, an eagle flying up toward the sun and looking like a tiny speck.

"Now," said the King, "if you can shoot that bird I will reward you."

Simon only smiled. He lifted his crossbow, took aim and fired, and the eagle fell. As it was falling, the sixth Simon ran up with a dish, caught the bird before it fell to earth and brought it to the King.

"Many thanks, my brave lads," said the King. "I see that each of you is indeed a master of his trade. You shall be richly rewarded. However, rest now and have your dinner."

The six Simons bowed and went to dinner. But they had hardly begun before a messenger came to say that the King wanted to see them. They obeyed at once and found him surrounded by all his court and councilors of state.

"Listen, my good fellows!" cried the King, as soon as he saw them. "Hear what my wise advisers have thought of. I am told that, far away, across many seas, is the great kingdom of the Island of Busan, and that the daughter of the King is the beautiful Princess Helena. As you, Simon the second, can see the whole world from the top of the great pillar, I want you to climb up and view the Island of Busan."

Off ran the second Simon and clambered quickly up the pillar. He gazed around, listened on all sides and then slid down to report to the King.

"Sire, I have obeyed your orders. Far away I saw the Island of Busan. The King is a mighty monarch but full of pride, harsh and cruel. He sits on his throne and declares that no prince or king on earth is good enough for his lovely daughter, that he will give her to none and if any king asks for her hand he will declare war against him and destroy his kingdom."

"Has the King of Busan a great army?" asked King Archidej. "Is his country far off?"

"As far as I could judge," replied Simon, "it would take you nearly ten years in fair weather to sail there. But if the weather were stormy it might be twelve. I saw the army being reviewed. It is not so very large— a hundred thousand men-at-arms and a hundred thousand knights. Besides these, he has a strong bodyguard and a good many crossbowmen. Altogether you might say another hundred thousand, and there is a picked body of heroes who reserve themselves for great occasions requiring particular courage."

The King sat for some time lost in thought. At last he said to the nobles and courtiers standing around, "I am determined to marry the Princess Helena, but how shall I do it?"

The nobles, courtiers and councilors said nothing, but tried to hide behind each other. Then the third Simon said: "Pardon me, Your Majesty, if I offer my advice. You wish to go to the Island of Busan? What can be easier? In my ship you will get there in a week instead of in ten years. But ask your council to advise you what you should do when you arrive—in one word, whether you will win the Princess peacefully or by war?"

But the wise men were as silent on this question as always.

The King frowned, and was about to say something sharp, when the court fool pushed his way to the front and said: "Dear me, what are all you clever people so puzzled about? The matter is quite clear. As it will not take long to reach the island, why not send the seventh Simon? He will steal the fair maiden fast enough, and then the King, her father, may consider how he is going to bring his army over here—it will take him ten years to do it! No less! What do you think of my plan?"

"What do I think? Why, that your idea is excellent and you shall be rewarded for it. Come, guards, hurry and bring the seventh Simon before me."

Not many minutes later, Simon the seventh stood before the King, who explained to him what he wished done, and also that to steal for the benefit of his King and country was by no means a wrong thing to do,

although it was very wrong to steal for his own advantage. The youngest Simon, who looked very pale and hungry, only nodded his head.

"Come," said the King, "tell me truly. Do you think you could steal the Princess Helena?"

"Why should I not steal her, sire? The thing is easy enough. Let my brother's ship be laden with rich brocades, Persian carpets, pearls and jewels. Send me in the ship. Give me my four middle brothers as companions and keep the two others as hostages."

When the King heard these words his heart became filled with longing for the Princess and he ordered all to be done as Simon wished. Everyone ran about to do his bidding, and in next to no time the wonder-ship was laden and ready to start.

The five Simons took leave of the King, went on board and had no sooner set sail than they were almost out of sight. The ship cut through the waters like a falcon through the air, and just a week after starting sighted the Island of Busan. The coast appeared to be strongly guarded, and from afar the watchman on a high tower called out to them: "Halt and anchor! Who are you? Where do you come from and what do you want?"

The seventh Simon answered from the ship, "We are peaceful people. We come from the country of the great and good King Archidej and we bring foreign wares—rich brocades, carpets and costly jewels—

which we wish to show to your King and the Princess. We desire to trade—to sell, to buy and to exchange."

The brothers launched a small boat, took some of their valuable goods with them, rowed to shore and went up to the palace. The Princess sat in a rose-red room, and when she saw the brothers coming near she told her lady-in-waiting to inquire who these people were and what they wanted.

The seventh Simon answered the lady-in-waiting. "We come from the country of the wise and good King Archidej," said he, "and we have brought all sorts of goods for sale. We trust the King of this country may condescend to welcome us and let his servants take charge of our wares. If he considers them worthy to adorn his followers, we shall be content."

This speech was repeated to the Princess, who ordered the brothers to be brought to the rose-red room at once. They bowed respectfully to her and displayed some splendid velvets and brocades, and opened cases of pearls and precious stones. Such beautiful things had never been seen in the island, and the ladies of the court stood bewildered by the magnificence. They whispered together that they had never beheld anything like that. The Princess, too, saw and wondered. Her eyes could not weary of looking at the lovely things nor her fingers of stroking the rich, soft velvets and of holding up the sparkling jewels to the light.

"Fairest of Princesses," said Simon, "be pleased to

order these gracious ladies to accept the silks and velvets and let them trim their headdresses with the jewels; these are no special treasures. But permit me to
say that they are as nothing to the many-colored tapestries, the gorgeous stones and ropes of pearls in our
ship. We did not like to bring more with us, not knowing what your royal taste might be. But if it seems good
to you to give honor to our ship with a visit, you might
condescend to choose such things as are pleasing in
your eyes."

This polite speech pleased the Princess very much.
She went to the King and said, "Dear Father, some
merchants have arrived with the most splendid wares.
I pray you to allow me to go to their ship and choose
what I like."

The King thought and thought, frowned hard and
rubbed his ear. At last he gave consent and ordered
out his royal yacht, with a hundred crossbowmen, a
hundred knights and a thousand soldiers to escort the
Princess Helena.

Off sailed the yacht with the Princess and her escort.
The brothers Simon came on board to conduct the
Princess to their ship and, led by the brothers and
followed by her lady-in-waiting and other women, she
crossed the crystal plank which led from one vessel to
the other.

The seventh Simon spread out his goods. He had so
many curious and interesting tales to tell about them

that the Princess forgot everything else in looking and listening, so she did not know that the fourth Simon had seized the prow of the ship and that all of a sudden it had vanished from sight and was racing along in the depths of the sea.

The crew of the royal yacht shouted aloud, the knights stood still with terror, the soldiers were struck dumb and hung their heads. There was nothing to be done but to sail back and tell the King of his loss.

How he wept and stormed! "Oh, light of my eyes," he sobbed, "I am indeed punished for my pride! I thought no one good enough to be your husband and now you are lost in the depths of the sea and have left me alone! As for all of those who saw this thing— away with them! Let them be put in irons and locked in prison while I think how I can best put them to death!"

While the King of Busan was raging and lamenting in this fashion, Simon's ship was swimming like a fish under the sea. When the island was well out of sight he brought the ship up to the surface again. At that moment the Princess recollected herself.

"We have been gazing at these wonders too long," she said to her lady-in-waiting. "I hope my father won't be vexed at our delay."

She tore herself away from the treasures and stepped on deck. Neither the yacht nor the island was in sight! Helena wrung her hands and beat her breast.

Then she changed herself into a white swan and flew up. But the fifth Simon seized his bow and shot the swan, and the sixth Simon did not let it fall into the water but caught it on the ship. Then the swan turned into a silver fish, but Simon lost no time and caught the fish, when, quick as thought, the fish turned into a black mouse and ran about the ship. It darted toward a hole, but before it reached it, Simon sprang upon it more swiftly than any cat, and then the little mouse turned once more into the beautiful Princess Helena.

Early one morning, just two weeks after the ship had left his kingdom, King Archidej sat thoughtfully at his window gazing out to sea. His heart was sad and he would neither eat nor drink. His thoughts were full of the Princess Helena, who was as lovely as a dream. When, suddenly—is that a white gull approaching the shore or is it a sail? No, it is no gull, it is the wonder-ship flying along with billowing sails. Its flags waved, all the fiddlers played on the wire rigging, the anchor was thrown out and the crystal plank laid from the ship to the pier.

The lovely Helena stepped across the plank. She shone like the sun, and the stars of heaven seemed to sparkle in her eyes.

Up sprang King Archidej in haste. "Hurry, hurry!" he cried. "Let us hasten to meet her! Let the bugles sound and the joyful bells be rung!"

The whole court swarmed with courtiers and servants. Golden carpets were laid down and the great gates of the palace were thrown open to welcome the Princess.

King Archidej went out himself, took her by the hand and led her into the royal apartments.

"Madam," said he, "the fame of your beauty had reached me, but I did not dare to expect such loveliness. Still, I will not keep you here against your will. If you wish it, the wonder-ship shall take you back to your father and your own country. But if you will consent to stay here, then reign over me and my country as our Queen."

What more is there to tell? It is not hard to guess that the Princess listened to the King's wooing, and that their betrothal took place with great pomp and rejoicings.

The brothers Simon were sent again to the Island of Busan with a letter to the King from his daughter to invite him to their wedding. And the wonder-ship arrived at the Island of Busan just as all the knights and soldiers who had escorted the Princess were being led to their execution.

Then the seventh Simon cried out from the ship: "Stop! Stop! I bring a letter from the Princess Helena!"

The King of Busan read the letter over and over again and ordered the knights and soldiers to be set free. He entertained King Archidej's ambassadors hospitably and told them to return to his daughter with his blessing, but he could not be persuaded to attend the wedding.

When the wonder-ship came home again, King Archidej and Princess Helena were enchanted with the news it brought.

The King sent for the seven Simons. "A thousand thanks to you, my brave fellows!" he cried. "Take whatever gold, silver and precious stones you want from my treasury. Tell me if there is anything else you wish for and I will give it to you, my good friends. Do you wish to be made nobles or to govern towns? Only speak."

Then the eldest Simon bowed and said, "We are plain folk, Your Majesty, and understand simple things best. What figures would we cut as nobles or governors? Nor do we desire gold. We have our fields which give us food and as much money as we need. If you wish to reward us, then grant that our land may be free of taxes, and of your goodness pardon the seventh Simon. He is not the first who has been a thief by trade and he will certainly not be the last."

"So be it," said the King, "your land shall be free of all taxes, and Simon the seventh is pardoned."

Then the King gave each brother a goblet of wine and invited them all to the wedding feast. And what a feast that was!

OLD HUNGARIAN TALE, ANDREW LANG COLLECTION

609

THE LITTLE MATCH-GIRL

IT WAS BITTERLY cold, snow was falling and darkness was gathering, for it was the last evening of the old year—it was New Year's Eve.

In the cold and gloom a poor little girl walked, bareheaded and barefoot, through the streets. She was wearing slippers, it is true, when she left home, but what good were they? They had been her mother's, so you can imagine how big they were. The little girl had lost them as she ran across the street to escape from two carriages that were being driven terribly fast. One slipper could not be found, and a boy had run off with the other, saying that he could use it very nicely as a cradle some day when he had children of his own.

So the little girl walked about the streets on her naked feet, which were red and blue with the cold. In her old apron she carried a great many matches, and she had a packet of them in her hand as well. Nobody had bought any from her, and no one had given her a single penny all day long. She crept along, shivering and hungry, the picture of misery, poor little thing! The snowflakes fell on her long golden hair which curled so prettily about her neck, but she did not think of her appearance now. Lights were shining in every window, and there was a glorious smell of roast goose in the street, for it was New Year's Eve, and she could not think of anything else.

She huddled down in a heap in a corner formed by two houses, one of which projected farther out into the street than the other, but though she tucked her little legs up under her she felt colder and colder. She did not dare to go home, for she had sold no matches nor earned a single penny. Her father would be sure to beat her, and besides it was so cold at home, for they had nothing but the roof above them and the wind whistled through that, even though the largest cracks were stuffed with straw and rags. Her thin hands were almost numb with cold. If only she could dare pull just one small match from the packet, strike it on the wall and warm her fingers!

She pulled one out—scr-r-ratch!—how it spluttered and burned! It had a warm, bright flame like a tiny candle when she held her hand over it—but what a strange light! It seemed to the little girl as if she were sitting in front of a great iron stove with polished brass knobs and brass ornaments. The fire burned so beautifully and gave out such a lovely warmth. Oh, how wonderful that was! The child had already stretched

her feet to warm them, too, when—out went the flame, the stove vanished and there she sat with a bit of the burned match in her hand.

She struck another—it burned clearly, and, where the light fell upon the wall, the bricks became transparent, like gauze. She could see right into the room, where a shining white cloth was spread on the table. It was covered with beautiful china and in the center of it stood a roast goose, stuffed with prunes and apples, steaming deliciously. And what was even more wonderful was that the goose hopped down from the dish, waddled across the floor with carving knife and fork in its back, waddled straight up to the poor child! Then—out went the match, and nothing could be seen but the thick, cold wall.

She struck another match, and suddenly she was sitting under the most beautiful Christmas tree. It was much larger and much lovelier than the one she had seen last year through the glass doors of the rich merchant's house. A thousand candles lit up the green branches, and gaily colored balls like those in the shop windows looked down upon her. The little girl reached forward with both hands—then, out went the match. The many candles on the Christmas tree rose higher and higher through the air, and she saw that they had now turned into bright stars. One of them fell, streaking the sky with light.

"Now someone is dying," said the little girl, for old

Granny, the only one who had ever been good to her but who was dead, had said, "Whenever a star falls, a soul goes up to God."

She struck another match on the wall. Once more there was light, and in the glow stood her old Granny, oh, so bright and shining, and looking so gentle, kind and loving. "Granny!" cried the little girl. "Oh, take me with you! I know you will disappear when the match is burned out; you will vanish like the warm stove, the lovely roast goose and the great glorious Christmas tree!"

Then she quickly struck all the rest of the matches she had in the packet, for she did so want to keep Granny with her.

The matches flared up with such a blaze that it was brighter than broad daylight, and her old Granny had never seemed so beautiful nor so stately before. She took the little girl in her arms and flew with her high up, oh, so high, toward glory and joy! Now they knew neither cold nor hunger nor fear, for they were both with God.

But in the cold dawn, in the corner formed by the two houses, sat the little girl with rosy cheeks and smiling lips, dead—frozen to death on the last evening of the old year. The dawn of the new year rose on the huddled figure of the girl. She was still holding the matches, of which a packet had been burned more than halfway down.

"She was evidently trying to warm herself," people said. But no one knew what beautiful visions she had seen and in what a blaze of glory she had entered with her dear old Granny into the heavenly joy and gladness of a new year.

HANS CHRISTIAN ANDERSEN, TRANSLATED BY PAUL LEYSSAC

EAST OF THE SUN
AND WEST OF THE MOON

ONCE UPON a time there was a poor countryman who had many children and little to give them either of food or clothing. They were all very pretty, but the prettiest was the youngest daughter.

Once, late on a Thursday evening in autumn, with wild weather outside, they were sitting together by the fireside, each busy with something or other, when suddenly someone rapped three times against the windowpane. The man went outside to see what could be the matter, and there in front of him stood a great big White Bear.

"Good evening to you," said the White Bear.

"Good evening," said the man.

"Will you give me your youngest daughter?" said the White Bear. "If you will, you shall be as rich as you are now poor."

Truly, the man had no objection to being rich, but he said to himself, "I must first ask my daughter about this." So he went in and told them all that a great White Bear was outside, who had promised to make them rich if he could have the youngest daughter.

But she said no, she would not hear of it. So the man went out again and settled with the White Bear that he should come again the next Thursday evening and get her answer. Then the man talked so much to her about the wealth they would have, and what a good thing it would be for herself, that at last she made up her mind to go, and washed and mended her rags to make herself as stylish as she could. Little enough had she to take away with her.

Next Thursday evening, the White Bear came to fetch her. She seated herself on his back with her bundle, and thus they departed. When they had gone a great part of the way, the White Bear said, "Are you afraid?"

"No, I am not," said she.

"Keep tight hold of my fur and then there is no danger," said he.

And thus she rode far, far away, until they came to

a great mountain. When the White Bear knocked on it, a door opened, and they went into a castle where there were many brilliantly lighted rooms which shone with gold and silver. There was a well-spread table, so magnificent it would be hard to make anyone understand how splendid it was.

The White Bear gave her a silver bell, which she had only to ring when she needed anything. After her supper she grew sleepy and thought she would like to go to bed. So she rang the bell, and scarcely had it sounded before she found herself in a chamber where a bed stood ready. It had pillows of silk, and curtains of silk fringed with gold, and everything in the room was of gold or silver. But when she had lain down and put out the light a man came and lay down beside her, and—behold!—it was the White Bear, who cast off the form of a beast during the night. She never saw him, however, for he always appeared after she had put out her light and went away before daylight.

So everything went well for a time, but then she began to be very sad and sorrowful. All day long she was alone; and she did so wish to go home to her father and mother and brothers and sisters. Then the White Bear asked what it was she wanted, and she told him it was because she could not see her brothers and sisters that she was so sorrowful.

"There might be a cure for that," said the White Bear, "if you would but promise me never to talk with your mother alone, as she will wish. If you do you will bring great misery on both of us."

So one Sunday the White Bear said they could now set out to see her father and mother. With the girl sitting on his back, they went a long, long way, and it took a long, long time. But at last they came to a large white farmhouse, and her brothers and sisters were running about outside, playing, and it was so pretty it was a pleasure to look at.

"Your parents dwell here now," said the White Bear. "But do not forget what I said to you, or you will do much harm both to yourself and me."

"No, indeed," said she, "I shall never forget." And as soon as she was at home the White Bear turned around and went away.

There were such rejoicings when she went in to her parents that it seemed as if they would never come to an end. Everyone thought he could never be sufficiently grateful to her for all she had done for them. Now they had everything they wanted, and everything was as good as it could be. All was well with her, too, she said, and she had everything she could want, but what other answers she gave did not tell them much about her.

In the afternoon, after they had dined at midday, it happened just as the White Bear had said. Her mother wanted to walk with her alone, but she remembered what the White Bear had told her and would on no account go. "What we have to say can be said at any time," she answered. But somehow or other her mother at last persuaded her, and she was forced to tell the whole story. She told how she continually went about in sadness, thinking how happy she would be if she could only see the White Bear when he was a man, and how all day long she was alone and it was so dull.

"Oh," cried the mother, in horror, "he is very likely a troll! You shall have a bit of one of my candles. Look at him with the candle when he is asleep. Take care, though, not to let any tallow drop upon him."

So she took the candle and hid it in her dress, and when evening drew near the White Bear came to take her away. When they had gone some distance, the White Bear asked her if everything had not happened just as he had suspected, and she had to admit to him that it had.

"Then, if you have done what your mother wished," he said, "you have brought great misery on both of us."

"No," she said, "I have not done anything at all."

When they reached home it was just the same as it had been before. A man came and lay down beside her, and late at night, when she knew he was sleeping, she rose and lit her candle. She saw he was the handsomest prince that eyes had ever beheld. She loved him so much it seemed she must die if she did not kiss him that moment. She did kiss him, but let three drops of hot tallow fall upon his shirt, and he awoke.

"What have you done now?" said he. "If you had just held out for the space of one year I should have been free. I have a stepmother who has bewitched me so I am a white bear by day and a man by night. Now all is at an end, and I must leave you and go to her. She lives in a castle which lies east of the sun and west of the moon. There is a Princess with a nose more than a yard long, and now she is the one I must marry."

She wept, but all in vain, for go he must. Then she asked him if she could not go with him. But no, that could not be. "Can you tell me the way then, and I will seek you—that I may surely be allowed to do!"

"Yes, you may do that," said he, "although there is no way to find it. It lies east of the sun and west of the moon, and never could you find your way there."

When she awoke in the morning, both the White Bear and the castle were gone and she was lying on a small green patch in the midst of a dark, thick wood. By her side lay the selfsame bundle of rags she had brought with her. When she had rubbed the sleep out of her eyes, and wept till she was weary, she set out on her way.

At last she came to a great mountain. At its foot an aged woman was sitting, playing with a golden apple. The girl asked her, "Do you know the way to the Prince who lives east of the sun and west of the moon, and who is to marry a Princess with a nose more than a yard long?"

"How do you happen to know about him?" inquired the old woman. "Maybe you are the one who should have had him."

"Yes, indeed, I am," she said.

"So it is you, then?" said the old woman. "I know only that he dwells in a castle east of the sun and west of the moon. You will be a long time reaching it, if ever you get there at all. But you shall have the loan of my horse. Ride on it to an old neighbor of mine; perhaps she can tell you. When you arrive there you must strike the horse beneath the left ear and bid it return home again. You may, however, take the golden apple with you."

The girl rode for a long, long way, and at last she came to another mountain, where an aged woman was sitting with a gold carding comb. The girl asked her if she knew the way to the castle which lay east of the sun and west of the moon. But she said what the first old woman had said: "I know nothing about it but that it is east of the sun and west of the moon, and you will be a long time in reaching it, if ever you get there at all. You shall have the loan of my horse to ride to the old woman who lives beyond me; perhaps she may know where the castle is. When you have reached her, just strike the horse beneath the left ear and bid it go home again."

Then she gave her the gold carding comb, for it might be of use to her, she said.

So the girl seated herself on the horse and rode a wearisome way onward again, and after a long, long time she came to a great mountain where an aged woman was sitting, spinning at a golden spinning wheel. She inquired if she knew the way to the castle which lay east of the sun and west of the moon.

"Maybe you should have had the Prince," said the old woman.

"Yes, I should have been the one," said the girl.

But this old crone knew the way no better than the others did.

It was east of the sun and west of the moon, she knew that. "And you will be a long time reaching it, if ever you get there at all," she said. "But you may have the loan of my horse, and I think you had better ride to the East Wind and ask him; perhaps he may know where the castle is and will blow you there. When you have reached him you must strike the horse beneath the left ear and he will come home again."

And then she gave her the golden spinning wheel, saying, "Perhaps you may find you have a use for it."

The girl had to ride for a great many days, for long hours, before she found the East Wind. But at last she did arrive, and then she asked him if he could tell her the way to the Prince who dwelt east of the sun and west of the moon.

"Well," said the East Wind, "I have heard tell of the Prince and his castle, but I do not know the way to it, for I have never blown so far. But, if you like, I will go with you to my brother the West Wind; he may know, for he is much stronger than I am. You may sit on my back and then I can carry you there."

She seated herself on his back, and off they went—so very swiftly! When they arrived, the East Wind went in and told his brother that the girl he had brought was the one who should have had the Prince at the castle which lay east of the sun and west of the moon, and now she was traveling about to find him again, and he had brought her to ask if the West Wind knew where the castle was.

"No," said the West Wind, "as far as that I have never blown. But, if you like, I will go with you to the South Wind, for he is much stronger than either of us and has roamed far and wide. Perhaps he can tell you what you want to know. You may seat yourself on my back and I will carry you to him."

They journeyed to the South Wind, nor were they long on the way, and the West Wind asked his brother if he could tell her the way to the castle that lay east of the sun and west of the moon, for she was the girl who should marry the Prince who lived there.

"Oh, indeed!" said the South Wind. "Well," said he, "I have wandered about a great deal in my time, and in all kinds of places, but I have never blown so far as that. If you like, however, I will go with you to my brother the North Wind. He is the oldest and strongest of us all, and if he does not know where the castle is, no one in the whole world will be able to tell you. You may sit upon my back and I will carry you there."

So she seated herself on his back, and off he went from his house in great haste, and they were not long on the way. When they came near his dwelling, the North Wind was so wild and frantic that they felt cold gusts long before they reached it.

"What do you want?" he roared out from afar, and they froze as they heard his voice.

Said the South Wind, "It is I, and this is the girl who should have had the Prince who lives in the castle which lies east of the sun and west of the moon. And now she wishes to ask you if you have been there and can tell her the way, for she would gladly find him."

"Yes," said the North Wind, "I know where it is. I once blew an aspen leaf there, but I was so tired that for many days afterward I was not able to blow at all. However, if you really are anxious to go there and are not afraid to go with me, I will take you on my back and try to carry you there."

"Go there I must," said she, "and if there is any way I will. I have no fear, no matter how fast you go."

"Very well then," said the North Wind, "but you must sleep here tonight, for we must have the day before us."

The North Wind woke her early the next morning,

and puffed himself up and made himself so big and so strong that it was frightful to see him, and away they went, high up through the air, as if they would not stop until they had reached the very end of the world. Below there was such a storm! It blew down woods and houses and, when they were above the sea, ships were wrecked by the hundreds.

Thus they tore on and on, and a long time went by, and then yet more time passed, and still they were above the sea, and the North Wind grew tired, and more tired, and at last so utterly weary he was scarcely able to blow any longer, and he sank and sank, lower and lower, until at last he went so low that the crest of the waves dashed against the heels of the poor girl he was carrying.

"Are you not afraid?" asked the North Wind.

"I have no fear," said she; and it was true.

They were not very far from land, and there was just enough strength left in the North Wind to enable him to throw her onto the shore, immediately under the windows of a castle which lay east of the sun and west of the moon. But then he was so weary and worn out he was forced to rest for several days before he could go to his own home again.

Next morning, the girl sat down beneath the walls of the castle to play with the golden apple, and the first person she saw was the maiden with the long nose who was to marry the Prince.

"How much do you want for that golden apple of yours, girl?" she asked, opening the window.

"It cannot be bought either for gold or money," answered the girl.

"If it cannot be bought either for gold or money, what will buy it? You may say what you please," said the Princess.

"Well, if I may go to the Prince who is here, and be with him tonight, you shall have it," said the girl who had come with the North Wind.

"You may do that," said the Princess, for she had made up her mind what she would do.

So the Princess got the golden apple, but when the girl went up to the Prince's apartment that night he was asleep, for the Princess had so contrived it by giving him a sleeping potion. The poor girl called to him and shook him, and between whiles she wept, but she could not wake him. In the morning, as soon as day dawned, in came the Princess with the long nose and drove her out again.

In the daytime she sat down once more beneath the windows of the castle and began to card with her golden carding comb; and then all happened as it had before. The Princess asked her what she wanted for it, and the girl replied it was not for sale, either for gold or money, but if she could have leave to go to the Prince and be with him during the night, she should have it. But when she went up to the Prince's room he was again asleep, and let her call him or shake him or weep as she would, he still slept on, and she could not put any life in him. When daylight came in the morning, the Princess with the long nose came too, and once more drove her away.

When day had come the girl seated herself under the castle windows, to spin with her golden spinning wheel, and the Princess with the long nose wanted to have that also. So she opened the window, and asked what she would take for it. The girl said what she had said on each of the former occasions—that it was not for sale either for gold or for money, but if she could have leave to go to the Prince who lived there, and be with him during the night, the Princess should have it. "Yes," said the Princess, "I will gladly consent to that."

In that palace there were some decent folk who had been sitting in the chamber which was next to that of the Prince and had heard how a woman had been there, weeping and calling on him two nights running, and they told the Prince of this. So that evening, when the Princess came once more with her potion, he pretended to drink but threw it away behind him instead, for he suspected that it was a sleeping drink. When the girl went into the Prince's room, this time he was awake, and she had to tell him how she had come to find her way there.

"You have come just in time," said the Prince, "for

I should have been married tomorrow. But I will not have the long-nosed Princess; and you alone can save me. I will say that I want to see what my bride can do and bid her wash the shirt which has the three drops of tallow on it. This she will consent to, for she does not know it is you who let them fall on it. No one can wash them out but one born of real folk; it cannot be done by a troll. Then I will say that no one shall ever be my bride but the woman who can succeed at this, and I know that you can."

There was great joy and gladness between them, and the next day, when the wedding was to take place, the Prince said to his stepmother, "I must see what my bride can do."

"That you may," said she.

"I have a fine shirt which I want to wear at my wedding, but three drops of tallow have got upon it which I want to have washed off, and I have vowed to marry no one but the woman who is able to do it. If she cannot, she is not worth having."

Well, that was a very small matter, they thought, and agreed to it.

The Princess with the long nose began to wash as well as she could, but the more she washed and rubbed, the larger the spots grew.

"Ah, you cannot wash at all," said the old troll who was her mother. "Give it to me."

But she too had not had the shirt very long in her

hands before it looked worse still, and the more she washed it and rubbed it, the larger and blacker grew the spots.

The other trolls had to come and wash, but the more they did, the blacker and uglier grew the shirt, until at length it was as black as if it had been up the chimney.

"Oh," cried the Prince, "not one of you is good for anything at all! There is a beggar girl sitting outside the window, and I'll be bound she can wash better than any of you! Come in, you girl there!" he cried.

So she came in.

"Can you wash this shirt clean?" he cried.

"Oh, I don't know," she said. "But I will try."

And no sooner had she taken the shirt and dipped it in the water than it was white as driven snow, and even whiter than that.

"I will marry you," said the Prince.

Then the old troll flew into such a rage that she burst, and the Princess with the long nose and all the little trolls must have burst too, for they have never been heard of since.

The Prince and his bride set free all the good people who were imprisoned there, and took with them all the gold and silver they could carry and moved far away from the castle which lay east of the sun and west of the moon.   PETER C. ASBJÖRNSEN AND JÖRGEN E. MOE,
ANDREW LANG COLLECTION

THE MUSICIANS OF BREMEN

A CERTAIN MAN had a Donkey that had served him faithfully for many long years, but whose strength was so far gone that at last he was quite unfit for work. So his master began to consider how much he could get for the Donkey's skin, but the beast, perceiving that something was up, ran away along the road to Bremen. There, thought he, I can be town musician. When he had run some way, he found a Hound lying by the roadside, yawning like one who was very tired. "Why are you doing that, you big fellow?" asked the Donkey.

"Ah," replied the Hound, "because every day I grow older and weaker. I can no longer run with the hunt, and my master has almost beaten me to death. So I took flight, and now I do not know where to turn in order to earn my bread."

"Well," said the Donkey, "I am going to Bremen, to be town musician there. Suppose you go with me and take a share in the music. I will play the lute, and you shall beat the kettledrums." The Hound was pleased with the plan, and off they set.

Presently they came to a Cat, sitting in the middle of the path, with a face like three rainy days! "Now, then, Old Whiskers, what is bothering you?" asked the Donkey.

"How can one be merry when one's neck is in danger?" answered the Cat. "Because I am growing old, and my teeth are all worn to stumps, and because I would rather sit by the fire than run after mice, my mistress wanted to drown me; and so I ran away. But good advice is hard to find, and now I do not know what to do."

"Come with us to Bremen. You are an expert at night music, so you can be a town musician, too." The Cat agreed, and went along with them. The three vagabonds soon came to a farmyard, where a Cock was sitting on a barn door crowing with all his might. "Your crowing can pierce through marrow and bone," said the Donkey. "What do you do that for?"

"That is the way I prophesy fine weather," said the Cock. "But important guests are coming for Sunday dinner tomorrow and my mistress has told the cook to make me into soup. Tonight I shall lose my head, so I am crowing with a full throat as long as I can."

"Ah, but you, Red-Comb, should come away with us," replied the Donkey. "We are going to Bremen, to find something better than death. You have a good voice, and if we four make music together it will have full play."

The Cock was delighted with the idea, and so all four traveled on together.

They could not, however, reach Bremen in one day, and at evening they came to a forest, where they meant to pass the night. The Donkey and the Hound lay down under a large tree. The Cat and the Cock climbed up into the branches, but the latter flew right to the top, where he was most safe. Before he went to sleep he looked around the countryside and thought he saw a little spark in the distance; so, calling his companions, he said they were not far from a house, for he saw a light. The Donkey said, "If it is so, we had better get up and go toward it, for it's not very comfortable here in this place." And the Hound continued, "Yes, indeed! A couple of bones with meat on them would be very acceptable!"

So they made haste toward the spot where the light was, and which shone brighter and brighter, until they came to a well-lighted robber's den. The Donkey, as the biggest, went to the window and peeped in. "What do you see, Gray Horse?" asked the Cock.

"What do I see?" replied the Donkey. "I see a table laid out with savory meats and drinks, and robbers sitting around enjoying themselves."

"That would be the right sort of thing for us," said the Cock.

"Yes, yes, I wish we were sitting there," replied the Donkey. Then the animals took counsel together on how to drive away the robbers, and at last they thought of a plan.

The Donkey placed his forefeet upon the window ledge, the Hound got on his back, the Cat climbed up upon the Hound, and, lastly, the Cock flew up and perched upon the Cat. When this was accomplished, at a given signal they commenced to perform their music. The Donkey brayed, the Hound barked, the Cat meowed, and the Cock crowed; and they made such a tremendous noise that the windowpanes splintered and crashed. Terrified at these unearthly sounds, the robbers jumped up, thinking that some demons had burst in on them, and fled off into the forest. The four musicians immediately made themselves at home, and quickly ate all that was left, as if they had been fasting for six weeks.

As soon as they had finished, they put out the light, and each sought for himself a sleeping place according to his nature and custom. The Donkey stretched out upon some straw, the Hound behind the door, the Cat upon the hearth near the warm ashes, and the Cock flew up on a beam which ran across the room. Weary with their long walk, they soon went to sleep.

At midnight the robbers could see from their retreat that no light was burning in their house, and everything appeared quiet. The captain said, "We need not have been frightened into fits," and, calling one of the band, he sent him forward to reconnoiter. The

messenger, finding all still, went into the kitchen to strike a light, and, taking the glistening, fiery eyes of the Cat for live coals, he held a match to them, expecting the match to take fire. But the Cat flew in his face, spitting and scratching, and frightening him so dreadfully that he made for the back door; then the Hound, who lay nearby, sprang up and bit his leg; and as he limped over the straw where the Donkey was stretched out, it gave him a powerful kick with its hind foot. This was not all, for the Cock, awakened by the noise around him, cried from his perch on the beam, "Cock-a-doodle-doo, cock-a-doodle-doo!"

Then the robber ran back as fast as he could to his captain and cried, "Ah, my master, there dwells a horrible witch in the house, who spat on me and scratched my face with her long nails. In front of the door stands a man with a knife, who chopped at my leg, and in the yard there lies a black monster, who beat me with a great wooden club. In addition to all that, upon the roof sits a judge, who called out, 'Bring the knave up, do!'—so I ran away as fast as I could."

After this the robbers dared not go near their house again, but everything prospered so well with the four town musicians of Bremen that they never left their new home. And there they have been, from that day to this, for all I know.

OLD GERMAN TALE, COLLECTION OF
KATE DOUGLAS WIGGIN AND NORA ARCHIBALD SMITH

BLUE BEARD

THERE WAS once a man who had fine houses, both in town and country, a great deal of silver and gold plate, embroidered furniture and gilded coaches. But this man was unlucky enough to have a blue beard, which made him so frightfully ugly that all the women and girls ran away from him.

One of his neighbors, a lady of quality, had two daughters who were perfect beauties. He asked her for one of them in marriage, leaving to her choice which of the two she would bestow on him. Neither of them would have him. Another reason, besides the beard, for their disgust and aversion was his having been married to several wives; and nobody knew what had become of them.

To win their affection, Blue Beard took them, with their mother, three or four ladies of their acquaintance and some young people of the neighborhood, to one of his country houses, where they all stayed for a week. There was nothing but parties, hunting, fishing, dancing, mirth and feasting. Nobody went to bed, for they spent the night playing games and joking with one another. In short, everything went so well that the younger daughter began to think the master of the house was an agreeable gentleman after all.

As soon as they returned home, the marriage took place, and about a month afterward, Blue Beard told his wife he was obliged to take a journey for six weeks at least, about affairs of very great consequence. He begged her to amuse herself in his absence, and suggested that she invite some of her friends to the country, if she pleased, and to enjoy herself wherever she might be.

"Here," said he, "are the keys to the large storerooms wherein I have my best furniture; these are for my silver and gold plate, which is not in use every day; these open my strongboxes, which hold my money, both gold and silver; these, my caskets of jewels; and this is the master key to all my apartments. But this little one is the key to the closet at the end of the gallery on the ground floor. Open any of them you wish; you may go into every one, except that little closet, which I forbid you."

She promised to observe exactly what he had ordered. Then, having embraced her, he got into his coach and started on his journey.

Her neighbors and good friends did not wait to be sent for, so great was their impatience to see the rich furnishings of her house. Not daring to do so while her husband was at home, they ran through the rooms and looked into the closets and wardrobes, all fine and rich.

They praised and envied the happiness of their friend, who hardly greeted them—such was her eagerness to open the closet on the ground floor. She was so driven by her curiosity that she went down a little back staircase with such excessive haste that twice or thrice she nearly broke her neck.

When she reached the closet door, she stopped for some time, thinking of her husband's orders, but the temptation was strong and she could not overcome it. She took the little key and opened the door, trembling, but could not at first see anything plainly, because the shutters were closed. After some moments she perceived a bloodstained floor on which lay the bodies of several dead women. These were the wives Blue Beard had married and murdered, one after another. She thought she would die of fear, and the key, which she had pulled out of the lock, fell from her hand.

When she had somewhat regained her courage, she picked up the key, locked the door and went upstairs into her room to recover herself, but she could not, so frightened was she. Having observed that the key of the closet was stained with blood, she tried two or three times to wipe it off. In vain did she wash it and even rub it with soap and sand—but the blood still remained, for the key was magical and she could never make it quite clean. When the blood was gone from one side, it appeared again on the other.

Blue Beard returned from his journey that same evening, saying he had received letters on the way informing him the business matter had ended to his advantage. Next morning he asked her for the keys, which she gave him, but with such a trembling hand he easily guessed what happened. "What!" said he. "How comes this blood upon the key?"

"I do not know," cried the poor woman, paler than death.

"You do not know!" replied Blue Beard. "I know very well. You were resolved to go into the closet, were you not? Very well, madam, you shall go in and take your place among the ladies you saw there."

Hearing this, she threw herself at her husband's feet. She would have melted a rock, so beautiful and sorrowful was she, but Blue Beard had a heart harder than any rock!

"You must die, madam," said he, "and very soon."

"Since I must die," answered she, looking upon him with her eyes filled with tears, "give me some little time to say my prayers."

"I give you," replied Blue Beard, "half a quarter of an hour, but not one moment more."

When she was alone she called out to her sister, who was still visiting with her, and said, "Sister Anne, go up, I beg you, to the top of the tower, and look if our brothers are not coming. They promised me they would come today. If you see them, give them a sign to make haste."

Her sister Anne went up on the top of the tower, and the poor, afflicted wife called, "Anne, sister Anne, do you see anyone coming?"

And sister Anne said, "I see nothing but the sun, which makes a dust, and the grass, which looks green."

Meanwhile Blue Beard, holding a great saber in his hand, shouted to his wife, "Come down instantly, or I shall come up to you."

"One moment longer, if you please," said his wife. And then she cried out very softly, "Anne, sister Anne, do you see anyone coming?"

And sister Anne answered, "I see nothing but the sun, which makes a dust, and the grass, which is green."

"Come down quickly," cried Blue Beard, "or I will come up to you."

"I am coming, I am coming," answered his wife. And then she called, "Anne, sister Anne, do you not see anyone coming?"

"I see," replied sister Anne, "a great dust, which comes on this side here."

"Are they our brothers?"

"Alas, no, my dear sister, I see a flock of sheep."

"Will you not come down?" cried Blue Beard.

"One moment longer," said his wife. And then she

cried out, "Anne, sister Anne, do you see nobody coming?"

"I see," said she, "two horsemen, but they are still a great distance away."

"Heaven be praised," replied the poor wife joyfully. "They are our brothers; I will make a sign, as well as I can, for them to make haste."

Then Blue Beard bawled out so loud that he made the whole house tremble. The distressed wife came down and threw herself at his feet, all in tears, with her hair about her shoulders.

"This means nothing to me," said Blue Beard. "You must die." Then, taking hold of her hair with one hand and lifting up the sword with the other, he was about to take off her head. The poor lady, looking at him with pleading eyes, begged him for one moment more to collect herself. "No, no," said he, "commend yourself to God," and was just ready to strike.

At this very instant, there was such a loud knocking at the gate that Blue Beard stopped short. Two horsemen entered, drawing their swords. Blue Beard knew them to be his wife's brothers and he immediately dashed off to save himself. But the two brothers pursued so closely that they overtook him before he reached the steps, where they ran their swords through him and left him dead. The poor wife was almost as dead as her husband and had not strength enough to rise and welcome her brothers.

Blue Beard's wife became mistress of all his estate. She made use of one part of it to marry her sister Anne to a young gentleman who had loved her a long while; another part to buy captains' commissions for her brothers; and the rest to marry herself to a very worthy gentleman, who soon made her forget the ill time she had passed in the house of Blue Beard.

CHARLES PERRAULT, ANDREW LANG COLLECTION

THE PRINCESS
ON THE GLASS HILL

ONCE UPON a time there was a man who had a meadow which lay on the side of a mountain, and in the meadow there was a barn in which he stored hay. Every St. John's Eve, when the grass was at its height, it was all eaten clean up—just as if a flock of sheep had gnawed it down to the ground during the night. This happened once, and it happened twice, but then the man grew tired of losing his crop and said to his sons—he had three of them, and the third was called Cinderlad—that one of them must go and sleep in the barn on St. John's Eve, for it was absurd to let the grass be eaten up again, blade and stalk.

The eldest was quite willing to go to the meadow; he would watch the grass, he said, and he would do it so well that neither man nor beast nor even the devil himself should have any of it. So he went to the barn and lay down to sleep, but when night was drawing near there was such a rumbling and such an earthquake that the walls and roof shook, and the lad jumped up and took to his heels, and the barn remained empty again that year.

Next St. John's Eve, the second son was willing to show what he could do. He went to the barn and lay down to sleep, as his brother had, but when night fell there was a great rumbling, and then an earthquake, which was even worse. When the youth heard it, he was terrified and went off, running as if his life depended upon it.

The year after, it was Cinderlad's turn, but when he made ready to go, the others laughed at him. "Well, you are just the right one to watch the hay, you who have never learned anything but how to sit among the ashes and toast yourself by the fire!" said they. Cinderlad, however, did not trouble himself about what they said, and when evening drew near he rambled away to the outlying field.

He went into the barn and lay down, but in about

an hour's time the rumbling and creaking began, and it was frightful to hear. "Well, if it gets no worse than that, I can stand it," said Cinderlad. In a little time the creaking began again, and the earth quaked so that all the hay flew around the boy.

"Oh, if it gets no worse than that I can stand it," said Cinderlad. Then came a third rumbling and a third earthquake, so violent that the boy thought the walls and roof had fallen in; when that was over everything suddenly grew as still as death around him. Cinderlad thought the upheaval would come again, but everything was quiet, and everything stayed quiet. After a short time, he heard something that sounded as if a horse were chewing just outside the barn door. He crept to the door to see what it was, and there stood a horse eating away. It was so big and fat and fine a horse that Cinderlad had never seen one like it before; a saddle and bridle lay upon it, and a complete suit of armor for a knight, and everything was of copper so bright that it sparkled.

"Ha, ha! It is you who eats our hay then," said the boy. "I will stop that." So he made haste and took out his flint for striking fire, for it has a power over animals. He threw a spark over the horse, and then it could not stir from the spot and the boy could do what he liked with it. He mounted and rode away to a place no one knew of but himself, and tied the horse up. When he went home, his brothers laughed and asked

646

how he had got on. "You did not lie long in the barn if you have been even as far as the field!" said they.

"I lay in the barn till the sun rose," said the boy. "What made you two so frightened?"

"Well, we shall soon see whether you have watched the meadow or not," answered the brothers. But they found the grass just as long and as thick as it had been the night before!

The next St. John's Eve, neither of the two older brothers dared go to the outlying field to watch the crop, but Cinderlad went, and everything happened exactly as before. There was a rumbling and an earthquake, and then there was another, and then a third. All three earthquakes were much, very much more violent than they had been the year before. Everything became still as death again, and the boy heard something chomping outside the barn. When he went to look through a crack in the door, there was a horse standing close by the wall of the house, eating and chewing. It was far larger and fatter than the first horse, and it had a saddle on its back and a bridle, too, and a full suit of armor for a knight, bright silver and as beautiful as anyone could wish to see.

"Ho, ho!" said the boy. "Is it you who eats our hay in the night? I will put a stop to that." So he took out his flint for striking fire and threw a spark over the horse's mane, and the beast stood there as quiet as a lamb. Then the boy rode this horse, too, away to the place where he kept the other and then went back to his house again.

"I suppose you will tell us the grass hasn't been touched this time either," said the brothers.

"Well, so it hasn't," said Cinderlad. And there it was—the grass standing as high and as thick as it had been before; but that did not make them any kinder to Cinderlad.

When the next St. John's Eve came, neither of the older brothers was brave enough to go to the outlying barn to watch the grass, but Cinderlad dared to go. There were three earthquakes, each worse than the other, and the last flung the boy all the way across the barn, then everything suddenly became still as death. When he had lain quietly a short time, he heard the chewing sound outside the barn. He peeped through the crack in the door, and, behold—there stood a horse just outside, much larger and fatter than the two others he had caught. The saddle and bridle were gold, and there was a suit of golden armor, too.

"Ho, ho! It is you, then, who eats our hay this time," said the boy, "but I will put a stop to that." So he pulled out his flint for striking fire and threw a spark over the horse, and it stood as still as if it had been nailed to the field, and the boy could do just what he liked with it. He mounted the horse and rode away to the place where he kept the two others, and then he went home again.

The two brothers mocked him just as they had done before, but Cinderlad did not trouble himself about that, telling them to go to the field and see. This time, also, the grass was standing, looking as fine and as thick as ever.

Now it happened that the King had a daughter whom he offered to give to the one who could ride to the top of a very high hill of glass, slippery as ice, which stood close to his palace. Upon the top of this the King's daughter was to sit with three golden apples in her lap, and the man who was able to ride up and carry off the three apples could marry her and have half the kingdom. The King had this proclaimed throughout the whole kingdom, and in many other kingdoms, too.

The Princess was very beautiful, and all who saw her fell in love with her, in spite of themselves. It is needless to say that the princes and knights were eager to win her—and half the kingdom besides. They came riding from the ends of the world, dressed so splendidly that their raiments gleamed in the sunshine, and riding on horses which seemed to dance as they went. There was not one of these princes who did not think he was sure to win the Princess.

When the day of the contest arrived, there was such a host of knights and princes at the foot of the glass hill that it made one dizzy to look at them. Everyone who could walk or even crawl was there to see who would win the King's daughter. Cinderlad's two brothers were there too, but they would not hear of letting him go with them, for he was so dusty and grimy from sleeping among the ashes that they said everyone would laugh at them if they were seen in the company of such an oaf.

Then I will go by myself, thought Cinderlad.

When the two brothers appeared at the scene, the princes and knights were trying so hard to ride up the glass hill that their horses were in a foam. It was all in vain, for no sooner did the horses set foot upon the hill than down they slipped. Not one could get even so much as a couple of yards, for the hill was as smooth as a glass windowpane and as steep as the side of a house. But they were eager to win the King's daughter and half the kingdom, so they kept riding and kept slipping. At length all the horses were so tired they could do no more, and so hot that the foam dropped from them, and the princes and knights were forced to stop.

The King was just about to proclaim that the riding should begin afresh on the following day, when suddenly a knight came riding up on a horse of such beauty that no one had ever seen its like before. The knight had on armor of copper, and his bridle was of copper too, so bright that it sparkled. The other knights called out to him that he might just as well spare himself the trouble of trying to ride up the glass hill, for it was of no use; but he did not heed them and rode straight off to it and went up as if it were nothing at all. Thus he rode for a long time—it may have been a third of the way to the top—but turned his horse around and rode down again.

The Princess thought she had never seen so handsome a knight, and while he was riding up she was thinking: Oh, how I hope he will be able to come to the top! When she saw that he was turning his horse back, she threw down one of the golden apples after him, and it rolled into his shoe. But when he reached the bottom of the hill he rode away so fast no one knew what had become of him.

All the princes and knights were bidden to present themselves before the King that night in order that he who had ridden so far up the glass hill might show the golden apple which the King's daughter had thrown down. But no one had anything to show. One knight after another presented himself, and none could show the apple.

That same night, Cinderlad's brothers came back and had a long story to tell. At first, they said, there was no one able to get even so much as one step up the hill, but then came a knight who had armor of copper and a bridle of copper, and his armor and trappings were so bright they shone for a great distance, and it was a grand sight to see him riding. He rode one third of the way up the glass hill, and he could easily have ridden the whole of it if he had liked. But he had made up his mind that that was enough.

"Oh, I should have liked to see him too—that I should," said Cinderlad.

Next day, the brothers were about to set out again, and this time, too, Cinderlad begged to go with them and see who rode. But no, they said—he was not fit to do that, for he was much too ugly and dirty. Well, well, then I will go all by myself, thought Cinderlad. So the brothers went to the glass hill, and all the princes and knights began to ride again. Not one could even get so far as a yard up the hill. When they had tired out their horses so they could do no more, they again had to stop altogether.

Just as the King was thinking it would be well to proclaim that the riding should continue next day so they might have one last chance, he suddenly thought it would be well to wait a little longer to see if the knight in copper armor would come on this day, too. Nothing was to be seen of him, but just as they had stopped looking for him, a knight came riding up on a steed that was much, much finer than the one the knight in copper armor had ridden. This knight had silver armor and a silver saddle and bridle, and all were so bright they shone and glistened when he was still a long way off.

Again the other knights called to him and said he might just as well give up the attempt to ride up the glass hill, for it was useless to try. But the silver knight paid no heed to them and rode straight away to the glass hill, and went farther than the knight in copper armor had gone; when he had ridden two thirds of the way to the top, however, he turned his horse around and rode down again.

The Princess sat longing that he might be able to reach her, and when she saw him turning back she threw the second apple after him, and it rolled into his shoe also, and as soon as he reached the bottom of the glass hill he rode away so fast that no one could see what had become of him.

In the evening, when everyone was to appear before the King and Princess, one knight after another went in, but none of them had a golden apple to show.

The two brothers went home as they had the night before and told Cinderlad how everyone had ridden, but that no one had been able to get up the hill.

"But last of all," they said, "came a knight in silver armor, and he had a silver bridle on his horse and a silver saddle, and oh, but he could ride! He took his horse two thirds of the way up the hill, but then he turned back. He was a fine fellow indeed," said the brothers, "and the Princess threw the second golden apple to him!"

"Oh, how I should have liked to see him too!" said Cinderlad.

On the third day, everything happened as it had

before. Everyone waited for the knight in silver armor, but he was nowhere in sight. At last, after a long time, came a knight riding upon a horse that was so fine its equal had never yet been seen. The knight had golden armor, and the horse a golden saddle and bridle, and these were all so bright they shone and dazzled everyone, even while the knight was still at a great distance. The other princes and knights did not think to call to him how useless it was to try, so amazed were they at his magnificence. He rode straight away to the glass hill and galloped up as if it were no hill at all, and the Princess had no time even to wish he might reach the top. As soon as he had ridden to the top, he took the third golden apple from the lap of the Princess and then turned his horse around and rode down again. He vanished from sight before anyone was able to say a word to him.

When the two brothers came home that night, they had much to tell of how the riding had gone that day, and at last they told about the knight in the golden armor too.

"He was a grand fellow! Another such splendid knight is not to be found anywhere in the world!" said the brothers.

"Oh, how I should have liked to see him too!" said Cinderlad.

Next day, all the knights and princes were to appear before the King and the Princess so that he who had the third golden apple might produce it. They all went in turn, first princes, and then knights, but none of them had a golden apple.

"But somebody must have it," said the King, "for with our own eyes we all saw a man ride up and take it." So he commanded that every man in the kingdom should come to the palace, to see if he could show the apple. And one after the other they all came, but no one had the golden apple, and after a long, long time Cinderlad's two brothers came likewise. They were the last of all, so the King inquired of them if anyone else in the kingdom was left to come.

"Oh, yes. We have a brother," said the two, "but he couldn't have the golden apple! He never left the cinder heap on any of the three days."

"Never mind that," said the King. "As everyone else has come to the palace, let him come, too."

So Cinderlad was forced to go and appear at the King's palace.

"Have you the golden apple?" asked the King.

"Yes," said Cinderlad. "Here is the first, and here is the second, and here is the third, too." And he took all three apples out of his pocket and with that threw off his sooty rags and appeared before them in his bright golden armor, which gleamed as he stood.

"You shall have my daughter, and the half of my kingdom as well, and you have truly earned both," said the King.

So there was a wedding, and Cinderlad married the King's daughter, and everyone made merry at the feast. For all of them could make merry, though they could not ride up the glass hill; and if they have not left off their merrymaking they must be at it still.

PETER C. ASBJÖRNSEN AND JÖRGEN E. MOE,
ANDREW LANG COLLECTION

THE HALF-CHICK

THERE WAS once upon a time a handsome, black Spanish hen who had a large brood of chickens. They were all fine, plump little birds, except the youngest, who was quite unlike his sisters and brothers. This one looked just as if he had been cut in two. He had only one leg, and one wing, and one eye; and he had half a head and half a beak.

His mother shook her head sadly as she looked at him and said: "My youngest born is only a half-chick. He can never grow up a tall, handsome cock like his brothers. They will go out into the world and rule over poultry yards of their own. But this poor little fellow

will always have to stay at home with his mother."
And she called him Medio Pollito, which is Spanish
for half-chick.

Now, though Medio Pollito was such an odd, help-
less-looking little thing, his mother soon found he was
not at all willing to remain under her wing and protec-
tion. Indeed, in character he was as unlike his brothers
and sisters as he was in appearance. They were good,
obedient chickens, and when the old hen called them
they chirped and ran back to her side. But Medio Pollito had a roving spirit in spite of his one leg, and when
his mother called him to return to the coop, he pretended he could not hear because he had only one ear.

When she took the whole family out for a walk,
Medio Pollito would hop away by himself and hide
among the Indian corn. His brothers and sisters had
many an anxious moment searching for him, while his
mother ran to and fro cackling in fear and dismay.

As he grew older, he became more self-willed and
disobedient. His manner to his mother was often rude
and his temper to the other chickens disagreeable.

One day, he had been out for a longer expedition
than usual in the fields. On his return, he strutted up
to his mother with a peculiar little hop and kick which
was his way of walking and, cocking his one eye at her
in a very bold way, he said: "Mother, I am tired of this
life in a dull farmyard with nothing but a dreary cornfield to look at. I'm off to Madrid to see the King."

"To Madrid, Medio Pollito!" exclaimed his mother. "Why, you silly chick, it would be a long journey even for a grown-up cock; a poor thing like you would be tired out before you had gone half the distance. No, no. Stay here at home with your mother, and some day, when you are bigger, we will go on a little journey together."

But Medio Pollito had made up his mind. He would not listen to his mother's advice, nor to the prayers and entreaties of his brothers and sisters.

"What is the use of our crowding each other in this poky little place?" he said. "When I have a fine court-yard of my own at the King's palace, I shall perhaps ask some of you to come and pay me a short visit." And scarcely waiting to say good-bye to his mother and his brothers and sisters, away he stumped down the highroad that led to Madrid.

"Be sure you are kind and civil to everyone you meet," called his mother, running after him. But he was in such a hurry to be off he did not wait to answer her or even to look back.

A little later in the day, as he was taking a short cut through a field, he passed a stream. Now the stream was choked and overgrown with weeds and water plants so its waters could not flow freely. "Oh, Medio Pollito!" it cried, as the half-chick hopped along its banks. "Do come here and help me by clearing away these weeds."

"Help you, indeed!" exclaimed Medio Pollito, tossing his head and shaking the few feathers in his tail. "Do you think I have nothing to do but waste my time on such trifles? Help yourself, and don't trouble busy travelers. I am off to Madrid to see the King." And hoppity-kick, hoppity-kick, hoppity-kick, away stumped Medio Pollito.

A little later, he came to a fire that had been left by some gypsies in a wood. It was burning very low and would soon be out. "Oh, Medio Pollito," cried the fire in a weak, wavering voice as the half-chick approached, "in a few minutes I shall go out completely unless you put some sticks and dry leaves upon me. Do help me or I shall die!"

"Help you, indeed!" answered Medio Pollito. "I have other things to do. Gather sticks for yourself and don't trouble me. I am off to Madrid to see the King." And hoppity-kick, hoppity-kick, away stumped Medio Pollito.

The next morning, as Medio Pollito was nearing Madrid, he passed a large tree in whose branches the wind was caught and entangled. "Oh, Medio Pollito," called the wind, "do hop up here and help me get free of these branches. I cannot tear myself away, and it is so uncomfortable."

"It is your own fault for going there," answered Medio Pollito. "I can't waste all my morning stopping here to help you. Just shake yourself off and don't

hinder me, for I am off to Madrid to see the King."
And hoppity-kick, hoppity-kick, away stumped Medio
Pollito in great glee, for the towers and roofs of
Madrid were now in sight.

When he entered the town, he saw before him a
great splendid house, with soldiers standing before the
gates. This he knew must be the royal palace, and he
determined to hop up to the front gate and wait until
the King appeared. But as he was hopping past one
of the back windows, the King's cook looked out
and saw him.

"Here is the very thing I want," he exclaimed, "for
the King has just sent a message that he must have
chicken broth for his dinner!" And, opening the window, he stretched out his arm, caught Medio Pollito
and popped him into the soup pot standing next to
the fire.

Oh, how wet and clammy the water felt as it went
over Medio Pollito's head, making his feathers and his
one wing cling to his side.

"Water, water," he cried in his despair, "do have
pity upon me and do not wet me like this."

"Ah, Medio Pollito," replied the water, "you would
not help me when I was a little stream away off in the
fields, and now you must be punished."

Then the fire began to burn and scald Medio Pollito.
He danced and hopped from one side of the pot to the
other, trying to get away from the heat and crying out

in pain: "Fire, fire! Do not scorch me like this. You cannot think how it hurts."

"Ah, Medio Pollito," answered the fire, "you would not help me when I was dying in the wood; and now you are being punished."

At last, just when the pain was so great Medio Pollito thought he was going to die, the cook lifted up the lid of the pot to see if the broth was ready for the King's dinner.

"Look here," he cried in horror, "this chicken is quite useless! It is burned to a cinder. I can't send it up to the royal table." And, opening the window, he threw Medio Pollito out into the street. But the wind caught him up and whirled him through the air so quickly that Medio Pollito could scarcely breathe, and his heart beat against his side till he thought it would surely break.

"Oh, wind," he gasped out, "if you hurry me along like this you will kill me. Do let me rest for just a moment, or ——" But he was so breathless he could not finish his sentence.

"Ah, Medio Pollito," replied the wind, "when I was caught in the branches of the tree you would not help me, and now you are being punished." And he swirled Medio Pollito over the roofs of the houses till they reached the highest church in the city, and there he left him fastened to the top of the steeple.

And there stands Medio Pollito to this day. If you

go to Madrid and walk through the streets till you come to the highest church, there you will see Medio Pollito perched on his one leg on the steeple, with his one wing drooping at his side, gazing sadly out of his one eye over the city.

OLD SPANISH TALE, ANDREW LANG COLLECTION

SLEEPING BEAUTY

THERE ONCE lived a King and a Queen who were sorry they had no children— so sorry that it cannot be expressed. They tried all the curative waters in the world, vows and pilgrimages, but to no purpose.

At last, however, the Queen gave birth to a daughter. There was a very fine christening; and the Princess had for her godmothers all the fairies they could find in the whole kingdom. They managed to locate seven, and so the Princess was endowed with all the perfections imaginable.

After the christening, the company returned to the King's palace, where a great feast was prepared for the fairies. Before every one of them was placed a magnificent casket of massive gold, wherein were a spoon, knife and fork of pure gold set with diamonds and rubies. But, as they were sitting down at table, they saw come into the hall a very old fairy who had not been invited. It was more than fifty years since she had been seen, and everyone believed that she was either dead or enchanted.

The King ordered a place set for her, but could not furnish her with a casket of gold because only seven had been made for the seven fairies. The old fairy felt she was intentionally slighted, and muttered some threats between her teeth. One of the young fairies, who sat by her, overheard her grumbling. Judging that she might give the little Princess some unlucky gift, the young fairy went, as soon as they rose from table, and hid herself behind the drapes so that she might speak last and repair, as much as she could, any evil which the old fairy intended.

Meanwhile all the fairies began to offer their gifts to the Princess. The youngest, for her gift, said that the Princess should be the most beautiful person in the world; the next, that she should have the wit of an angel; the third, that she should have wonderful grace in everything she did; the fourth, that she should dance perfectly; the fifth, that she should sing like a nightingale; and the sixth, that she should play all kinds of music to perfection.

The old fairy's turn came next. With her head shaking more with spite than age, she said that the Princess should have her hand pierced with a spindle and die of the wound. This terrible gift made the whole company tremble, and everybody began to weep.

At this very instant the young fairy came out from behind the drapes and spoke these words:

"Assure yourselves, O King and Queen, that your daughter shall not die. It is true, I have no power to undo entirely what my elder has done. The Princess shall indeed pierce her hand with a spindle. But instead of dying, she shall only fall into a profound sleep, which shall last for a hundred years. After that time a king's son shall come and wake her."

The King, to avoid the misfortune, immediately forbade spinning with a distaff and spindle, or to have so much as a spindle in the house.

About fifteen or sixteen years later, the King and Queen happened to be visiting one of their other castles, and the young Princess was diverting herself by running up and down the palace. She came into a little room at the top of the tower, where an old servingwoman was spinning with her spindle. This woman had never heard of the King's proclamation against spindles.

"What are you doing there, my good woman?" said the Princess.

"I am spinning, my dear child," said the old woman.

"Ha," said the Princess, "this is very pretty. How do you do it? Give it to me so I may see."

She had no sooner taken the spindle than it ran into her hand and she fell down in a swoon.

The good old woman cried out for help. People came and threw water upon the Princess' face, unlaced her dress and rubbed her hands and temples with perfume. But nothing would bring her to herself.

And now the King, who had returned to the palace, came up at the noise, remembered the prediction of the fairies and, judging very well that this must necessarily come to pass since the fairies had said it, had the Princess carried into the finest apartment in his palace and laid upon a bed all embroidered with gold.

One would have taken her for a little angel, she was so very beautiful. Her swooning had not dimmed her complexion, for her cheeks were carnation and her lips were coral. Indeed, her eyes were shut, but she was heard to breathe softly, which satisfied those about her that she was not dead. The King commanded that she be left to sleep quietly till her hour of awakening should come.

The good fairy who had saved the life of the Princess by condemning her to sleep a hundred years was in the kingdom of Matakin, twelve thousand miles off, when this accident befell the Princess. But she was instantly informed of it by a little dwarf who had boots with which he could go seven leagues in one stride.

The fairy came immediately, riding in a fiery chariot drawn by dragons.

The King handed her out of the chariot, and she approved everything he had done. But she touched with her wand everything in the palace—except the King and the Queen—governesses, maids of honor, ladies of the bedchamber, gentlemen, officers, stewards, cooks, undercooks, scullions, guards, pages, footmen. She likewise touched the horses in the stables, the great dogs in the courtyard and even pretty little Mopsey, the Princess' spaniel, which lay at the foot of her bed.

The minute she touched them they all fell asleep that they might not awake before their mistress and might be ready to wait upon her when she wanted them. The very spits at the fire, loaded with partridges and pheasants, fell asleep also, as did the fire. This was done in a moment, for fairies are not long in doing their magic.

And now the King and the Queen, having kissed their dear child without waking her, went out of the palace, and in a quarter of an hour's time there grew up all around about the park such a vast number of trees, great and small, bushes and brambles, twining so thickly one within another, that neither man nor beast could pass through. Nothing could be seen of the castle but the very tops of the towers, and those only from a great distance

When a hundred years had passed, another family ruled the kingdom. The son of the king then reigning chanced to go hunting and asked about the towers which he saw in the middle of a great thick wood.

All answered according to the stories they had heard. Some said it was a ruined old castle, haunted by spirits; others that it was where sorcerers and witches held their night meetings. The common opinion was that it belonged to an ogre who carried there as many little children as he could catch.

The Prince was at a loss, not knowing what to believe, when a very aged countryman spoke to him: "May it please Your Royal Highness, about fifty years ago I heard from my father, who heard my grandfather say, there was in this castle a Princess, the most beautiful ever seen, who must sleep there a hundred years and should be awakened by a king's son."

The young Prince was fired by these words. Thinking it a gay and rare adventure and inspired by a wish for love and honor, he resolved that moment to look into it. Hardly had he advanced toward the wood when all the great trees, the bushes and brambles gave way of themselves to let him pass. He walked up a long avenue to the castle. What surprised him was that he saw none of his people could follow him. The trees closed behind him as soon as he had passed through. A young prince is always valiant, however, and he continued on his way.

He came into a spacious outer court, where everything he saw might have frozen the most fearless person with horror. There was a frightful silence, and nothing was to be seen but the stretched-out bodies of men and animals, all seeming to be dead. He knew, however, by the ruddy faces of the porters, that they were only asleep. And their goblets, wherein still remained some drops of wine, showed plainly that they had fallen asleep in their cups.

The Prince then crossed a court paved with marble, went up the stairs and came into the guardroom, where guards were lined up, their muskets upon their shoulders, and snoring as loudly as they could. After that he went through several rooms full of gentlemen and ladies, all asleep, some standing, others sitting. At last he came into a chamber gilded with gold, where he saw upon a bed, the curtains of which were open, the finest sight the young Prince ever beheld—a Princess, who appeared to be about fifteen or sixteen years old and whose radiant beauty had a somewhat unearthly quality. He approached, trembling with admiration, and fell down before her upon his knees.

And now, as the enchantment was at an end, the Princess awoke and, looking on the Prince with eyes more tender than a first glance might seem to admit, "Is it you, my Prince?" said she. "I have waited a long while."

The Prince, charmed with these words, and much

more with the manner in which they were spoken, knew not how to show his joy and gratitude. He assured her he loved her better than he did himself. There was little eloquence but a great deal of love in their talk. He was more at a loss than she, and we need not wonder at it. She had had time to think on what to say to him; for it is very probable—though history mentions nothing of it—that the good fairy, during so long a sleep, had given her very agreeable dreams. In short, they talked for hours together, and yet they said not half what they had to say.

Meanwhile the rest of the palace awoke; everyone went about his own business, and as they were not in love they were ready to die of hunger. The chief lady-in-waiting grew very impatient and told the Princess loudly that supper was served. The Prince helped the Princess to rise. She was dressed magnificently, but His Royal Highness took care not to tell her she was dressed like his great-grandmother in pictures he had seen—even to the lace band peeping over her collar. She looked not a bit less charming and beautiful for all that.

They went into the great hall of mirrors where they supped and were served by the Princess' officers. The musicians played old tunes, very excellently, even though it was now over a hundred years since they had touched their instruments. When supper was over they were married in the chapel of the castle, and though the bride was one hundred years older than the groom nobody would ever have guessed it.

A few days later the Prince took his bride to live with him in his own palace, and the enchanted castle and wood vanished, never to be seen again.

OLD FRENCH TALE, ANDREW LANG COLLECTION

THE MAGIC CARPET

THERE WAS a Sultan who had three sons and a niece. The eldest of the Princes was called Houssain, the second Ali, the youngest Ahmed, and the Princess, his niece, Nouronnihar.

The Princess Nouronnihar was the daughter of the Sultan's younger brother, who had died when the Princess was very young. The Sultan took upon himself the care of his niece's education and brought her up in his palace with the three Princes.

To his dismay, he discovered one day that each of his sons loved the Princess passionately. He was very much concerned and devised a plan to settle the predicament. The next day he sent for all three together

673

and said to them, "I think it would be advisable for each of you to travel separately into different countries. As you know, I have great curiosity and delight in everything that is unusual. I therefore promise my niece in marriage to him who shall bring me the most extraordinary rarity. For the purchase of the rarity and the expense of traveling I will give each of you a sum of money."

As the three Princes were always submissive and obedient to the Sultan's will and flattered themselves that Fortune might prove favorable to them, they consented. The Sultan gave them the money he had promised them; and that very day they gave orders for the preparations for their travels and took leave of their father.

Accordingly, they set out the next morning from the same gate of the city, each outfitted like a merchant, attended by an aide dressed like a slave, and all well mounted and equipped.

They went the first day's journey together and stopped at an inn where the road divided into three different directions. That night, when they were at supper, they agreed to travel for one year and meet in the inn at the end of that time. The first one who came should wait for the rest; since they had all taken their leave of the Sultan together, they would return together. The next morning, just as the sun was rising, after they had embraced and wished one another success, each mounted his horse and started off on a different road.

Prince Houssain, the eldest brother, arrived at Bisnagar, the capital of the kingdom of that name and the residence of its king. He lodged at an inn patronized by foreign merchants. Having learned that there were four principal sections in the city where merchants sold their various commodities, he went to one of these the next day.

He wandered through several streets, all vaulted and shaded from the sun, and yet very light too. He noted that those men who dealt in the same sort of goods lived in one street; as did the handicrafts men, who had their shops in the smaller streets.

The Prince's admiration was quickened when he beheld the multitude of shops stocked with a variety of merchandise, such as the finest linens from India, some painted in the most lively colors and representing beasts, trees and flowers; silks, brocades and tapestries from Persia and China; and porcelain from China and Japan. But when he came to the goldsmiths and jewelers he was in an ecstasy to behold such prodigious quantities of wrought gold and silver and was dazzled by the luster of the pearls, diamonds, rubies, emeralds and other jewels exposed for sale.

Another thing Prince Houssain particularly liked was the great number of rose sellers who crowded the streets, for the people of Bisnagar are such great lovers of that flower that not one will stir without a nosegay in his hand or a garland on his head, and the merchants keep them in pots in their shops so the air is perfectly perfumed.

After Prince Houssain had gone through that first section street by street, he was very tired, and a merchant, noticing this, invited him to sit down in his shop. He accepted and had not been there long before he saw a peddler passing by with a piece of carpet, about six feet in length, on his arm, proclaiming its price at forty purses of gold.

The Prince called to the peddler and asked to see the carpet, which seemed to him to be valued at an exorbitant price not only for its size but for its inferior quality. When he had examined it well he told the peddler he could not comprehend how he could expect to sell so small and mediocre a piece of carpet at so high a price.

The peddler, who took Prince Houssain for a merchant, replied, "If this price seems so extravagant to you, your amazement will be greater when I tell you I have strict orders not to bargain and not to part with the carpet for anything less than the forty purses."

"Certainly," answered Prince Houssain, "it must have something very extraordinary in it, which I am not aware of."

"You have guessed it, sir," replied the peddler, "and you will admit its value when you come to know that whoever sits on this piece of carpet may be transported in an instant to wherever he desires to be, without being stopped by any obstacle."

When he heard this, the Prince, considering that the principal motive of his travel was to bring to the Sultan, his father, some singular rarity, thought he would never find anything in the world which would give him more satisfaction.

"If the carpet," said he to the peddler, "has the quality you assign it, I shall not think forty purses of gold too much for its price and I shall make you a present besides."

"Sir," replied the crier, "I have told you the truth, and it is an easy matter to convince you of it. With the permission of the owner of the shop we will go into the back and I will spread the carpet. When we have both sat down, you will form the wish to be transported to your room at the inn—if we are not taken to it there will be no sale and you are released from our bargain. As to your present, though I am paid for my trouble by the seller, I shall receive it as a favor and be very much obliged to you."

The Prince accepted the peddler's conditions and they concluded the bargain. Having the owner's leave, they went into the back of his shop, where they both sat down on the carpet.

As soon as the Prince had formed his wish to be transported to his room at the inn, he presently found himself and the peddler there. He needed no more proof of the value of the carpet and counted out forty purses of gold for the peddler, giving him twenty pieces for himself.

In this manner Prince Houssain became the possessor of the magic carpet and was overjoyed that he had found so rare a piece, which he never doubted would gain him the hand of Nouronnihar. In short, to him it appeared impossible for his younger brothers to find anything to compare with it. It was in his power, by sitting on his carpet, to be at the place of meeting that very day. But as he was obliged to wait there at the inn for his brothers and, being curious to see the King of Bisnagar and to inform himself of the strength, laws, customs and religion of the kingdom, he chose instead to spend some months in satisfying his curiosity. After traveling around Bisnagar for a time he transported himself and his aide to the inn where he and his brothers were to meet and where he passed for a merchant till they came.

Prince Ali, the middle brother, had decided to travel into Persia and joined a caravan three days after he parted from his brothers. After four days' travel he arrived at Shiraz, which was the capital of the kingdom of Persia. Here he decided to pass for a jeweler.

The morning after his arrival, Prince Ali, who had brought nothing but necessities along with him, took a walk into that part of the town which the natives called the bazaar.

Among all the peddlers who passed back and forth with various sorts of goods, he was surprised to see one who held in his hand an ivory telescope with black binding, about a foot in length and the thickness of a man's thumb, for sale at thirty purses of gold.

At first Prince Ali thought the peddler mad. To inform himself, he went to a shop and said to the merchant who stood at the door:

"Pray, sir, is not that man mad who hawks the ivory telescope at thirty purses of gold? If he is not, then I do not understand."

"Indeed, sir," answered the merchant, "he was in his right senses yesterday. I can assure you he is one of the ablest peddlers we have and the one most often employed when anything valuable is to be sold. If he asks thirty purses of gold for the ivory telescope it must be worth at least that much or more. He is sure to come by presently; we will call him and you shall be satisfied. But in the meantime sit down and rest yourself."

Prince Ali accepted the merchant's offer, and presently the peddler passed by. The merchant called to him by name and, pointing to the Prince, said, "This gentleman asked me if you were in your right senses. Tell him what you mean by selling an ivory telescope, which seems not to be worth much, at thirty purses of gold. I should be very much amazed myself if I did not know you."

The peddler, addressing himself to Prince Ali, said, "Sir, you are not the only person that takes me for a madman on account of this glass. You shall judge yourself whether I am or not. When I have told you its merits I hope you will value it as do those to whom I have shown it already, who had a worse opinion of me than you do.

"First, sir," pursued the peddler, presenting the telescope to the Prince, "observe that this pipe is furnished with a glass at both ends and consider that by looking through one of them you see whatever object you wish to behold."

"I am," replied the Prince, "ready to make you profound apologies if you will demonstrate the truth of what you said." The Prince glanced at both ends of the ivory telescope and added, "Show me through which of these ends I must look that I may be satisfied."

The peddler presently showed him, and he peered through, wishing at the same time to see the Sultan, his father, whom he immediately beheld in perfect health on his throne in the midst of his council. And, since there was nothing in the world so dear to him after his father as the Princess Nouronnihar, he wished to see her also, and beheld her seated at her dressing table, smiling, with her ladies-in-waiting grouped about her.

Prince Ali needed no other proof to be persuaded that this telescope was the most valuable thing in the world and believed that if he did not purchase it he would never meet again with such a rarity. He therefore took the peddler with him to the inn where he was lodging, paid him the money and received the telescope.

The Prince was overjoyed at his bargain. He persuaded himself that his brothers would not be able to meet with anything so rare and admirable, and therefore the Princess Nouronnihar would be his. So he visited the Court of Persia, incognito, seeing whatever was curious in Shiraz and thereabouts till he rejoined the caravan which was then returning to the Indies. The Prince arrived happily without accident or trouble at the place of rendezvous, where he found Prince Houssain, and both prepared to wait for Prince Ahmed.

When the three brothers had parted, Prince Ahmed took the road to Samarkand. The day after his arrival there, he went, as his brothers had done, into the great bazaar. He had not walked long before he heard a peddler, who had an artificial apple in his hand, offer it for sale at thirty-five purses of gold.

Upon hearing this, Ahmed stopped the man and said to him, "Let me see that apple and pray tell me what extraordinary properties it has to be valued at so high a price."

"Sir," said the peddler, putting it into his hand, "if you look at the outside of this apple it seems worthless, but if you consider the great use and benefit it is to mankind, you will say thirty-five purses of gold is no price for it and that he who possesses it is master of a great treasure. In short, it cures all sick persons of the most mortal diseases; if the patient is dying it will cause him to recover immediately and restore him to perfect health. And this is done in the easiest manner in the world—simply through the patient's smelling the apple."

"If I may believe you," replied Prince Ahmed, "the virtues of this apple are wonderful, and it is invaluable. But what ground have I, for all you tell me, to be persuaded of the truth of this matter?"

"Sir," replied the peddler, "the truth is known by the whole city of Samarkand. Without going farther, just ask all these merchants you see here and listen to what they say. You will find several who will tell you they would not be alive this day if they had not made use of this excellent remedy.

"And, that you may better comprehend what it is, I must tell you that this apple is the fruit of the experiments of a celebrated philosopher of this city, who applied himself during his entire lifetime to the study and knowledge of plants and minerals and at last attained this fruit, by which he performed such surprising cures in this town as will never be forgotten.

However, he died suddenly, before he could apply his own remedy, and left his wife and young children in difficult circumstances. She, to support her family and provide for her children, has resolved to sell the apple."

While the peddler informed Prince Ahmed of the virtues of the artificial apple, a great many persons surrounded them and confirmed what he said. One gentleman said he had a friend, dangerously ill, who was sure to die.

Here, the man suggested, was a favorable opportunity to show Prince Ahmed the experiment; upon which the Prince told the peddler that he would give him forty purses of gold for the apple if he cured the sick person.

The peddler, who was delighted at this generous price, said to Prince Ahmed, "Come, sir, let us go and make the experiment, and the apple shall become yours. I can assure you that it will always have the desired effect."

The experiment succeeded, and the Prince, after he had counted out to the peddler forty purses of gold and had received the apple, waited patiently for the first caravan that was returning to the Indies, and arrived in perfect health at the inn where the Princes Houssain and Ali waited for him.

When the Princes met, they showed each other their treasures. While peering through Prince Ali's tele-

scope, they saw that the Princess was dying. They all immediately sat down on the magic carpet, wished themselves with her and were there in a moment.

Prince Ahmed no sooner perceived himself in Nouronnihar's chamber than he rose from the carpet, as his brothers did also, went to the bedside and put the apple under the Princess' nose. Some moments afterward she opened her eyes and turned her head from side to side, looking at the people who stood around her. She then rose from the bed and asked to be dressed, just as if she had waked out of a sound sleep. Her ladies-in-waiting joyfully informed her that she was obliged to the three Princes for the sudden recovery of her health, especially to Prince Ahmed. Thereupon she immediately expressed her joy at seeing them and thanked them, and afterward thanked Prince Ahmed in particular.

While Princess Nouronnihar was dressing, the Princes went to throw themselves at the feet of the Sultan, their father, and to pay their respects to him. When they came before him they found he had already been informed by the chief of the Princess' eunuchs of their arrival and by what means the Princess had been perfectly cured. The Sultan embraced them with the greatest joy, both for their return and the recovery of his niece, who had been given up by the physicians.

After the usual ceremonies and compliments, each of the Princes presented his rarity: Prince Houssain his magic carpet, Prince Ali his ivory telescope and Prince Ahmed his artificial apple. And after each had extolled his present when he put it into the Sultan's hands, they begged him to pronounce their fate and declare to which of them he would give the Princess Nouronnihar as his wife.

The Sultan of the Indies, having heard without interrupting all that the Princes had to report about their rarities, remained silent for some time as if he were thinking of what answer he should make.

At last he broke the silence and said to them, "I would declare for one of you children with a great deal of pleasure if I could do it with justice, but consider whether I can do it or not. 'Tis true, Prince Ahmed, the Princess is obliged to your artificial apple for her cure, but I must ask you whether or not you could have been so useful to her if you had not known by Prince Ali's telescope the danger she was in and if Prince Houssain's carpet had not brought you so soon. Your telescope, Prince Ali, informed you and your brothers that you were about to lose your cousin, and so you are owed a great obligation. You must also grant that the knowledge would have been of no service without the artificial apple and the magic carpet.

"And lastly, Prince Houssain, the Princess would be very ungrateful if she did not show her appreciation for your carpet, which was so necessary a means toward her cure. But consider, it would have been of little use if you had not learned of her illness through Prince Ali's glass and if Prince Ahmed had not applied his apple. Therefore, magic carpet, ivory telescope and artificial apple have not the least preference one before the other. In fact, there's a perfect equality, and I cannot grant the Princess to any one of you. All you have reaped from your travels is the glory of having equally contributed to restoring her health.

"If this be true," added the Sultan, "you see that I must have recourse to other means to determine the choice I ought to make among you. As there is time enough before nightfall, I'll do it today. Each of you is to get a bow and arrow and go out to the great plain where they exercise horses. I'll soon join you and I will give the Princess to him who shoots the farthest."

The three Princes had nothing to say against the Sultan's decision. When they had provided themselves with bows and arrows, they went to the appointed plain, followed by a great number of people.

The Sultan did not make them wait long for him. As soon as he arrived, Prince Houssain, as the eldest, took his bow and arrow and shot first; Prince Ali was next and shot much farther than his brother; and Prince Ahmed shot last of all. It so happened that nobody could see where Prince Ahmed's arrow fell; notwithstanding all the diligence used by himself and everybody else, it was not to be found far or near. And though it was believed that he had shot the far-

THE WORLD'S BEST FAIRY TALES

thest and therefore deserved the Princess Nouronnihar, it was, however, necessary that his arrow should
be found to make this certain. And, despite Prince
Ahmed's strong protests, the Sultan judged in favor of
Prince Ali and ordered preparations to be made for
the wedding, which was celebrated a few days later.

Prince Houssain would not honor the feast with his
presence. In short, his grief was so violent and in-
supportable that he left the court and, renouncing all
right of succession to the crown, became a hermit.

Prince Ahmed, also, did not go to the wedding of
Prince Ali and the Princess Nouronnihar, but he did
not renounce the world as Prince Houssain had done.
He still could not imagine what had become of his
arrow and he stole away from his attendants one night,
resolved to search for it, that he might not have anything to reproach himself with. He went to the place
where his brothers' arrows had been gathered up and,
going straight forward from there, searched carefully
on both sides of him. He went so far that at last he
began to think his labor was all in vain. Yet he
continued till he came to some steep, craggy rocks
which cut off his progress and were situated in barren
country about four leagues from where he had set out.

When Prince Ahmed came close to these rocks he
saw an arrow, which he picked up. After examining
it carefully he was greatly astonished to find it was the
same one he had shot off.

"Certainly," said he to himself, "neither I nor any man living could shoot an arrow so far." Having found it lying flat, not sticking into the ground, he judged that it had rebounded against the rock. There must be some mystery in this, he thought. Perhaps Fortune, to make amends for my loss of Nouronnihar, may have reserved a greater happiness for me.

The rocks were full of caves, some of them deep, and the Prince entered one. Looking about, he cast his eyes on an iron door which seemed to have no lock, but he feared it was fastened. When he thrust against it, the door opened and revealed an easy descent along an incline, down which he walked, carrying his arrow in his hand. At first it was very dark and difficult going, but presently a quite different light succeeded that out of which he came. Advancing into a spacious area he perceived a magnificent palace, which he had not then time enough to look at, for at the same moment a lady of majestic bearing appeared at the entrance, attended by a group of ladies so finely dressed and beautiful that it was difficult to distinguish which was the mistress.

The moment Prince Ahmed noticed the lady, he hastened to pay his respects. She, seeing him, said, "Come nearer, Prince Ahmed, you are welcome."

It was no small surprise to the Prince to hear himself named in a place he had never heard of and by a lady who was a stranger to him. At last he returned the lady's compliment by throwing himself at her feet and, rising again, said to her, "Madam, a thousand thanks for the assurance you give me of a welcome to a place where I believe my curiosity has made me penetrate too far. But, madam, may I, without being guilty of ill manners, dare ask you by what chance you know me? And how you, who live in the same neighborhood with me, should be a stranger to me?"

"Prince," said the lady, "let us go inside. There I will gratify you in your request."

After these words the lady led Prince Ahmed into the great hall of the palace. Then she sat down on a sofa, and when the Prince, with her permission, had done the same, she said, "You are surprised, you say, that I should know you and not be known by you, but you will no longer be surprised when I inform you who I am.

"You are undoubtedly aware that the world is inhabited by genies as well as by men. I am the daughter of one of the most powerful and distinguished of genies. My name is Paribanou. You seemed to me to be worthy of a happier fate than that of marrying the Princess Nouronnihar. In order that you might attain it, I was present when you drew your arrow. I seized it in the air and gave it the necessary motion to strike against the rocks near which you found it. Now it lies in your power to make use of the favorable opportunity which presents itself to make you happy."

The fairy Paribanou pronounced these last words with a different tone and looked tenderly upon Prince Ahmed. It was therefore no hard matter for the Prince to comprehend what happiness she meant. He realized also that Princess Nouronnihar could never be his, and that the fairy Paribanou excelled her in beauty, wit and, as much as he could conjecture by the magnificence of the palace, in immense riches. He blessed the moment that he thought of seeking his arrow a second time and yielded to his love.

"Madam," replied he, "if all my life I should have the happiness of being your slave and the admirer of the many charms which ravish my soul, I should think myself the most blessed of men. Pardon the boldness which inspires me to ask you to admit into your court a Prince who is entirely devoted to you."

"Prince," answered the fairy, "will you not pledge your faith to me as I give mine to you?"

"Yes, madam," replied the Prince, ecstatically, "what can I do better and with greater pleasure? Yes, I'll give you my heart without the least reserve."

"Then," answered the fairy, "you are my husband and I am your wife. But I suppose you have eaten nothing today; a slight repast shall be served up for you while preparations are being made for our wedding feast tonight, and then I will show you the apartments of my palace and you shall judge if this hall is not the meanest part of it."

Some of the fairy's ladies-in-waiting who had come into the hall with them went out immediately, returning presently with some excellent meats and wines. When Prince Ahmed had eaten and drunk, Paribanou took him through all the apartments, where he saw diamonds, rubies and emeralds intermixed with pearls, agate, jasper and porphyry, together with the most precious marbles. There was such rich profusion throughout that the Prince said that he could not have imagined there was anything in the world that could come up to it.

"Prince," said the fairy, "if you admire my palace so much—it is very beautiful, indeed—I could also charm you with my gardens, but we will let that alone till another day. Night draws near, and it will soon be time to go to supper."

The next hall into which the fairy led the Prince, and where the table had been arranged for the wedding feast, was the only apartment he had not yet seen. He admired the infinite number of sconces of wax candles perfumed with ambergris, the multitude of which were placed with a symmetry that formed an agreeable and pleasant sight. A large side table was set out with all sorts of gold plate so finely wrought that the workmanship was much more valuable than the weight of the gold. Several choruses of beautiful women, whose voices were ravishing, began a concert, accompanied by many kinds of the most harmonious instruments.

When they were eating, the fairy Paribanou took care to serve Prince Ahmed with the most delicate meats, which the Prince found to be delicious. He found the same excellence in the wines, which neither he nor Paribanou tasted till the dessert, consisting of the choicest sweets and fruits, was served.

The wedding feast was continued the next day, and the days following the celebration were a continual round of feasts.

At the end of six months Prince Ahmed, who had always loved and honored his father, conceived a great desire to know how he was. He told Paribanou of it and asked if she would give him leave to visit his father, saying that he would return in a short time.

"Prince," she said, "go when you wish. But please don't take it amiss that I give you some advice. First, I don't think it proper for you to tell the Sultan, your father, of our marriage, nor of my quality, nor the place where you have been. Beg of him to be satisfied in knowing simply that you are happy, and let him understand that the sole purpose of your visit is to assure him of this."

She then appointed twenty gentlemen, well mounted and equipped, to attend him. When all was ready, Prince Ahmed took his leave of Paribanou, embraced her and renewed his promise to return soon. Then his horse, which was as beautiful a creature as any in the Sultan of the Indies' stables, was led to him, and he mounted it with extraordinary grace. After bidding Paribanou a last adieu he set forth on his journey.

It was not a great distance to his father's capital, and Prince Ahmed soon arrived there. The people, glad to see him again, received him with acclamations of joy and followed him in large crowds to the Sultan's palace. The Sultan received and embraced him with great rejoicing, complaining at the same time with a fatherly tenderness of the sadness his long absence had caused him, for he had feared the Prince might have committed some rash action.

Prince Ahmed told the story of his adventures, but without speaking of the fairy Paribanou, and added, "The only favor I ask of Your Majesty is to give me leave to come often in order to pay my respects and to know how you are."

"Son," answered the Sultan of the Indies, "I cannot refuse what you ask of me, but I should much rather you would resolve to stay with me. At least tell me where I may send for you if you should fail to come or when I may think your presence necessary."

"Sir," replied Prince Ahmed, "what Your Majesty asks of me is part of the mystery I spoke of. I beg of you to give me leave to remain silent on this point, for I shall come so frequently that I am afraid I shall sooner be thought troublesome than be accused of negligence in my duty."

The Sultan of the Indies pressed Prince Ahmed no

more but said to him, "Son, I penetrate no further into your secrets. However, I can tell you that your presence restores to me the joy I have not felt this long time. You shall always be welcome when you come, without interrupting your business or pleasure."

Prince Ahmed stayed three days at his father's court, and on the fourth returned to the fairy Paribanou, who did not expect him so soon.

A month after Prince Ahmed's return from his visit to his father, the fairy observed that the Prince, since the time that he gave her an account of his journey, never talked of the Sultan, as if there were no such person in the world, whereas before he was always speaking of him. She thought his silence was on her account; therefore she took an opportunity to say to him one day: "Prince, don't you remember the promise you made to go and see the Sultan, your father? I have not forgotten what you told me on your return and so I am reminding you not to delay too long in fulfilling your vow."

So Prince Ahmed went the next morning with the same attendants as before, but he himself was more magnificently mounted and dressed, and he was received by the Sultan with the same joy and satisfaction. For several months he constantly paid his visits, each time looking richer and finer.

At last some Viziers, the Sultan's favorites, who judged Prince Ahmed's grandeur and power by the figure he cut, made the Sultan jealous of his son, saying it was to be feared he might inveigle himself into the people's favor and dethrone him.

The Sultan of the Indies refused to believe Prince Ahmed capable of so evil a design as his favorites would make him believe, and he said to the Viziers, "You are mistaken. My son loves me, and I am certain of his tenderness and fidelity because I have given him no reason to be otherwise."

But the favorites went on defaming Prince Ahmed till the Sultan said, "Be it as it may, I don't believe my son Ahmed is as wicked as you would persuade me he is. However, I am obliged to you for your good advice and don't doubt that it proceeds from your good intentions."

The Sultan of the Indies said this in order that his favorites might not know the impression their charges had made on his mind. They had so alarmed him that he resolved to have Prince Ahmed watched, unknown to his Grand Vizier. He sent for a noted sorceress and said, "Go immediately. Follow my son and watch him so well that you find out where he retires. Then return and bring me word."

The sorceress left the Sultan and, knowing the place where Prince Ahmed had found his arrow, went there immediately and hid herself near the rocks in order not to be seen.

The next morning Prince Ahmed left at daybreak

to return to the fairy palace, without taking leave either of the Sultan or any of his court, according to the established custom.

The sorceress, seeing him coming, followed him with her eyes till suddenly she lost sight of him and his attendants. The rocks were steep and craggy, making an insurmountable barrier, and she judged that the Prince either retired into some cavern or an abode of genies or fairies.

Thereupon, the sorceress left the place where she had been hiding and looked carefully about on all sides. But she could detect no opening, certainly not the iron door that Prince Ahmed had discovered, which was to be seen and opened by none but men and only by those whose presence was agreeable to the fairy Paribanou.

The sorceress, who saw it was in vain for her to search any further, had to be satisfied with the discovery she had made and returned to give the Sultan an account.

The Sultan was well pleased with the sorceress' conduct and said to her, "Do as you think fit. I'll await the outcome patiently." And to encourage her he gave her a diamond of great value.

As Prince Ahmed had obtained the fairy Paribanou's leave to visit the Sultan of the Indies once a month, he never failed, and the sorceress, knowing the time of his visits, went a day or two before to the foot of the rock where she had lost sight of the Prince and his attendants, and waited there.

The next morning Prince Ahmed went out of the iron door, as usual, with the same attendants as before, and passed by the sorceress. Seeing her lying with her head against the rock, complaining as if she were in great pain, he took pity, turned his horse about and went to her. He asked what was the matter and what he could do to ease her pain.

The artful sorceress looked at the Prince in a pathetic manner, without ever lifting her head, and answered in broken words and sighs. She told him that she was on her way to the capital city, but had been taken by so violent a fever that her strength failed her and she was forced to lie down where he saw her, far from any habitation and without any hopes of assistance.

"Good woman," replied Prince Ahmed, "you are not so far from help as you imagine. I am ready to assist you and convey you to where you will meet with a speedy cure; only get up and let one of my people support you."

At these words the sorceress, who pretended sickness only to know where the Prince lived and what he did, accepted the charitable offer he made her. Two of the Prince's attendants, alighting from their horses, helped her up, set her behind another horseman and remounted, following the Prince, who turned back to the iron door, which was opened by one of his retinue who rode in front. And when he came into the fairy's outer court, without dismounting himself, he sent one of his attendants to tell her he wanted to speak with her.

The fairy Paribanou came with all imaginable haste, not knowing what made the Prince return so soon.

Without giving her time to ask the reason, he said, pointing to the sorceress, "Princess, I desire you would have compassion on this good woman. I found her in the condition you see her in and promised her assistance. I know that you, out of your goodness as well as upon my entreaty, will not abandon her."

Paribanou, who had her eyes fixed upon the sorceress all the time the Prince was talking to her, ordered two of her ladies-in-waiting to carry her into an apartment of the palace and take as much care of the woman as they would of herself.

While the two women executed the fairy's commands she went up to Prince Ahmed and whispered in his ear, "Prince, this woman is not sick as she pretends to be. I am very much mistaken if she is not an impostor who will be the cause of great trouble to you. But don't be concerned; be assured that I will deliver you out of all the snares that shall be laid for you. Go and pursue your journey."

This discourse of the fairy's did not in the least frighten Prince Ahmed. "My Princess," said he, "I do not remember ever doing anybody an injury and I cannot believe that anybody can have a thought of doing me harm. But if someone should, I shall nevertheless not forbear doing good whenever I have an opportunity." Then he started out again for his father's palace.

In the meantime, the two ladies-in-waiting had carried the sorceress into a richly furnished apartment. First they sat her down upon a sofa with her back supported by a cushion of gold brocade, while they made a bed for her; the quilt was finely embroidered with silk, the sheets were of the finest linen, and the coverlet cloth of gold. When they had put her into bed —for the old sorceress pretended that her fever was so violent she could not help herself in the least—one of the women went out and returned soon again with a china dish in her hand, full of a certain liquor, which she presented to the sorceress while the other helped her to sit up.

"Drink this," she said. "It is the Water of the Fountain of Lions and a certain remedy against all fevers whatsoever. You will feel the effect of it in less than an hour's time."

The sorceress, to dissemble the better, refused it despite a great deal of entreaty, but at last, holding back her head, swallowed down the medicine. When she was laid down again the women covered her up. "Lie quiet and get a little sleep if you can," they said.

"We'll leave you and hope to find you perfectly cured when we come again an hour from now."

When the two women returned they found the sorceress up and dressed, sitting upon a sofa. "O admirable potion!" she said. "It wrought its cure much sooner than you told me it would. I shall be able to continue my journey." The two fairies then conducted her through several apartments and into a large hall, the most elaborate and magnificently furnished of all the rooms in the palace.

Paribanou sat in this hall on a throne of massive gold, enriched with diamonds, rubies and pearls of extraordinary size, attended on each hand by a great number of beautiful fairies, all richly clothed. At the sight of so much majesty, the sorceress was not only dazzled but was so amazed that after she had prostrated herself before the throne she could not open her lips to thank the fairy as she proposed.

However, Paribanou saved her the trouble, and said to her, "Good woman, I am glad I had an opportunity to oblige you and to see you are able to continue your journey. I won't detain you, but perhaps it would please you to see my palace; follow my women and they will show it to you."

Then the sorceress went back and related to the Sultan of the Indies all that had happened and how very rich Prince Ahmed was since his marriage with the fairy, richer than all the kings in the world, and how there was danger that he might come and take the throne from his father.

Though the Sultan knew very well that Prince Ahmed's natural disposition was good, yet he could not help being concerned about the report made by the old sorceress. When she was taking her leave, he said, "I thank you for the pains you have taken and for your wholesome advice. I am so aware of its great importance that I shall deliberate upon it in council."

Now, the favorite Viziers warned that the Prince should be killed, but the sorceress advised differently. "Make him give you all kinds of wonderful things with the fairy's help," she said, "till she tires of him and sends him away. For example, every time Your Majesty goes into the field you are at great expense, not only in tents for your army but in mules and camels to carry their baggage. Now, persuade Prince Ahmed to use his influence with the fairy to procure you a tent which might be carried in a man's hand and would be large enough to shelter your whole army against bad weather."

When the sorceress had finished her speech the Sultan asked his favorites if they had anything better to propose. Finding them all silent, he determined to follow the sorceress' advice as the most reasonable and agreeable to him.

Next day the Sultan did as the sorceress had told him and asked his son for the tent. Prince Ahmed realized then that the old woman had informed the Sultan of his marriage to the fairy Paribanou. And, although he didn't know how great the power of genies and fairies was, he doubted whether it extended so far as to produce a tent such as his father desired.

At last he replied, "Though it is with the greatest reluctance imaginable, I will not fail to ask of my wife the favor Your Majesty desires but will not promise you to obtain it. If I should not have the honor to come again to pay you my respects, that shall be the sign I have not had success. But, beforehand, I desire you to forgive me and remember that you yourself have reduced me to this extremity."

"Son," replied the Sultan of the Indies, "I would be very sorry if what I ask of you should cause me the displeasure of never seeing you again. I find you don't know the power a husband has over a wife. Yours would prove that her love for you was very indifferent if she, with the power of a fairy, would refuse you so trifling a request. I desire you to ask this for my sake."

The Prince went back and was very sad for fear of offending the fairy. She kept pressing him to tell her what was the matter, and at last he said, "Madam, you may have observed that hitherto I have been content with your love and have never asked you any favor. Consider, then, that it is not I but the Sultan, my father, who unwisely, or at least so it seems to me, begs of you a tent large enough to shelter him, his court and his army from the violence of the weather, but which a man may carry in his hand. Remember it is my father who asks this favor."

"Prince," replied the fairy, smiling, "I am sorry that so small a matter should disturb you and make you as uneasy as you appear to be."

Then the fairy sent for her treasurer, to whom she said, "Nourgihan, bring me the largest tent in my treasury." Nourgihan returned presently with the tent, which she could hold in the palm of her hand when she shut her fingers, and presented it to her mistress, who gave it to Prince Ahmed to look at.

When Prince Ahmed saw the tent which the fairy called the largest in her treasury, a look of surprise appeared on his face.

Paribanou burst out laughing. "Prince," she cried, "do you think I jest with you? You'll see presently that I am in earnest. Nourgihan," she said to her treasurer, taking the tent out of Prince Ahmed's hands, "go and set it up, that the Prince may judge whether it is large enough for the Sultan, his father."

The treasurer immediately went out of the palace and carried the tent a great way off. When she had set it up, one end reached all the way to the palace. The Prince, after investigating it, found the tent was large enough to shelter two armies greater than his father's. He then said to Paribanou: "I ask my Princess a thousand pardons for my incredulity. After what I have seen I believe there is nothing impossible to you."

"You see," said the fairy, "that the tent is larger than your father may have occasion for, but you must know that it has one property—it is larger or smaller according to the army it is to cover."

The treasurer took down the tent and brought it to the Prince. Without staying any longer than the next day, he mounted his horse and went with the same attendants to visit his father.

The Sultan, who was persuaded there could not be any such tent as he had asked for, was greatly surprised at the Prince's diligence. He took the tent and admired its smallness. His amazement was boundless when it was set up in the great plain and he found it big enough to shelter an army twice as large as he could bring into the field. But the Sultan was not yet satisfied.

"Son," said he, "I have already expressed how much I am obliged for the present of the tent that you have procured for me. I look upon it as the most valuable thing in all my treasury. But you must do one thing more which will be just as agreeable to me. I am informed that the fairy, your spouse, makes use of a certain water, called the Water of the Fountain of Lions, which cures all sorts of fevers, even the most dangerous. Since I am perfectly certain that my health is dear to you, I don't doubt that you will ask her for a bottle of that water and bring it to me as a medicine which I may make use of when I have occasion. Do me this other important service and thereby complete the duty of a good son toward a tender father."

The Prince returned and told the fairy what his father had said.

"There's a great deal of wickedness in this demand," she answered, "as you will understand by what I am going to tell you. The Fountain of Lions is situated in the middle of a court of a great castle. The entrance is guarded by four fierce lions, two of which sleep alternately while the other two are awake. But don't let that frighten you; I'll give you means to pass by them without any danger."

The fairy Paribanou had several balls of thread by her side. She took up one and, presenting it to Prince Ahmed, said, "First, take this ball of thread. I'll tell you the use of it presently. Secondly, you must have two horses: one you are to ride yourself and the other you must lead; the latter must be loaded with a freshly slaughtered sheep cut into four quarters. Third, I will give you a bottle in which to bring back the water.

"Set out early tomorrow morning and, when you have passed the iron door, throw the ball of thread before you; it will roll till it comes to the gates of the castle. Follow it, and when it stops at the open gates, you will see the four lions; the two that are awake will wake the other two by their roaring, but don't be frightened. Throw each of them a quarter of the sheep and then clap spurs to your horse and ride to the fountain; fill your bottle without alighting and return here with speed. The lions will be so busy eating they will let you pass by them."

Prince Ahmed set out the next morning at the time appointed by the fairy and followed her directions carefully. When he arrived at the gates of the castle, he distributed the quarters of the sheep among the four lions and, passing among them bravely, went to the fountain, filled his bottle and got away from the castle safe and sound.

When he had gone a little distance from the castle gates he turned around and, seeing two of the lions coming after him, he drew his saber and prepared himself for defense. As he rode forward one of the lions turned off the road at some distance and showed that he had not come to do him harm but only to go before him, and the other lion stayed behind to follow. Guarded in this manner, Prince Ahmed arrived at the capital of the Indies, and the lions never left him till they had conducted him to the gates of the Sultan's palace. This done, they returned the same way they had come, but not without frightening all who saw them, even though they went in a very gentle manner and showed no fierceness.

A great many officers came to attend the Prince while he dismounted from his horse, and afterward they conducted him into the Sultan's apartment. Prince Ahmed approached the throne, laid the bottle at the Sultan's feet, kissed the rich tapestry which covered his footstool and then said: "I have brought you the healthful water which Your Majesty desired so much to keep among the other rarities in your treasury, but at the same time I wish you such extraordinary health as never to have occasion to make use of it."

After the Prince had paid his respects the Sultan placed him at his right hand and said to him, "Son, I am very much obliged to you for this valuable present. I am also aware of the great danger you have exposed yourself to upon my account, which I have been informed of by a sorceress who knows the Fountain of Lions. But do me the pleasure," he continued, "to inform me by what incredible power you have been so fortunate."

"Sir," replied Prince Ahmed, "I have no share in the compliment Your Majesty is pleased to make me; all the honor is due to my wife, whose good advice I followed." Then he informed the Sultan what those directions were and, by so doing, let him know how well he had behaved himself. When he had finished, the Sultan, who showed outwardly all the demonstrations of great joy but secretly was becoming more and more jealous, retired to a private apartment, where he sent for the sorceress.

The sorceress saved the Sultan the trouble of telling

her of the success of Prince Ahmed's journey; she had heard of it before she came and had prepared an infallible means to destroy the Prince. This she communicated to the Sultan, who declared it the next day to the Prince in the presence of all his courtiers. "Son," said he, "I have one thing more to ask of you, after which I shall expect nothing further. This request is that you bring me a man not above a foot-and-a-half high, whose beard is thirty feet long, who carries a bar of iron upon his shoulders weighing five hundred pounds, which he uses as a weapon."

Prince Ahmed, who did not believe there was such a man in the world as his father described, would gladly have excused himself. But the Sultan persisted in his demand and told him the fairy could do more incredible things.

The next day the Prince returned to his dear Paribanou, to whom he told his father's new demand, which he looked upon as more impossible than the first two. "For," he added, "I cannot imagine there is such a man in the world. Without doubt, my father has a mind to see whether or not I am so silly as to go about it, or he has a scheme for my ruin. How does he suppose that I can lay hold of such a man? If there are any means, I beg you will tell me them and let me come off with honor."

"Do not alarm yourself, Prince," replied the fairy. "You ran a risk in fetching the Water of the Fountain

of Lions for your father. But there's no danger in finding this man, for he is my brother Schaibar. However,
he is far from being like me though we both had the
same father. He is of so violent a nature that nothing
can prevent his showing cruelty for a slight offense;
yet, on the other hand, he is so good as to oblige everyone in whatever they desire. He is made exactly as your
father has described him and has no other weapon than
a bar of iron of five hundred pounds' weight, without
which he never stirs and which makes him respected.
I'll send for him, and you shall judge the truth of what
I am telling you. But be sure to prepare yourself
against being frightened at his extraordinary figure
when you see him."

"What, my Queen!" replied Prince Ahmed. "Do
you say Schaibar is your brother? Let him be ever so
ugly or deformed, I shall never be frightened at the
sight of him, and as your brother I shall honor and
love him."

The fairy ordered that a fire be set in a gold chafing
dish placed in the courtyard of her palace. From a
metal box she took a perfume and, after her throwing
it into the fire, there arose a thick cloud of smoke.

Some moments afterward the fairy said to Prince
Ahmed, "There comes my brother." The Prince immediately saw Schaibar approaching gravely, with his
heavy bar on his shoulder, his long beard, which he
held up before him, and a pair of thick mustaches,

which were tucked behind his ears and almost covered his face. His eyes were very small and set deep in his head, which was far from being of the smallest size, and on his head he wore a grenadier's cap. Besides all this, he was very humpbacked.

If Prince Ahmed had not known that Schaibar was Paribanou's brother, he would not have been able to look at him without fear but, knowing first who he was, he stood by the fairy without the least concern.

Schaibar, as he came forward, looked at the Prince frightfully enough to have chilled the blood in his veins and asked Paribanou, when he first addressed her, who that man was.

To which she replied, "He is my husband, brother. His name is Ahmed. He is the son of the Sultan of the Indies. The reason I did not invite you to my wedding was because I was unwilling to divert you from an expedition you were engaged in and from which, I heard with pleasure, you returned victorious; so I took the liberty now to call for you."

At these words, Schaibar, looking on Prince Ahmed favorably, said, "Is there anything, sister, wherein I can serve him? It is enough for me that he is your husband to do for him whatever he desires."

"The Sultan, his father," replied Paribanou, "is curious to see you, and I desire the Prince may be your guide to the Sultan's court."

"He needs but lead the way: I'll follow him."

"Brother," replied Paribanou, "it is too late to go today, therefore stay till tomorrow morning. In the meantime, I will inform you of all that has passed between the Sultan of the Indies and Prince Ahmed since our marriage."

The next morning, after Schaibar had been informed of the affair, he and Prince Ahmed set out for the Sultan's court. When they arrived at the gates of the capital the people no sooner saw Schaibar than they ran and hid themselves; some shut up their shops and locked themselves in their houses, while others, fleeing, communicated their fear to all they met, who stayed not to look behind them but ran too. So that as Schaibar and Prince Ahmed went along they found the streets deserted till they came to the palace, where the porters, instead of minding the gates, also ran away. Prince Ahmed and Schaibar advanced without any obstacle to the council hall, where the Sultan was seated on his throne, giving audience. Here, likewise, the ushers at the approach of Schaibar abandoned their posts and gave them free admittance.

Schaibar went boldly and fiercely up to the throne, without waiting to be presented by Prince Ahmed, and accosted the Sultan of the Indies in these words: "You have asked for me. See, here I am. What would you have with me?"

The Sultan, instead of answering him, clapped his hands before his eyes to avoid the sight of so terrible an object. At this uncivil and rude reception Schaibar was so much provoked, after the Sultan had given him the trouble of coming this far, that he instantly raised his iron bar and killed the Sultan before Prince Ahmed could intercede in his behalf. All that he could do was to prevent Schaibar's killing the Grand Vizier, who sat not far from him, insisting that he had always given the Sultan, his father, good advice.

"These are the ones, then," said Schaibar, "who gave him bad advice," and as he pronounced these words he killed the other Viziers and favorites of the Sultan who were Prince Ahmed's enemies. Every time he struck he killed someone or other, and none escaped but those who were not so frightened as to stand staring and gaping and who saved themselves by flight.

When this terrible execution was over, Schaibar came out of the council hall into the middle of the courtyard with the iron bar upon his shoulder and, looking hard at the Grand Vizier who owed his life to Prince Ahmed, he said, "I know there is a certain sorceress who is a greater enemy of my brother-in-law than these base favorites I have chastised. Let the sorceress be brought to me."

The Grand Vizier immediately dragged her forward, and Schaibar struck her with his iron bar, saying, "Take the reward of your pernicious counsel and learn not to feign sickness again."

After that he said, "This is not yet enough; I will use the whole town after the same manner if it does not immediately acknowledge Prince Ahmed, my brother-in-law, as its Sultan and the Sultan of the Indies." Then all who were present made the air echo with the repeated acclamations of "Long life to Sultan Ahmed!" and, immediately after, he was proclaimed through the whole town.

Schaibar had him clothed in the royal vestments, installed him on the throne and, after he had caused everyone to swear homage and fidelity to Ahmed, went and brought his sister, Paribanou, with great pomp and grandeur, and made her be acknowledged Sultana of the Indies.

As for Prince Ali and Princess Nouronnihar, since they had had no hand in the conspiracy against Prince Ahmed and knew nothing of it, they were assigned a large province with a capital, where they spent the rest of their lives. The new Sultan sent an officer to Prince Houssain to acquaint him with the change and make him an offer of which province he liked best. But that Prince thought himself so happy in his solitude that he bade the officer give his brother thanks for the kindness he offered him, assuring the new Sultan of his submission and that the only favor he desired was to be given leave to live in retirement in the place he had chosen for his retreat.

ARABIAN NIGHTS, TRANSLATED BY ANTOINE GALLAND

JACK THE GIANT KILLER

IN THE REIGN of the famous King Arthur there lived in Cornwall a lad named Jack, who was a boy of bold temper and took delight in hearing or reading of conjurers, giants and fairies. He used to listen eagerly to the deeds of the knights of King Arthur's Round Table.

In those days there lived on St. Michael's Mount, off Cornwall, a huge giant, eighteen feet high and nine feet round. His fierce and savage looks were the terror of all who beheld him. His name was Cormoran and he dwelled in a gloomy cavern on the top of the mountain and used to wade over to the mainland in search of prey. He would throw half a dozen oxen upon his back, tie three times as many sheep and hogs around his waist and march back to his own abode. The giant had been doing this for many years when Jack resolved to destroy him.

Jack took a horn, a shovel, a pickaxe, his armor and a dark lantern and, one winter's evening, he went to the Mount. There he dug a pit twenty-two feet deep and twenty broad. He covered the top over to make it look like solid ground and then blew such a loud and long tantara that the giant awoke and came out of his den, roaring: "You saucy villain, you shall pay for this. I shall broil you for my breakfast."

He had scarcely spoken when, taking one step farther, he tumbled into the pit, and Jack struck him such a blow on the head with his pickaxe that he killed him. Jack then returned home to cheer his friends with the news.

When the townsfolk heard of this valiant action they declared that henceforth he should be called Jack the Giant Killer and gave him a sword and belt upon which was written in letters of gold:

> This is the valiant Cornishman
> Who slew the giant Cormoran.

Another giant, called Blunderbore, vowed revenge if ever he should have Jack in his power. This giant kept an enchanted castle which stood in the midst of a lonely wood. One day, some time after the death of Cormoran, Jack was passing through this wood while on his way to Wales and, being weary, sat down and went to sleep.

The giant, walking by and seeing the words on Jack's belt, carried him off to his castle, where he locked him up in a large room, the floor of which was covered with the bones of men and women. Soon after, he went to fetch his brother, likewise a giant, to make a meal of

Jack. Through the bars of his prison, Jack, terrified, could see the two giants approaching.

Perceiving in one corner of the room a strong cord, Jack took courage and, making a slipknot at each end, threw it over the giants' heads and tied it to the window bars. He then pulled with all his might till he had choked them. Quickly, he slid down the rope and stabbed them to the heart.

Jack next took a great bunch of keys from the pocket of Blunderbore and went into the castle again. He made a thorough search through all the rooms, and in one of them found three ladies tied up by the hair of their heads and almost starved to death. They told him their husbands had been killed by the giants, who then condemned them to be starved to death because they would not eat the flesh of their dead husbands.

"Ladies," said Jack, "I have put an end to the monster and his wicked brother. I give you this castle and all the riches it contains, to make some amends for the dreadful pain you have felt."

He then very politely gave them the keys of the castle and went farther on his journey. As Jack had but little money, he went on as fast as possible. At length he came to a handsome house, knocked at the door, and there came forth a Welsh giant. Jack said he was a traveler who had lost his way, at which the giant made him welcome and led him into a room where there was a good bed.

Jack took off his clothes quickly, but though he was weary he could not sleep. Soon after this he heard the giant walking back and forth in the next room, saying:

> Though here you lodge with me this night,
> You shall not see the morning light;
> My club shall dash your brains out quite.

Well, thought Jack, so these are the tricks you play upon travelers? But I hope to prove as cunning as you.

Then, getting out of bed, he groped about the room, and at last found a large wooden log. He laid it in his own place in the bed and then hid himself in a dark corner of the room.

About midnight the giant entered the room and with his bludgeon struck many blows on the bed, in the very place where Jack had laid the log. Then he went back to his own room, thinking he had broken all Jack's bones.

Early in the morning Jack boldly walked into the giant's room to thank him for his lodging. The giant started when he saw him and began to stammer, "Oh, dear me, is it you? Pray, how did you sleep? Did you hear or see anything in the dead of the night?"

"Nothing worth speaking of," said Jack carelessly. "A rat, I believe, gave me three or four slaps with its tail and disturbed me a little. But I soon went back to sleep again."

The giant wondered more and more at this, yet he

did not answer a word, but went to bring two great bowls of hasty pudding for their breakfast. Jack wanted to make the giant believe he could eat as much as himself, so he contrived to button a leather bag inside his coat and slip the pudding into this bag while pretending to put it all into his mouth. When breakfast was over he said to the giant: "Now I will show you a fine trick. I can cure all wounds with a touch. I could cut off my head in one minute, and the next put it sound again on my shoulders. You shall see." He then took hold of a knife, with one stroke ripped up the leather bag, and all the pudding tumbled out upon the floor.

"I can do that myself!" cried the Welsh giant, who was ashamed to be surpassed by such a little fellow as Jack. So he snatched up the knife, plunged it into his own stomach and in a moment dropped down dead on the floor.

Having thus far been successful in all his undertakings, Jack resolved not to be idle in the future. He therefore furnished himself with a horse, a cap of knowledge, a sword of sharpness, shoes of swiftness and an invisible coat, the better to perform the wonderful enterprises that lay before him.

He traveled over high hills, and on the third day he came to a large and spacious forest through which his road lay. Scarcely had he entered the forest when he beheld a monstrous giant dragging along a handsome

knight and his lady by the hair of their heads. Jack alighted from his horse and, after tying him to an oak tree, put on his invisible coat, under which he carried his sword of sharpness.

When he came up to the giant he made several slashes at him. He could not reach his body, but wounded his thighs in several places. At length, putting both hands to his sword and aiming with all his might, Jack cut off both the giant's legs. Then, setting his foot upon his neck, he plunged his sword into the giant's body, and the monster gave a groan and expired.

The knight and his lady invited Jack to their house, to receive a proper reward for his services.

"No," said Jack, "I cannot be easy till I find out this monster's habitation." So he mounted his horse and soon after came in sight of another giant, who was sitting on a block of timber.

Jack alighted from his horse and, putting on his invisible coat, approached and aimed a blow at the giant's head, but he only cut off his nose. On this the giant seized his club and thrashed about unmercifully.

"Nay," said Jack, "if this be the case I'd better dispatch you!" So, jumping upon the block, he stabbed him in the back, and the giant dropped down dead.

Jack then proceeded on his journey and traveled over hills and dales. Arriving at the foot of a high mountain, he knocked at the door of a lonely house, where an old man let him in. When Jack was seated the hermit addressed him thus: "My son, on the top of this mountain is an enchanted castle kept by the giant Galligantus and a vile magician. I lament the fate of a Duke's daughter, whom they seized as she was walking in her father's garden, and brought here after transforming her into a deer." Jack promised that in the morning, at the risk of his own life, he would break the enchantment.

When he had climbed to the top of the mountain he saw two fiery griffins: but he passed between them without the least fear, for they could not see him in his invisible coat. On the castle gate he found a golden trumpet, under which were written these lines:

> Whoever can this trumpet blow
> Shall cause the giant's overthrow.

As soon as Jack had read this he seized the trumpet and blew a shrill blast which made the gate fly open and the very castle itself tremble.

The giant and the conjurer now knew their wicked course was at an end, and they stood biting their nails and shaking with fear. With his sword of sharpness Jack soon killed the giant, and the magician was then carried away by a whirlwind. Every knight and beautiful lady who had been changed into a bird or a beast returned to the proper shape. The castle vanished away like smoke, and the head of the giant Galligantus was sent to King Arthur.

The knights and ladies rested that night at the old man's hermitage, and the next day they set out for the court. Jack went up to the King and gave His Majesty an account of all his fierce battles.

Jack's fame had now spread through the whole country, and at the King's desire the Duke gave Jack his daughter in marriage, to the joy of the entire kingdom. After this the King gave him a large estate, on which he and his lady lived the rest of their days in joy and contentment.

OLD CHAPBOOK, ANDREW LANG COLLECTION

TWELVE DANCING PRINCESSES

ONCE UPON a time there lived in the village of Montignies-sur-Roc a little cowherd, without either father or mother. His real name was Michael, but he was always called the Star Gazer because he went along with his head in the air when he drove his cows over the meadows to seek pasture.

He had white skin, blue eyes and hair that curled all over his head, and the village girls used to cry after him, "Well, Star Gazer, what are you doing?" and Michael would answer, "Oh, nothing," and go on his way without even turning to look at them.

One morning about the middle of August, just at midday when the sun was hottest, Michael ate his dinner of a piece of dry bread and went to sleep under an oak tree. And while he slept he dreamed that a beautiful lady, dressed in a robe made of gold, came and said to him, "Go to the castle of Belœil, and there you shall marry a princess."

That evening the little cowherd told his dream to the farm people. But, as was natural, they only laughed at the Star Gazer.

The next day at the same hour he went to sleep again under the same tree. The lady appeared a second time, and said, "Go to the castle of Belœil, and there you shall marry a princess."

In the evening Michael told his friends that he had dreamed the same dream again, but they only laughed at him more than before.

"Never mind," he said to himself, "if the lady appears to me a third time, I will do as she tells me."

The following day, to the great astonishment of all the village, about two o'clock in the afternoon a voice was heard singing:

Raleô, raleô,
How the cattle go!

It was the little cowherd driving his cattle back to the barn.

The farmer began to scold him furiously, but he answered quietly, "I am going away." He made his clothes into a bundle, said good-bye to his friends and boldly set out to seek his fortune.

There was great excitement throughout the village, and on the top of the hill the people stood, holding their sides with laughter, as they watched the Star Gazer trudge bravely along the valley with his bundle at the end of his stick.

It was well known for full twenty miles around that in the castle of Belœil lived twelve Princesses of wonderful beauty, as proud as they were comely, and so sensitive and of such truly royal blood that they would have felt at once the presence of a pea in their beds, even if ten mattresses were laid over it.

They had twelve beds all in the same room, but what was very extraordinary was the fact that, though they were locked in by triple bolts, every morning their satin shoes were worn into holes. No noise was ever heard in the room, yet how could the shoes wear themselves out alone?

At last the Duke of Belœil ordered the trumpet sounded and a proclamation made that whoever could discover how his daughters wore out their shoes should choose one of them for his wife.

On hearing the proclamation, a number of Princes

arrived at the castle to try their luck. They watched all night at the door of the Princesses, but when the morning came the Princes had disappeared, and no one could tell what had become of them.

When he reached the castle, Michael went straight to the gardener and offered his services. Now it happened the garden boy had just been sent away, and though the Star Gazer did not look very sturdy, the gardener agreed to take him, as he thought his pretty face and golden curls would please the Princesses.

The first thing he was to do, when the Princesses awoke, was to present each one with a bouquet. So Michael placed himself behind the door of the Princesses' room, with the twelve bouquets in a basket. He gave one to each of the sisters, who took them without even deigning to look at the lad, except Lina, the youngest, who fixed on him her large black eyes as soft as velvet and exclaimed, "Oh, how pretty he is—our new flower boy!" The others burst out laughing, and the eldest said that a princess ought never to lower herself by looking at a garden boy.

Now Michael knew that all the Princes had disappeared, but the beautiful eyes of the Princess called Lina inspired him with a violent longing to try his fate. Unhappily he did not dare to come forward, being afraid he should only be jeered at or even turned away from the castle on account of his impudence.

Then the Star Gazer had another dream. The lady

in the golden dress appeared to him once more, holding in one hand two young laurel trees, a cherry laurel and a rose laurel, and in the other hand a little golden rake, a little golden bucket and a silken towel. She said, "Plant these two laurels in two large pots, rake them over with the rake, water them with the bucket and wipe them with the towel. When they have grown as tall as a girl of fifteen, say to each of them, 'My beautiful laurel, with the golden rake I have raked you, with the golden bucket I have watered you, with the silken towel I have wiped you.' Then, after you have done that, ask anything you choose, and the laurels will give it to you."

Michael thanked the lady in the golden dress, and when he woke he found the two laurel trees beside him. So he carefully obeyed the orders given to him by her.

The trees grew very fast and, when they were as tall as a girl of fifteen, he said to the cherry laurel, "My lovely cherry laurel, with the golden rake I have raked you, with the golden bucket I have watered you, with the silken towel I have wiped you. Teach me how to become invisible."

Instantly there appeared on the laurel a pretty white flower, which Michael gathered and stuck into his buttonhole and, true enough, it made him invisible.

That evening, when the Princesses went upstairs to bed, he followed them barefoot, so that he would

make no noise, and hid himself under one of the beds.

The Princesses began at once to open their wardrobes and boxes. They took out of them the most magnificent dresses, which they put on before their mirrors, turning themselves to admire their appearance. Michael could see nothing from his hiding place, but he could hear everything, and he listened to the Princesses laughing and talking with pleasure.

At last the eldest said, "Be quick, my sisters; our partners will be impatient."

When the Star Gazer peeped out, he saw the twelve sisters in splendid garments, with satin shoes on their feet, and in their hands the bouquets he had brought for them.

"Are you ready?" asked the eldest.

"Yes," replied the other eleven in chorus, and they took their places one by one behind her.

Then the eldest Princess clapped her hands three times and a trapdoor opened. All the Princesses disappeared down a secret staircase, and Michael hastily followed them. As he was following on the steps of the Princess Lina, he carelessly trod on her dress. "There is somebody behind me," cried the Princess, "holding my dress."

"You foolish thing," said her eldest sister, "you are always afraid of something. It is only a nail which caught you."

They went down, down, down, till at last they came

to a passage with a door at one end, which was only fastened with a latch. The eldest Princess opened it, and they found themselves immediately in a lovely little wood, where the leaves were spangled with drops of silver which shone in the brilliant light of the moon. Next they crossed another wood, where the leaves were sprinkled with gold, and after that still another, where the leaves glittered with diamonds.

At last the Star Gazer perceived a large lake, and on the shore were twelve little boats with awnings, in which were seated twelve Princes who, grasping their oars, awaited the Princesses.

Each Princess entered one of the boats, and Michael slipped in with the youngest. The boats glided along rapidly, but Lina's, being heavier, was always behind the rest.

"We never went so slowly before," said the Princess. "What can be the reason?"

"I don't know," answered the Prince. "I assure you I am rowing as hard as I can."

On the other side of the lake the Star Gazer saw a beautiful castle, splendidly illuminated, from which came the lively music of fiddles and kettledrums and trumpets. In a moment they touched land, and the company jumped ashore. The Princes, after having securely fastened their boats, gave their arms to the Princesses and conducted them to the castle.

Michael followed and entered the ballroom in their

train. Everywhere were mirrors, lights, flowers and damask hangings. The Star Gazer was quite bewildered at the magnificence of the sight.

He placed himself out of the way in a corner, admiring the grace and beauty of the Princesses. Some were fair and some were dark; some had chestnut hair, or curls darker still, and some had golden locks. Never were so many beautiful Princesses seen together at one time, but the one the garden boy thought the most beautiful and the most fascinating was the little Princess with the velvet eyes.

With what eagerness she danced! Leaning on her partner's shoulder she swept by like a whirlwind. Her cheeks flushed, her eyes sparkled, and it was plain that she loved dancing better than anything else. The poor garden boy envied those handsome young men with whom she danced so gracefully, but he did not know how little reason he had to be jealous of them.

The young men were really the Princes who, to the number of fifty at least, had tried to steal the Princesses' secret. The Princesses had made them drink a potion which froze the heart and left nothing but the love of dancing.

They danced on until the shoes of the Princesses were worn into holes. When the cock crowed the third time, the fiddles stopped, and a delicious supper was served, of sugared orange flowers, crystallized rose leaves, powdered violets, cracknels and wafers, which are, as everyone knows, the favorite foods of princesses.

After supper, the dancers all went back to their boats, and this time the Star Gazer entered that of the eldest Princess. They crossed once again the wood with the diamond-spangled leaves, the wood with the gold-sprinkled leaves and the wood whose leaves glittered with drops of silver, and as a proof of what he had seen, the boy broke a small bough from a tree in the last wood. Lina turned as she heard the noise made by the breaking of the branch.

"What was that noise?" she asked.

"It was nothing," replied her eldest sister. "It was only the screech of the barn owl that roosts in one of the turrets of the castle."

While she was speaking, Michael managed to slip ahead and, running up the staircase, he reached the Princesses' room first. He flung open the window and, sliding down the vine which climbed up the wall, found himself in the garden just as the sun was rising and it was time for him to set to his work.

That day, when he made up the bouquets, Michael hid the branch with the silver drops in the nosegay intended for the youngest Princess. When Lina discovered it she was much surprised. However, she said nothing to her sisters, but when she met the boy while she was walking under the shade of the elms she suddenly stopped as if to speak to him. Then, changing her mind, she went on her way.

In the evening the twelve sisters went again to the ball, and once more the Star Gazer followed them, crossing the lake in Lina's boat. This time it was the Prince who complained that the boat seemed very heavy. "It is the heat," replied the Princess. "I, too, have been feeling very warm."

During the ball she looked everywhere for the garden boy, but she never saw him.

As they came back, Michael gathered a branch from the wood with the gold-sprinkled leaves, and now it was the eldest Princess who heard the noise it made in breaking.

"It is nothing," said Lina, "only the cry of the owl which roosts in the turrets of the castle."

The next morning Lina found the branch in her bouquet. When the sisters went down she stayed a little behind and said to the garden boy, "Where does this branch come from?"

"Your Royal Highness knows well enough," answered Michael.

"So you have followed us?"

"Yes, Princess."

"How did you manage it? We never saw you."

"I hid myself," replied the Star Gazer quietly.

The Princess was silent a moment and then said, "You know our secret—keep it! Here is the reward for your discretion." And she flung the boy a purse of gold.

"I do not sell my silence," answered Michael, and he went away without picking up the purse.

For three nights Lina neither saw nor heard anything extraordinary. On the fourth she heard a rustling among the diamond-spangled leaves of the wood. The next day there was a branch of the trees in her bouquet.

She took the Star Gazer aside and said to him in a harsh voice, "You know what price my father has promised to pay for our secret?"

"I know, Princess," answered Michael.

"Don't you mean to tell him?"

"That is not my intention."

"Are you afraid?"

"No, Princess."

"What makes you so discreet, then?"

But Michael was silent.

Lina's sisters had seen her talking to the garden boy, and ridiculed her for it.

"What prevents your marrying him?" asked the eldest. "You would become a gardener too; it is a charming profession. You could live in a cottage at the end of the park, and help your husband draw up water from the well, and bring us our bouquets."

The Princess Lina was very angry, and when the Star Gazer presented her bouquet she received it in a disdainful manner. Michael behaved most respectfully. He never raised his eyes to her, but nearly all day she felt him at her side without ever seeing him.

One day she made up her mind to tell everything to her eldest sister. "What!" said she. "This rogue knows our secret and you never told me! I must lose no time in getting rid of him."

"But how?"

"Why, by having him taken to the tower with the dungeons, of course."

For this was the way in old times that beautiful princesses rid themselves of people who knew too much. But the astonishing part of it was that the youngest sister did not seem to relish this method of stopping the mouth of the garden boy, who, after all, had said nothing to their father. They agreed to ask their ten sisters. Each was on the side of the eldest. Then the youngest sister declared that, if they laid a finger on the garden boy, she would herself go and tell their father the secret of the holes in their shoes.

At last it was decided that Michael should be put to the test; they would take him to the ball, and at the end of supper would give him the potion which was to enchant him like the rest. They sent for the Star Gazer and asked him how he had contrived to learn their secret, but still he remained silent. Then, in commanding tones, the eldest sister gave him the order they had agreed upon. He only answered, "I will obey."

He had been present, invisible, at the council of Princesses and had heard all. But he had made up his mind to drink of the potion and sacrifice himself for the happiness of her he loved. Not wishing, however, to cut a poor figure at the ball by the side of the other dancers, he went at once to the laurels and said, "My lovely rose laurel, with the golden rake I have raked you, with the golden bucket I have watered you, with the silken towel I have wiped you. Dress me like a prince."

A beautiful pink flower appeared. Michael plucked it, and in a moment found himself clothed in velvet which was as black as the eyes of the little Princess, with a cap to match, a diamond aigrette and a blossom of the rose laurel in his buttonhole.

Thus dressed, he presented himself that evening before the Duke of Belœil and obtained leave to try and discover his daughters' secret. He looked so distinguished that hardly anyone would have known who he was.

The twelve Princesses went upstairs to bed. Michael followed them and waited behind the open door till they gave the signal for departure. This time he did not cross in Lina's boat. He gave his arm to the eldest sister, danced with each in turn and was so graceful that everyone was delighted with him. At last the time came for him to dance with the little Princess. She found him the best partner in the world, but he did not dare speak a single word to her. When he was taking her back to her place she said to him in a mocking voice, "Here you are at the summit of your wishes; you are being treated like a prince."

"Don't be afraid," replied the Star Gazer gently. "You shall never be a gardener's wife."

The little Princess stared at him with a frightened face, and he left her without waiting for an answer.

When the satin slippers were worn through, the fiddles stopped and they were at the banquet table, Michael was placed next to the eldest sister and opposite the youngest.

They gave him the most exquisite dishes to eat and the most delicate wines to drink; and in order to turn his head more completely, compliments and flattery were heaped on him from every side.

At last the eldest sister made a sign, and one of the pages brought in a large golden cup. "The enchanted castle has no further secrets for you," she said to the Star Gazer. "Let us drink to your triumph."

He cast a lingering glance at the little Princess and without hesitation lifted the cup.

"Don't drink!" the Princess Lina suddenly cried out. "I would rather marry a gardener." And she burst into tears. Michael flung the contents of the cup behind him, sprang over the table and fell at Lina's feet. The rest of the Princes fell likewise at the knees of the Princesses, each of whom chose a husband and raised him to her side. The charm was broken.

The twelve couples embarked in the boats, which

crossed back many times in order to carry over the other Princes. Then they all went through the three woods, and when they had entered the underground passage a great noise was heard as if the enchanted castle were crumbling to the earth.

They went straight to the room of the Duke of Belœil, who had just awakened. Michael held in his hand the golden cup and he revealed the secret of the holes in the shoes. "Choose, then," said the Duke, "whichever one you prefer."

"My choice is already made," replied Michael, and he offered his hand to the youngest Princess, who blushed and lowered her eyes.

The Princess Lina did not become a gardener's wife; on the contrary, it was the Star Gazer who became a prince. But before the marriage ceremony the Princess insisted that Michael tell her how he came to discover the secret.

So he showed her the two laurels which had helped him, and she, being a prudent girl and thinking they gave him too much advantage over his wife, cut them off at the root and threw them into the fire.

And this is why the country girls go about singing:

> We won't go to the woods anymore,
> The laurel trees are cut—

and dance in summer by the light of the moon.

OLD GERMAN TALE, ANDREW LANG COLLECTION

LITTLE CLAUS AND BIG CLAUS

THERE WERE two men in one village, both of whom had the very same name. They were both called Claus, but one of them owned four horses, and the other only one; so to tell them apart, people called the man who had four horses Big Claus and the man who had only one horse Little Claus. We are going to hear what happened to these two, for this is a true story.

The whole week long, Little Claus had to plow for Big Claus and lend him his one horse; in return, Big Claus lent him his four horses, but only once a week, and that was on Sundays. Hooray! How Little Claus did crack his whip over all the five horses, for they were as good as his own on that one day. The sun shone brightly, and the church bells rang merrily as the people passed by. Dressed in their best clothes and with their prayer books under their arms, they were on their way to hear the parson preach. They looked at Little Claus plowing away with all the five horses, and he was so happy that he cracked his whip and shouted, "Gee up, all my good horses!"

"I don't want you to shout that," said Big Claus. "Only one of the horses is yours, remember!"

But when some more people passed by on their way to church, Little Claus forgot, and he shouted again, "Gee up, all my good horses!"

"Look here; kindly stop that," said Big Claus. "If you say that once again, I'll knock your horse on the head and kill him on the spot, and that will be the end of him."

"All right, I won't say it again," said Little Claus, but when another lot of people went by and nodded "Good morning," it pleased him so much and he thought he looked so grand to be plowing with five horses that he cracked his whip once more and shouted, "Gee up, all my good horses!"

"I'll gee up your horses for you!" said Big Claus, and he took the tethering mallet and gave Little Claus's only horse such a knock on the head that it fell down, stone dead.

"What a shame! Now I haven't got any horse at all!" said Little Claus, and he began to cry. By and by he flayed the horse and took the hide and let it dry thoroughly in the wind. Then he stuffed the skin into a bag, which he slung over his shoulder, and went off to town to sell it.

He had a very long way to go and had to pass through a big, gloomy forest. Presently a terrible storm came up. He lost his way, and before he could find it again it was too far for him to get either to the town or back home before night fell.

Close to the road there was a large farmhouse; the shutters had already been put up over the windows for the evening, but a ray of light still escaped at the top. I suppose they won't mind letting me spend the night here, thought Little Claus and he knocked at the front door.

The farmer's wife opened it, but when she heard what he wanted, she told him to go away. Her husband was not at home, and she wasn't having any strangers on the place.

"Very well, then I shall have to sleep out of doors," said Little Claus, and the farmer's wife slammed the door in his face.

Close by stood a big haystack, and between this and the house was a little shed with a flat thatched roof.

"I can sleep up there," said Little Claus when he saw the roof. "It will make a fine bed. I hope the stork won't fly down and bite my legs!"—for a real live stork was standing on the roof, where it had its nest.

Little Claus climbed up onto the shed, and he tossed and turned about until at last he found a comfortable position. When he faced the farmhouse, he could see that the wooden shutters didn't quite fit the windows at the top, and so he was able to look straight into the dining room of the house.

There was a large table laid with wine and roast

meat and a delicious-looking fish. The farmer's wife and the parish clerk were sitting at the table; she kept helping him to wine, and he kept helping himself to the fish—for it was one of his favorite dishes.

"If only I could get a bite of that!" said Little Claus and he poked his head quite close to the window. Heavens, what a glorious cake he could see now! That was a feast and no mistake!

Suddenly he heard someone riding along the road toward the house. It was the woman's husband coming back home.

He was an excellent man, but he had one strange prejudice—he couldn't for the life of him bear the sight of a parish clerk; if he ever set eyes on one he got mad with rage. That's why the parish clerk had come to pass the time of day with the farmer's wife, knowing that her husband would be away; and the good woman had put before him the best food she had in the house. All of a sudden they heard the husband coming, and they were so frightened that the woman begged the clerk to creep into a great empty chest which stood against the wall. He did as he was told, for he knew very well how the poor husband felt at the sight of a parish clerk. The woman quickly hid the delicious food and wine in her oven, for if her husband were to see it he would certainly ask what it all meant.

"Oh, dear," sighed Little Claus up on the shed, when he saw all the food disappear.

"Is there anybody there?" asked the farmer, looking up at Little Claus. "What are you doing on the roof? You'd better come inside with me."

Little Claus then told him how he had lost his way, and asked if he might stay the night.

"Why, certainly!" said the farmer. "But first let's have a bite to eat."

The farmer's wife welcomed them in a most friendly way, laid the long table and gave them a large bowl of porridge. The farmer was hungry and set to with right good will, but Little Claus couldn't help thinking about the delicious roast meat, the fish and the cake which he knew were in the oven.

He had put the bag with the horsehide under his feet—for you remember he had left home to sell the horsehide in the town. He had no appetite at all for porridge, so he trod on the bag and the dry hide gave quite a loud squeak.

"Ssh!" said Little Claus to his bag, but at the same time treading on it again, and it squeaked much louder than before.

"Why, what on earth have you got in your bag?" asked the farmer.

"Oh, it's a wizard," said Little Claus. "He tells me that we shouldn't be eating porridge, when he's conjured the whole oven full of meat, fish and cake."

"You don't say so!" said the farmer, and in less than no time he had opened the oven and seen all the delicious food his wife had hidden—but he thought it was the wizard in the bag who had conjured it there. The wife didn't dare say a word but at once she put the food on the table, and they had their fill of the meat, the fish and the cake.

Little Claus again trod on his bag and made the hide squeak.

"What does he say now?" asked the farmer.

"He says," answered Little Claus, "that he's also conjured up three bottles of wine, and that they are in the oven too." Then the wife had to bring out the wine she had hidden, and the farmer drank and got quite merry. He thought what fun it would be to have a wizard like the one Little Claus had in his bag.

"Can he conjure up the devil too?" asked the farmer. "I should like to see him, for now I'm just in the mood for it."

"Certainly," said Little Claus. "My wizard can do anything I ask him to. Can't you?" he asked, and he trod on the bag so that it squeaked again. "Did you hear? He said 'Yes!' But the devil is so terrifying to look at that I should advise you not to try."

"Oh, I'm not a bit afraid. I wonder what he looks like."

"Well, he's going to appear in the shape of a parish clerk."

"Ugh!" said the farmer. "How horrible! I can't bear the sight of parish clerks. But never mind—so long as I know it's the devil, I can stand it better. I've plucked up my courage now, but don't let him come too close."

"Just let me ask my wizard," said Little Claus, treading on the bag and putting his ear up against it.

"What does he say?"

"He says you must open the chest over there against the wall, and you'll see the devil crouching inside, but mind you hold on to the lid, otherwise he'll slip out."

"Will you help me to hold it?" asked the farmer, going to the chest in which his wife had hidden the real clerk, who was trembling with fear.

The farmer lifted the lid ever so little and peeped under it. "Ugh!" he gasped out, jumping backward. "I did see him; he looked exactly like our own clerk. It was too awful!"

So they had to have another go at the wine, and then another one after that, and there they sat drinking till late into the night.

"You must sell me that wizard," said the farmer. "Ask as much as you like for him. I'll give you a whole bushel of money right away."

"No, I couldn't do that," said Little Claus. "Just think how useful this wizard can be to me."

"Oh, but I must have him," said the farmer, and he went on insisting.

"Well," said Little Claus, giving in at last, "as you've been kind enough to give me a night's lodging, all right. You shall have the wizard for a bushel of money, but you must give me full measure."

"Don't worry about that," said the farmer, "but you'll have to take the chest away with you. I won't keep it in the house another hour. The devil might still be in it."

So Little Claus gave the farmer the bag with the dried hide in it, and got a whole bushel of money—and full measure too—in exchange for it. The farmer also gave him a big wheelbarrow to take away the money and the chest.

"Good-bye," said Little Claus, and off he went with his money and the chest with the clerk still in it.

On the other side of the wood ran a deep river; the current was so strong that it was hardly possible to swim against it, and a fine new bridge had been built over it. Little Claus stopped halfway across, and said loud enough for the clerk to hear him: "What good is that stupid chest to me? It's heavy enough to be full of stones. I shall be tired out if I wheel it any longer. I'll just throw it into the river; if it sails home to me, well and good; but if it doesn't, no matter!"

Then he took hold of the chest with one hand and lifted it up a little as if he meant to throw it into the water.

"Stop! Stop!" shouted the clerk inside. "Let me out first!"

"Oh!" exclaimed Little Claus, pretending to be

frightened. "He's still there! I'd better be quick and push the chest into the river and let him drown."

"Oh, no, no!" screamed the clerk. "I'll give you a whole bushel of money if you don't."

"Well, that's another story," said Little Claus, opening the chest. The clerk crept out at once and pushed the empty chest into the water. They went off to his home, where Little Claus got his bushel of money. Since he'd already gotten a bushel from the farmer, he now had his whole wheelbarrow quite full of money.

"Anyway, I call that a good price for my horse," he said to himself when he got home to his room and emptied all the money in a heap on the floor. "Big Claus will be as cross as two sticks when he hears what a lot I've made out of my one and only horse, but I'm not going to tell him the whole truth about it."

Then he sent a boy over to Big Claus to borrow a bushel measure.

What can he want with that? thought Big Claus, and he smeared tar on the bottom of it, so that a little of whatever was being measured might stick to it. And that's exactly what happened, for when the measure was returned to him there were three silver coins sticking to the bottom.

"What's this?" said Big Claus, and he immediately went rushing over to Little Claus's home. "How did you get all that money?"

"Oh, I got it for my horsehide which I sold last night," Little Claus explained.

"My word, that's a thundering good price, I must say!" exclaimed Big Claus. Then he ran home, took an axe and knocked all his four horses on the head, ripped off their hides and drove off to the town with them.

"Hides! Hides! Who'll buy hides?" he shouted through the streets.

The shoemakers and tanners came running up and asked him how much he wanted for them.

"A bushel of money apiece!" said Big Claus.

"Are you mad?" they all said. "Do you think we've got money by the bushel?"

"Hides! Hides! Who'll buy hides?" he shouted again, and to everyone who asked him the price, he answered, "A bushel of money."

"He's trying to make fools of us," they all said, and the shoemakers took their straps, and the tanners their leather aprons, and they all began to beat Big Claus.

"Hides, hides!" they mocked at him. "Yes, we'll give your hide a good tanning! Out of the town with him!" they shouted, and Big Claus ran away as fast as he could, for he'd never received such a beating in his life before.

"Well," he said when he got home, "Little Claus shall pay for this. I'll slay him for it."

Now at Little Claus's home his old grandmother had died; true enough, she had been bad-tempered and nasty to him, but all the same he was very sorry, so he took the dead woman and put her into his own warm bed, to see if she might not possibly come to life again. She was to lie there until morning, while he himself meant to sit in the corner and sleep in a chair, as he had often done before.

As he sat there in the night, the door opened and Big Claus came in with an axe. He knew well enough where to find Little Claus's bed, so he went straight up to it and knocked the dead grandmother on the head, thinking she was Little Claus.

"There now," he said, "you won't fool me anymore." And he went home again.

"What a wicked man he is, wanting to kill me," said Little Claus. "It's lucky for poor old Granny that she was dead already, otherwise he would have finished her off."

Then he dressed his old grandmother in her Sunday best and, having borrowed a horse from his neighbor, harnessed it to his cart and planted her bolt upright on the back seat in such a way that she couldn't possibly fall out when the horse began to trot—and off they bowled through the woods. When the sun rose, they were near a big inn. Little Claus pulled up and went in to get something to eat.

The innkeeper had heaps and heaps of money, and was quite a good sort, but he was very hot-tempered, almost as if he were filled with pepper and snuff.

"Good morning," he said to Little Claus. "You've got into your Sunday best early today."

"Yes," said Little Claus. "I'm going to town with my old grandmother. She's out there in the cart; I can't get her to come in. Would you mind taking her a glass of cider? But you'll have to speak pretty loud, for she's hard of hearing."

"Right you are!" said the innkeeper, and he filled a large glass full of cider and took it out to the dead grandmother, who was still propped up in the cart.

"The young man has sent you a glass of cider," said the innkeeper, but the dead woman never uttered a word or moved.

"Can't you hear?" shouted the innkeeper just as loud as he could. "The young man has sent you a glass of cider!"

Once more he shouted the same thing, and then again for the fourth time, but when she never even stirred, he lost his temper and flung the glass right into her face, so that the cider ran down her nose, and she tumbled over backward into the cart, for she was only propped up, and not tied at all.

"Hi! What are you doing there?" shouted Little Claus, rushing out and grabbing the innkeeper by the throat. "You've killed my grandmother. Just look, there's a great hole in her forehead."

"Oh, what a tragedy!" cried the innkeeper, clasping his hands in despair. "It's all because of my hot temper. Dear Little Claus, I'll give you a whole bushel of money and have your grandmother buried as if she was my own; but mum's the word, or they'll cut my head off, and that's very unpleasant, you know."

So Little Claus got another bushel of money, and the innkeeper buried the old grandmother as if she'd been his own.

When Little Claus came back home with his money, he immediately sent his boy over to Big Claus to borrow a bushel measure.

"What the devil does this mean?" exclaimed Big Claus. "Didn't I kill him after all? I'd better go and find out for myself." And he went over to Little Claus with the measure.

"Where in the world did you get all that money from?" he asked, opening his eyes wider and wider when he saw the money that had been added to Little Claus's heap.

"It was my grandmother you killed, not me," said Little Claus, "so I have just sold her for a bushel of money!"

"My word, that's a thundering good price!" said Big Claus, so he hurried home, took an axe and quickly killed his own old grandmother. Then he put her in his cart, drove to the hospital in town and asked a doctor if he wanted to buy a dead body.

"Who is it and where did you get it from?" asked the doctor.

"It's my grandmother," said Big Claus. "I've killed her to get a bushel of money."

"Good Lord!" said the doctor. "You must be raving, man! You'd better not say that, or they'll have your head off." And then he told him what a terribly wicked thing he had done, and what a scoundrel he was, and that he ought to go to prison. At this Big Claus got so frightened that he dashed straight from the hospital into his cart, whipped up the horses and galloped home. But the doctor and everyone else thought he must be mad, so they let him drive wherever he liked.

"You shall pay for this," said Big Claus, once he had reached the highroad. "Yes, indeed, you shall pay for this, Little Claus." So as soon as he got home he took the biggest sack he could find, went over to Little Claus's home and said, "You've fooled me again. First I killed my horses and now I've killed my old grandmother. It's all your fault, but you shan't make a fool of me anymore." Then he grabbed Little Claus by the middle, thrust him into the sack and threw him over his shoulder, shouting, "Now I'm going to take you out and drown you!"

The river was some distance away, and Little Claus wasn't at all light to carry. The road went past the church, where the organ was playing and the people were singing very beautifully. Big Claus put the sack down close to the church door and thought it might be a good thing to go in and hear a hymn before he went any farther. There was no chance for Little Claus to get out of the sack, and everybody else was in church, so in he went.

"Oh, dear, oh, dear!" sighed Little Claus in the sack. He twisted and turned, but he couldn't manage to loosen the cord. At that very moment, an old cattle drover with chalk-white hair passed by, leaning on a big stick. He was driving a whole herd of cows and oxen in front of him, and they bumped into the sack in which Little Claus was sitting and pushed it over.

"Oh, dear!" sighed Little Claus. "I'm so young to go to Heaven already."

"And poor me," said the drover, "I'm so old and yet I can't get there!"

"Open the sack!" shouted Little Claus. "Crawl in and take my place, and you'll be in Heaven before you know it."

"That's just what I want!" said the cattle drover, and he untied the sack for Little Claus, who jumped out at once.

"You'll take care of the cattle for me, won't you?" said the old man, and he crawled into the sack. Little Claus tied it up again and went off with all the cows and oxen.

Soon after this, Big Claus came out of church and threw the sack over his shoulder again. He couldn't help noticing that it had gotten very light during his absence, for the old drover was not more than half the weight of Little Claus.

"How light he is to carry now! I'm sure it must be because I've been listening to a hymn." Then he went to the broad, deep river, threw the sack with the old drover in it into the water and shouted after him, thinking that it was Little Claus, "There now! You shan't fool me anymore."

So he started off for home, but when he came to the crossroads he met Little Claus coming along with all the cattle.

"I'll be blowed!" exclaimed Big Claus. "Didn't I drown you?"

"To be sure you did!" said Little Claus. "You threw me into the river less than half an hour ago."

"But where on earth did you get all these fine cattle from?" asked Big Claus.

"They're sea cattle," said Little Claus. "I'm going to tell you the whole story, and I'm going to thank you for drowning me. I'm at the top of the ladder now; I'm really rich, I tell you. I was scared to death in the sack when the wind whistled about my ears as you threw me down from the bridge into the cold water. I sank straight to the bottom, but I didn't hurt myself, for the finest soft grass grows down there. I fell on that, and the sack was opened at once. The loveliest maiden in snow-white garments, with a green wreath on her wet hair, took my hand and said, 'Is that you,

Little Claus? Here are some cattle for you to begin with. Four miles farther up the road there's another herd of them which I will also give you for a present.' Then I discovered that the river is a great highroad for the sea people. Down there at the bottom they walk straight in from the sea and far up into the land, where the river is lost to sight. It was lovely down there with flowers and the freshest of grass. Fishes darted past my ears as birds do in the air up here. I can't tell you how nice looking the people were, and what a lot of cattle there were grazing along the ditches and fences!"

"But why have you come back so soon?" asked Big Claus. "I shouldn't have done that if it was so beautiful down there."

"Why," said Little Claus, "that's where I've been very clever! Don't you remember what I told you? The sea maiden said that four miles farther up the road—and by the road she meant the river, for she can't get anywhere else—there was another herd of cattle waiting for me. But I know how the river meanders in and out; it would be a terribly roundabout way. No, the shortest way, if you can manage it, is to come up on land and go straight across to the river again. It saves about two miles, and so I get to my sea cattle that much more quickly."

"Oh, you are a lucky fellow," said Big Claus. "Do you think I shall get some sea cattle too, if I go down to the bottom of the river?"

"I'm sure of it," said Little Claus, "but I can't carry you in the sack to the river, you're too heavy. If you'll go there yourself and crawl into the sack, I'll throw you in with the greatest of pleasure."

"Thanks very much," said Big Claus, "but if I don't find any sea cattle when I get down there, I'll give you a walloping such as you'll never forget."

"Now don't be so hard on me!" said Little Claus—and down they went to the river.

When the thirsty cattle saw the water, they ran as fast as they could to reach it and drink.

"Look what a hurry the cattle are in," said Little Claus. "They're longing to go down to the bottom of the river again."

"Yes, but help me first," said Big Claus, "or you'll get a good beating." And then he crawled into the big sack which had been lying across the back of one of the oxen.

"Put a stone in it, or I'm afraid I shan't sink," said Big Claus.

"You'll sink fast enough," said Little Claus, but still he put a good big stone in the sack, tied the rope tight and gave it a good push—plump! There was Big Claus out in the river, and he sank straight to the bottom.

"I'm afraid he won't find his cattle," said Little Claus, and he drove home the ones he had.

HANS CHRISTIAN ANDERSEN, TRANSLATED BY PAUL LEYSSAC

Long, long ago, as far back as the time when animals spoke, there lived a community of cats in a deserted house not far from a large town. They had everything they could possibly desire for their comfort. They were well fed and well lodged, and if by any chance an unlucky mouse was stupid enough to venture in their way, they caught it, not to eat but for the pure pleasure of catching it.

The old people of the town related how they had heard their parents speak of a time when the whole country was so overrun with rats and mice that not so much as a grain of corn was to be gathered in the fields; and it might be out of gratitude to the cats who had rid the country of these plagues that their descendants were allowed to live in peace.

No one knows where the cats got the money to pay for everything, or who paid it, for all this happened so very long ago. But one thing is certain: they were rich enough to keep a servant, for though they lived very happily together and did not scratch or fight more than human beings would have done, they were not

clever enough to do the housework themselves and pre-
ferred at all events to have someone to cook their meat,
which they scorned to eat raw.

Not only were they very difficult to please about the
housework, but most women quickly tired of living
alone with only cats for companions, and consequently
they never kept a servant long. It had become a saying
in the town, when anyone found herself reduced to her
last penny: "I will go and live with the cats," and
many a poor woman actually did so.

Now Lizina was not happy at home, for her mother,
who was a widow, was much fonder of her elder
daughter. Often the younger one fared very badly and
had not enough to eat, while her sister could have
everything she desired, and if Lizina dared to complain
she was certain to receive a good beating.

At last the day came when she was at the end of her
patience, and she exclaimed to her mother and sister,
"Since you hate me so much, you will be glad to be rid
of me—so I am going to live with the cats!"

"Away with you!" cried her mother, seizing an old
broom handle from behind the door.

Poor Lizina did not wait to be told twice, but ran
off at once and never stopped till she reached the door
of the cats' house. Their cook had left them that very
morning with her face all scratched, the result of such
a quarrel with the head of the house that he had nearly
clawed out her eyes. Lizina therefore was warmly wel-

comed, and she set to work at once to prepare the dinner, not without many misgivings as to the tastes of the cats and whether she would be able to satisfy them.

Going to and fro about her work, she found herself frequently hindered by a constant succession of cats who appeared one after another in the kitchen to inspect the new servant. She had one in front of her feet, another perched on the back of her chair while she peeled vegetables, a third sat on the table beside her and five or six others prowled about among the pots and pans on the shelves against the wall.

The air resounded with their purring, which meant they were pleased with their new maid, but Lizina had not yet learned to understand their language, and often she did not know what they wanted her to do. However, as she was a good, kindhearted girl, she set to work to pick up the little kittens which tumbled about on the floor, she patched up quarrels and nursed on her lap a big tabby—the oldest of the community—which had a lame paw.

All these kindnesses could hardly fail to make a favorable impression on the cats, and it was even better after a while, when Lizina had become accustomed to their strange ways. Never had the house been kept so clean, the meats so well served nor the sick cats so well cared for.

Some weeks later they had a visit from an old cat whom they called their father, who lived by himself in a barn at the top of the hill and came down from time to time to inspect the little colony. He too was much taken with Lizina, and on seeing her, asked, "Are you well served by this nice, black-eyed little person?" and the cats answered with one voice, "Oh, yes, Father Gatto, we have never had so good a servant!"

At each of his visits the answer was always the same; but after a time the old cat, who was very observant, noticed that the little maid was looking sadder and sadder.

"What is the matter, my child—has anyone been unkind to you?" he asked one day, when he found her almost crying in her kitchen.

She burst into tears and answered between her sobs, "Oh, no! They are all very good to me. But I long for news of home and I pine to see my mother and sister."

Gatto, being a sensible old cat, understood the little servant's feelings. "You shall go home," he said, "and you shall not come back here unless you please. But first you must be rewarded for your kind services to my children. Follow me down into the inner cellar, where you have never been before, for I always keep it locked and carry the key away with me."

Lizina looked around her in astonishment as they went down into the great vaulted cellar underneath the kitchen. Before her stood two big earthenware water jars, one of which contained oil, the other a liquid shining like gold.

"Into which of these jars shall I dip you?" asked Father Gatto, with a grin that showed all his sharp white teeth, while his mustaches stood out straight on either side of his face.

The little maid looked at the two jars from under her long dark lashes. "In the oil jar!" she answered timidly, thinking to herself, I could not ask to be bathed in gold.

But Father Gatto replied, "No, no; you have deserved something better than that." And seizing her in his strong paws he plunged her into the liquid gold.

Wonder of wonders! When Lizina came out of the jar she shone from head to foot like the sun in the heavens on a fine summer's day. Her pretty pink cheeks and long black hair alone kept their natural color, but otherwise she had become like a statue of pure gold.

Father Gatto purred loudly with satisfaction. "Go home," he said, "and see your mother and sister; but take care if you hear the cock crow to turn toward it; if on the contrary the donkey brays, you must look the other way."

The little maid, having gratefully kissed the white paw of the old cat, set off for home. Just as she got near her mother's house the cock crowed, and quickly she turned toward it. Immediately a beautiful golden star appeared on her forehead, crowning her glossy black hair. At the same time the donkey began to bray,

but Lizina took care not to look over the fence into the field where the donkey was feeding. Her mother and sister, who were in front of their house, uttered cries of admiration and astonishment when they saw her, and their cries became still louder when Lizina, taking her handkerchief from her pocket, drew out a handful of gold also.

For some days the mother and her two daughters lived very happily together, for Lizina had given them everything she had brought away except her golden clothing, for that would not come off, in spite of all the efforts of her sister, who was madly jealous of her good fortune. The golden star, too, could not be removed from her forehead. But the gold pieces she drew from her pockets had found their way to her mother and sister.

"I will go now and see what I can get out of the pussies," said Peppina, the elder girl, one morning, as she took Lizina's basket and fastened her purses into her own skirt. I should like some of the cats' gold for myself, she thought, as she left her mother's house before the sun rose.

The cat colony had not yet hired another servant, for they knew they could never get one to replace Lizina, whose loss they had not ceased to mourn. When they heard that Peppina was her sister, they ran to meet her. "She is not the least like her," the kittens whispered among themselves.

"Hush, be quiet!" the older cats said. "All servants cannot be pretty."

No, decidedly she was not at all like Lizina. Even the most reasonable and generous of the cats soon acknowledged that.

The very first day she shut the kitchen door in the faces of the tomcats, who used to enjoy watching Lizina at her work, and a young and mischievous cat who jumped in by the open kitchen window and alighted on the table got such a blow with the rolling pin that he squalled for an hour.

With every day that passed the household became more and more aware of its misfortune.

The work was as badly done as the servant was surly and disagreeable. Heaps of dust collected in the corners of the rooms; spiders' webs hung from the ceilings and in front of the windowpanes; the beds were hardly ever made; and the feather beds, so beloved by the old and feeble cats, had never once been shaken since Lizina left the house. At Father Gatto's next visit he found the whole colony in a great state of uproar.

"Caesar has one paw so badly swollen that it looks as if it were broken," said one. "Peppina kicked him with her great wooden shoes. Hector has an abscess on his back where a wooden chair was flung at him, and Agrippina's three little kittens have died of hunger beside their mother, because Peppina forgot them in their basket up in the attic. There is no putting up with the creature—do send her away, Father Gatto! Lizina herself would not be angry with us; she must know very well what her sister is like."

"Come here," said Father Gatto in his most severe tones to Peppina. And he took her down into the cellar and showed her the same two great jars that he had shown Lizina. "Into which of these shall I dip you?" he asked; and she made haste to answer, "In the liquid gold," for she was no more modest than she was good and kind.

Father Gatto's yellow eyes darted fire. "You have not deserved it," he uttered in a voice like thunder and, seizing her, he flung her into the jar of oil, where she was nearly suffocated.

When she came to the surface screaming and struggling, the vengeful cat seized her again and rolled her in the ash heap on the floor; then when she rose, dirty, blinded and disgusting to behold, he thrust her from the door, saying, "Begone! When you meet a braying donkey be careful to turn your head toward it."

Stumbling and raging, Peppina set off for home, thinking herself fortunate to find a stick by the wayside with which to support herself. She was within sight of her mother's house when she heard the voice of a donkey loudly braying in the meadow on the right. Quickly she turned her head toward it, and at the same time put her hand up to her forehead where, waving like a plume, was a donkey's tail. She ran home to her mother at full speed, yelling with rage and despair; and it took Lizina two hours with a big basin of hot water and two cakes of soap to wash off the layer of oil and ashes with which Father Gatto had adorned her. As for the donkey's tail, it was impossible to get rid of that; it was as firmly fixed on her forehead as was the golden star on Lizina's.

Their mother was furious. She first beat Lizina unmercifully with the broom. Then she took her to the mouth of the well and lowered her into it. She went away, leaving her stranded at the bottom, weeping and crying for help.

Before this happened, however, the King's son in passing the mother's house one day had seen Lizina sitting and sewing in the parlor and had been dazzled by her beauty. After coming back two or three times, he at last ventured to approach the window and to whisper in the softest voice, "Lovely maiden, will you be my bride?"

And she had answered, "I will."

Next morning, when the Prince arrived to claim his bride, he found her wrapped in a large white veil. "It is thus that maidens are received from their parents' hands," said the mother, who hoped to make the King's son marry Peppina in place of her sister, and had fastened the donkey's tail around her head like a lock of hair under the veil. The Prince was young and a little timid, so he made no objections, and he seated Peppina in the carriage beside him.

Their way led past the old house inhabited by the cats, who were all at the window, for the report had got about that the Prince was going to marry the most beautiful maiden in the world, on whose forehead shone a golden star, and they knew that this could only be their adored Lizina. As the carriage slowly passed in front of the old house, where cats from all parts of the world seemed to be gathered, a song burst from every throat:

> Mew, mew, mew!
> Prince, look quick behind you!
> In the well is fair Lizina,
> And you have nothing but Peppina.

When he heard this, the coachman, who understood the cats' language better than the Prince did, stopped his horses and asked, "Does Your Highness know what the grimalkins are saying?"

The song broke forth again, louder than ever.

With a turn of his hand, the Prince threw back the white veil and discovered beneath it the puffed-up, swollen face of Peppina, with the donkey's tail twisted around her head.

"Ah, traitoress!" he exclaimed, quivering with rage, and, ordering the horses to be turned around, he drove the elder daughter back to the woman who had sought to deceive him. With his hand on the hilt of his sword he demanded Lizina in so fierce a voice that the mother hastened to the well to draw her prisoner out.

Lizina's clothing and her star shone so brilliantly that when the Prince led her home to the King, his father, the whole palace was lit up. Next day they were married, and lived happily ever after; and all the cats, headed by old Father Gatto, were at the wedding.

ITALIAN FAIRY TALE, ANDREW LANG COLLECTION

SINDBAD THE SAILOR

IN THE TIMES of Caliph Haroun al Raschid there lived in Baghdad a poor porter named Hindbad who, on a very hot day, was sent to carry a heavy load from one end of the city to the other. Before he had accomplished half the distance, he was so tired that, finding himself in a quiet street where the pavement was sprinkled with rosewater and a cool breeze was blowing, he set his burden upon the ground and sat down to rest in the shade of a grand palace.

Very soon he decided he could not have chosen a pleasanter place; a delicious perfume of aloes wood and pastilles came from the open windows and mingled with the scent of the rosewater which steamed up from the hot pavement. Within the palace he heard music, as of many instruments cunningly played, and the melodious warble of nightingales and other birds; and by this, and the appetizing smell of many dainty dishes, he judged that feasting and merrymaking were going on.

He wondered who lived in this magnificent place he had never seen before, the street in which it stood being one which he seldom had occasion to pass. To satisfy his curiosity he went up to one of the splendidly dressed servants who stood outside the door and asked the name of the master of the mansion.

"What," replied he, "do you live in Baghdad and not know that here lives Sindbad the Sailor, that famous traveler who has sailed over every sea upon which the sun shines?"

The porter could not help feeling envious of one whose lot seemed to be as happy as his own was miserable. Casting his eyes up to the sky he exclaimed aloud: "Consider, Mighty Creator of all things, the difference between Sindbad's life and mine. Every day I suffer a thousand hardships and misfortunes and have hard work to get even enough barley bread to keep myself and my family alive, while the lucky Sindbad spends money right and left and lives upon the fat of the land! What has he done that you should give him this pleasant life—what have I done to deserve so hard a fate?"

Saying this, he stamped upon the ground like one beside himself with misery and despair. Just at this moment a servant came out of the palace and, taking him by the arm, said, "Come with me. The noble Sindbad, my master, wishes to speak to you."

Hindbad was not a little surprised at this summons and feared that his unguarded words might have drawn upon him the displeasure of Sindbad, and he tried to excuse himself upon the pretext that he could not leave the burden which had been entrusted to him in the street. However, the lackey promised him it should be taken care of and urged him to obey the call so pressingly that, at last, the porter was obliged to yield.

He followed the servant into a vast room, where a great company was seated around a table covered with all sorts of delicacies. In the place of honor sat a tall, grave man whose long white beard gave him a venerable air. Behind his chair stood a crowd of attendants ready to minister to his wants. This was the famous Sindbad himself.

Sindbad, making a sign to him to approach, caused him to be seated and heaped many choice morsels upon his plate. Presently, when the banquet drew to a close, he addressed the noble company and the humble porter.

"Since you have, perhaps, heard but confused accounts of my seven voyages, and the dangers and wonders that I have met with by sea and land, I will now give you a full and true account of them, which I think you will be well pleased to hear."

As Sindbad was relating his adventures chiefly on account of the porter, he ordered, before beginning his tale, that the burden which had been left in the street should be carried by some of his own servants to the place for which Hindbad had set out at first, while he remained to listen to the story.

First Voyage

I inherited considerable wealth from my parents and, being young and foolish, I squandered it recklessly upon every kind of pleasure. But before long, finding that riches speedily take to themselves wings if managed as badly as I was managing mine, and remembering also that to be old and poor is misery indeed, I began to think of how I could make the best of what still remained to me. I sold all my household goods by public auction, joined a company of merchants who traded by sea and embarked with them at Balsora in a ship which we had fitted out among us.

We set sail and took our course toward the East

Indies by the Persian Gulf, having the coast of Persia upon our left hand and upon our right the shores of Arabia Felix. I was at first much troubled by the uneasy motion of the vessel but speedily recovered my health, and since that hour have been no more plagued by sickness.

From time to time we landed at various islands where we sold or exchanged our merchandise, and one day when the wind dropped suddenly we found ourselves becalmed close to a small island which rose only slightly above the surface of the water. Our sails were furled, and the captain gave all who wished permission to land for a while and amuse themselves. I was among the number, but when, after strolling about for some time, we lighted a fire and sat down to enjoy a repast, we were startled by a sudden and violent trembling of the island. At the same moment those left upon the ship set up an outcry, bidding us come on board for our lives, since what we had taken for an island was nothing but the back of a sleeping whale. Those who were nearest to the boat jumped into it, others leaped into the sea, but before I could save myself, the whale plunged suddenly into the depths of the ocean, leaving me clinging to a piece of wood which we had brought to make our fire.

Meanwhile a breeze had sprung up, and in the confusion of hoisting the sails and collecting those who were near the boat and clinging to its sides, no one missed me and I was left at the mercy of the waves. All that day I floated, now beaten this way, now that, and when night fell I despaired for my life. But weary and spent as I was, I clung to my frail support, and great was my joy when the morning light showed that I had drifted against an island.

The cliffs were high and steep, but luckily for me some tree roots protruded in places, and by their aid I climbed up at last and stretched myself upon the turf at the top, where I lay, more dead than alive, till the sun was high in the heavens. By that time I was very hungry, but after some searching I came upon edible herbs and a spring of clear water, and much refreshed I set out to explore the island.

Presently I reached a great plain where a grazing horse was tethered and, as I stood looking at it, I heard voices talking, apparently underground. In a moment a man appeared who asked me how I had come to be on the island.

I told him my adventures and heard in return that he was one of the grooms of Mihrage, the King of the island, and that each year they came to feed their master's horses on this plain. He took me to a cave where his companions were assembled. When I had eaten the food they set before me, they bade me think myself fortunate to have come upon them when I did, since they were going back to their master, the King, on the following day and without their aid I could certainly never have found my way, alone, to the inhabited part of the island.

Early the next morning we accordingly set out, and when we reached the capital I was graciously received by the King, to whom I related my adventures. He ordered that I should be well cared for and provided with such things as I needed. The capital was situated upon the seashore and was visited by vessels from all parts of the world. Being a merchant, I sought out men of my own profession, particularly those who came from foreign countries, as I hoped in this way to hear any news from Baghdad and find some means of returning there.

In the meantime I heard many curious things and answered many questions concerning my own country, for I talked with everyone who came to me. Also, to while away the time of waiting, I explored a little island named Cassel, which belonged to King Mihrage and was supposed to be inhabited by a spirit named Deggial. Indeed, the sailors assured me that often at night the playing of timbals could be heard upon it. However, I saw nothing strange on my voyage, saving some fish that were a full three hundred feet long, but were fortunately even more in dread of us than we of them, and fled from us if we did but strike upon a board to frighten them. Other fishes there were only a cubit long and these had heads like owls.

One day, down on the quay, I saw a ship which

had just cast anchor and was discharging her cargo, while the merchants to whom it belonged were busily directing the removal of it to their warehouses. Drawing nearer I presently noticed that my own name was marked upon some of the packages and, after having carefully examined them, I felt sure that they were indeed those which I had put on board our ship at Balsora. I then recognized the captain of the vessel, but as I was certain that he believed me to be dead, I went up to him and asked who owned the packages at which I was looking.

"There was on board my ship," he replied, "a merchant of Baghdad named Sindbad. One day he and several of my other passengers landed upon what we supposed to be an island but which was really an enormous whale floating asleep upon the waves. No sooner did it feel the heat of the fire which had been kindled upon its back, than it plunged into the depths of the sea. Several of the people who were upon it perished in the waters and, among others, was this unlucky Sindbad. This merchandise is his, but I have resolved to dispose of it for the benefit of his family should I ever chance to meet with them."

"Captain," I said, "I am that Sindbad whom you believe to be dead, and these are my possessions!"

When the captain heard these words he cried out in amazement, "Lackaday! What is the world coming to? In these days there is not an honest man to be met with. Did I not with my own eyes see Sindbad drown, and now you have the audacity to tell me that you are he! I should have taken you to be a just man, and yet for the sake of obtaining what does not belong to you, you are ready to invent this horrible falsehood."

"Have patience and do me the favor of hearing my story," said I.

"Speak then," the captain replied to me, "I am all attention."

So I told him of my escape and of my fortunate meeting with the King's grooms and how kindly I had been treated at the palace. Very soon I began to see that I had made some impression upon him, and after the arrival of some of the other merchants who showed great joy at once more seeing me alive, he declared that he also recognized me.

Throwing himself upon my neck, he exclaimed, "Heaven be praised that you have escaped from so great a danger. As to your goods, I pray you take them and dispose of them as you please."

I thanked him and praised his honesty, begging him to accept several bales of my merchandise in token of my gratitude, but he would take nothing. Of the choicest of my goods I prepared a present for King Mihrage, who was amazed, having known that I had lost all of my possessions. When I explained how my bales had been miraculously restored to me, he accepted my gifts and in return gave me many valuable things. I then took leave of him and, exchanging my merchandise for sandal and aloes wood, camphor, nutmegs, cloves, pepper and ginger, I embarked upon the same vessel and traded so successfully during our homeward voyage that I arrived in Balsora with about one hundred thousand pieces of gold.

My brothers and sisters received me with joy. I bought land and slaves, and built a great house in which I resolved to live happily and, in the enjoyment of all the pleasures of life, to forget my past sufferings.

Here Sindbad paused and commanded the musicians to play again, while the feasting continued until evening. When the time came for the porter to depart, Sindbad gave him a purse containing one hundred pieces of gold, saying, "Take this, Hindbad, and go home, but tomorrow come again and you shall hear more of my adventures."

The porter retired, quite overcome by so much generosity, and you may imagine that he was well received at home, where his wife and children thanked their lucky stars that he had found such a benefactor as the wealthy Sindbad.

The next day, Hindbad, dressed in his best, returned to the voyager's house and was received with open arms. As soon as all the guests had arrived the banquet began as before, and when they had feasted long and merrily, Sindbad addressed them.

"My friends, I beg that you will give me your attention while I relate the adventures of my second voyage, which you will surely find even more astonishing than the first."

Second Voyage

I had resolved, as you know, on my return from the first voyage, to spend the rest of my days quietly in Baghdad, but very soon I grew tired of such an idle life and longed once more to find myself upon the sea. I procured, therefore, goods that were suitable for the places I intended to visit and embarked for the second time in a good ship with other merchants whom I knew to be honorable men.

We went from island to island, often making excellent bargains, until one day we landed at a spot which appeared to possess neither houses nor people. While my companions wandered here and there gathering flowers and fruit, I sat down in a shady place and, having heartily enjoyed the provisions and the wine I had brought with me, I soon fell asleep, lulled by the murmur of a brook which flowed by.

How long I slept I know not, but when I opened my eyes I perceived with horror that I was alone and the ship was gone. I rushed to and fro like one distracted, uttering cries of despair, and when I saw the vessel under full sail just disappearing upon the horizon, I wished bitterly enough that I had been content to stay at home in safety.

Since wishes could do me no good, I presently took courage and looked about me for a means of escape. I climbed a tall tree and first of all directed my anxious glances toward the sea; but, finding nothing hopeful there, I turned landward and my curiosity was excited by a huge dazzling white object, so far away that I could not make out what it might be.

Descending from the tree, I hastily collected what remained of my provisions and set off as fast as I could. As I drew near, it seemed to me to be a white ball of immense size and height, and when I could touch it I found it marvelously smooth and soft. Since it was impossible to climb—for it presented no foothold—I walked around it, seeking some opening, but there was none. I counted, however, that it was at least fifty paces round.

By this time the sun was near setting, but quite suddenly something like a huge black cloud came swiftly over me, and I saw with amazement that it was a bird of extraordinary size which was hovering near. Then I remembered I had often heard the sailors speak of a wonderful bird called a roc, and it occurred to me that the white object which had so puzzled me must be its egg.

Sure enough the bird settled slowly down upon it, covering it with its wings to keep it warm, and I cow-

ered close beside the egg in such a position that one
of the bird's feet, which was as large as the trunk of a
tree, was just in front of me. Taking off my turban, I
bound myself securely to the foot with the linen in the
hope that the roc, when it took flight next morning,
would bear me away with it from the island. And this
was precisely what did happen.

As soon as the dawn appeared, the bird soared into
the air, carrying me up and up till I could no longer
see the earth and then suddenly descended so swiftly
that I almost lost consciousness. When I became aware
that the roc had settled and I was once again upon
solid ground, I hastily unbound my turban from its
foot, and not a moment too soon; for the bird, pounc-
ing upon a huge snake, grasped it with its powerful
beak, rose into the air and soon had disappeared from
my view. After I had looked about me I began to
doubt if I had gained anything at all by quitting the
desolate island.

The valley in which I found myself was deep and
narrow and surrounded by mountains which towered
into the clouds and were so steep and rocky there was
no way of climbing up their sides.

As I wandered about, seeking for some means of
escaping from this trap, I observed that the ground
was strewn with diamonds, many of them of an
astonishing size.

This sight gave me great pleasure, but my delight

was speedily dampened when I also saw numbers of horrible snakes so long and so large that the smallest of them could have swallowed an elephant with ease. Fortunately for me they seemed to hide in caverns in the rocks by day, and only came out by night, probably because of their enemy the roc.

All day long I wandered up and down the valley, and when it grew dusk I crept into a small cave. Having blocked up the entrance to it with a stone, I ate part of my little store of food and lay down to sleep, but all through the night the serpents crawled to and fro, hissing horribly, so that I could scarcely close my eyes for terror.

I was thankful when the morning light appeared and, when I judged by the silence that the serpents had retreated to their dens, I came tremblingly out of my cave and wandered up and down the valley once more, kicking the diamonds contemptuously out of my path, for I felt that they were indeed vain things to a man in my situation.

At last, overcome with weariness, I sat down upon a rock, but I had hardly closed my eyes when I was startled by something which fell to the ground with a thud close beside me.

It was a huge piece of fresh meat, and as I stared at it several more pieces rolled over the cliffs in different places. I had always thought that the stories the sailors told of the famous Valley of Diamonds, and of the cunning way which some merchants had devised for getting at the precious stones, were mere travelers' tales invented to give pleasure to the hearers, but now I perceived that they were surely true.

These merchants came to the valley at the time when the eagles, which keep their aeries in the rocks, had hatched their young. The merchants then threw great lumps of meat into the valley. These, falling with so much force upon the diamonds, were sure to take up some of the precious stones with them when the eagles pounced upon the meat and carried it off to their nests to feed their hungry broods. Then the merchants, scaring away the parent birds with shouts and outcries, would secure their treasures.

Until this moment I had looked upon the valley as my grave, for I had seen no possibility of getting out of it alive, but now I took courage and began by picking up all the largest diamonds I could find and storing them carefully in the leather pouch which had held my provisions; this I tied securely to my belt. I then chose the piece of meat which seemed most suited to my purpose, and with the aid of my turban bound it firmly to my back. This done, I lay down upon my face and awaited the coming of the eagles. I soon heard the flapping of their mighty wings above me, and had the satisfaction of feeling one of them seize upon the meat and me with it, and rise slowly toward his nest, into which he presently dropped me.

Luckily for me the merchants were on the watch and, setting up their usual outcries, they rushed to the nest, scaring away the eagle. Their amazement was great when they discovered me, also their disappointment, and with one accord they fell to abusing me for having robbed them of their usual profit.

Addressing myself to the one who seemed most aggrieved, I said, "I am sure, if you knew all I have suffered, you would show more kindness toward me, and as for diamonds, I have enough here of the very best for you and me and your entire company." So saying I showed them to him.

The others all crowded around me, wondering at my adventures and admiring the device by which I had escaped from the valley. When they had led me to their camp and examined my diamonds, they assured me that, in the many years they had carried on their trade, they had seen no stones to be compared with them for size and beauty.

I found that each merchant chose a particular nest, so I begged the one who owned the nest to which I had been carried to take as much as he would of my treasure, but he contented himself with one stone and that by no means the largest, assuring me that with such a gem his fortune was made and he need toil no more. I stayed with the merchants several days, and then, as they were journeying homeward, I gladly accompanied them.

Our path lay across high mountains and came at last to the seashore. We sailed to the Isle of Roha, where the camphor trees grow to such size that a hundred men could shelter under one of them with ease. The sap flows from an incision made high up in the tree into a vessel hung there to receive it and soon hardens into the substance called camphor, but the camphor tree itself withers up and dies when it has been so treated.

In this same island we saw the rhinoceros, an animal smaller than the elephant and larger than the buffalo. It has a horn a foot and a half long which is solid but has a furrow from the base to the tip. Upon it is traced in white lines the figure of a man. The rhinoceros fights with the elephant and, transfixing him with his horn, carries him off upon his head, but becoming blinded with the blood of his enemy, he falls to the ground. Then comes the roc and he clutches them both in his talons, taking them to feed his young.

This doubtless astonishes you, but if you do not believe my tale go to Roha and see for yourself. For fear of wearying you, I pass over in silence many other wonderful things which we saw on this island. Before we left I exchanged one of my diamonds for much goodly merchandise by which I profited greatly on our homeward way. At last we reached Balsora, whence I hastened to Baghdad, where my first action was to bestow large sums of money upon the poor, after which I settled down to enjoy tranquilly the riches I had gained with so much toil and pain.

Having thus related the adventures of his second voyage, Sindbad again bestowed a hundred pieces of gold upon Hindbad, inviting him and all the other guests to return on the following day and hear how he fared upon his third voyage. The other guests also departed for their homes but returned at the same hour the next day, including the porter, whose former life of hard work and poverty already seemed to him like a bad dream. Once more, when the feast was over, Sindbad claimed the attention of his guests and began the account of his third voyage.

Third Voyage

After a very short time, the pleasant, easy life I led made me quite forget the perils of my two voyages. So once more providing myself with the rarest and choicest merchandise of Baghdad, I set sail with other merchants of my acquaintance for distant lands. We had touched at many ports and made much profit, when one day upon the open sea we were caught by a terrible wind which blew us completely out of our reckoning and lasted for several days, finally driving us into harbor on a strange island.

"I would rather have come to anchor anywhere than

here," cried our captain. "This island and those adjoining it are inhabited by hairy savages who are certain to attack us. Whatever these dwarfs may do we dare not resist, since they swarm like locusts, and if one of them is killed the rest will fall upon us and speedily make an end of us."

These words caused great consternation among all the ship's company and only too soon we were to find out that the captain spoke truly. There appeared a vast multitude of hideous savages, not more than two feet high and covered with reddish fur. Throwing themselves into the waves, they surrounded our vessel. Chattering meanwhile in a language which we could not understand, and clutching at ropes and gangways, they swarmed up the ship's side with such speed and agility that they almost seemed to fly.

You may imagine the terror that seized us as we watched them, neither daring to hinder them nor able to speak a word to deter them from their purpose, whatever it may be. Of this we were not left long in doubt. Hoisting the sails and cutting the anchor cable, they sailed our vessel to an island which lay a little farther off, where they drove us ashore. Then, taking possession of the ship, they made off to the place from which they had come, leaving us stranded upon a shore avoided with horror by mariners for a reason you will learn before long.

Turning away from the sea we wandered miserably

inland, finding as we went various herbs and fruits which we ate, feeling that we might as well live as long as possible though we had no hope of escape. Presently we saw in the distance what seemed to be a splendid palace, toward which we turned our weary steps. When we reached it we saw that it was a castle, lofty and strongly built. Pushing back the heavy ebony doors we entered the courtyard, but upon the threshold of the great hall beyond it we paused, frozen with horror at the sight which greeted us. On one side lay a huge pile of bones—human bones, and on the other numberless spits for roasting!

Overcome with despair we sank trembling to the ground and lay there without speech or motion. The sun was setting when a loud noise aroused us, the door of the hall was violently burst open and a hideous giant entered. He was as tall as a palm tree and had but one eye, which flamed like a burning coal in the middle of his forehead. His teeth were long and sharp and he grinned horribly, while his lower lip hung down upon his chest, and he had ears like elephant's ears, which covered his shoulders, and his nails were like the claws of some fierce bird.

At this terrible sight our senses left us and we lay like dead men. When at last we came to ourselves the giant sat examining us attentively with his fearful eye. Before long, having looked at us enough, he came toward us and, stretching out his hand, took me by the back of the neck, turning me this way and that, but feeling that I was mere skin and bone he set me down again and went on to the next, whom he treated in the same fashion. At last he came to the captain and, finding him the fattest of us all, he took him up in one hand and stuck him upon a spit and proceeded to kindle a huge fire at which he presently roasted him. After the giant had supped he went to sleep, snoring like the loudest thunder, while the rest of us lay shivering with horror the whole night through. When day finally broke the giant awoke and went out, leaving us alone in the castle.

When we believed him to be really gone, we started up, bemoaning our horrible fate until the hall echoed with our despairing cries. Though we were many and our enemy was alone, it did not occur to us to kill him. Indeed we should have found that a hard task even if we had thought of it, but no plan could we devise to deliver ourselves. So at last, submitting to our sad fate, we spent the day in wandering up and down the island, eating such fruits as we could find, and when night came we returned to the castle, having sought in vain for any other place of shelter.

At sunset the giant returned, supped upon one of our unhappy comrades, slept and snored till dawn and then left us as before. Our condition seemed to us so frightful that several of my companions thought it would be better to leap from the cliffs and perish in the waves at once, rather than await so miserable an end; but I had a plan of escape which I now unfolded to them, and which they immediately agreed to attempt with me.

"Listen, my brothers," I said, "you know that plenty of driftwood lies along the shore. Let us make several rafts and carry them to a suitable place. If our plot succeeds, we can wait patiently for the chance of some passing ship which would rescue us. If it fails, we must quickly take to our rafts; frail as they are, we have more chance of saving our lives with them than we have if we remain here."

All agreed with me, and we spent the day in building rafts, each capable of carrying three persons. At nightfall we returned to the castle, and very soon in came the giant, and one more of our number was sacrificed. As soon as he had finished his horrible repast, he lay down to sleep as before, and when we heard him begin to snore, I, and nine of the boldest of my comrades, rose softly. Each of us took a spit, which we made red-hot in the fire, and then at a given signal we plunged it with one accord into the giant's eye, completely blinding him.

Uttering a terrible cry, the giant sprang to his feet reaching about in every direction to try to seize one of us, but we had all fled different ways as soon as the deed was done and thrown ourselves flat upon the ground in corners where he was not likely to touch us with his feet. After a vain search he fumbled about till he found the door leading from the castle and fled out of it, howling frightfully. As for us, my companions and I immediately made haste to leave the fatal place and, stationing ourselves beside our rafts, we waited to see what would happen.

Our idea was that if, when the sun rose, we saw nothing of the giant and no longer heard his howls, which still came faintly through the darkness, growing more and more distant, we should conclude that he was dead and that we might safely stay on the island and need not risk our lives upon the frail rafts. But alas, morning light showed us our enemy approaching, supported on either hand by two giants nearly as large and fearful as himself, while a crowd of others followed close upon their heels. Hesitating no longer, we clambered onto our rafts and rowed out to sea as fast as we could.

The giants, seeing their prey escaping them, seized huge pieces of rock and, wading into the water, hurled them after us. So good was their aim that all rafts except the one I was on were swamped and their luckless crews drowned, without our being able to do anything to help them. Indeed, I and my two companions had all we could do to keep our own raft beyond the reach of the giants, but by dint of hard rowing we at last gained the open sea. Here we were at the mercy of the winds and waves, which tossed us to and fro that entire day and night, but the next day we found ourselves near an island, upon which we gladly landed.

There we picked delicious fruits and, having satisfied our hunger, we presently lay down to rest upon the shore. Suddenly we were aroused by a loud rustling noise and, starting up, saw that it was caused by an immense snake which was rapidly gliding toward us over the sand.

So swiftly it came that it had seized one of my comrades before he had time to fly and, in spite of his struggles and cries, speedily crushed him in its mighty coils and proceeded to swallow him.

By this time my other companion and I were running for our lives to some place where we might hope to be safe from this new horror. Seeing a tall tree, we climbed up into it, having first provided ourselves with a store of fruit from the surrounding bushes. When night came I fell asleep, only to be awakened once more by the terrible snake, which coiled itself around the tree and, finding my comrade who was perched just below me, swallowed him and crawled away, leaving me half dead with terror.

When the sun rose I crept down from the tree, with hardly a hope of escaping the dreadful fate which had overtaken my comrades; but life is sweet, and I determined to do everything I could to save myself. All day long I toiled with frantic haste and collected quantities of dry brushwood which I bound with reeds and, making a circle of them under my tree, I piled them firmly one upon another until I had a kind of tent in which I crouched, like a mouse in a hole when she sees the cat coming.

You may imagine what a fearful night I passed, for the snake returned eager to devour me and glided around and around my frail shelter seeking an entrance. Every moment I feared that it would succeed in pushing aside some of the brushwood, but happily for me it held together, and when it grew light my enemy retired, baffled and hungry, to his den. As for me, I was more dead than alive!

Shaking with fright and half suffocated by the poisonous breath of the monster, I came out of my tent and crawled down to the sea. I felt that it would be better to plunge from the cliffs and end my life at once than pass another night of such horror. But to my joy and relief I saw a ship in the distance and, shouting wildly and waving my turban, I managed to attract the attention of her crew.

A boat was sent to rescue me, and very soon I found myself on board surrounded by a wondering crowd of sailors and merchants eager to know by what chance I found myself on that desolate island. After I had told my story they regaled me with the choicest food the ship afforded, and the captain, seeing that I was dressed in rags, generously bestowed upon me one of his own coats. After sailing about for some time and touching at many ports the ship came at last to the Island of Salahat, where sandalwood grows in great abundance.

Here we anchored, and, as I stood watching the merchants preparing to sell or exchange their goods, the captain came up to me and said, "I have here some merchandise belonging to a passenger of mine who has died. Will you do me the favor to trade with it, and when I meet with his heirs I shall be able to give them the money, though it will be only just that you shall have a portion for your trouble."

I consented gladly, for I did not like standing by idle. Whereupon he pointed the bales out to me and sent for the person whose duty it was to keep a list of the goods that were upon the ship. When this man came he asked in what name the merchandise was to be registered.

"In the name of Sindbad the Sailor," replied the captain.

At this I was greatly surprised but, looking carefully at him, I recognized him to be the captain of the ship upon which I had made my second voyage, though he had altered much since that time. As for him, believing me to be dead, it was no wonder that he had not recognized me.

"So, captain," said I, "the merchant who owned those bales was called Sindbad?"

"Yes," he replied, "he was so named. He was from

Baghdad and joined my ship at Balsora, but by mischance he was left behind upon a deserted island where we had landed to fill up our water casks, and it was not until four hours later that he was missed. By that time the wind had freshened and it was impossible to put back for him."

"You suppose him to have perished, then?" said I.

"Alas, yes," he answered.

"Why, captain," I cried, "look well at me! I am that Sindbad who fell asleep upon the island and awoke to find himself abandoned."

The captain stared at me in amazement, but was presently convinced that I was indeed speaking the truth and rejoiced greatly at my escape.

"I am glad to have that piece of carelessness off my conscience at any rate," said he. "Now take your goods and the profit I have made for you upon them, and may you prosper in the future."

I took them gratefully and, as we went from one island to another, I laid in stores of cloves, cinnamon and other spices. In one place I saw a tortoise which was twenty cubits long and as many broad, also a fish that was like a cow and had skin so thick it was used to make shields. Another fish I saw was like a camel in shape and color. By degrees we came back to Balsora, and I returned to Baghdad with so much money that I could not myself count it, besides treasures without end. I gave largely to the poor and bought much land to add to what I already possessed, and thus ended my third voyage.

When Sindbad had finished his story he gave another hundred pieces of gold to Hindbad, who then departed with the other guests. The next day, when they had all reassembled and the banquet was ended, their host continued his adventures.

Fourth Voyage

Rich and happy as I was after my third voyage, I could not make up my mind to stay at home altogether. My love of trading and the pleasure I took in anything that was new and strange made me set my affairs in order and begin my journeying again. I took ship at a distant seaport, and for some time all went well, but at last, being caught in a violent hurricane, our vessel became a total wreck and many of our company perished in the waves. I, with a few others, had the good fortune to be washed ashore clinging to pieces of the wreck, for the storm had driven us near an island, and, scrambling up beyond the reach of the waves, we threw ourselves down to wait for morning.

At daylight we wandered inland and soon saw some huts, to which we directed our steps. As we drew near, their inhabitants swarmed out in great numbers and surrounded us, and we were led to their houses and divided among our captors. I with five others was taken into a hut, where we were made to sit upon the ground, and certain herbs were given to us which our captors made signs for us to eat.

Observing that they themselves did not touch them, I was careful only to pretend to taste my portion; but my companions, being very hungry, rashly ate all that was set before them, and very soon I had the horror of seeing them become perfectly mad. Though they chattered incessantly, I could not understand a word they said, nor did they heed when I spoke to them. The savages now produced large bowls full of rice prepared with coconut oil, of which my crazy comrades ate eagerly, but I tasted just a few grains, understanding clearly that the object of our captors was to fatten us speedily for their own eating, and this was exactly what happened.

My unlucky companions, having lost their reason, felt neither anxiety nor fear and ate greedily whatever was offered them. So they were soon fat and there was an end of them, but I grew leaner day by day, for I ate but little, and even that little did me no good by reason of my fear of what lay before me. However, as I was far from being a tempting morsel, I was allowed to wander about freely, and one day, when the savages had gone off upon some expedition, leaving only an old man to guard me, I managed to escape from him and plunged into the forest, running faster the more he cried to me to come back, until I completely outdistanced him.

For seven days I hurried on, resting only when the darkness stopped me, and living chiefly upon coconuts, which afforded me both meat and drink; and on the eighth day I reached the seashore and saw a party of men gathering pepper, which grew abundantly. I advanced toward them and they greeted me in Arabic, asking who I was and whence I came. My delight was great on hearing this familiar speech, and I willingly satisfied their curiosity, telling them how I had been shipwrecked and captured.

"But these savages devour men!" said they. "How did you escape?" I repeated to them what I have just told you, at which they were mightily astonished. I stayed with them until they had collected as much pepper as they wished, and then they took me back to their own country and presented me to their King. To him also I had to relate my adventures, which surprised him much, and when I had finished he ordered that I should be supplied with food and raiment and treated with consideration.

The island on which I found myself abounded in all sorts of desirable things, and a great deal of traffic went on in the capital, where I soon began to feel at home and contented. Moreover, the King treated me with special favor and in consequence of this everyone, whether at the court or in the town, sought to make life pleasant for me.

One thing I remarked which I thought very strange: from the greatest to the least, all men rode their horses without bridle or stirrups. One day I presumed to ask His Majesty why he did not use them, to which he replied, "You speak to me of things of which I have never before heard!"

This gave me an idea. I found a clever workman and made him cut out, under my direction, a bridle, reins and the foundation of a saddle, which I wadded and covered with choice leather, adorning it with rich gold embroidery. I then had a locksmith make me a bit, stirrups and a pair of spurs after a pattern that I drew for him, and when these things were completed I presented them to the King and showed him how to use them.

When I had saddled one of his horses he mounted it and rode about, quite delighted with the novelty, and to show his gratitude he rewarded me with many gifts. After this I had to make saddles for all the principal officers of the King's household, and as they gave me rich presents I soon became very wealthy and quite an important person in the city.

One day the King sent for me and said, "Sindbad, I am going to ask a favor of you. Both I and my subjects esteem you, and wish you to end your days among us. Therefore, I desire you to marry a rich and beautiful lady I will find for you, and think no more of your own country."

As the King's will was law I accepted the charming bride he presented to me and lived happily with her. Nevertheless, I had every intention of escaping at the first opportunity and going back to Baghdad. Things were thus going prosperously with me when it happened that the wife of one of my neighbors, with whom I had struck up quite a friendship, fell ill and presently died. I went to his house to offer my consolations and found him in the depths of woe.

"Heaven preserve you," said I, "and send you a long life!"

"Alas!" he replied. "What is the good of saying that when I have but an hour left to live!"

"Come, come!" said I. "Surely it is not so bad as all that. I trust that your life may be spared for many years."

"I hope," answered he, "that your life may be long, but as for me, all is finished. I have set my house in order, and today I shall be buried with my wife. This has been the law upon our island from the earliest ages—the living husband goes to the grave with his dead wife, the living wife with her dead husband. So did our fathers and so must we do. The law changes not and all must submit to it!"

As he spoke, the friends and relations of the unhappy pair began to assemble. The body, decked in rich robes and sparkling with jewels, was laid upon an open bier, and the procession started, making its way to a high mountain at some distance from the city; the wretched husband, clothed from head to foot in a black mantle, followed mournfully.

When the burial place was reached, the corpse was lowered, just as it was, into a deep pit. Then the husband, bidding farewell to all his friends, stretched himself upon another bier, on which were laid seven little loaves of bread and a pitcher of water, and he was also let down, down, down to the depths of the horrible cavern. A stone was then laid over the opening, and the melancholy company wended its way back to the city.

You may imagine that I was no unmoved spectator of these proceedings. All the others were accustomed to it from their youth up, but I was so horrified that I could not help telling the King how it struck me.

"Sire," I said, "I am more astonished than I can express to you at the strange custom which exists in your dominions of burying the living with the dead. In all my travels I have never before met with so cruel and horrible a law."

"What would you have, Sindbad?" he replied. "It is the law for everybody. I myself should be buried with the Queen if she were the first to die."

"But, Your Majesty," said I, "dare I ask if this law applies to foreigners also?"

"Why, yes," replied the King, smiling in what I could but consider a very heartless manner, "they are no exception to the rule if they have married in the country."

From that time forward my mind was never easy. If only my wife's little finger ached I fancied she was going to die, and sure enough before very long she fell really ill and within a few days she had breathed her last.

My dismay was great, for it seemed that to be buried alive was even a worse fate than to be devoured by cannibals. The body of my wife, arrayed in her richest robes and decked with all her jewels, was laid upon the bier. I followed it, and after me came a great procession, headed by the King and all his nobles, and in this order we reached the fatal mountain, one of a lofty chain bordering the sea.

Here I made one more frantic effort to excite the pity of the King and those who stood by, hoping to save myself at this last moment, but it was of no avail. No one spoke to me, they even appeared to hasten over their dreadful task, and I speedily found myself descending into the gloomy pit, with my seven loaves and pitcher of water beside me. Almost before I reached the bottom the stone was rolled into its place above my head, and I was left to my fate.

A feeble ray of light shone into the cavern through some chink, and when I had the courage to look about me I could see that I was in a vast vault, strewn with the bones of the dead. I even fancied that I heard the expiring sighs of those who, like myself, had come into this dismal place alive. All in vain did I shriek aloud with rage and despair, reproaching myself for the love of gain and adventure which had brought me to such a pass; but at length growing calmer, I took up my bread and water and, wrapping my face in my mantle, groped my way toward the end of the cavern, where the air was fresher.

Here I lived in darkness and misery until my provisions were nearly exhausted. One day I fancied that I heard something near me which breathed loudly. Turning to the place from which the sound came I dimly saw a shadowy form which fled at my movement, squeezing itself through a cranny in the wall. I pursued it as fast as I could and found myself in a narrow crack among the rocks, along which I was just able to force my way. I followed it for what seemed to me many miles and, at last, saw before me a glimmer of light which grew clearer every moment until I emerged upon the seashore with a joy which I cannot describe.

When I was sure that I was not dreaming, I realized that it was doubtless some little animal which had found its way into the cavern from the sea and when disturbed had fled, showing me a means of escape which I could never have discovered for myself. I hastily surveyed my surroundings and saw that I was safe from all pursuit from the town.

The mountains sloped sheer down to the sea and there was no road across them. Being assured of this I returned to the cavern and amassed a rich treasure of diamonds, rubies, emeralds and jewels of all kinds which were scattered over the ground. These I made up into bales, stored them in a safe place upon the beach, then sat down and waited hopefully for the passing of a ship.

I had looked out for two days, however, before a single sail appeared, so it was with much delight that I at last saw a vessel not very far from the shore, and by waving my arms and uttering loud cries succeeded in attracting the attention of the crew. A boat was sent off to me, and in answer to the questions of the sailors as to how I came to be in such a plight, I replied that I had been shipwrecked two days before but had managed to scramble ashore with the bales which I pointed out to them.

Luckily for me they believed my story and, without even looking at the place where they found me, took up my bundles and rowed me back to the ship. Once on board, I soon saw that the captain was too much occupied with the difficulties of navigation to pay much heed to me, though he generously made me welcome and would not even accept the jewels with which I offered to pay my passage.

Our voyage was prosperous, and after visiting many lands and collecting in each place a great store of goodly merchandise, I found myself at last in Baghdad once more with unheard-of riches of every description.

Here Sindbad paused, and his audience took their leave, followed by Hindbad, who had once more received a hundred pieces of gold and with the rest had been bidden to return next day for the story of the fifth voyage.

When the time came all were in their places and, when they had eaten and drunk what was set before them, Sindbad began his tale.

Fifth Voyage

Not even all that I had gone through could make me contented with a quiet life. I soon wearied of its pleasures and longed for change and adventure. Therefore I set out once more, but this time in a ship of my own; but as I did not intend carrying enough goods for a full cargo, I invited several merchants of different nations to join me. We set sail with the first favorable wind, and after a long voyage upon the open seas we finally landed upon an unknown island which proved to be uninhabited.

We determined to explore it, but had not gone far when we found a roc's egg, as large as the one I had seen before and evidently very nearly hatched, for the beak of the young bird had already pierced the shell.

In spite of all I could say to deter them, the merchants who were with me fell upon it with their hatchets, breaking the shell and killing the young roc. Then, lighting a fire upon the ground, they hacked morsels from the bird and proceeded to roast them while I stood by, aghast.

Scarcely had they finished their ill-omened repast, when the air above us was darkened by two mighty shadows. The captain of my ship, knowing by experience what this meant, cried out to us that the parent birds were coming and urged us to get on board with all speed. This we did, and the sails were hoisted, but before we had made any headway, the rocs reached their despoiled nest and hovered about it, uttering frightful cries when they discovered the mangled remains of their young one. For a moment we lost sight of them and were flattering ourselves that we had escaped, when they reappeared and soared into the air directly over our vessel, and we saw that each held in its claws an immense rock ready to crush us.

There was a moment of breathless suspense, then one bird loosed its hold and the huge block of stone hurtled through the air, but thanks to the presence of mind of the helmsman, who turned our ship violently in another direction, it fell into the sea close beside us, cleaving it asunder till we could nearly see the bottom. We had hardly time to draw a breath of relief before the other rock fell with a mighty crash right in the midst of our luckless vessel, smashing it into a thousand fragments and hurling passengers and crew into the sea.

I myself went down with the rest, but had the good fortune to rise unhurt and, by holding on to a piece of driftwood with one hand and swimming with the other, I kept myself afloat and was presently washed up by the tide onto an island. Its shores were steep and rocky, but I scrambled up safely and threw myself down to rest upon the green turf.

When I had somewhat recovered I began to examine the spot in which I found myself, and truly it seemed to me that I had reached a garden of delights. There were trees everywhere, laden with flowers and fruit, while a crystal stream wandered in and out under their shadow. When night came I lay down and slept in a cozy nook, though the remembrance that I was alone in a strange land made me sometimes start up and look around me in alarm, and then I wished heartily that I had stayed at home.

The morning sunlight restored my courage and I once more wandered among the trees. I had penetrated some distance into the island when I saw an old man, bent and feeble, sitting upon the river bank. At first I took him to be some shipwrecked mariner like myself. Going up to him I greeted him in a friendly way but he only nodded his head at me in reply. I then asked what he did there, and he made signs to me that he wished to get across the river to gather some fruit and seemed to beg me to carry him on my back.

Pitying his age and feebleness, I took him up and, wading across the stream, I bent down that he might more easily reach the bank and bade him get down. But instead of allowing himself to be set upon his feet, this creature, who had seemed so decrepit, leaped nimbly upon my shoulders and, hooking his legs around my neck, gripped me so tightly that I was well-nigh choked, and so overcome with terror that I fell insensible to the ground.

When I recovered, my enemy was still in his place, though he had released his hold enough to allow me breathing space, and seeing me revive he prodded me adroitly first with one foot and then with the other, until I was forced to get up and stagger about with him under the trees while he gathered and ate the choicest fruits. This went on all day, and even at night, when I threw myself down half dead with weariness, the terrible old man held on tight to my neck. Nor did he fail to greet the first glimmer of morning light by drumming upon me with his heels, until I perforce awoke and resumed my dreary march with rage and bitterness in my heart.

It happened one day that I passed a tree under which lay several dry gourds. Catching one up I amused myself with scooping out its contents and pressing into it the juice of several bunches of the

grapes which hung from every vine. When it was full
I left it propped in the fork of a tree, and a few days
later, carrying the hateful old man that way, I snatched
at my gourd as I passed it and had the satisfaction of
a draught of excellent wine so good and refreshing that
I even forgot my detestable burden and began to sing
and caper.

The old monster was not slow to perceive the effect
which my draught had produced and that I carried him
more lightly than usual, so he stretched out his skinny
hand and, seizing the gourd, first tasted its contents
cautiously, then drained it to the very last drop.
The wine was strong and the gourd capacious, so he
also began to sing after a fashion. Soon I had the
delight of feeling the iron grip of his goblin legs un-
clasp, and with one vigorous effort I threw him to the
ground, from which he did not move again. I was so
delighted to have at last got rid of this old man that I
ran leaping and bounding down to the seashore where,
by the greatest good luck, I met with some mariners
who had anchored off the island to enjoy the delicious
fruits and to renew their supply of water.

They heard the story of my escape with amazement,
saying, "You fell into the hands of the Old Man of the
Sea, and it is a mercy that he did not strangle you as he
has everyone else upon whose shoulders he has managed to perch himself. This island is well known as the
scene of his evil deeds, and no merchant or sailor who

lands upon it cares to stray far away from his comrades."

After we had talked for a while they took me back with them on board their ship, where the captain received me kindly. We soon set sail, and after several days reached a large and prosperous-looking town where all the houses were built of stone. Here we anchored, and one of the merchants, who had been very friendly to me on the way, took me ashore with him and showed me a lodging set apart for strange merchants. He then provided me with a large sack and pointed out to me a party of other men equipped in like manner.

"Go with them," he said, "and do as they do, but beware of losing sight of them, for if you stray your life would be in danger."

I set out with my new companions and soon learned that the object of our expedition was to fill our sacks with coconuts. The crowns of the coco palms were alive with monkeys, big and little, which skipped from one to the other with surprising agility, seeming to be curious about us and disturbed at our appearance. I was at first surprised when my companions, after collecting stones, began to throw them at the lively creatures, which seemed to me quite harmless. But very soon I saw the reason of it and joined them heartily, for the monkeys, annoyed and wishing to pay us back in our own coin, began to tear the nuts from the trees and cast them at us with angry gestures, so after little labor on our part our sacks were filled with the fruit which we could not otherwise have obtained.

As soon as we had all the coconuts that we could carry, we went back to the town, where my friend bought my share and advised me to continue the same occupation until I had earned money enough to carry me to my own country. This I did and before long had amassed a considerable sum.

Just then I heard that there was a trading ship ready to sail. Taking leave of my friend I went on board, carrying with me a goodly store of coconuts; and we sailed first to the islands where pepper grows, then to Comari where the best aloes wood is found and where men drink no wine by an unalterable law. Here I exchanged my nuts for pepper and aloes wood, and went searching for pearls with some of the other merchants, and the divers I engaged were so lucky that very soon I had an immense number of pearls and those very large and perfect. With all these treasures I came joyfully back to Baghdad, where I disposed of them for large sums of money, of which I did not fail as before to give the tenth part to the poor, and after that I rested from my labors and comforted myself with the many pleasures that my riches could give me.

Having thus ended his story, Sindbad ordered that one hundred pieces of gold should be given to Hindbad, and the guests then withdrew; but after the next day's feast he began the account of his sixth voyage.

Sixth Voyage

It must be a marvel to you how, after having five times met with shipwreck and unheard-of perils, I could again tempt fortune, but evidently it was my fate to rove, and after a year of repose I prepared to make a sixth voyage. Instead of going by the Persian Gulf, I traveled a considerable way overland and finally embarked from a distant Indian port with a captain who meant to make a long voyage. One day we fell in with stormy weather which drove us completely off our course, and for many days neither the captain nor the pilot knew where we were nor where we were going.

When they did at last discover our position we had small ground for rejoicing, for the captain, casting his turban upon the deck and tearing his beard, declared that we were in the most dangerous spot upon the whole wide sea and had been caught by a current which was at that minute sweeping us to destruction. It was too true! In spite of all the sailors could do we were driven with frightful rapidity toward the foot of a mountain which rose sheer out of the sea, and our vessel was dashed to pieces upon the rocks at its base, not, however, before we had managed to scramble onto the shore, carrying with us the most precious of our possessions.

When we had done this the captain said to us, "Now that we are here we may as well begin to dig our graves at once, since from this fatal spot no shipwrecked mariner has ever returned."

This speech discouraged us much, and we began to lament over our sad fate.

The mountain formed the seaward boundary of a large island, and the narrow strip of rocky shore upon which we stood was strewn with the wreckage of a thousand gallant ships, while the bones of luckless mariners shone white in the sunshine, and we shuddered to think how soon our own would be added to the heap.

All around, too, lay vast quantities of the costliest merchandise, and treasures were heaped in every cranny of the rocks, but these things only added to the desolation of the scene. It struck me as very strange that a river of clear fresh water, which gushed from the mountain not far from where we stood, instead of flowing into the sea as rivers generally do, turned off sharply and flowed out of sight under a natural archway of rock. When I went to examine it more closely, I found that inside the cave the walls were thick with diamonds and rubies and masses of crystal and the floor was strewn with ambergris.

Here, then, upon this barren shore we abandoned

ourselves to our fate, for there was no possibility of scaling the mountain, and if a ship had appeared it could only have shared our doom. The first thing our captain did was to divide equally among us all the food we possessed, and then the length of each man's life depended on the time he could make his portion last. I myself could live upon very little.

Nevertheless, by the time I had buried the last of my companions my stock of provisions was so small I hardly thought I should live long enough to dig my own grave. I regretted bitterly the roving disposition which was always bringing me into such straits and thought longingly of all the comfort and luxury I had left. But luckily the fancy took me to stand once more beside the river where it plunged out of sight into the depths of the cavern, and as I did so an idea struck me.

This river which hid itself underground doubtless emerged again at some distant spot. Why should I not build a raft and trust myself to its swiftly flowing waters? If I perished before I could reach the light of day again I should be no worse off than I was now, for death was staring me in the face. I decided at any rate to risk it, and speedily built myself a stout raft of driftwood and strong cords, of which enough and to spare lay strewn upon the beach. I then made up many packages of rubies, emeralds, rock crystal, ambergris and precious stuffs, and bound them upon my raft. Then I seated myself upon it and loosed the cord which held it to the bank.

In the strong current my raft flew swiftly under the gloomy archway, and I found myself in total darkness, carried smoothly forward by the rapid river. On I went, as it seemed to me, for many nights and days. Once the channel became so small that I had a narrow escape from being crushed against the rock roof, and after that I took the precaution of lying flat upon my precious bales. Though I ate only what was absolutely necessary to keep myself alive, the inevitable moment came when, after swallowing my last morsel of food, I began to wonder if I must, after all, die of hunger.

Then, worn out with anxiety and fatigue, I fell into a deep sleep and when I again opened my eyes I was in the light of day. A beautiful country lay before me, and my raft, which was tied to the riverbank, was surrounded by friendly dark men. I rose and saluted them, and they spoke to me in return, but I could not understand a word of their language. But one of the natives, who spoke Arabic, came forward, saying, "My brother, be not surprised to see us; this is our land, and as we came to get water from the river we noticed your raft floating down it, and swam out and brought you to the shore. We have waited for your awakening; tell us whence you come and where you were going by that dangerous way?"

I replied that nothing would please me better than

to tell them, but that I was starving and would like to eat something first. I was soon supplied with all I needed and, having satisfied my hunger, I told them faithfully what had befallen me.

They were lost in wonder at my tale when it was interpreted to them and said that adventures so amazing must be related to their King only by the man to whom they had happened. So, procuring a horse, they mounted me upon it, and we set out, followed by several strong men carrying my raft just as it was upon their shoulders. In this order we marched into the city of Serendib, where the natives presented me to their King, whom I saluted in the Indian fashion, prostrating myself at his feet and kissing the ground; but the monarch bade me rise and sit beside him, asking what was my name. "I am Sindbad," I said, "whom men call 'the Sailor,' for I have voyaged much on many seas."

"And how come you here?" asked the King.

I told my story, concealing nothing, and his wonder and delight were so great that he ordered my adventures to be written in letters of gold and laid up in the archives of his kingdom.

Presently my raft was brought in, the bales were opened, and the King declared that in all his treasury there were no such rubies and emeralds as those which lay in great heaps before him.

Seeing that he looked at them with interest, I ventured to say that I myself and my possessions were at his disposal, but he answered me, smiling, "Nay, Sind-bad. Heaven forbid that I should covet your riches; I will rather add to them, for I desire that you shall not leave my kingdom without taking with you some tokens of my goodwill."

After many days I petitioned the King that I might return to my own country, to which he graciously con-sented. Moreover, he loaded me with rich gifts, and when I went to take leave of him he entrusted me with royal presents and a letter to the Commander of the Faithful, our sovereign lord, saying, "I pray you give these to the Caliph Haroun al Raschid, and assure him of my friendship."

I accepted the charge respectfully and soon em-barked upon the vessel which the King himself had chosen for me. The King's letter to the Caliph was written in beautiful blue characters upon a very rare and precious skin of yellow color, and these were the words of it:

The King of the Indies—before whom walk a thousand elephants, who lives in a palace, the roof of which blazes with a hundred thousand rubies, and whose treasurehouse contains twenty thousand diamond crowns—to the Caliph Ha-roun al Raschid sends greeting. Though the offer-ings we present to you are unworthy of your notice, we pray you to accept them as a mark of the esteem and friendship which we cherish for

you, and of which we gladly send you these tokens, and we ask of you a like regard if you deem
us worthy of it. Adieu, brother.

The presents consisted of a vase carved from a single
ruby, six inches high and as thick as my finger; this
was filled with the choicest pearls, large and of perfect
shape and luster; secondly, a huge snakeskin which
would preserve from sickness those who slept upon it;
then quantities of aloes wood, camphor and pistachio
nuts; and, lastly, a beautiful slave girl, whose robes
glittered with precious stones.

After a long and prosperous voyage we landed at
Balsora, and I made haste to reach Baghdad. Taking
the King's letter I presented myself at the palace gate,
followed by the beautiful slave and various members
of my own family, bearing the treasure.

As soon as I had declared my errand I was conducted into the presence of the Caliph Haroun al
Raschid, to whom, after I had made my obeisance, I
presented the letter and the King's gifts. When he had
examined these closely he demanded of me whether
the King of Serendib was really as rich and powerful
as he claimed to be.

"Commander of the Faithful," I replied, again bowing humbly before him, "I can assure Your Majesty
that the King of Serendib has in no way exaggerated
his wealth and grandeur. Nothing can equal the magnificence of his palace. When he goes abroad, his throne

is prepared upon the back of an elephant, and on either side of him ride his ministers, his favorites and courtiers. On his elephant's neck sits an officer, his golden lance in his hand, and behind him stands another bearing a pillar of gold, at the top of which is an emerald as long as my hand.

"A thousand men in cloth of gold, mounted upon richly caparisoned elephants, go before him, and as the procession moves onward the officer who guides his elephant cries aloud, 'Behold the mighty monarch, the powerful and valiant Sultan of Serendib, whose palace is covered with a hundred thousand rubies, who possesses twenty thousand diamond crowns. Behold a monarch greater than Solomon and Mihrage in all their glory.' Further, my lord, in Serendib no judge is needed, for to the King himself his people come for justice."

The Caliph was well satisfied with my report. "From the King's letter," said he, "I judge that he is a wise man. It seems that he is worthy of his people, and his people of him." So saying he dismissed me with rich presents and I returned in peace to my own house.

When Sindbad had done speaking, his guests withdrew, Hindbad having first received a hundred pieces of gold; but all returned next day to hear the story of the seventh voyage. Sindbad thus began.

Seventh Voyage

After my sixth voyage I was determined to go to sea no more. I was now of an age to appreciate a quiet life and I had run risks enough. I only wished to end my days in peace. One day, however, when I was entertaining a number of my friends, I was told that an officer of the Caliph wished to speak to me. When he had been admitted he bade me follow him into the presence of Haroun al Raschid, which I did.

I saluted him, and the Caliph said, "I have sent for you, Sindbad, because I need your services. I have chosen you to bear a letter and gifts to the King of Serendib in return for his message of friendship."

The Caliph's commandment fell upon me like a thunderbolt. "Commander of the Faithful," I answered, "I am ready to do all that you command, but I humbly pray you to remember that I am utterly disheartened by the sufferings I have undergone. Indeed, I have made a vow never again to leave Baghdad."

"I admit," said he, "that you have indeed had some extraordinary experiences, but I do not see why they should hinder you from doing as I wish. You have only to go straight to Serendib and give my message, then you are free to come back and do as you will. But go you must; my honor and dignity demand it."

Seeing there was no help for it, I declared myself

willing to obey; and the Caliph, delighted at having his own way, gave me a thousand gold pieces for the expenses of the voyage. I soon embarked at Balsora and sailed quickly and safely to Serendib. Here, when I had disclosed my errand, I was well received and brought into the presence of the King, who greeted me with joy.

"Welcome, Sindbad," he cried. "I have thought of you often, and rejoice to see you once more."

After thanking him for the honor he did me, I displayed the Caliph's gifts: first a bed with complete hangings of cloth of gold, and another like it of crimson stuff; fifty robes of rich embroidery; a hundred fine white linens from Cairo, Suez, Kufa and Alexandria; an agate vase carved with the figure of a man aiming an arrow at a lion; and finally a costly table which had once belonged to King Solomon.

The King of Serendib received with satisfaction the assurance of the Caliph's friendliness toward him. And now my task being accomplished I was anxious to depart, although it was some time before the King would think of letting me go. At last, however, he dismissed me with many presents and I lost no time in going on board a ship, which sailed that very hour, and for four days all went well.

On the fifth day we had the misfortune to come upon pirates, who seized our vessel, killing all who resisted and making prisoners of those who were prudent enough to submit at once, of whom I was one. When they had despoiled us of all we possessed, they forced us to put on vile raiment and, sailing to a distant island, there sold us for slaves.

I fell into the hands of a rich merchant, who took me home with him, clothed and fed me, and after some days sent for me and questioned me about what I could do. I answered that I too was a rich merchant, who had been captured by pirates, and therefore did not know a trade.

"Tell me," said he, "can you shoot with a bow?"

I replied that this had been a pastime of my youth, and that doubtless with practice my skill would come back to me.

Upon this he provided me with a bow and arrows and, mounting me with him upon his own elephant, took the way to a vast forest which lay far from the town. When we had reached the wildest part of the forest, we stopped, and my master said, "This forest swarms with elephants. Hide yourself in this great tree and shoot at any that pass you. When you have succeeded in killing one, come and tell me."

So saying he gave me a supply of food and returned to the town. I perched myself high up in the tree and kept watch. That night I saw nothing, but just after sunrise the next day a large herd of elephants came crashing by. You may be sure that I immediately let fly several arrows, and at last one of the great animals fell to the ground, dead. The others retreated, leaving me free to come down from my hiding place and run back to tell my master of my success, for which I was praised and regaled with good things. Then we went back to the forest together and dug a mighty trench in which we buried the elephant I had killed, in order that when it became a skeleton my master might return and secure its tusks.

For two months I hunted thus, and no day passed without my getting an elephant. Of course I did not always station myself in the same tree, but sometimes here, sometimes there. One morning as I watched the coming of the elephants I was surprised to see that, instead of passing the tree I was in, as they usually did, they paused and completely surrounded it, trumpeting horribly and shaking the very ground with their heavy tread. When I saw that their eyes were fixed upon me I was terrified, and my arrows dropped from my trembling hand.

I had indeed good reason for my terror when, an instant later, the largest of the animals wrapped his trunk around the tree, and with one mighty effort tore it up by the roots, bringing me to the ground entangled in its branches. I thought now my last hour was surely come; but the huge creature, picking me up gently enough, set me upon its back, where I clung more dead than alive. Then, followed by the whole herd, it turned and crashed into the dense forest.

It seemed to me a long time before I was once more set upon my feet, and I stood as if in a dream watching the herd which trampled off in another direction and were soon hidden in the heavy underbrush. Then, recovering myself, I looked about me and found that I was standing upon the side of a great hill, strewn as far as I could see on either hand with bones and tusks of elephants. "This then must be the elephants' burying place," I murmured to myself, "and they must have brought me here that I might cease to persecute them, seeing that I want nothing but their tusks, and here lie more than I could carry away with me in a lifetime."

Whereupon I turned and made for the city as fast as I could go, not seeing a single elephant as I went. This convinced me that they had retired deeper into the forest to leave the way open to the ivory hill, and I did not know how to admire their sagacity sufficiently. After a day and a night I reached my master's house and was received by him with joyful surprise.

"Ah, poor Sindbad," he cried, "I was wondering what could have become of you. When I went to the forest I found the tree newly uprooted, the arrows lying beside it, and I feared I should never see you again. Pray tell me how you escaped death."

I soon satisfied his curiosity, and the next day we went together to the ivory hill, and he was overjoyed to find that I had told him nothing but the truth. When we had loaded our elephant with as many tusks as it could carry and were going back to the city, he said: "My brother—since I can no longer treat as a slave one who has enriched me thus—take your liberty and may Heaven prosper you. I will no longer conceal from you that these elephants have killed numbers of our slaves. You alone have escaped their wiles; therefore you shall not only receive your freedom, but I will also bestow fortune and honors upon you."

So I stayed with him till the time of the monsoon, which would bring the ivory ships, and every day we added to our store of ivory till his warehouses were overflowing with it. By this time the other merchants knew the secret, but there was enough and to spare for all. When the ships finally arrived, my master put on board for me a great store of choice provisions, also ivory in abundance and some of the costliest curiosities of the country.

I left the ship at the first port we came to, not feeling at ease upon the sea after what had happened to me by reason of it. Having disposed of my ivory for much gold and having bought many rare and costly presents, I loaded my pack animals and joined a caravan of merchants. Our journey was long and tedious, but I bore it patiently, reflecting that at least I had not to fear tempests, nor pirates, nor serpents, nor any of the other perils from which I suffered before. After a time we reached Baghdad.

My first care was to present myself before the Caliph and give him an account of my journey.

By his orders this story and the others I had told him were written by his scribes in letters of gold and laid up among his treasures. I took my leave of him, well satisfied with the honors and rewards he bestowed upon me; and since that time I have rested from my labors and given myself up wholly to my family and my friends.

Thus Sindbad ended the story of his seventh and last voyage. Turning to Hindbad he added, "Well, my friend, what do you think now? Have you ever heard of anyone who has suffered more or had more narrow escapes than I have? Is it not just that I should now enjoy a life of ease and tranquillity?"

Hindbad drew near and, kissing his hand respectfully, replied, "Sir, you have indeed known fearful perils; my troubles have been nothing compared to yours. Moreover, the generous use you make of your wealth proves that you deserve it. May you live long and happily in the enjoyment of it."

Sindbad then gave him a hundred pieces of gold and henceforward counted Hindbad among his friends. Also he caused him to give up his profession as a porter and to eat daily at his table that he might all his life remember Sindbad the Sailor.

ARABIAN NIGHTS, TRANSLATED BY ANTOINE GALLAND

ABOUT THE ORIGINAL AUTHORS AND COLLECTORS
OF STORIES IN THIS BOOK

HANS CHRISTIAN ANDERSEN Biographers of Hans Christian Andersen have suggested that the real story of his life is reflected in two of his fairy tales, "The Ugly Duckling" and "Little Fir Tree." He was a big, awkward duckling of a boy who refused to learn a modest trade, became first an actor and then was transformed into one of the most famous of writers. And, like the little fir tree, Andersen was always yearning for change.

Born in Odense, Denmark, in 1805, the son of a cobbler, he left home at the age of fourteen to seek his fortune in Copenhagen. There, after a period of extreme hardship, he came to the attention of several prominent people, including the King. Through their influence, he obtained an education and began to write. He turned out poems, novels and plays, but it was his fairy tales—some based on folk legends, others original—that became his great legacy to mankind.

Even during his lifetime, Andersen was appreciated all over the world. His admirers included many of the important literary figures of the day: Henry Wadsworth Longfellow, Elizabeth Barrett Browning, Walt Whitman, Oscar Wilde and Charles Dickens. Dickens once wrote to him: "Whatever you do, don't leave off writing, for we cannot afford to lose any of your thoughts. They are too purely and simply beautiful to be kept in your own head."

Nor was Andersen a prophet without honor in his own country. In 1867, eight years before his death, Odense gave him the key to the city, staging a mammoth torchlight parade to celebrate its most famous and beloved son.

JAKOB and WILHELM GRIMM In the year 1812, two brothers quietly published a slim volume that went on to become the most widely read book in the world except for the Bible. Called *Tales for Children and the Hearth,* it contained stories which, until the brothers Grimm put them on paper, had existed only by word of mouth. Painstakingly interviewing elderly German peasants, shepherds and others who had heard these ancient tales from their forebears, they made a collection that included such popular favorites as "Snow White and the Seven Dwarfs," "Hansel and Gretel," "The Frog Prince" and "Rapunzel."

Jakob and Wilhelm Grimm, born in 1785 and 1786 respectively, studied law in college but became interested in early German epics and folktales, beginning their research in this field in their early twenties. The two were at first interested only because of what the stories revealed about primitive man's thinking and language, and they might have remained unpublished had not a friend chanced to read them. He immediately arranged for their publication. Their simplicity, the swiftness of narrative, the triumph of weak "little people," the presence of magic, enchantments, talking animals—all made the stories an instant success with children.

The two brothers later became great scholars of antiquity and linguistics, at work on a vast dictionary when they died, Wilhelm in 1858 and Jakob in 1863. But the name Grimm will always stand for fairy tales.

PETER CHRISTEN ASBJÖRNSEN and JÖRGEN ENGER-BRETSEN MOE   Europe in the middle of the nineteenth century was bursting with national rebirth. Country after country was becoming aware of its own individual cultural heritage. One aspect of this was the work of Peter Christen Asbjörnsen and Jörgen Engerbretsen Moe, who produced extensive collections of Norwegian folktales.

Asbjörnsen, born in 1812, and Moe, a year later, met as boys at the Norderhov School north of Oslo in 1826, becoming lifelong friends and collaborators. Asbjörnsen became a zoologist; Moe, after some years as a tutor, entered the clergy. On voyages through Norway's majestic fjords, Asbjörnsen saw the setting of "Why the Sea Is Salt" and encountered the North Wind, "oldest and strongest . . . frightful to see," that is described in "East of the Sun and West of the Moon." Moe, on holiday expeditions into wild mountain areas, beheld the rugged terrain of the trolls who appear in so many of their stories.

Their first collection of native tales appeared in 1843, the second in 1844, including such famous stories as "Three Billy Goats Gruff" and "The Princess on the Glass Hill."

Moe became the bishop of Christiansand and died in 1882. Asbjörnsen died in 1885.

CHARLES PERRAULT   France's greatest contributor to the literature of fairy tales was a man born into a prominent family in 1628. He studied for the bar and served as secretary to Jean Baptiste Colbert, the powerful finance minister of King Louis XIV. After Colbert's death in 1683, Perrault, by then an honored member of the *Académie Française,* devoted his time primarily to literature, writing scholarly essays, poems and his memoirs. In 1697, he collected a volume called *Histoires ou contes du temps passé avec les moralités* (Stories or Tales of Times Past With Morals). Included in this book were some of the most famous fairy tales we know: "Puss in Boots," "Blue Beard" and "Cinderella." Some of these stories were original, written as much to entertain the frivolous ladies of the French court as to instruct and amuse children. Perrault died in 1703.

ANDREW LANG   "There was a touch of the elf about him," is the way James M. Barrie described his friend Andrew Lang, who made the most extensive collection of fairy tales in the English language. He gathered his stories from the literature of almost every country in the world. About himself Lang said: "Some are born soldiers from the cradle, some merchants, some orators; nothing but a love of books was given me by the fairies." However, his father had been a business partner of Sir Walter Scott, and the household into which he was born, in Selkirk, Scotland, in 1844, was an influential literary one.

After graduation from Oxford and a few years as a don at the university, Lang found his way to London's center of journalism, Fleet Street. Here he enjoyed a forty-year career as one of the greatest authors of his era, writing news articles, literary criticism, poetry and novels.

All of his life the world of the past fascinated Lang—Scottish and French history, the literature of ancient Greece, especially Homer, and finally the folktales and fairy tales that appeared in his many collections. The first of these—the *Blue Fairy Book*—was published in 1889. He died in 1912.

In one of his prefaces to the fairy-tale books Lang made this quiet comment about whether fairies really exist: "The editor never saw any himself, but he knows several people who have seen them—in the Highlands—and heard their music."

ACKNOWLEDGMENTS Collected and edited by Andrew Lang: THE PIED PIPER OF HAMELIN, THE GOLDEN GOOSE, JACK AND THE BEANSTALK, SIX SILLIES, SNOW WHITE AND THE SEVEN DWARFS, RAPUNZEL, TWELVE DANCING PRINCESSES, from *Red Fairy Book*, © 1948; SNOW WHITE AND ROSE RED, CINDERELLA, WHY THE SEA IS SALT, THE GOOSE-GIRL, BEAUTY AND THE BEAST, THE BRONZE RING, DICK WHITTINGTON AND HIS CAT, RUMPELSTILTZKIN, HANSEL AND GRETEL, EAST OF THE SUN AND WEST OF THE MOON, BLUE BEARD, THE PRINCESS ON THE GLASS HILL, SLEEPING BEAUTY, JACK THE GIANT KILLER, from *Blue Fairy Book*, © 1948; THE NIGHTINGALE, THUMBELINA, THE TINDERBOX, THE EMPEROR'S NEW CLOTHES, THE STEADFAST TIN SOLDIER, THE SIX SWANS, from *Yellow Fairy Book*, © 1948; JORINDA AND JORINGEL, LITTLE ONE EYE, LITTLE TWO EYES AND LITTLE THREE EYES, THE HALF-CHICK, from *Green Fairy Book*, © 1948; ALI BABA AND THE FORTY THIEVES, ALADDIN AND THE WONDERFUL LAMP, THE MAGIC CARPET, SINBAD THE SAILOR, from *Arabian Nights*, © 1898, 1946; the aforementioned books are copyrighted and published by David McKay Company, Inc. FIVE WISE WORDS, THE GOLDEN-HEADED FISH, from *Olive Fairy Book*, first published by David McKay Company, Inc., in 1950. All the aforementioned books are published in Great Britain by Longmans, Green & Co. Ltd. THE SNOW QUEEN, LITTLE FIR TREE, from *Pink Fairy Book*, © 1897 and published by Longmans, Green and Co. Ltd. TWO FROGS, from *Violet Fairy Book;* THE BOY WHO KEPT A SECRET, THE MAGIC KETTLE, SEVEN SIMONS, THE COLONY OF CATS, from *Crimson Fairy Book;* both first published by Longmans, Green and Co. Ltd. in 1951.

THE FROG PRINCE, DOCTOR KNOW-IT-ALL, from *Tales From Grimm*, © 1936, Wanda Gág; THE HEDGEHOG AND THE RABBIT, THE SORCERER'S APPRENTICE, from *More Tales From Grimm*, © 1947, Estate of Wanda Gág; both translated by Wanda Gág, published by Coward-McCann, Inc. and Faber & Faber Ltd. IT'S PERFECTLY TRUE!, THE UGLY DUCKLING, THE LITTLE MERMAID, THE RED SHOES, THE LITTLE MATCH-GIRL, LITTLE CLAUS AND BIG CLAUS, from *It's Perfectly True and Other Stories*, by Hans Christian Andersen, translated by Paul Leyssac, © 1937, Paul Leyssac; renewed, 1965, Mary Rehan, published by Harcourt, Brace & World, Inc. TOM THUMB, THE THREE LITTLE PIGS. from *English Fairy Tales*, by Joseph Jacobs, published by G. P. Putnam's Sons. CHICKEN LITTLE, from *For the Children's Hour*, by Carolyn S. Bailey and Clara M. Lewis, © 1906, 1926 and published by Milton Bradley Company. THE PRINCESS AND THE PEA, THE TOWN MOUSE AND THE COUNTRY MOUSE, THE SHOEMAKER AND THE ELVES, THE BRAVE LITTLE TAILOR, THE MUSICIANS OF BREMEN, from *Tales of Laughter*, edited by Kate Douglas Wiggin and Nora Archibald Smith, © 1908, 1926 and published by Doubleday & Company, Inc. RED RIDING HOOD, from *Grimms' Fairy Tales*, translated by Mrs. E. V. Lucas, Lucy Crane and Marian Edwardes, © 1945 and published by Grosset & Dunlap, Inc. and J. M. Dent & Sons Ltd. THREE BILLY GOATS GRUFF, BILLY BEG AND HIS BULL, from *Chimney Corner Stories*, by Veronica S. Hutchinson, © 1925 and published by G. P. Putnam's Sons. PUSS IN BOOTS, from *Perrault's Complete Fairy Tales*, translated by A. E. Johnson and others, © 1961 and published by Dodd, Mead & Company, Inc. and Constable & Co. Ltd. SNEGOURKA, THE SNOW MAIDEN, from *Favorite Fairy Tales Told in Russia*, by Virginia Haviland, © 1961, Virginia Haviland, published by Little, Brown and Co. and the Bodley Head Ltd. THE THREE BEARS, from *The Golden Goose and the Three Bears*, by L. Leslie Brooke, published by Frederick Warne and Co. Ltd. THE GINGERBREAD MAN, from *Stories to Tell to Children*, by Sara Cone Bryant, © 1907, Sara Cone Bryant, published by Houghton Mifflin Company and George G. Harrap & Co. Ltd. A HORNED GOAT, from *The Jolly Tailor and Other Fairy Tales*, translated by Lucia Merecka Borski (Lucia Merecka Szcepanowice) and Kate B. Miller, © 1928 and published by Longmans, Green and Co.